BEDFORDSHIRE LIBRARIES

KT

BOOKS SHOULD BE RETURNED
BY LAST DATE STAMPED ABOVE

9

D0230450

By Emma Hannigan

Keeping Mum
The Pink Ladies Club
Miss Conceived
Designer Genes
Driving Home for Christmas
Perfect Wives
The Summer Guest
The Heart of Winter
The Secrets We Share
The Perfect Gift

The Wedding Weekend (e-short)

Talk to the Headscarf

Readers love *The Perfect Gift* . . .

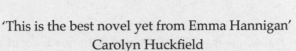

'This is the best novel yet from Emma Hannigan'
Carolyn Huckfield

'This novel was a joy to read; strong female characters who I felt
I knew like friends blended with a cosy setting I was very happy
to escape to . . . A multi-generational story of hope'
Emily Wright

'What I loved about the book was how real the characters felt . . .
more than once I found myself holding back tears or bursting out
laughing . . . This book was a sheer joy the entire way through'
Edel Waugh

'Loved the story, this is the best book I have read in a long time!'
Sophie Ufton

'The book grabs you from the beginning and doesn't let go . . .
A good book to curl up with on a cold night and be transported
to a lighthouse and bakery in rural Ireland'
Janet Gilliard

'Emma Hannigan is a storyteller from the Maeve Binchy stable;
like Ms Binchy she is warm and welcoming, sympathetic and
kindly towards her characters and manages to restore one's
faith in human nature'
Clare Turner

'This is a truly adorable story; I loved the quaint coastal
village setting, the close-knit community feel and the lovely,
lovely characters'
Nikki Clark

Reader reviews all provided by Lovereading

Praise for Emma Hannigan.
Stories you'll want to share . . .

'A glorious read . . . A wonderfully uplifting novel about women's
friendship by a writer who understands exactly how women think'
Cathy Kelly

'Hannigan's novel, much like the vivacious author herself, is
brimming with hope, joy and inspiration'
Sunday Independent

'Emotional and heartbreaking . . . A fast-paced story with
endearingly warm characters – you'll savour this touching tale'
Candis Magazine, Book of the Month

'A moving tale celebrating the bonds between women, Emma
Hannigan beautifully captures the difficult and wondrous thing that
is loving and learning to let go . . . just a little. An excellent read'
Irish Tatler

'This fast-paced and endearing novel is about friendship between
women, accepting yourself and trusting your own judgement'
Belfast Telegraph

'This is her best novel yet. Her heart and soul was poured into
every word of this story and it just radiates from the pages . . . a
wonderful, heartfelt, emotive book'
Shaz's Book Blog

'I didn't just like it, I really LOVED it . . . grab this book, curl up on the
couch and prepare to have a few lump in your throat moments too'
Celeste Loves Books

'[T]he author deals with some hard-hitting and sensitive issues,
giving the story a depth that I really did not expect . . .
Emma Hannigan is a gifted storyteller'
Random Things Through My Letterbox

Emma Hannigan

The Perfect Gift

headline
review

First published in Great Britain in 2016
by HEADLINE REVIEW
An imprint of HEADLINE PUBLISHING GROUP

First published in paperback in Great Britain in 2016
by HEADLINE REVIEW
An imprint of HEADLINE PUBLISHING GROUP

Cataloguing in Publication Data is available from the British Library

ISBN 978 1 4722 3011 9

Typeset in Palatino by Palimpsest Book Production Limited,
Falkirk, Stirlingshire

Printed and bound in Great Britain by
Clays Ltd, St Ives plc

HEADLINE PUBLISHING GROUP
An Hachette UK Company
Carmelite House
50 Victoria Embankment
London EC4Y 0DZ

www.headline.co.uk
www.hachette.co.uk

For the two most important women in my world:
my mum Denise and my daughter Kim.

And for the men who keep us smiling:
my dad Philip, my husband Cian and my son
Sacha.

Together you are my perfect gifts.

My darling, my beautiful, my daughter,
You are ten days old and we don't have long left together.
Panic is a terrible thing. It takes away all rationale. But my
love for you has spurred me on and helped me find a way to
leave you a part of myself.

Beside me on the bed sit twenty-nine cards, to be sent to you
each year on your birthday. I want you to know that I am
thinking of you always. You must have so many questions about
me and the circumstances of your birth. The most important
thing you need to know is this: I love you as only a mother can.

What I want more than anything else is to stay, to watch
you grow up, learn to walk and talk. To see you find happiness.
To know you've found love.

The truth is, I am dying. A large part of me wants to scream
and throw things violently at the walls and let all the anger
out at the injustice of it all. But I cannot waste the energy I
have left. I want to cherish each and every moment I have left
with you, my darling girl.

Being pregnant with you, feeling those tiny flutters in the
beginning as you grew, then bringing you into this world,
holding you, feeding you – this has been the perfect finale
before I go. All my life I have been weakened by my illness.
So knowing that I defied the odds and you are here has made
it all worthwhile.

The Perfect Gift

Being your mother has given me the greatest sense of achievement and happiness. I will never tire of stroking your cheek and watching your solemn eyes gazing purposefully back at me. Having you has made sense of everything. I now know my main purpose in life was to bring you into the world. And I know you were brought here to carry on where I've had to leave off. Live for us both and seize every moment. For me and, most of all, for you, my little miracle, just as I have been doing for these past nine months. Enjoy the scent of every flower, dance to every song, laugh until you cry, walk barefoot by the sea, but no matter what, let your passions soar.

I will watch over you always and I know we will meet again some day. There is nothing more I can say except that I love you. I love you. I love you. I love you, my darling girl, my perfect gift.

Mam

Chapter 1

RÓISÍN STIFLED A YAWN AS SHE STRETCHED UP HER arms and rose to the tips of her toes to engage the pole with the shutter in order to close her shop for the night. Well, Nourriture – Food For The Soul might be just a shop to the passing gaze of a tourist, but it was Róisín's entire world.

Clicking the sturdy padlock in place, she grinned at her own suspiciousness. The sleepy fishing village of Ballyshore was hardly up there with the crime hotspots of the world. As she turned and inhaled the damp saltiness of the early evening air, she closed her eyes momentarily. Her time away from her home village had made her appreciate the rugged west of Ireland beauty that surrounded her all the more.

A spatter of fat raindrops plopping onto her cheeks dragged her from her reverie. Stooping to grab the bottle and the box of Sushi she'd swiped from her well-stocked food emporium, she slung her battered soft leather fringed bag over her shoulder. She knew all too well that the heavens could open and drench her with a chilly late spring shower. The cottage she shared with her oldest and best friend Jill was a ten minute walk at a brisk pace. Róisín had grown up at the other side of the bay, a short drive away, but she preferred living near the hub of the village.

Despite the low temperature the air was unmistakably soft. Róisín could almost hear the kinks forming in her dark, glossy hair as the salty air worked its magic. Glad of the sturdy comfort of her scuffed Dr Martens black boots, she wished she'd brought a downy puffa coat instead of the leather biker jacket she'd paired with her pale pink tulle skirt today. The watered-down lemony sunshine this morning had lulled her into a false sense of summer.

Balancing the shopping bag containing the wine bottle and Sushi in the crook of her arm, she wrestled with the jacket zip. The cross-over cardigan with flimsy tank top underneath was adequate while she ran from the kitchen to the counter and back up to her office in Nourriture during the busy working day, but it was no match for the now squalling rain.

At a trot she passed the sharply curving stone wall that separated the narrow country road from the sea. Darting across to the other side, she hoped the overhanging trees might offer more shelter. In another few weeks the tiny buds that dotted the hedgerows would flourish and ripen into juice-laden blackberries. She licked her lips, longing to taste the rich jam she'd make from her pickings.

Róisín sighed in grateful relief as she rounded the corner and saw the small white-washed cottage shining like a beacon through the rain. Bellows of grey smoke belched from the chimney and Róisín trotted happily towards the door.

'Hi honey, I'm home!' she called out, then started coughing. The open-plan kitchen-cum-living room was smokey from the fire and her friend was nowhere to be seen.

'Jill?'

Setting her bag and wine on the kitchen table, she rushed to the potbellied stove and snatched up the poker. Shoving the single log and pyramid of peat briquettes into the back of the grate, she secured the door shut. She was too cold to open the windows and doors, so instead Róisín escaped into her bedroom. Too small to host a double bed as well as the wardrobe and dressing-table, she'd opted for an iron-framed single bed.

'It's not as if I'm entertaining queues of hot lovers,' she had joked with Jill. 'For the moment, a single bed with a feather duvet and a pile of pillows will do me nicely.'

Jill, on the other hand, had said she'd rather hang her clothes on the floor than pass up her double bed.

'I mightn't have a steady boyfriend yet,' she'd said, hands on hips, as they'd moved in together three years ago, 'but I've every intention of interviewing for the post.'

A teacher in the local primary school, Jill was vivacious and enthusiastic. From the time they'd held hands in the Montessori room in Ballyshore National aged three, she and Róisín had been inseparable.

'That you, Ro?' Jill called out now.

'No, I'm a masked murderer.'

'Stop it!' Jill said, bursting into the bedroom and flinging herself onto the end of Róisín's bed with her hair turbaned in a towel. 'How's it going? Good day at the office?'

'Yeah, it was really busy. That burst of sunshine this morning brought the tourists and locals out in force.'

'So aren't you going to ask me how I got on last night?' Jill said, eyes shining.

'I heard how you got on,' Róisín grinned. 'You weren't exactly keeping it to yourself last night.'

'I know! And on a school night, too. I'm such a rebel.'

She sighed. 'I was a bit hung-over this morning. Dreadful idea when there are twenty-five pairs of eyes squinting suspiciously at yours for six hours.'

'I don't know how you work as a teacher, but doing it with a hangover and very little sleep seems like self-inflicted torture to me.'

'Gordon was worth it,' she said dreamily.

'Gordon? With a name like that he hardly sounds too rock 'n' roll.'

'He didn't seem it either when we first met. He was at the enrolment for the summer evening classes. He's not actually taking part, he was simply there to set up the computer for one of the lecturers. I enrolled for bird-watching.'

'Bird-watching? You? Don't you need to be quiet and still for that?'

'Yeah,' she sighed and rolled onto her back while rubbing her damp hair with the towel. 'I'll call and say I've changed my mind. I really wanted to do Italian. But the woman enrolling that course was like an ancient little shrivelled person who'd been exhumed after the disaster in Pompeii.' Róisín laughed and shook her head. Jill was incorrigible, but she adored her.

'I brought Sushi for you to try,' Róisín said. 'And some delicious white wine. It's a Riesling. A really special Spätlese to be precise.'

'A who?'

'Spätlese, or sweet wine from the Rhone valley. It's usually served with desserts, but I think it'll work magically with the fish and rice along with the pickled ginger.'

'You're not selling this to me, Róisín,' Jill said, looking mildly disgusted. 'I'm hankering after a bowl of creamy pasta or a bag of chipper chips.'

'Trust me, you'll love this. I'll get it sorted while you get dressed.'

She padded into the kitchen and waved her hand to try and clear the settling smoke. Róisín prepared a platter with the Sushi, hoping the pretty array of pinks and white would entice Jill. She popped the cork on the wine just as Jill appeared in a rabbit onesie and snuggled into the sofa.

'Let's eat in here, by the stove,' she said. 'The chairs are too hard and upright for my poor body.'

Róisín brought the platter to the coffee table and instructed Jill to remove the pile of corrections she'd flung there.

With the encouragement of the glass of wine and Róisín's earnest nods, Jill popped a piece of Sushi into her mouth. Grimacing, she held it there without chewing.

'For crying out loud, you're acting as if I'm feeding you slugs! Eat it, you goon!'

As she chewed, Jill's eyes popped open in surprise. 'Wow,' she said swallowing. 'That's really tasty.'

'I know,' Róisín said in mild exasperation.

'Wine is divine too,' she said, drinking greedily. 'Looks like that time in France wasn't a total waste after all. You know your gargle, my friend,' she said, helping herself to another piece of sushi.

Róisín smiled, because that was what Jill expected. But whenever France was mentioned, and specifically her time spent there in an exclusive French culinary school after she had graduated from university, it was as if Róisín had been punched in the gut. She had learned far more than wine appreciation in her time there. Over the two-year period she'd spent near Bordeaux she'd probably experienced every emotion known. But she knew the best policy was to keep France and all the events that had unfolded there to the back of her mind.

'Looking forward to your party tomorrow?' Jill asked, with a fresh look of glee in her eyes. 'Do you feel old? I can't believe you're leaving your twenties behind and heading for your thirties,' she teased.

'Jill, I'm two months older than you. Enough of the old talk,' she said. She tried to keep her tone light-hearted, but Róisín was actually dreading hitting the big 3-0. She glanced at Jill, who was horsing into the Sushi and making appreciative noises. She wished she shared her friend's carefree attitude to life.

'Touchy, touchy,' Jill said. 'So answer my question. Are you looking forward to the party or not?'

'So-so.' Róisín hesitated. 'Actually, I'm dreading it. I feel like a total wipe-out. What have I got to show for myself at thirty? Look at Liv. She's younger than me and she's married with two children. I thought I'd be settled and happy too, by now.'

'Oh bloody hell, Ro, let's tune the violin. Seriously? Are you really saying you'd be happier if you were surrounded by nappies and whinging?'

'Well, when you put it like that . . .'

'Take it from me. I'm with small children day in, day out. They're gorgeous and funny and full of life and completely head-wrecking. Thirty is young, for God's sake. It's only the beginning. We have years ahead for worrying about body clocks or wiping noses all day. There are places to see, wine to drink, men to shag and a whole host of nonsense we need to get involved with. So enough of your depressing talk. Tomorrow is the beginning of the next decade. Grab it by the balls and live your life, my friend!'

In spite of her inward gloom, Róisín couldn't help laughing at Jill. Her *joie de vivre* was infectious. Jill filled their glasses and raised hers up high. 'To you,' she said. 'May your thirties be flirty and fabulous!'

Róisín stood up, clinked her glass against Jill's and smiled.

Chapter 2

RÓISÍN WOKE BEFORE THE ALARM CLOCK NEXT morning, which wasn't unusual for her. She hadn't finished her wine last night, knowing today was going to be busy. There were two deliveries due and Róisín knew she'd probably have to leave work early to go over to her parents' house for birthday cake.

'I'm thirty, Mum,' she whispered to the ceiling. 'Does that make you feel old? It makes me feel old.'

After a quick shower she stepped into her white with red polka dots 1950s tea dress. Hoping for some warm weather, she left off her tights and slipped into a pair of red ballerina pumps. Her thick, dark hair was still a little wild after the night before, so she pulled it back with a scarlet Alice band and put some crystal studs in her ears. Popping in a matching nose-stud, she moisturised and smoothed a little BB cream on her face. A perfectly formed tick of black liquid eyeliner added to the mascara she layered on her long lashes.

After brushing her teeth she applied ruby red lip-gloss and ran to her car. Her baby blue Fiat 500 never failed to make her smile. She preferred to walk, but knowing she'd need her car later at some point for nipping across to her parents' B&B, she fired it up and sped toward the village.

This was Róisín's favourite time of the day. The fishing

boats could be seen bobbing on the ocean, already well into their day's work. The postman was cycling laboriously on his round and there was a traffic jam consisting of her little car and a tractor. As Róisín pulled in beside Nourriture, the farmer waved out the window of his tractor and trundled on.

Delighted that she was already ahead of herself, Róisín unlocked the shutters and flicked on the lights. Her chef and main assistant, Brigid, would be along at any moment, so she switched on the ovens, the computer and cash till.

As she often did when the shop was empty, Róisín took a little walk about to see if she should make any changes. She liked to try and look at the shop from a newcomer's perspective. The main counter was placed toward the rear of the store, with a full glass section that let customers see the fresh salads and delicatessen goods. The breads and cakes section was a little to the right, in a glass display unit topped by large hand-made baskets. Soon, Brigid would fill each one with croissants, brown yeast bread, rock salt-encrusted white plaits, plain and fruit scones and oozing *pain au chocolat*.

The new sushi counter was over near the wall that led to the wine shop. Róisín was always looking for new and tasty offerings and she had a great feeling about this one. If she could convert Jill to sushi, she could convert anyone. Jill's idea of gourmet involved a plastic pot of dried noodles and boiling water.

The space by the window would house the new smoothie station. She'd ordered state-of-the-art machines to create nutritious juices. Her plan was to offer them at a set price with a healthy granola bar for the school children.

The navy-and-white theme throughout the café was

accented by little red wooden hearts and pretty trinkets. The fresh flowers at each wooden table were meticulously replaced and arranged with stylish simplicity each day.

When she'd taken over the building four years ago, it had been dishevelled and damp and badly in need of renovation. Her landlord, Mr Grace, had given her free rein to do whatever she felt was right.

It had taken three months of hard graft every single day, much of it carried out with her own fair hands, but finally it had come together and Nourriture had opened to great local fanfare. Róisín had thought of everything, from home-made lemonade for the non-bubbly drinkers to sugar-free and gluten-free snacks for the food allergy sufferers.

The eager photographer from the local newspaper had verged on intrusive as he'd trailed her for the night, snapping shots constantly.

'I don't suppose you'd like to go on a date next week?' he asked, blushing furiously to the roots of his sandy, spiky hair.

'Eh,' she'd been totally caught out. 'I don't think I'll have time. I need to try and make money so I don't end up living on the side of the road,' she joked.

'Can't your boss give you a day off then?' he asked.

'I am the boss,' she said.

'Huh? Really? You look too young . . . I thought you were only helping out.'

'Thanks,' she beamed. 'I'm actually twenty-six. Nearly twenty-seven, in fact.'

'No way!' he said, shaking his head and laughing. 'You're well old! I thought you were around my age. That shows you what a bad judge of women I am. My last girlfriend was twenty-one and I broke up with her because she was too old. She was too serious. I'm still looking for fun.' He went to walk away, but turned back. 'If I ever consider an older woman, you'll be well up there. You're totally hot. Do you wear coloured contact lenses? Your eyes are a wild shade of blue. A bit like the fishes my da catches, only prettier.'

'Thanks,' she said, laughing. 'I've never been compared to a dead fish before. I'll take all the compliments I can get, though.'

'Yeah, cheers!' he said, walking off.

Little did he know that he had given Róisín the tiny boost of confidence she needed. Dead fish or anything else was fine with her. She'd take it. After what she'd been through with Jacques, she certainly wasn't choosy.

Since the opening night, when all the locals for a ten-mile radius had gathered to wish her well, Nourriture had flourished.

'Who knew such a diverse and cosmopolitan food emporium could do so well in this little backwater,' her dad, Doug, had chuckled. 'I'm ever so proud of you, love. You always did have an eye for things. You're always a step ahead of the rest of us.'

Those words rang through Róisín's head for a long time after. Her dad truly believed she was totally together and sorted, following a definite plan of action. If only he knew the mess she'd made of just about every aspect of her life in France . . . Jacques, with his sexy smile, his ability to whisper sweet nothings in her eager ear and his empty promises . . . But for all his faults and for all the hurt he'd caused her, no man had even come close to breaking down the wall of ice she'd created around her heart since then.

As she was opening the side-door to the kitchen, ready for the morning deliveries, Brigid pitched up. A local woman in her early fifties, she was the backbone of Nourriture. She could turn any ingredient into something delectable and had an uncanny knack for estimating quantities of food for each day. She made meticulous notes in her little red diary and had built up a steady reference base for them to draw upon as the years passed.

'Morning, Róisín. How are you today?'

'Well, thanks Brigid. I like your outfit!'

'Me too,' Brigid said with a wink. She always wore a crisp white chef's jacket, ironed and starched to within an inch of its life, but Brigid had a quirky habit of making her own cotton baggy trousers. Her argument was that they were cool in the heat of the kitchen and she could express her personality without looking a mess. Today's trousers had comical-looking penguins all over them.

'I have a headscarf to match,' she said, pulling a bandana styled piece onto her head and knotting it at the back.

Róisín fired up the coffee machine and dropped an espresso beside Brigid's mixing bowl, before making one for herself. The rich aroma of freshly brewed coffee seemed to alert her senses long before the caffeine had a chance to kick in. The creamy bitter crème on top left a delicious frothy moustache. Róisín flicked on the stereo and selected that day's music compilation.

'I think it's a jazzy rather than a classical sort of day today,' Róisín said, hitting her selection.

'You know me,' Brigid said. 'Give me One Direction or Usher or Mozart and I'll be just as happy!'

The fruit man and then the fish man deposited crates of fresh food inside the door and the rest of the staff ambled in one by one. By the time the doors officially opened at eight thirty, the shop was filled with the smell of fresh baking breads, cakes and quiches, instantly making the early customers feel welcome.

Róisín was always warmed by the strong local support she received. Everyone from sheep-shearers to commuting office workers to families on holiday frequented the shop. Knowing she needed to continually add to her range and remove the things that weren't so popular kept her mind sharp. She was always on the lookout for new products and initiatives.

As she planned the day's specials, Brigid called her to the back kitchen, sounding uncharacteristically hassled.

'What's up?' Róisín asked running into the kitchen where Brigid was holding her hand wrapped in a thick tea towel.

'I think I've burned my hand. I clunked it off the top of the bread oven. I think it might need a doctor to look at it.'

'Oh no, Brigid,' she cried. 'We should have some ointment in the first aid kit.' Róisín rummaged in a drawer, discarding bandages and plasters. 'Found it,' she turned to Brigid.

'Can you show me where it hurts?'

'Oh, I don't know,' Brigid said staggering sideways and heading jerkily towards the counter.

'Wait,' Róisín said in alarm, following her, 'let me help you.'

To her utter astonishment, the previously calm shop was filled with rows of smiling faces.

'One, two, three,' Jill said.

The gaggle of small children burst into an excited rendition of 'Happy Birthday', joined by Brigid, waving her very unburnt hand at Róisín. As the children finished singing, all the staff clapped and Brigid produced a chocolate cake with a tiny marzipan figurine with an astonishing likeness to Róisín on top.

'I didn't think you'd want too many candles,' she said. 'So I put you on there instead.'

Róisín was still standing there, open-mouthed. 'Thank you all!' she said at last. 'You are the best birthday choir ever. What a wonderful surprise! Jill, you're a mad woman,' she said, shaking her head at her friend.

'Do we get cake now?' one of the little boys asked.

'Of course,' Brigid said. 'Here's one I prepared earlier,' she said with a laugh. From behind the counter she brought out slices of cake on paper plates, with plastic forks and napkins – as organised as ever. 'There aren't enough seats, so we'll all sit cross-legged on the floor and have our cake,' Jill said in her teacher voice. Róisín, Jill and Brigid had a chat and a laugh while the children ate up their cake and then piled up their plates for the recycling bin. 'Right, we'd better skedaddle so we don't scare off the actual customers,' Jill said. 'Happy birthday you,' she said, giving Róisín a tight hug.

Jill clapped her hands and the children formed a perfect line and followed her out like little ducklings. Róisín and Brigid waved them off.

'You'd never think that Jill could command such order when you see what she's like at home,' Róisín said to Brigid. 'She can't even make tea and toast. She sits and waits like a baby bird for me to come back to the nest and feed her.'

'Yeah, there's one fool living in that cottage, and it's not Jill,' Brigid said with a grin.

Work resumed and, as she and Brigid had predicted, the sunshine brought hordes of people. The white sandy beach at Seal's Rest Bay a mile and a half beyond Ballyshore was Róisín's all-time favourite. She'd travelled to many corners of the globe and had yet to find one more beautiful. The green fields and rugged coastline seemed to be stooping to frame and protect the golden sands as the glittery black rocks provided perfect perches for sunbathing and diving. The smooth beach welcomed picnickers in summer and bracing walkers in winter. Today, it would be playing host to a crowd of people anxious for any little bit of summer they could get.

It wasn't unusual for Mr Grace, Róisín's landlord, to drop by Nourriture for a creamy cappuccino late morning. Róisín smiled as he approached the counter and reached for a take-out cup.

'Lovely morning out there from what I can see,' she said. 'How are you today, Mr Grace?'

'Indeed it is,' he said, looking edgy.

'Is everything OK?' she asked, dropping her smile instantly.

'I'd like a word, if I may?' he said.

'Sure, will you have a cappuccino and a fresh Danish? They're the ones with the cinnamon, just the way you like them.'

'Ah no. Thanks all the same, but I'm on the run today. Just a quick word.'

Róisín followed as he made his way to a small table beside the window.

'So what can I do for you, Mr Grace?'

He lifted his head and made momentary eye contact. 'I'm afraid . . . I need to give you notice, Róisín.'

'Notice of what?'

'I've had a bad run of it these past few years. What with my boys being without a mother, Lord rest her, and all the responsibility resting on my shoulders. I've had to make a difficult decision.'

'I don't understand,' she said.

'I've had an offer. Someone wants to buy this place,' he said. 'I know you like it here and your food is lovely. But it's an offer I can't refuse. I'd be mad to . . .'

Róisín's head was reeling, trying to catch up with the meaning of what he was saying. 'But Mr Grace . . . what am I meant to do about Nourriture? Do you think the person who's buying the building would let me continue renting?'

'No, lass. To be honest with you, I'd be fairly certain he's thinking of knocking it all down and starting again. There's the small garden to the rear and the strip of land to the side. Well, it seems he thinks he can put a big building in.'

Róisín swallowed. She hadn't seen this coming.

'I know you took the place in good faith four years ago.'

'At a time when it was falling down and nobody wanted it,' Róisín added.

He closed his eyes momentarily. 'This isn't easy for me,' he said. 'But I can't look a gift-horse in the mouth. I need to secure my sons' futures. I've no other way of going about it.'

Róisín wanted to yell in his face. She wanted to tell his two adult sons to get up off their lazy asses and stop drinking their father's money and get a life and a job each. But her mother had always told her to say nothing in moments of raw anger. To keep her mouth shut and wait for the torrent of anger to pass. She took deep breaths and tried to maintain her composure.

'I'll have to give you this now,' Mr Grace said, putting an envelope on the table between them. 'There are pieces of paper in there that explain when you need to be out and all those sorts of things. Seeing as our lease was only for a year at a go, it'll be up in four months' time.'

Róisín looked into the old man's eyes. He looked shamed and saddened and she hated herself for hating him.

'I wish there'd been another way,' he said, pushing his chair back.

Róisín got up too and they moved towards the door. Just then Steve, one of the college students Róisín had hired for the summer, burst in.

'Happy birthday, boss!' he said, sweeping her into a twirling hug. 'Sorry I missed the cake earlier. Did you nearly wet yourself with shock? Have you brought a big pressie for Róisín, Mr Grace?' He dropped her and elbowed the man playfully.

'I didn't know it was your birthday,' Mr Grace said.

'She's really old, too,' Steve teased, drawing a big thirty with his finger in the air.

Mr Grace turned abruptly and strode out the door.

'What did I say?' Steve said, flushing. 'Sorry if I overstepped the mark,' he said holding his hands up. 'My mother is always telling me I have the subtlety of a brick.'

'You're grand,' Róisín said, forcing a smile. 'I think Mr Grace is having one of those days. He can be a bit like that. No harm done. There's cake left at the back for you, so enjoy that and then get started on setting up the fruit. I'm expecting the smoothie machines any minute now.'

'Deadly, I can't wait for this,' he said. 'I've told my

mates in college and they're all well up for coming down. Will we be doing wheatgrass shots? Apparently they're rank but really good for you. A huge group of the lads will be coming round here for the surf and the birds, if you know what I mean?'

'Ah, the bathing beauties that Seal's Rest attracts in their droves,' Róisín grinned. 'Yeah, I've ordered a little hand machine to crush wheatgrass. So you can take charge of feeding those to your body beautiful mates.'

'Nice one,' he said, running to grab Brigid and swing her around too. She swatted him away.

'Put those muscles to good use and lift the big flour bags to the dry store room for me,' she said.

Róisín wanted to cry. Instead, she fixed a smile on her face and made it through the shop to the back stairs. Taking them two at a time, she managed to close the door to her office before she fell onto her chair. The tears came quick then, as she slid the pages from the envelope. How could this be happening? What would she do without Nourriture? This place was her life, her sanity and most of all her greatest achievement. She'd mourned the fact she'd no husband or children last night. Now it was looking as if she'd have no business either. Nothing. Happy bloody birthday, she said biting her finger in a vain attempt to stop her sobbing.

When her mobile phone rang a few minutes later, Róisín glanced at the screen and knew she needed to gather herself, and quickly. Wiping her eyes and blowing her nose, she answered with as much cheer as she could muster.

'Hi Mum,' she managed.

'Happy birthday, love! How are you?'

'Good, thanks,' she lied.

'You sound a bit muffled. Is everything OK?'

'Oh I've just had a sneezing fit. I'll have to start taking spoons of Manuka honey again. I'd say it's that blasted hayfever starting up.'

'Oh,' Keeley said. 'Poor you.'

'I'll be fine, Mum.'

'Now, I know we'll be seeing you this evening at our place, but I wanted to hear your voice before then. I wish you could take the day off. Do you think you can?'

'I'd love to,' she said. 'But there's so much to do and I wouldn't relax.'

'Alright then. I'd better let you go. You're sounding very distracted there.'

'Sorry, Mum. I'll chat to you properly later, OK?'

'Of course.'

Róisín hung up. Her head was thumping and she was feeling totally overwhelmed. She wished she could go home after work and curl into a ball and cry. She couldn't let her mum and dad down, though. She thought of Keeley and Doug. They were the one constant in her life. With her corkscrew chestnut-coloured curls and her warm smiling brown eyes, Keeley Daly was one of life's true ladies. Róisín's dad, Doug, was her mum's perfect companion and she hadn't lost hope that some day she'd find a love like they had.

'You two are like two peas in a pod,' she said, at their ruby wedding anniversary dinner last year.

'More like Tweedle-Dum and Tweedle-Dee,' joked Keeley.

'Or Homer and Marge,' said Doug.

'You're as wonderful to me as Laurence Olivier and Vivien Leigh,' Róisín said.

'Or Baby and Johnny from *Dirty Dancing*,' Róisín's sister Liv piped up, to much laughter.

Róisín couldn't ruin the birthday get-together her parents had planned so she'd just have to push the shock of Mr Grace's announcement to the back of her mind for now. After all, she thought as an image of Jacques passed through her mind, she was the queen of keeping secrets.

When Róisín had envisaged her thirtieth birthday ten or twenty years ago, she hadn't imagined it taking place in her parents' back garden in Ballyshore with her sister Liv's four-year-old son and two-year-old daughter as the main attraction. Although she adored Billy and Jess, a sedate gathering with the inevitable discount-store bunting threaded gaudily around the trees and music by her mother's idol, Barry Manilow, being pumped from a crackly speaker at the kitchen window wasn't even close to what she'd thought would happen.

Having spent two years immersed in the culinary culture of Bordeaux and the surrounding areas, she knew she had almost alienated herself from her childhood environment in the west of Ireland. She'd loved everything about Bordeaux, from the cuisine to the fiery dark-eyed men who had entertained her. She'd struggled to settle back here in the rugged isolation and simplicity of Ballyshore, and her initial frustration hadn't been helped by the heartbreak and disappointment at having to exit her life in France so suddenly.

For a moment in time she'd genuinely believed her future happiness could be found by marrying Jacques, and having beautiful, bronzed Breton children with names like Fabienne and Stéphane. But it had turned out that Jacques wasn't ready to commit to her. When things had gone pear-shaped, she'd packed up everything bar her pride and returned home shattered but tight-lipped about the events leading to her return.

Her parents and younger sister were thrilled to see her back and welcomed her with open arms. Not for the first time, she saw how amazing her family truly were. They pulled out all the stops to ensure she stayed around, too. Her childhood bedroom had been renovated to become part of her mother's B&B, but it was instantly removed from the busy rental list and she was assured she could stay as long as she wished.

The excitement of starting a new business a year after she'd returned home had taken the heat off the fact she was dying inside. Róisín couldn't tell anyone the real reason she'd left France and nobody pushed the point. But why would they? Any time Jacques was mentioned, she'd firmly assure people it was all for the best.

'It's difficult to mix two cultures. It wasn't meant to be so it was best to face the music sooner rather than later,' she'd assured her mother, arranging her face in a convincing smile.

'But don't you miss him, love?' Keeley asked, not long after she returned.

'Of course,' she'd sighed. 'But it's more of a case of breaking the habit than being heartbroken.'

When her mother had nodded and looked as if she understood, Róisín had learned something new — it was easy to hide her feelings once she did it with a smile. The same lie had worked on Jill. She was astonished that her best friend had swallowed it hook, line and sinker. But she had. Smiling and making herself go on a few boozy nights out, where she giggled in company and cried herself to sleep in private, was all it took to convince everyone that she was glad and even relieved to be home.

Her main therapy at the time was to throw herself into

her new business. Sourcing special cured meats, tasty cheeses and delectable wines for her emporium had been such a joy. Róisín eventually managed to convince herself that Nourriture was her reward, and her exchange for the life she'd lost in France. She'd even tried to convince herself that she'd get over Jacques some day. That he would seem like a distant and very sweet memory. She was still waiting for that closure.

Channelling the smile she'd grown so accustomed to plastering across her face, Róisín took a deep breath and resolved not to talk to anyone about the bombshell Mr Grace had just lobbed at her. But deep down, she wasn't sure how long she could continue with the façade if Nourriture was taken from her.

Chapter 3

THE SOUND OF MO'S KEY TURNING IN THE FRONT door made Nell jump. She'd been recording the tides and taking snapshots of the bay and time had run away with her. She'd always been an early riser, but after forty-six years of running Ballyshore lighthouse she was well and truly a servant of the sea.

'Good morning to you, Nell my love,' said Mo cheerfully. 'That's a grey start out there, but I don't need to tell you that.'

'Hello Mo,' she said politely. 'The light has changed, mind you. We'll start to see an even longer stretch in the evenings before long.'

'True, not that it bothers me,' Mo said as she hung up her coat. 'Once I get to see my soaps and read my books, I don't care if it's winter or summer.'

'Fair enough,' Nell said as she hid a smile. By 'books' Mo wasn't referring to a Russian spy novel or the latest bestseller, she meant the weekly women's magazines she pored over and whose information she regurgitated at Nell from time to time. 'Now if you'll excuse me, Mo, I'll go and have a look at the garden.'

'I'll call you for your cup of coffee when I'm on my break,' Mo called after her.

Nell knew she could probably manage perfectly well

without Mo. In fact, for several weeks after she'd started, she'd told the woman not to return. But Mo had selective hearing along with an unquenchable desire to witter on, no matter who her audience might be.

Most of the lighthouses in Ireland were the responsibility of the Commissioners of Irish Lights, but a small number, including Ballyshore lighthouse, were run by local authorities. So although Nell didn't actually own the place, nobody would dream of asking her to leave. Her job was specific and constant and very few people would survive the isolation. Mo's little Micra was one of the only vehicles besides Nell's to bumble along the rugged coast road to the lighthouse. Mo was always at pains to remind Nell just how secluded it was, as if she could coax her to live in the town.

'If it was any more windy out there, I'd be swept away,' Mo would announce. 'And Lord only knows how long I'd be bobbing about in that sea before my John-Joe would notice. But he's still the light of my life.'

'I'd notice that canary yellow car you insist on driving in a split second,' Nell said. 'And your John-Joe would realise fairly swiftly if his dinner wasn't on the table.'

Mo laughed when she said things like that, but Nell wasn't trying to be funny. She detested Mo's car. It was one of those gimmicky, new-fangled ones that was only really useful for one person, and the colour made her eyes water. As for her husband, John-Joe . . . he was the most useless creature on God's earth. He'd been 'unable to find work' for the past forty years and had no problem sending his wife off cleaning pubs, houses and indeed her lighthouse. Nell often wondered where the worthless creature had actually looked for a job – at the bottom of a pint glass? On the pattern on his dinner plate? He moaned if his dinner was five minutes late and continuously visited the doctor with invented illnesses that sent poor Mo into a panic.

'He's really unwell today, Nell,' she'd said just before Christmas. 'He thinks he has gallstones. He's in terrible pain.'

'Has his skin turned yellow? Is he doubled over in pain and unable to move?' Nell asked.

'Well, his poor eyes were very glassy and he said he couldn't manage another piece of bacon and French toast this morning. He's headed for the doctor as soon as I finish my work and get back to fetch him.'

'Why can't he go by himself? It's only a few hundred yards away from your house.'

'Ah now Nell, I couldn't let him walk when he's got suspected gallstones, could I, love?'

Nell wanted to grunt that she would happily get that man moving with the help of a cattle prod, but she kept her thoughts to herself.

Needless to say, the following week there was no mention of gallstones. It had turned out John-Joe had gotten a clean bill of health from the doctor – again.

'He put the pain down to a dodgy hot port at the pub,' Mo said innocently. For a perfectly intelligent woman, Mo baffled Nell at times. How could she accept her good-for-nothing husband's guff? All she could concede was that love was blind. In her opinion, in this instance love also seemed to be deaf and dumb, but at the end of the day John-Joe wasn't her concern, thank the Lord for small mercies.

Nell kept her cool by not asking about John-Joe (ever)

or even commenting when Mo told her about him. He only came to the lighthouse once a year for mince pies. That gesture was purely for Mo as Nell knew she looked forward to the occasion. On that one day a year, Nell resisted the urge to put arsenic in the mincemeat and did her best not to scowl at John-Joe as he chomped open-mouthed at her kitchen table.

Today as she made her way outside, pulling on her favourite bright green waterproof overalls, Nell closed her eyes and inhaled. She'd never tire of the fresh saltiness of the west of Ireland air. She knew the people in the village thought she was some sort of madwoman, living out in a lighthouse all alone, but quite frankly she didn't give a toss what anyone thought of her. This was the best move she'd ever made and she didn't regret a single day she'd spent here.

From Dublin originally, Nell had grown up in a very different setting. Instead of the magical expanse of the Wild Atlantic Way, she'd been raised in the concrete bunkers of the inner-city flats. The only view she'd known was shrouded in pollution and decorated with graffiti. Then, on that fateful day all those years ago, she'd made the decision to leave Dublin and everyone she knew. Scouring the papers, she'd come across the advert for a lighthouse-keeper. Her geography wasn't the best, but even she knew that Ballyshore was in the middle of nowhere.

The interview for the job was different from most in that the man, a local government representative, had pretty much asked her if she could stick living there.

'With this post, it's not really a case of whether or not we want you, more to the point it's if you think you can bear to be stationed out here. I'm not going to lie to you, it can be pretty bleak. You'll be the fourth person in as many months to take this post.'

'How much would you pay me?' she asked.

The wage seemed too good to be true, but Nell held her poker face and said she was happy to give it a shot.

The man handed her a thin book with the order of work typed up and wished her well. She raised an eyebrow as he drove off at high speed but looking back on it, he'd probably thought she wouldn't last spitting time. Back then she hadn't looked the way she did now. Her waist-length hair had been ash blonde rather than snow-white. Her weather-worn skin had been blemish-free and she certainly hadn't half the wrinkles she saw staring back at her these days. Her now calloused hands were smooth with just a hint of yellowing from nicotine staining.

In the greater scheme of things, not much had changed. She'd given up her twenty-a-day smoking habit purely because it was far too much hassle walking to the nearest shop, which was six miles away. She'd grown into her angular features and was fairly uninterested in the finer details, such as blemishes or lines.

Still, she mused, she'd no desire to look like one of those women who put all their energy into looking twenty years younger. What was the point? She was in her mid-seventies, whoop-di-do. Weren't women of her age supposed to have lines and white hair?

She hadn't planned on staying here for ever, but somehow that's what had come to pass. Once she'd proven she could hack the job, the council offered her a car.

'A little run-around would give you a lot more freedom. It would help with access to schools for your daughter, too.'

She'd raised an eyebrow and nodded. The thought of going to the village and having to sit in a car with some nosey instructor didn't appeal to her, but she knew she needed to do it for Laura.

It still hurt her to think of Laura . . . That was the most notable difference between now and back then: Nell wasn't alone in those days. She'd had her baby girl to keep her company. In actual fact, Laura was the main reason Nell had moved to Ballyshore. All she'd ever wanted was to protect her. Being shunned by her father was something her daughter had to deal with, but Nell couldn't allow her to grow up in a small-minded community where pitying stares and hushed whispers followed them. She'd only ever done what she'd thought was right.

As she pulled on her woolly hat and gardening gloves, she forced all thoughts of the past from her mind. The wind felt icy, even though it was May. She crouched to inspect her garden. She hadn't known the first thing about growing stuff until she came here. Living in the inner-city it wasn't something her family had ever thought of doing, but here, with the scenery and the rural setting, it seemed rude not to join in. She was glad of it now. Gardening was her therapy. She could plant things and look forward to seeing them flourish and grow. It was like having friends who didn't pass comment or judge her.

Today she'd planned on planting the huge bucket of late-flowering bulbs she'd bought. Daffodils were Laura's favourite, but she liked to keep the colours going as far into the autumn as possible. She rested on the handle of her shovel and gazed out at the sea and up at the sky. The water looked like rolling mercury as the wind herded it in. A proper bit of sun would be a welcome luxury for sure.

Knowing Mo would be delighted with a cup of coffee and a chat, she decided to go back inside. Her back was acting up a bit anyway.

'I think there might be a spot of rain on the way,' she told Mo.

'I was going to say . . . but I know you well enough at this point to hold my own counsel.'

Nell grinned at the irony of the comment as she removed her heavy boots. The day Mo learned to hold her tongue, there'd be snowballs in hell.

'Coffee?' Nell said.

'Oh yes, dear. That'd be lovely. I don't suppose you've any of those nutty chocolate biscuits in your tin?' Mo asked, eyeing the goodies cupboard hopefully.

'As a matter of fact, I do,' she said. 'Did your John-Joe enjoy the ones I sent him?'

'Oh I'm so rude, I should've told you. He gobbled the whole packet inside a single afternoon. He said to tell you they were your best find yet.'

'He says that every time I send him anything,' Nell said dryly. 'I suppose I should only worry when he doesn't say it.'

'That's true,' said Mo as she accepted a plate of the cookies and a mug of tea. It always intrigued her that Mo and John-Jo seemed to believe she had some kind of talent for finding things. Nor would it ever occur to them to purchase the things themselves. Mo bought the same products every week, so Nell's bit of diversion was always greeted with awe.

'I took your advice and we ate that Christmas pudding I won at bingo back in December. I'm ever so glad you told me not to throw it away. It was quite delicious. John-Jo loved it once he got his head around eating it at the wrong time of the year,' Mo said.

'There's never a wrong time of the year to eat pudding, if you ask me,' Nell said. Mo nodded. 'I'm not a massive fan of microwaves as you know,' Nell said, 'but nothing else heats pudding quite like it.'

'Unless you fry it in bubbly butter,' Mo said licking her lips at the thought of it. As she laughed, Mo's chins wobbled and her large tummy bobbed up and down.

Nell offered Mo some squirty cream from a can to put in her coffee, which she accepted. This was one of the only throwbacks to her time in the flats in Dublin. Her ma used to buy it for special occasions, along with a tub of sugar strands.

Nell squirted a large rosette of cream into her coffee.

'I've never met another person who does that,' Mo said, shaking her head. 'And there'd be more fat on a sparrow's knee than your entire body.'

'I don't know about that now, Mo,' she said. 'I have more wobbly bits than you'd realise. That's the advantage to dressing in baggy clothing. I'm always warm and comfy and nobody has the first idea of what lurks underneath.'

There was a convivial silence as Mo tucked into the cookies and Nell enjoyed her coffee. Mo looked up at Nell and back down at the table. She did it twice more and Nell knew there was a question coming.

'I know I've asked you before,' Mo said, 'but would you reconsider your decision and come to the bingo with me, Nell? I think you'd enjoy it. There's a lovely crew of over sixties at it and it's great fun.'

'Thank you, Mo,' she said carefully. 'You're kind to ask, but as I said before, I couldn't think of anything worse than sitting in a hall with a bunch of wrinklies squinting at a sheet of paper.'

'Ah Nell,' she laughed. 'You're a terror. You don't have to make it sound so horrendous!'

'And it isn't?' she asked, raising an eyebrow.

'No, you dreadful woman, it isn't.'

Nell scraped her chair back from the table, letting Mo know in no uncertain terms that their chat was now over.

It had taken years for her to get to this point with Mo and as far as she was concerned, they were as close as they needed to be. She'd purposely hidden away from people and it had served her well. But Mo was one of those women who craved the company and conversation of others. Nell found some of her stories exhausting. She was always off on bus tours and the like. It seemed to please her no end, so Nell made the right noises and wished her well each time. But as for joining in, Nell couldn't bear the idea. She knew what folk were like. She knew the bitter and mean thoughts they harboured in their heads. She'd borne the brunt of it all those years ago and she wasn't going to be burned twice.

'If you'll excuse me,' she said to Mo. 'I need to set up some of my observation equipment and I need to finish off my books. The council will send one of their minions any day now. I like to have all the paperwork in order so I can simply hand the file over.'

'Do you invite the poor sod in?'

'What poor sod?' she asked.

'The one given the job of trekking over here to see you,' Mo said.

'I've never seen the need,' she said. 'If they want to conduct an inspection, I'd be happy to oblige. But I see no reason why I'd let some random stranger into my home.'

Nell cleared away the few dishes and made her way up to the observatory. She was fond of Mo and, more than that, she was very used to her now. But it irked her when she started trying to organise her or make her conform.

As she sat at her desk and turned on the computer, Nell sighed. Plucking the photo of smiling Laura from its little stand, she allowed a couple of tears to escape. As soon as she felt them wriggle warmly down her cheeks, she put the picture back and rubbed her eyes roughly.

'I hope you're happy my beautiful girl,' she whispered into the silence as she closed her eyes and took a deep breath before turning her attention to her work.

What seemed like moments later, Mo shouted up the narrow spiral staircase to say she was going.

'All done for this week then?' Nell said appearing at the top of the stairs.

'That's it, my dear. Unless there's anything else you need?'

'No, thank you kindly, Mo. I'm sure you've done a sterling job as usual. Thanks and see you next week. Oh, I almost forgot. I made a batch of Jerusalem artichoke soup. It's in the fridge, on the second shelf.'

'Ah you're a sweetheart,' Mo said. 'John-Joe will be delighted. Your soups put him in a good mood for days!'

Nell hadn't the patience for cooking in general. She didn't find it therapeutic like the gardening, but she did gain considerable satisfaction from eating the vegetables she grew. She had two great big pots that usually had some sort of stew or a vat of soup on the go. She only had a tiny compartment freezer tucked into the top of the fridge, so any spare soups or stews were put into plastic containers and given to Mo. She'd gotten into a little routine where she cooked on a Thursday and gave part of the results to Mo on a Friday.

'Bye Mo,' she said with a grunt. She doubted anything bar a pint of Guinness put that dreadful man in good form.

'Oh, and I have your newspapers. I'll leave them at the hall door.'

'Thank you, my dear,' she said.

Each week Mo brought the local and national news-papers from the previous week. While Nell enjoyed reading them, she'd never got into the habit of driving to the local shop on a daily basis for them.

On the whole, she only left the lighthouse on a Monday. On that day she'd go to Ballyshore and visit the supermarket on the outskirts of the village and then sort whatever bank business needed doing. Her only treat, and by now it was more of a ritual than anything, was to stop by Mrs Mangan's coffee shop. Each week she ordered the exact same thing, a custard slice and a cappuccino. Each week she and Mrs Mangan had the same conversation.

'Hello Nell.'

'Hello Mrs Mangan.'

'Will it be your usual?'

'Yes, please.'

'Any news with yourself, Nell?'

'Not a thing, what about you?'

'Ah divil a bit, Nell.'

Nell would sit in the same window seat, at a tiny table that faced the wall with the space for a single chair. Mrs Mangan would serve her drink and cake, she'd hand over the exact change and that was it until Nell waved goodbye.

The exchange always gave Nell a little lift. She enjoyed the crumbly pastry and the frothy coffee and her small snippet of village life through the window. Nobody annoyed her. Nobody questioned her. It was just the right amount of human contact.

Sitting at her desk, Nell strained to the left to see if Mo's car was out of sight. When she was certain that it was, she tiptoed down the stairs to retrieve the clod of newspapers.

Instead of reading each and every news story, Nell did what she always did and scanned the pages quickly. The third paper she picked up made her stop. Grabbing her scissors from the desk drawer, she carefully snipped around her chosen article and photograph. With trembling hands she found the precious scrapbook that she kept in the back of her only filing cabinet. Taking her glue stick, she gummed the reverse side of the article and secured it in place.

Chapter 4

RÓISÍN WAS STILL FEELING SHELL-SHOCKED BY THE time she left Nourriture at three o'clock. The best birthday gift she could've gotten was a night of peace to sit and think clearly about how she could possibly save her business and stop her entire life unravelling.

As she pulled up outside her parents' B&B, she was horrified to see a load of cars she recognised. As she stepped out, she could hear excited chatter coming from the back garden.

'Róisín!' Keeley appeared with a wicked grin lighting her pretty features. 'Surprise! We have a lovely gathering of family and friends and they're all thrilled to be here.'

'Oh no, Mum, I didn't realise you would have so many people here. I thought it'd only be us.' The words tumbled from her lips before she could engage her brain.

'Oh.' Keeley's face dropped. 'But what will I tell all the neighbours?'

'I'm kidding, obviously!' she said hugging her and forcing a dry laugh. 'I'm actually just in a bit of shock, that's all. You know me and surprises! I'm not exactly what you'd call spontaneous, now am I?'

'I wouldn't say that,' Keeley said. 'You dashed off to France after all. Stayed there far too long as well. But,' she brightened, 'you ran back home just as quickly, so here we all are,' she said leading her around the side of the house and into a full round of applause as party poppers went off, creating little floaty rainbows of paper.

Her brother-in-law, Martin, was the first to wrench her from Keeley as he wrapped her in a hug.

'Happy birthday, Róisín. It's warming up a bit now. You seem to bring the sunshine with you, even though it's only May.'

'Last year was a total washout,' she reminded him. 'Remember, poor Mum organised a picnic and the rain came down in diagonal sheets and we ended up sitting in the car at the edge of Seal's Rest Bay eating sandwiches on our laps.'

Martin nodded as he slowly recalled the scene. 'Yeah, I was mixing it up with something else . . . Now I remember . . . I was home from Florida and seemed to be the only one who was delighted with the rain!'

'How long are you back for this time, Martin?' she asked.

'Only a few days,' he said. 'I wish I could be here more, but Liv and I need the money and most of my adverts need to be shot in sunny climates. This swimwear company we've taken on seem to have an endless budget, but it's hardly feasible to do bikini shots here in the damp chill.'

'Well, at least you have the work and, more to the point, you have your own family to rush back to,' Róisín said. She could feel her lip tremble and she bit into the inside of her cheek. She was not going to start blubbing at Martin.

'You enjoy the good times while you have them,' Martin whispered into her ear. 'Once you're married and saddled with kids and a mortgage and all that nonsense, your life isn't your own any longer. Take it from me, you're doing the right thing. Enjoy your birthday. I totally envy you.'

She watched him, agog, as he weaved his way to the other side of the garden to chat to Eamonn, an old school friend. Róisín was puzzled. She hoped Martin was simply a bit tipsy, or maybe he was missing Liv and the children terribly.

'Happy birthday, love,' her father said, coming over to plant a kiss on her cheek. 'Did I tell you I'm making a proper workshop out at the back shed?'

'No, Dad, you didn't, but that's a great plan,' she said hugging him tightly. 'It'll keep you out of trouble now you're retired.'

'True,' he laughed. 'That and my fishing. The boat that Jimmy and I bought is really coming into its own. I honestly dreaded retiring and thought I'd be bored stupid by not working. But so far I love being able to concentrate on the things I enjoy doing.'

'Well it's only a few weeks into it all,' Liv warned, joining them. 'If you find you're going out of your mind, you're always welcome to drop over to our house and build things.'

'Thanks, Liv, you're so thoughtful,' he said, laughing.

'How's Mum coping with having you around more?' Róisín asked.

'Ah, she's busy as usual with the B&B. It never stops, but she absolutely loves it. Every spare moment she has is spent in that box room doing her painting too. She's very independent and content in her own world.'

Róisín blanched as she spied Jill staggering under the weight of a massive cake that looked like it could start a forest fire and take out all the trees in a mile radius should she drop it.

'Happy birthday, Ro-Ro,' she said as the neighbours burst into song.

'What's the story with you today? Are you intent on leaping out at every opportunity and shoving a cake at me?'

'Blow out the candles, for crying out loud,' Jill begged. 'This thing weighs more than I do.'

To her utter dismay Róisín realised the cake was in the shape of a bikini.

'I was going to do something fun like a willy,' Jill whispered, 'but then your mother said the elderly neighbours were coming so the next best thing at the cake shop was the itsy-bitsy-teeny-weeny-yellow . . .'

'Polka-dot-bikini,' Róisín finished with a grin. 'Thanks Jill, you complete and utter nutter.'

'I'd have given anything to serve a slice of willy to Miss Dean, though. She's the embodiment of misery. Look at her over there, chewing the ear off your poor mother.' Róisín glanced over at the elderly neighbour. She'd worn the same housecoat over a floral shirt-waister dress for as long as Róisín could recall. As an eighty-odd-year-old spinster, she'd turned into a bitter and cross old woman. Fleetingly, Róisín hoped she wasn't looking at her future self.

Once the bikini was chopped up and doled out, Róisín did a tour of the garden, thanking the neighbours for coming. She ended up with a strange collection of gifts, from rosary beads to a book token for a shop that had closed down at least a decade ago, to a voucher for two chicks from Mrs Hagerty who owned the free-range hen farm.

'I was going to bring them along in a shoebox, but I wasn't sure if you'd have a run at your cottage. I'll happily keep them at the farm and deliver their eggs to you once a week if that would suit you better?'

'That would be wonderful, if you don't mind,' Róisín said. 'Jill and I are out at work a lot of the time, so I don't think we'd be great at looking after hens.'

'They don't need to watch the television or be brought for a walk,' Mrs Hagerty barked. 'But you do need a proper pen to save them from the fox and knowing you and that mad one Jill, they'd end up doused in hairspray and nail varnish.'

As she walked off muttering, with the token still firmly clasped in her hand, Mrs Hagerty seemed very cross.

'I don't know what I did wrong,' Róisín whispered to Keeley. 'She gave me a gift and more or less told me I can't have it now.'

'The poor pet isn't too well,' Keeley said. 'She brings that voucher everywhere. It helps her to feel important and it has her name and address on it in case she gets lost. Her Brian was telling your father she was delivered home by the Rentokil van last week. A little ironic, but terrible sad.'

While Róisín felt for Mrs Hagerty, she was beginning to feel exhausted. Her mother bustled off to make more teas and coffees and Liv came up to her and gave her a hug.

'How are you bearing up?' Liv asked.

'Would it sound horrible if I said I'd rather be sitting on the sofa with you, having a glass of wine?'

'That, my darling sister, is exactly what I wanted you to say!'

'What do you mean?'

'Come on, follow me. I have your birthday gift in here.'

Intrigued, Róisín followed Liv inside to the sitting room and they shut the door gently.

'I don't have a huge amount of cash at the moment,' Liv said. 'So I've made a little video. I've put it on a disc so you'll have it always.'

Róisín sat on the sofa as Liv set up the DVD. Pulling the curtains shut, Liv perched beside her and took her hand. On-screen, jerky images of them as tots made her smile instantly. Her smiles soon turned to tears as 'You are the Sunshine of my Life' played in the background. There was photo after photo of the two sisters, hugging, playing and sharing special moments. Finally, the screen went blank and as the song played out, a message appeared on the screen: *Thank you for being my soul and my sister.*

Róisín couldn't hold back her tears. 'Oh Liv, that's the most incredible gift you could possibly have given me. We have such amazing memories, don't we? Things that nobody else will ever know about. Things that we will never forget.'

'Thanks for always being there,' Liv said and she began to cry, too. She covered her face.

'Hey, is everything OK?' Róisín asked.

'Yeah,' Liv said a little too quickly. 'Everything is fine. I'm just totally emotional after putting that together. I really enjoyed researching it and making the little movie.'

'I love it,' Róisín said.

The door pushed open and Keeley peered in at them. 'There you are! I was looking for you.'

'Liv made me the most thoughtful gift, Mum,' Róisín said. 'I'll show you once the guests have gone.'

'Lovely,' Keeley said. 'I have some champagne and Liv and Martin are staying over with the children. We're all making a little holiday of your birthday, so you can show me in a while. People are starting to leave, so I thought you might come and say goodbye?'

As they followed Keeley back out into the garden, Róisín spotted Jill drinking bottles of her awful blue vodka alcopop by the neck. She was obviously out for the night. Keeley nudged her. 'You've barely spoken to Colm. He was so pleased about coming today. He's a lovely man, Róisín. You could do a lot worse, you know?'

'Mum,' she said, finding it tough to hide her irritation. 'I'm sure Colm is a lovely bloke.'

'He is. He's a pillar of society, in fact.'

'So I can clearly see,' Róisín said. 'But he wears a brown suit every day of the year. For all I know he sleeps in the darn thing. He also looks at his mother as if she's a super model. Nobody could ever compare to Mrs Burke in his eyes. And to top it all off, he's far too nice for me. I'd kill him within a week. Now you don't want to spend the rest of your days visiting me in prison, do you?'

'No,' Keeley said tightly. 'You don't need to speak to him if you don't want to, Róisín. It's your birthday after all.'

Róisín sighed and walked over to Colm.

'Hello Róisín,' he said and bowed forward slightly. 'Thanks ever so much for inviting me. It's a fantastic party.'

'Really?' she said doubtfully. 'I think it's a nice party, but it's not really my thing . . .'

'A bit wild for you, is it?' Colm said, elbowing her sharply. 'I know the feeling. Mammy can be a bit of a mad woman when she gets at the Limoncello. We bought a bottle in duty-free on the way home from a trip to the Holy City in Rome. That was only eight months ago and she's polished off the whole lot already.'

'How many bottles did you buy?' Róisín asked with a

grin, images of Mrs Burke doing the can-can around their home making her want to laugh.

'Just the one bottle,' Colm said. 'But it was a big one. Mammy is wild as a boar,' he said, suddenly grabbing her forearm in a vice-grip. 'Come on a date with me, Róisín. I'll take you for fish and chips and we'll have wine. Red or white, or even both in the one glass if you want.'

'Colm,' she said evenly, 'I know you mean well, but I'm afraid I'll have to let you down gently. As I've mentioned once or twice before, I'm not really on the market for a new man.'

'But if you were?' He stared hopefully at her. It would be easier to tell him he'd be first in line, but she couldn't do that to him. There wasn't a hope in hell she'd date him, even if the rest of the male population had been wiped out in a chemical spill.

'Colm, I don't think we're compatible. Having heard the stories of wild nights, drinking and trips to the Vatican, I don't see how I'd ever fit in.'

'Ah you would. I'd convince Mammy, eventually . . .'

'No, Colm. I think we should leave it at just friends, OK?'

'Ah now!' he said slapping his leg. 'I see what you're at, Róisín, you little minx. You're playing hard to get, aren't you? I know your sort. Mammy warned me. Well, have it your way. I'll get you again. Friends for now?' he asked winking. 'See you again!'

'Not if I see you first,' she muttered, wanting to box him.

'All good over here?' Keeley asked casually.

'Not if hell freezes over or if pigs do indeed grow wings will I ever date Colm. So do me a favour and stop trying to push us together.'

'What's eating you?' Keeley asked.

'He's a total dweeb, Mum. If that's all I have to look forward to on my birthday, it's a sorry state of affairs!'

Liv joined her and they watched Colm lumbering away.

'Bless him, he's like a cross between Adrian Mole and an overly sympathetic social worker,' Liv said.

'He's found his mammy now,' Róisín said. They both tried to stifle a giggle as he stood gazing at Mrs Burke with his hands clasped and his head tilted so far to the right it was in danger of rolling across the garden like a boule.

'You did well with your Martin,' Róisín said as she linked Liv's arm. 'He's such a dote and adores you and the kids.'

'Do you think?' Liv said sadly.

'Hey,' Róisín stopped and looked at her sister. 'What's going on?'

'Ah, I'm probably imagining it, but he seems less and less bothered by the weeks he's having to spend away.'

'He's probably trying to make the best of it,' Róisín reasoned.

'Yeah, probably,' Liv said. As they looked around for Martin, they expected to see him swinging out of a tree with Billy or chasing Jess, but he was perched on a rock, chatting to Doug's mate Jimmy.

'Things will look up for you guys,' Róisín said firmly. 'Once you get your finances sorted, you'll be back on track. You'll see.'

The last of the guests were saying their goodbyes and while Liv went over to talk to Jill, Róisín started on the tidying up. She knew Keeley wouldn't be able to relax until it was done. She filled a black sack with paper waste and went through the kitchen to bring it to the garage. On her way back, Róisín spotted an A5 brown envelope propped up at the end of the kitchen counter. It was addressed to her, and the stamp was from Galway, the nearest large city. Róisín smiled to herself. It looked like it came from the convent, so it must be this year's card.

Every year since she was born, Róisín had received a birthday card from her birth mother. Keeley and Doug had made it very clear from the beginning that Róisín was adopted.

'You are the most precious gift we could've received. Our hearts were crying out for a baby to love and we were blessed to get you.'

Two years after Róisín arrived, Keeley was astonished to discover she was pregnant with Liv. Their family was complete.

All Róisín knew about herself was that she'd come from Galway and her mother had died soon after she was born. The birthday cards arrived every year, and her parents told her the convent where they had adopted her had been instructed by her mother to send them on. It was such a thoughtful and loving gesture, it made Róisín feel very special. She would have loved to find out more, maybe even go to the convent, but even the cards brought a look of fear and hurt into Keeley's eyes, so she had made the choice long ago to accept that her birth mother was dead and that Keeley and Doug were all the mother and father she'd ever need. There was no point hurting everyone by trying to dig up the past.

Róisín took the brown envelope and slipped into the sitting room again.

She could never have guessed what was inside. It wasn't a card this time. It was a proper letter. It was dated May

1986 and began with the words: *My darling, my beautiful, my daughter . . .*

By the time she'd finished reading, Róisín was struggling for breath. She'd no idea she was crying so loudly and she jumped when Liv came into the room and rushed to her side.

'What's wrong?' she asked, looking pale with worry.

'I . . .' Róisín handed her the letter, unable to speak through her tears. Liv read it, silently. When she came to the end, she read the last lines aloud:

I will watch over you always and I know we will meet again some day. There is nothing more I can say except that I love you. I love you. I love you. I love you, my darling girl, my perfect gift.

Liv looked up at her with tears welling in her eyes. 'Oh Ro,' she said. 'What an incredible letter to receive. But why did this come now, instead of the usual card? I don't understand.'

Róisín took a shaky deep breath. 'The writing is different. It looks as if it were written with a shaky hand. I wonder if I should ask Mum about it.'

As she said it, the girls heard their mother calling down the hall. 'Come when you're finished chatting, my darlings. We're about to open the champagne. Everyone else is gone now.'

The sense of excitement and joy in Keeley's voice gave Róisín her answer.

'Let's say nothing for the moment,' Róisín said and Liv nodded.

'Can you give me a minute?' Róisín asked. 'Do I look as if I've been crying?'

'You look like you've been boxed,' Liv said honestly. 'Why don't you have a shower and put on something comfy and I'll fob the others off for a few minutes.'

'Thanks Liv, you're the best.'

As she climbed out of the shower, Róisín's mobile phone rang. It was Brigid, full of apologies because she needed Róisín to come and lock up.

'I was so intent on getting your cake to work this morning, I left without my keys.'

'No hassle. I'm on my way.'

Róisín couldn't face a long-winded explanation so she popped her head in the kitchen door, where Keeley had gathered the children, Liv and Martin, Doug and Jill, and told them she'd be back in two shakes of a lamb's tail, emergency at Nourriture. Then she raced out of the house and into the sanctuary of her car.

Chapter 5

KEELEY WAS LIVID WITH HER GIRLS. RÓISÍN WAS always in a hurry and never seemed to have time to sit and chat like most normal people. Liv could be downright rude and, although she hated to admit it, slightly selfish too.

Take the party this afternoon, for instance. Everyone was busy in this day and age, but they'd all taken the time to come along. Róisín had made it quite obvious that she wasn't exactly thrilled with the whole thing. Keeley had a million other things to do herself, it wasn't easy running a B&B and being there for her two daughters as well, but she managed to do it without making people feel they were boxes she had to tick. That was important to her. Her girls were her world and she wanted to be there for them.

It bothered her that Róisín was too busy to make time for herself, and for meeting someone new. She wasn't going to make a fuss about her daughter's single status, but she wasn't getting any younger. If she wanted to have children and make a life outside of that business, she'd need to get cracking. Jill was a great girl and always had been, but she had mad ideas about what life should be, and Keeley didn't feel the singleton path would lead Róisín to happiness. Since she was little, Róisín had loved company, was interested in people and was just so full of love.

Keeley felt her anger melting as she thought back over her daughter's childhood. It had been a magical time. They had tried so hard for a baby, but it just wasn't happening for them. When Doug suggested adoption, she had said no at first, but as each month came and went and the pregnancy test in the drawer went unused, she decided it was worth thinking about. Once she'd set eyes on Róisín that day in 1986, that had been it: love at first sight. Of course, in the way of life, once she had relaxed and given up on all thought of children of her own, within two years of Róisín's arrival, she found out she was pregnant. When Liv was born, they'd felt like a proper family. Keeley wanted Róisín to feel all these things one day, too.

There was no shortage of admirers either. Colm was a wonderful guy, for example. Just because she'd been hurt by that arrogant French man, Róisín seemed to have written off the entire male sex. Keeley liked Colm. He was dependable, friendly and had a good job in an office in Galway. If he looked after his future wife the way he cared for his aging mother, he'd be nothing short of a saint.

During the party, she had been having a great chat with Colm when Liv had burst rudely into the kitchen and asked to talk to her in private. The poor man was in such a panic to excuse himself, he'd clobbered his head on an open cupboard door.

'Oh dear,' Keeley said, 'are you alright, Colm? Do you need an ice-pack?'

'Not at all. You're very kind, but I'm totally fine. I'll leave you ladies to your privacy.'

'Ah bless you, Colm,' Keeley said waving to him.

'Cripes, he's some dork,' Liv said shaking her head. 'The fact he thinks he stands a chance with our Róisín is a joke. No wonder she ran a mile from him earlier on.'

'Now, Liv, stop that horrible talk,' Keeley said. 'Colm is a lovely fellow and Róisín could do a lot worse.'

'Yeah right,' Liv said, chuckling. 'So, I need to run something by you.'

'Oh? What is it, love?' she asked with a sigh. At twenty-seven, Liv was the picture of health. She could see herself in her daughter more and more as the years passed. They had the same pale chestnut curls and deep brown eyes.

'I've been waiting a couple of weeks for a call, and it's Murphy's Law that they ring as soon as I'm at a party,' she said.

'Who?' Keeley asked.

'The foreign student agency,' she said. 'Martin's advertising job is certainly bringing in a lot more cash than in recent years. But with him away most of the time and me left behind to face the music with the kids and running the house, it's no picnic in the park. We've been chatting and I've let him know I'm sick of struggling constantly and doing the weekly grocery shop with a calculator.'

'Believe me, I've been in the same boat myself,' Keeley said. 'When you girls were little, before I opened the B&B, your dad and I were finding it really hard to make ends meet.'

'And you were practical to the last, Mum. Which is what I'm attempting to be too. It seems I would be eligible to have four students.'

'Four? Where on earth would you put them?'

'I've the box room spare at the moment. I could put Billy and Jess in there in a bunk bed. They're both small enough to not mind. Their rooms would fit two single beds each . . .'

'Well, four would bring in a good few euros,' Keeley said. 'And I suppose if you're doing all the work anyway, like cooking and cleaning and washing clothes, you may as well take in as many as you can.'

'I agree, and it'll mean the foreign children mightn't be as lonely. I'm not allowed to put two from the same country sharing a room. But I think that's fine.'

'Why don't you ask Dad to build you a bunk bed for the little ones? He'd be thrilled and it'd give him something purposeful to do while he's out in that shed.'

'Do you think he'd mind?' Liv asked.

'Mind what?' Doug asked as he arrived in the back door.

'Hi Dad,' Liv said. 'Mum and I were talking about my idea of taking on a few foreign students. It would mean moving Billy and Jess into the box room. I'll need to get bunk beds,' she said.

'I was offering your services,' Keeley said. 'You could build a bunk bed, couldn't you, love?' she asked.

'For my two darlings?' he said. 'I'll make the most fabulous bunk bed in the universe.' As if on cue, Billy and Jess ran in looking for them. Doug stooped to talk to them. 'Would you like me to build you two a bunk bed?' The children reacted the way they always did and rushed to hug their granddad, cheering happily.

'Can mine be the top bunk?' Billy asked. 'And can it be red like Spider-Man?'

'And me!' Jessie said. They all laughed.

'That's all she ever says,' Liv said with a grin. 'Just in case she's missing out on anything.'

Liv and the children went outside to tell Martin about the new beds.

'I think it's a good idea for Liv to take this on, don't you?' Keeley said.

'Absolutely,' Doug agreed. 'If she wants to stay at home with the kiddies while they're little, it's a good way of earning some funds.'

'If we can make the box room seem like a positive move, then at least Billy and Jess won't give you a hard time,' Keeley said. 'Now why don't you make yourself useful and bring the teapot around? I'm sure some of the neighbours are looking for a fresh drop.'

'Oh, I was going to make a list of what materials I'll need for the bunk-bed,' Doug said looking pained.

'What? Right this second? We have a garden full of visitors, in case you haven't noticed.'

It was typical of Doug to get distracted at just the wrong moment. Keeley wasn't one for complaining, but between Róisín showing signs of boredom, Liv never lifting a finger to help and Doug hiding out in his shed, they really did leave the work to her. Once everyone had left, the garden had needed tidying. Martin had been quite productive for a few minutes, gathering a few cups and plates and putting them in the kitchen sink, but then Doug had called him away to look at something. Jill and Liv were giggling together like schoolgirls at a table, oblivious to her efforts.

'Liv, maybe let them watch the television for a few minutes while we get this place back in order?'

'I'm not feeling the Mae West actually,' Jill said. 'I think I'll go and keep the kids company on the sofa.'

'I'll come with you,' Liv said and off they went, not a

care in the world. In the meantime, Róisín had disappeared too.

By the time Keeley had cleared the garden, on her own, it was raining softly. She hauled a black sack into the kitchen and surveyed the scene. The children were sitting on the sofa in the adjoining living area, contentedly sucking their thumbs, while Jill and Liv were both asleep, leaning against each other. Too much wine, no doubt.

The two men wandered in and began discussing fishing as they drank from bottles of beer.

'What's the story with dinner?' Doug asked as Keeley made a start on the mess in the kitchen.

'I was going to do pasta bolognaise with garlic bread,' she said. 'I have the sauce made. I'm waiting for Róisín to come back. She had to rush over to Nourriture for something.'

'So can we eat soon?' Doug asked. 'And can we ask Róisín to bring some parmesan cheese from Nourriture? It makes boring bolognaise a lot tastier.'

Keeley wanted to clobber him with the sweeping brush she was now using to collect the strands of paper streamers that had crept in from the garden.

'If you want parmesan cheese, you'd better call Róisín before she leaves the shop.'

'Right, can you do it, love? Martin and I are in the middle of this.'

Keeley strode from the kitchen to the hall and called Róisín, who answered immediately sounding as if she was on the defensive.

'Mum, I won't be too much longer, OK?'

'I wasn't calling to rush you,' Keeley explained. 'Your father is looking for parmesan, that's all. I'll put the pasta water on to boil.'

'Granny I'm hungry,' Billy said as he padded into the hallway.

'OK pet, come with me and we'll put the pasta on to cook. Auntie Róisín will be back soon and we can have a birthday dinner!'

Keeley halted as she walked back into the room.

'Jess!' she said in exasperation. 'What have you done, love?'

'I'm making snow like in *Frozen*,' Jess said. Keeley dropped Billy's hand and crouched down to scoop up the large bowl of popcorn her granddaughter was scrunching into the carpet.

'What about the pasta?' Billy whined.

'Liv?' Keeley said loudly. 'Can you help clear up?'

'Ah leave her to have a little chat with Jill,' Doug said from the kitchen. 'She's run ragged with the kiddies most of the time.'

'Well, will you come and pick this up while I make dinner then?' Keeley asked.

'I'll do it in a jiffy,' Doug said. 'Sure she's happy there.' He grinned across at Jess, who continued to roll on the popcorn.

'I love coming over here,' Jill said, stretching herself awake. 'It's so much nicer than our cottage and it's like being on holiday, even if it's only for a night.'

Keeley exhaled and rolled up her sleeves to fill the large pot with water for pasta. Then she cleared the rest of the kitchen and put the garlic bread in the oven.

The landline rang and thankfully Doug went to answer it. He came back a few moments later, scribbling into her large red accommodation book.

'There's a German couple coming in about an hour. Two

nights and they only want a continental breakfast in the morning but they need it at six. They're going off on a tour tomorrow,' he said leaving the book in a wet patch on the counter near the sink.

'What?' Keeley said in horror. 'Doug, I wasn't taking any bookings for tonight! We have everybody staying over and I wanted it to be a family gathering.'

'Oh.' He looked at her blankly. 'The little ones can go in with Liv and Martin, can't they?'

'But we want to stay in the blue room!' Billy moaned.

'I'll go in with Róisín if that helps?' Jill said.

'I have a spare room for the Germans,' Keeley said through her teeth. 'But I didn't want paying guests. Now I'll have to get up at five to bake scones.'

'Right you are, love,' Doug said, clearly not taking on board anything she was saying. He handed Martin another beer.

Keeley wanted to join Billy on the floor, crying and kicking her legs. She knew it was probably her own fault that she was exhausted. After all, she'd insisted on having people over today in an attempt to celebrate Róisín's birthday. But was it completely unreasonable of her to expect a bit of help?

Keeley hated feeling so negative, but lately she was really beginning to feel put upon. She adored her family and they were the centre of her universe, but for the first time in her life she was struggling to see exactly where she fit in with all of their lives, apart from as a cleaner and cook. When they were little, she'd worked through walls of exhaustion and didn't care – it only mattered that they were happy and well cared for. But no one had told her she'd still be doing it when they were adults. Did the tables never turn? She felt selfish even thinking it, but it would be nice to come first in other's people's minds sometimes. She shook herself – no point thinking like that. A mother's job was to put everyone else first, so she'd just have to put that self-pity out of her head. It was hard, though – there was Liv, zoned out, useless, and Róisín not even having the decency to stay in the house. Keeley tried to find her grateful thoughts again, but they were clouded over by dark thoughts she couldn't banish. Maybe she should write a guidebook, warning others just what being a mother was really like – so wonderful, but really, so unrelenting.

Chapter 6

BY THE TIME SHE MANAGED TO CLOSE NOURRITURE, Róisín was in no mood for driving back to the B&B and continuing her lame 'party'. She was too stressed to deal with Billy and Jess. Glancing at her watch, she knew her mother was waiting for her. Lord only knew what Jill was up to at this point, probably swinging from a light and looking for someone to go dancing with. She resented not having her evening to herself, but there was nothing else for it. She couldn't disappoint her family.

She drove down to the cottage first and put her pyjamas and some basics in a bag. To be on the safe side, she packed a few essentials for Jill, in case she ended up staying the night too.

The short drive, with the glittering vista of the bay to her right, made Róisín relax somewhat. No matter how many times she drove along this road, the view never grew stale. The sea birds were swooping and diving as the tide ebbed, revealing morsels for them to feed on. She drove on, past the farm run by Declan, who supplied her with organic beef. She knew her parents had been full of anticipation about him, but Róisín had never been interested. Keeley had made it clear she wanted a local husband for her, so she would stay put.

'Going to France for all that time was enough roaming.

We need you here from now on. We're not getting any younger you know.'

While Róisín was genuinely grateful that her parents were so loving, since returning from France, she'd often found them a little smothering. It wasn't their fault. They hadn't changed, it was Róisín who had done that.

After the events with Jacques in France, she'd had her eyes opened. She now viewed the world in a very different way. While she'd been growing up, Róisín was completely cocooned in her parents' love. So much so, she'd never so much as wondered about her birth mother. But when everything had happened with Jacques . . . well, it had changed her perspective on a lot of stuff. Suddenly the birthday cards she'd stored in a box over the years took on a whole new importance and she'd felt a growing desire to know more about the woman who'd given birth to her. She tried not to behave in a quiet or sullen manner, but the questions had been multiplying recently, and of course now that the letter had arrived, she felt an even greater need to know where she came from.

Sighing deeply, Róisín forced all thoughts of Jacques from her mind. She had enough worries today without allowing herself to dredge up all the past hurt.

In spite of her best efforts, a sob caught in her throat as her parents' house came into view. She pulled the car over and opened the window, taking big gulps of air. She couldn't think of what might have been. Not today. Not while they expected her to be the happy birthday girl.

Fresh terror washed over her as she thought of Mr Grace and Nourriture. She'd used her business as a sticking plaster to cover the emotional wounds Jacques had inflicted. What if that was taken away now? She'd be left with absolutely nothing. Róisín couldn't bear to imagine what kind of a state she'd end up in . . . Knowing she could possibly become hysterical, she forced herself to smile. She clenched her jaw and stopped her own tears.

She wished there was someone she could confide in. Someone who wouldn't judge her, and most of all someone she wouldn't hurt with her words.

Róisín knew there was no way she could tell her parents how she was feeling. Keeley would instantly jump to the wrong conclusion. She'd think she wasn't enough of a mother to her if Róisín said she wanted to trace her birth mother's roots and find out about her. And as for the trauma with Jacques – where would she even begin? Her parents would be horrified to know that she'd kept such a massive thing from them. She was in a hole of her own digging and she'd have to learn how to cope with it.

As soon as Róisín pulled up outside the B&B ten minutes later, Keeley opened the front door. She had Jess in her arms and they both waved.

'Hi,' Róisín called, hoping she didn't look as wretched as she felt. 'How are you girls?'

'I made snow on the carpet,' Jess said.

'Oh really?' Róisín looked to her mother.

'Popcorn,' Keeley said with a sigh.

Róisín was amazed by how quickly her mother had turned the house from mayhem to a calm, dinner-party atmosphere.

'Mum, have you sat down at all today?' she asked. Keeley didn't answer her, so she followed her. 'Hey,' she said finding her in one of the larger bedrooms that they'd built on in recent years. 'Who's staying in here tonight?'

'Oh your father took a booking from a couple earlier.

It didn't occur to him that I'd purposely avoided taking paying guests so we could have some family time.' Keeley began to pull fresh sheets from the wardrobe and Róisín automatically helped her make a fresh bed.

'When are the guests due to arrive?' she asked.

'Soon, I think. I do know that they need breakfast at six tomorrow morning, mind you.'

'I can get up and do it if you like? I'll be going to work and it won't be that much later than six.'

'Ah you're a good girl,' Keeley said with a smile. 'But I'll do it. You know me. I like things to be just so.'

'OK,' Róisín said. 'Is Jill staying over?'

'Yes I think so. Although nobody seems able to tell me exactly what they're doing until the last minute.'

'Are you tired, Mum? Why don't you go and sit down and have a glass of wine and I'll sort dinner?'

'I'm fine, love,' she said with a smile. 'I'm just having a moment. Don't mind me.' She came over and hugged her tightly.

Róisín put her small overnight bag in another room, pulled the piece of parmesan cheese from her bag and followed her mother to the kitchen, where she was dishing up big bowls of steaming bolognaise.

'That smells divine,' Róisín said. 'Come on you lot, dinner's ready.'

They all descended upon the large kitchen table and were happily passing out a basket of warm garlic bread when the doorbell rang.

'That'll be the guests,' Keeley said, shoving her chair back.

'I'll go,' Róisín said.

'No,' Keeley raised her hand, 'you're the birthday girl.

You stay put and I'll show them in. With a bit of luck they'll go straight to their room. They have tea- and coffee-making facilities and I've left a few home-made cookies in a basket beside their kettle.'

They'd all finished dinner and the conversation was on Liv's new venture when Keeley returned.

'Will I put your food in the microwave?' Róisín asked.

'No, I wasn't that hungry,' she said. 'I'll leave it.'

With all the excitement of the students' imminent arrival, Liv had skulled several glasses of red wine.

'Uh, who let me drink so much?' she moaned. 'I'm going to lie on the sofa for a bit. Martin, would you give the two kids a bath? Put them in together and they can play for a few minutes until bedtime.'

Martin looked up from his phone. 'Huh?'

'Can you put the kids in the bath, please? You won't see them for weeks. So have some quality time with them now, yeah?' Liv said.

'If it's a major issue I can do it,' Keeley said.

'Ah no!' Martin said pushing his chair back. 'I'm doing it now. I was only teasing you, Liv! Come on, you two. Let's go and have some fun in the tub!'

'What's a tub?' Billy asked.

'It's American for bath,' Liv said. 'Dad is getting all American on us.'

Martin glowered at Liv as he plucked Jess out of her seat and carried her upstairs.

Liv zigzagged her way to the sofa and Doug followed, scolding and teasing her good-naturedly for being a bad mother.

'I never get to relax,' she said. 'I'm run off my feet all the time. Don't give out to me, Dad. Martin will be gone again soon and he loves doing things with the kids while he's here.'

Keeley smiled at Róisín as they cleared the table with Jill's help and picked up strands of spaghetti from the floor.

'How does Liv stick the constant mess?' Róisín whispered.

'She gets Martin to sort it,' Keeley said. 'Or if he's away working, she calls me. She has it all sussed, that one.'

'Then who's going to do all the work with these students?' Jill asked.

'Lord only knows,' Keeley said. 'Probably me.'

Róisín knew she needed to tell her mum about the letter. She figured it would be easier to say it now, while they were busy. So she plunged in and gave Keeley the gist of what was written in it, making light of it all. Obviously realising that they needed a little mother and daughter time, Jill grabbed an open bottle of wine and went into the living room.

'How lovely it must have been to receive that letter,' Keeley said with a sigh.

'Is everything OK, Mum?' Róisín asked.

'You, it's just that . . .' A loud knock on the door leading to the hallway made Róisín rush to answer.

'I'm sorry to bother you . . . Ah, you're the woman from the Nourriture shop,' said the man, smiling widely at her.

'Yes,' Róisín said. 'This is my parents' house.'

'What a lovely coincidence,' said the man. 'I am Claus.' He had a distinctly German accent but his English was flawless.

'Róisín,' she introduced herself with a smile. He didn't

offer his hand for her to shake. 'So, we would like to make a cup of tea, but the tin in our room is empty,' he said holding it out.

'Oh, I beg your pardon,' Róisín said. 'Please, let me fill it up for you.' Claus waited patiently in the hallway until she returned. 'Have you everything else you need?'

'Yes, please let me know if you want anything else, or if your wife needs anything,' Keeley added as she joined them.

'Ah, so that's another small issue, but it doesn't matter totally,' he said. 'My travel companion is actually my sister . . .'

'And you have a king-sized bed in that room,' Keeley said instantly. 'I have another room with twin beds or else I have a smaller single room if one of you would prefer that?'

'I would take the single room if it's available,' the man said. 'We will pay the usual tariff for both rooms of course.'

'No problem,' Keeley said as she found the key of the single room in her cupboard in the kitchen. 'I'll show you where the other room is and I'll double-check that it has all you need.'

Róisín left her mum to it as she finished off cleaning the kitchen. There was still no sign of Keeley by the time she'd made tea and brought some of the leftover birthday cake to the others.

Eventually, Keeley arrived back with a smile on her face.

'What happened?' Róisín asked.

'Claus is very chatty,' she said. 'He complimented the little painting of the roses I put in the single room. When I told him I'd painted it, he wanted to see my art room.'

'So you've been in the box room with a strange fella,' Doug said with a smile. 'Is that what you're trying to tell me?'

'Who's been in a room with a strange fella?' Martin said as he carried Jess and led Billy by the hand back into the room.

'Mum was flirting with a German guest,' Liv said as she held her arms out to snuggle Jess.

'I was doing nothing of the sort,' Keeley said. As they enjoyed the tea and cake, Róisín longed to go to bed. She couldn't concentrate on any conversations without seeing the endless numbers from her calculator jumping about in her mind's eye.

'What's wrong, love?' Keeley asked. 'You're miles away. I know you don't really love surprises, but I hope you're not cross about earlier on? It was only a few neighbours. I didn't mean any harm.'

'Oh Mum,' she said feeling guilty. 'It was lovely of you to have the party. I think I'm just having a bit of a blue moment. Look at me, thirty years of age and nothing to show for myself.'

'That's just about the most ridiculous thing you've ever come out with,' Doug said. 'Aren't you a successful business-woman with a bright future?'

'Yeah, at least you earn your own money and have some sort of a life,' Liv said. 'I've spent the past few years stooped in half as I try to chase these two little monsters about. Martin and I haven't a spare cent to show for it all either.'

'That's all about to change, however,' Róisín said. 'Once you have your students in place, you'll have the best of both worlds. I, on the other hand, cannot come up with an instant husband and children overnight. There's no agency for that, is there?'

'Bloody Nora, what is this?' Jill asked, staring at them in amazement. 'The woe-is-me birthday contest! Give over, the two of you.'

'Dead right, Jill,' said Doug. 'You're all fantastic women. I won't hear another word of bad-mouthing from either of you. Now, who wants to play Scrabble?'

After an hour of Scrabble, Róisín was fit for nothing but bed. But she wasn't surprised when Jill announced that Gordon was on his way to collect her.

'We're heading to the Thatch for last drinks. Anyone coming?'

'No thanks,' Róisín said. 'Work in the morning.'

The others declined too, so Jill got herself ready to go. 'Keeley, thanks so much for a lovely afternoon and evening. It was all gorgeous. See you tomorrow after work, Ro-Ro.' She bounded out, as full of energy as when she'd arrived.

'She's the most lovely girl,' Keeley said.

'Ah she's a dote,' Róisín said. 'The only time we have any sort of friction is when she brings half of the Thatch pub home on a Monday night. She's as sensible as a nun during term time, but the minute she's on school holidays or even on the countdown to them, she goes wild.'

'Ah she's dead right,' Liv said. 'She picked the best job, too. She's always on holidays.'

'She works really hard, Liv,' Róisín said. 'She's really diligent and takes so much pride and interest in her students.'

'Works hard and plays hard,' Doug said.

'Exactly, Dad,' Róisín said with a smile. 'Right, I'm going to hit the hay.'

'I'll see you in the morning, love,' Keeley said. 'The others might be in the land of nod, but we can have a cup of tea together. That'll be lovely.'

'Unless there's a bomb, I'm staying put,' Liv said. 'Saturdays are sacred and we're only weeks away from the school holidays.'

'Imagine when they're older, they'll have even longer holidays,' Keeley said, referring to the secondary school summer holidays, which were three full months.

'I'm utterly exhausted after an entire year of dragging the children out of bed early,' Liv said. 'Roll on the long summer break when nobody will have to get up at the crack of dawn for a while.'

'What about the students?' Doug asked with a smirk.

'Oh yeah, I forgot about the early morning thing with them. Sure they can do their own. If they're old enough to go to a foreign country alone, they can surely pour out a bowl of cereal? I could set the table and leave the boxes of cereal on the counter and they could help themselves the way people do here.'

'And what about your own children?' Róisín asked. 'They hardly stay in bed until lunchtime, do they?'

'They go downstairs and watch television if Liv is tired,' Martin said.

'I don't actually leave our guests to their own devices in the mornings,' Keeley said. 'You need to think this through a little more.'

'I've thought it all through perfectly,' Liv said looking affronted.

Róisín excused herself and went to bed with a grin on her face. If there were an easy way out, Liv would find it. She'd never come across a more laidback person in her life. As children, even though she only three years older, Róisín had done everything for her little sister.

'You'll get my trainers won't you, Ro? You will,' she'd say, 'because you're the best big sister in the world and I love you.'

As she lay in bed and tried to go to sleep, Róisín's mind was in a whirl with the day's events. Eventually, she sat up and took the letter from her bag and read it again. Tears blurred her vision as she tried to imagine what her birth mother looked like. Would people be able to know they were related just by looking at them? Did she look like her father? Was he alive? Did he know she existed? Was there a proper birth certificate that her parents hadn't shown her, or maybe it was in the records office in Dublin? Was her adoption even legal? There were so many stories of babies that were taken from young mothers in those times. Was she one of those? Did her parents knowingly tear her from her mother? Was she really dead at all?

She felt so sad and frustrated by it all. One thing was for sure, though, she needed some answers. She had to speak to her parents and find out what they knew. She hadn't fully made her mind up, but she was also thinking that she'd finally like to try and trace her birth parents. As soon as she admitted this to herself, an image of Keeley and Doug flooded her mind . . . What if she never got anywhere? If the search was all a wild goose chase and yet she'd caused hurt and sorrow to her adoptive parents in the process. Should she do the selfless thing and let sleeping dogs lie?

A new and determined voice inside her head was telling her that she had every right to know where she came from. That her parents loved her with all their hearts. That she loved them back, just as much. So where was the problem? They were adults. All she wanted was answers. That was OK, right?

Minutes turned to hours as Róisín tossed and turned, unable to get comfortable and unable to stop her mind jumping from one question to the next.

Chapter 7

KEELEY NEVER SLEPT PARTICULARLY WELL WHEN the little ones were staying over. With the best will in the world, Martin was an extremely heavy sleeper. He was used to sleeping abroad with his earplugs and eye mask. No amount of crying or noise ever woke him. Liv simply didn't do getting up in the middle of the night, so Keeley felt the onus was on her to keep an ear out.

As she lay in the darkness, she wondered what was actually written in that letter Róisín had opened today. How many more letters or cards were there? Many years ago she'd tried to find out exactly where they were being held, but she'd met a brick wall. She was probably being paranoid, but she couldn't help feeling Róisín was out of sorts all day today. She hoped there wasn't anything awful or sad written in the letter.

Her dreams were exhausting - everything moving too fast, looking for people who weren't there, shouting herself hoarse trying to find them. She was relieved to get out of bed at five thirty. The early morning light was already peeking around her curtains, and she was actually glad Doug had taken that booking last night. At least she had a purpose this morning, rather than roaming aimlessly until someone woke up. She peeped in at the children, who were both curled up like little rabbits on the camp bed in their parents' room.

She turned on the oven and began to weigh up ingredients for scones. All her guests commented on the freshly baked delicacies she served. Róisín had a wonderful range of home-made jams at Nourriture that she paired with them.

She offered a full cooked breakfast and other delicious dishes, such as locally smoked salmon with free-range scrambled eggs. But Claus had seemed adamant that they only needed a continental breakfast today.

'Good morning!'

She almost dropped the mixing bowl in fright as she spun on her heel to see Claus standing there, looking pristine.

'Hello Claus,' she said. 'I hope you slept well?'

'Yes, I was most comfortable,' he said. His perfectly pressed chinos, white shirt and loosely tied cravat set him aside from the thrown-together farmers she was used to seeing about the place.

'I didn't realise you were awake. I would've gotten up earlier . . .'

'I'm a terrible sleeper. I have been for the past six years, since my wife died.'

'Oh I'm so sorry to hear that,' Keeley said.

'It was such a shock. I still miss her every day and I still think she's coming back. That probably sounds ridiculous,' he said looking at the floor.

'Of course it doesn't,' she said as she mixed the sour milk into the scone dough. 'How long were you married?'

'Thirty-four years,' he said. 'We met when we were eighteen, married when we were twenty. Heidi and I had a great time together.'

'Have you children?' she asked as she mixed the dough.

'No, we didn't have kids. That wasn't a conscious plan. It just didn't come about and we were busy with work. We owned a shop together and odd as it may sound now, that was our family.'

'Have you retired now?' Keeley asked.

'Not yet, although Heidi always said we must do that once we hit sixty.'

'I'm approaching sixty myself,' Keeley said with a sigh as she expertly stamped out scone shapes. 'Not for another while, mind you. But I'm sort of dreading it. I've no idea why. Silly really, isn't it? It's only a number after all.'

'I understand,' Claus said. 'Don't tell anyone, but it's my birthday today.'

'No!' she said. 'Your sixtieth?'

He nodded. 'That's part of the reason Ida, my sister, and I are in Ireland. I couldn't bear the thought of being at home or in the shop without Heidi . . .'

'So you came on a trip,' Keeley finished. She popped the scones onto a tray and into the oven.

He nodded. 'Ida has booked a special day out on a small cruise ship.'

'Ah yes, it goes from Seal's Rest Bay. It's fun, but it'll probably be cold. You'll hopefully see some dolphins and catch a fish or two.'

'We get our lunch on board and Ida has some wine.'

'That's great,' she said with a smile. Ida joined them, looking fresh and ready to go.

'Good morning,' Keeley said. 'Your brother is telling me about your plans for today. If you'd both like to take a seat in the dining room, I'll bring your breakfast. Coffee or tea?' she asked.

'Thank you,' Ida said. 'Coffee would be excellent.'

She showed them to the dining room at the front of the house, which was separate to their family kitchen. It housed six tables and a sideboard that was filled with small cereal boxes and some other breakfast staples.

She brought a jug of fresh milk and invited them to help themselves to cereal.

By the time coffee and toast were made, the scones were cooked. She piled them into a basket and presented them with some local country butter.

'Let me know if you need anything else,' she said, leaving them to their conversation. Twenty minutes later she heard Ida and Claus walk to their rooms to fetch their coats.

'Have a good day,' she said. 'There's always someone here, so there's no need to give you a key.'

'Sure,' Claus said. 'We've booked a table at the castle restaurant for eight o'clock this evening. Do you know where we might order a taxi to take us there and collect again at ten thirty? We would like to have some wine with our meal and don't want to cause an accident.'

'I'll organise something, don't worry,' Keeley promised. 'Enjoy your day.' She waved and watched as Ida drove gingerly toward the gate in their hired car.

When Róisín appeared a while later, Keeley was still smiling.

'Claus is such a charming man,' she said, filling her in on the news.

'Sounds as if he's lonely,' Róisín said. 'At least that's one plus to ending up as an old maid. I won't know how it feels to be a married woman, so I'll never feel bereft when I'm old.'

'Hey,' Keeley said. 'Less of the defeatist talk and no more of the "old" word. Claus is the same age as me, give or take a few months.'

'Oh yes, of course,' Róisín said banging her forehead with the heel of her hand. 'Your big six-oh is looming. What's the plan?' she asked. 'Will you have a big bash? We could do something in the church hall. Or we could enquire at the castle. They have that grand banqueting hall.'

'Oh no, I wouldn't relax in there. I'd like to mark the day in some shape or form, but I'm not sure if a great big party is what I'd like.'

'Ah Mum, you'd organise a bash with your eyes shut. What's stopping you?'

Keeley watched as Róisín helped herself to a scone and poured a mug of coffee.

'Coffee?' she asked, holding up the pot.

Keeley shook her head. What she would really love was if someone, anyone else, took the initiative and organised a party for her. Why was she always the one to do everything? Didn't any of her family ever stop and think that she would appreciate being treated for once?

'You OK, mama bear?' Róisín asked as she put her arm around her shoulders. Keeley nodded and smiled. 'Mmm, these scones are gorgeous. No matter what we do at Nourriture, they don't turn out like this. We use your recipe and I've seen you bake them a thousand times, but nobody else has your touch. If you're ever bored, I'll sign you up instantly as my chief baker!'

Róisín slugged the remainder of her coffee and kissed her. 'Thanks for everything. I have to fly. Chat to you later on, yeah?'

Keeley hid her tears until Róisín slammed the front door.

Feeling utterly ridiculous for crying and not really knowing what had set her off, she wandered into the guests' dining room. First she cleared the table Claus and Ida had used. Next she carried on to the kitchen and cleared the coffee pot, cup, side plate, jam and butter Róisín had used. She was about to sit and have a cup of tea when the two children appeared with rosy cheeks and their hair still fluffy from sleep.

'We're hungry,' Billy said as Jess nodded. Wiping her damp eyes with the back of her hand Keeley lifted each of them up to sit at the table and served their breakfast.

She normally enjoyed looking after others. More than that, she'd made a good living out of it. But lately she'd begun to feel like a dogsbody. As if she was some sort of unnoticed fairy godmother who flittered in and cooked, cleaned and washed things as everybody else got on with their lives.

'Keeley?' she heard Doug shouting from their bedroom. 'Any chance of a cup of coffee, love?' If the children weren't there she might have yelled back, 'Get it yourself'. Not sure what had come over her, she berated herself for being so cranky and rushed to set a little tray for her husband, and another for Liv and Martin.

She was ready to deliver both when Martin appeared.

'Morning, Keeley,' he said. 'Oh you're a step ahead of me.' He yawned and scratched himself agitatedly. 'Her hung-over Highness is in there acting as if the world is ending and wants breakfast in bed. I said I'd do it. It's either that or listen to her griping all day.'

Keeley looked over at Martin, expecting him to be grinning as he got a tray together. But instead he was scowling and muttering under his breath.

'I'll do it for her now. I'm bringing something to Doug anyway. Why don't you sit with the children and have a nice little breakfast party?'

'Cool, thanks Keeley, you're a doll,' he said. He poured a coffee and wandered into the living room and switched on the news.

'Jess!' Billy shouted. 'She poured the cereal all over the floor.'

'I didn't mean it,' she said, with tears forming.

'It was an accident,' Keeley said, leaving the tray and rushing to clear it up. 'Maybe if your daddy would come and sit here he could help a bit?' she said loudly.

Martin didn't respond, so Keeley poured more cereal and continued setting the tray.

She hurried to her own room and delivered Doug's tray, telling him she'd be back in five minutes, then she brought Liv hers.

'Thanks, Mum,' she said. 'I'm so wrecked. I've all these kids arriving in the next few weeks too. I don't know how I'm going to cope. It's worrying me so much that Martin is going to do the supermarket shop for me and take the kids with him. Would you be able to come over to mine for a bit? Just to give me a dig-out with the rooms? I have all the stuff there, but I'm not good at making them look nice the way you can. You love all that sort of thing really. I hate it, if I'm honest.'

'Yes, love,' Keeley said. 'Of course.'

She walked back to her own room, where Doug was sitting up, enjoying the scones.

'These are delicious. Are there many left? I know Jimmy would enjoy a few if you could see your way to splitting some and putting that lovely rhubarb and ginger jam inside. He didn't love the raspberry jam you used last time. He has trouble with his dentures and he said the pips from the raspberries stick in his gums.'

'Do they really?' she said. 'Poor Jimmy. I'll make sure I don't upset him with the scones today. How's that?'

If Doug noticed the sarcastic tone to her voice, he didn't acknowledge it.

So that was her husband's roundabout way of telling her he'd be off in a boat bobbing around the water talking rubbish to Jimmy for the day, she mused.

Martin was standing in the living room munching a scone, dropping crumbs all over the carpet. With a full mug of coffee in the other hand, he was glued to Sky News. The children started running around, also with food in their hands.

'Please sit at the table with your food or I'm going to have to vacuum the entire place again,' Keeley said weakly.

Nobody listened and by the time they all ran in to wake Liv and get ready to go out, Keeley knew she'd need to do the floors again.

'Would you mind stripping your bed so I can wash the sheets?' she called down to Liv. 'I need to freshen that room before a customer needs to use it.'

There was no answer, but Keeley's face dropped when Liv and Martin appeared with their bags a few moments later.

'I've to go and get the shopping done,' Martin said. 'Can you drop Liv over to ours?'

'I already told you Mum is coming to help me. I've been left with everything as usual,' Liv said with a pout.

'Where are the bed sheets I asked you to strip?'

Martin bundled the children out the door.

'Yeah, we only slept in them for a few hours, Mum. I pulled the duvet straight. Nobody would even know we'd been there.' Liv switched on the kettle as Keeley marched to the room and began to pull the duvet cover, sheets and pillowcases off the bed.

No matter what her daughter thought, Keeley was not going to sell a room with used sheets on the bed. She folded the small duvets the children had used and placed them in a blanket-box in her art room. Clicking the beds in thirds, she wheeled the camp-beds away too.

It would only take her a few minutes to freshen up the bathroom, so she decided to do it there and then.

'What are you doing, Mum?' Liv asked in shock.

'I'm cleaning the room, Liv. I know you don't think it needs it, but I have high standards and for all I know, I could have a tourist board inspector here tonight and I'd lose my high rating.'

Liv shrugged and left her to clean the bathroom and run the vacuum cleaner over the carpet.

By the time she had all the sheets in the washing machine, Doug was up and chatting to Liv.

'Ah there you are, love,' he said with a smile. 'I'm out of here. Jimmy is going to swing by and collect me. I'll be out for the day so you can put your feet up and relax.'

He kissed her on the head and clicked his fingers. 'Shoot, the scones! Did you manage to put some of that jam on for Jimmy?'

'No,' she said. 'But you can do it if you like. The jam is in the fridge and the scones are right there on the cooling rack.'

'I won't bother in that case,' he said. 'See you later.'

By the time they locked the house and drove to Liv's

place, Keeley was feeling completely disgruntled. She actually thought she'd cry when she saw the state of the duvet covers and sheets Liv was planning to use.

'They look as if you've put them through a mangle,' she said in horror. 'How on earth did you make them so creased?'

'I dunno,' Liv said defensively. 'Look, I'm not as good at all this stuff as you are. It'd probably be easier if I drop these to your place each week. You have that roller iron for doing the duvet covers . . .'

'Well I'll do this lot for you now,' she agreed. 'Help me put them into my car. I'll be back as soon as possible. Meanwhile I want you to put the fitted sheets on each bed.'

'But I've had gel nails put on,' Liv moaned. 'If I start tugging about with mattresses one will be whipped off and Lorna who does my nails is away at a wedding today.'

Keeley was still furious by the time she got all the linen into the boot of her car. As she slammed the door shut, Liv appeared looking like a string of misery.

'I can't keep this up, Liv,' she said. 'It's not my responsibility. I have the B&B to run. That's enough for me.'

'But you said it was a good idea,' she said bursting into tears.

Keeley sighed, then went over and put her arm around her daughter. 'I encouraged you to do something for yourself. That didn't mean I wanted to tear from my house to yours, working like a slave.'

'I'm never going to manage. Martin is going to hate me. We'll probably get divorced and I won't see my children any more. Why did I take this on board?'

'There now,' Keeley said. 'That's enough silly talk. You can cope with all of this just perfectly. It may mean breaking a nail the odd time, but that's not life-threatening. If you're taking the students in, you have to ensure you're able to look after them. Let me assure you, I will not be doing it for you. Now as I said, I'll do this for today, but after that it's down to you, OK?'

Liv nodded and stood leaning against the front door. Keeley went back to her car. From her rear-view mirror, Keeley watched her daughter for a moment. She was like a sulky teenager. Liv needed to grow up.

As she drove home, a thought struck her. Poor Claus had nobody in the world bar his sister, yet he seemed upbeat and cheerful. She'd dispel her rotten mood by baking him a birthday cake. Even though he was going out to eat that night, it would be a lovely surprise for him when he returned.

Taking advantage of the empty house, Keeley turned on the radio and tuned into an oldies music station. Slowly but surely she began to relax. She ironed the bedclothes for Liv and left the folded pile at the front door. She returned to the kitchen and made double the amount of cake mixture and divided some into mini bun trays. They'd be handy to have in the freezer for the grandchildren.

The phone rang a couple of times and she took bookings for overnight stays. She had very few vacancies for the next four months. She knew she ought to be proud of her business and how well she was doing, but Keeley was beginning to find all the work exhausting. The joy had seeped out of it over the years. Perhaps it was because her sixtieth birthday was approaching, she mused. Maybe it wasn't just a number after all? Maybe her body was going to suddenly shut down and not allow her to manage as well as before.

Once the cakes were out of the oven, she left them to cool while she drove back to Liv's house. It only took a few minutes to dress the beds, but the bathrooms were also in a state.

'You need to scrub this place from top to bottom, Liv,' she said. 'Have a bit of pride in your home. It's better for you and the children and Martin. Let them see what a lovely place they have to live. It teaches the children respect too.' Keeley thought of little Jess rolling around in the popcorn and Doug eating a scone with no plate, dropping crumbs all over the carpet.

'What's the point?' Liv shot back. 'They just trash the place after ten minutes and besides, Martin won't be here, so it's not going to impress him.'

Keeley sighed. It wasn't easy for Liv with Martin away so much, but she was an adult. A mother of two. Keeley knew that at some point she needed to take a small step back and encourage her daughter to take control of her own home. She decided that time had come.

'I'll go now, love. I've a lot to do in my own house. See you soon?'

'OK,' Liv said. 'See you.'

Keeley couldn't help feeling irritated again as she left Liv sitting on the sofa. There was no word of thanks or any kind of recognition that she'd dropped everything and driven over twice to help. The buck stops here, Liv, she thought.

Chapter 8

CLAUS RETURNED EARLY IN THE AFTERNOON, looking a little worried.

'Ida is in the car,' he said. 'She was so sick the boat had to turn and bring us back. She's never been on such a small vessel and unfortunately it didn't suit her.'

'Oh no, poor Ida,' Keeley said as she followed Claus outside. 'Let me help her inside. I'll make her a nice cup of tea. That should settle her tummy.'

Ida was green in the face and obviously very unwell. Between them they managed to bring her to her room and Claus waited outside while Keeley helped her into bed.

'I'm so sorry,' Ida said in a voice barely above a whisper. 'You barely know me and you are putting me to bed like a child.'

'Don't you worry,' she said. 'There's nothing worse than feeling seasick. I've been there and it's just awful. Will I bring you tea?'

'Do you know, I'd rather just sleep,' she said.

'No problem, call me if you need anything.'

When she found Claus, he was outside looking across the road at the view.

'How wonderful to have this beautiful scenery on your doorstep.'

'Yes, we love it here, I must say.'

She offered him a cup of tea, which he accepted grate-fully. Inviting him into the kitchen, she explained that guests didn't usually come to this part of the house.

He sat at the kitchen table and seemed instantly at home. She'd finished the birthday cake and as she held the fridge door open with her foot, she studded a single candle in the middle. Feeling slightly foolish, she lit it and then produced it.

'I won't sing, if you don't mind! I'm not blessed with a good voice.'

'You made this for me?' Claus looked up at her in total shock. 'Oh my . . .' He teared up and instantly fumbled a handkerchief from his trouser pocket. 'Oh silly me. I'm sorry, but Heidi used to bake for my birthday and I haven't had a cake since she died.'

'I honestly didn't mean to upset you,' she said in alarm.

'Oh no, Keeley, you haven't. You've made my day. Thank you so much.'

He blew out the candle and smiled at her. 'I thought my birthday was ruined, but it's turning out to be the best one in years.'

'Ah you're very easily pleased,' she said with a laugh.

The doorbell rang and she excused herself. Poking her head back into the kitchen, she grabbed keys and explained that she needed to check in some guests.

He waved to let her know that he was perfectly happy and had found a newspaper to read.

Once the first couple were settled, another car arrived with the remaining guests for the night. They too were happy with their rooms and explained that they were there for a wedding the following day at the castle. They were all heading over to the castle for the evening. Keeley gave them keys to the front door and left them to unpack, after checking breakfast times.

Claus looked a little worried when she found him later.

'I don't think Ida can come for dinner. She'd prefer to stay in bed,' he said. 'It's too late to cancel and besides, I've been looking forward to it. I don't suppose you and your good husband would join me?'

'Oh,' Keeley was flummoxed. 'I'm not sure I can get in touch with Doug now. Let me try.' She rushed toward the house before remembering her manners. 'Thank you, Claus, it's a lovely offer.'

She dialled Doug's number, but it went directly to voice-mail. She left a message, telling him about Claus's offer and asking him to call her back as soon as he could. She updated Claus and checked that Ida would be all right alone.

'She lives alone in Germany,' he confirmed. 'She's perfectly happy in her bed. She's not a needy woman.'

The other guests had left and the house was very quiet by six o'clock. There was still no word from Doug, so Keeley reluctantly told Claus she'd better not go.

'Oh, I see . . . I must tell you I am very disappointed. I thought it would make a nice evening.'

'It would, of course,' she said quickly. 'But I can't get an answer from Doug, and I've no idea what time he'll be back.'

'In that case, can't you leave him a note? He is not contactable. So why should you miss out on a dinner?'

When he put it that way, it seemed so straightforward to Keeley.

'Do you know, you're dead right!' she said. 'I'll have a quick shower and we can go. I'll drive.'

'Oh good,' he said, looking delighted. 'Who knows, maybe Doug will be back before we depart and can join us after all.'

Keeley pulled on her shower cap so as not to wet her hair. It was a clod of curls at the best of times, but when it was wet she felt like a poodle and she wasn't great at styling it at home. Opting for a simple white linen trouser suit with a brightly patterned camisole and sandals, she applied some make-up and decided she'd do.

'Wow,' Claus said looking truly awestruck. 'You look wonderful, Keeley. I am proud to walk into a castle with such an elegant woman.'

'Oh really?' she asked, looking down at her clothes. 'I was aiming for practical and comfortable. But if you think it goes as far as being elegant, I'm delighted.'

Doug wasn't a man for compliments. He was always kind and polite, but it wasn't really in his nature to comment on what she was wearing. Unless she had a streak of coal dust across her cheek or she'd tied her hair up with a pair of knickers and a guest was approaching the front door, he didn't comment on her appearance.

Keeley tried Doug's mobile phone one last time and left yet another voice message. She scribbled a note and left that on the kitchen table. As they drove the ten minutes to the castle along the winding coast road, she felt distinctly odd.

'It's a little uncomfortable for me being in this strange car with a woman I barely know,' Claus said as if reading her mind.

'Yes, I feel the same way!' She laughed and instantly the atmosphere lightened.

'I'm not in the habit of taking married women to dinner in castles,' he chuckled.

'I don't often go out with other men either,' she said.

'And so we'll put this awkwardness to one side and enjoy the evening, yes?'

'Totally,' she grinned. It was so refreshing to find a person who was straight-talking.

At the hotel reception, Marie raised an eyebrow. 'Hello there, Keeley,' she said, looking from her to Claus.

'Hi Marie,' she said with a smile. 'Claus is one of my guests and it's his birthday.'

'So Keeley agreed to accompany me,' he finished.

Marie looked Claus up and down with obvious disdain and tutted before leading them to a table. 'Enjoy your evening and give my regards to Doug, won't you?' she said. Then with a face that would stop a clock, she banged down the menus and strode away.

Keeley giggled softly. 'She thinks I've started some sort of escort agency at the B&B,' she whispered. 'Folks around here are very set in their ways. I've no doubt that Doug will hear about where we are well before he reads my note on the kitchen table. This is one of the remaining places in the world where whispers still travel on the wind!'

'Really?' he said, looking amused. 'And how do the locals take to new foreign residents?'

'Ah there are lots of holiday homes in the area. That's allowed. Welcomed even. But an old married lady like me pitching up here at the castle with a dashing foreign gentleman . . .' Her eyebrow shot up with the fun of it all. 'I'll be a social outcast by morning!'

'You don't look too perturbed by the prospect,' he said.

'Believe me, Claus, I have always done the right thing. It actually feels great to cause some innocent gossip.'

'Just wait until we start waltzing after dessert,' he said with a belly laugh.

As they ordered food and Keeley agreed she would have one glass of wine with her meal, she glanced around the dining room. There were many other couples, some of whom were barely speaking to each other. For the first time ever, Keeley wondered who they all were and why they weren't enjoying the company of the person sitting opposite. Did people think Claus was her husband? She glanced over at him. He looked tanned and relaxed and incredibly attractive. She felt a shiver of excitement as she caught a neighbouring female diner staring at him appreciatively.

Claus raised his glass to her. 'To a fantastic birthday with a wonderful hostess.'

Keeley clinked his glass, feeling like a teenager once more.

Chapter 9

NELL WAS ACCUSTOMED TO STORMS BY NOW. THEY rarely made her nervous any more. In the beginning, when she was getting used to the new noises and how the different conditions affected the lighthouse, she had felt anxious. Growing up in Dublin, she'd never truly known the full force of nature. Nor had she known its beauty.

When Laura was small she'd often crawl in beside her and cuddle under the covers.

'It sounds like the wind is trying to get in.'

'Don't worry, I won't let it. Inside is only for you and me, Laura.'

Nell didn't want to encourage her daughter to leave her own bed, feeling it was better for the child to have a sense of independence. But she'd loved those special nights when Laura's tiny body tucked in beside hers, long hair splayed across the pillow and her angelic face looking so calm. She often lay awake staring at her, while saying a silent prayer that she'd stay well.

For months and even years after Laura departed, Nell had carried her grief like a lead ball. The weight of the hollow pain in her heart was almost suffocating. The fact she lived alone in such remote surroundings meant she could wallow all the more.

'I know you won't thank me this minute,' Mo said,

'but I've brought a friend today. This is Dr Stephens. I call her Mary and that works just fine too.'

Nell had wanted to strangle Mo, and Mary. The intrusion was too much for her to handle but luckily for all concerned, her anger left her speechless. Mo had disappeared and left her eyeballing this stranger in her own kitchen.

As it turned out, Mary was a nice woman. Nell couldn't fault her and to give her her due, she was only trying to help. They talked for an hour and Nell agreed to take her business card and call her if she felt the need. The card was thrown in a drawer, where it still lay.

As time marched on and the seasons came and went, Nell knew she had a decision to make. A man in a suit from the local government office arrived, looking nervously at her, as if her reputation preceded her.

'In light of your bereavement, we felt it only right that we should come and check that you are all right,' he said. 'I . . . We at the council . . . Eh . . .'

'I'm fine,' she stated. 'I'm not going to throw myself into the raging sea. I don't want to leave the lighthouse. If and when I do, I'll give you plenty of notice. So you can go back to the other men in suits and tell them the box has been ticked.'

'Eh right . . . Thank you.'

'Goodbye.' She'd held the door open and the man scuttled to his car and drove off at such speed, no doubt with great relief.

As time passed Nell's heart had healed somewhat. She didn't feel truly lonely that often. She didn't allow herself. In fact, she'd gone so far as to have stern words with herself many years ago and made the conscious decision to make the most of her life at Ballyshore lighthouse. Nobody was holding a gun to her head, after all. This wasn't Hotel California; she could leave any time she liked.

But she was still human, so every once in a while a wave of aching loss swept over her without warning. On those occasions she liked to sit at the edge of the water and watch its awesome power. She'd think long and hard about all the places she hadn't visited. She had pots of money. Each month more of the stuff rolled into her bank account and she rarely spent a cent of it.

She could go on a cruise or travel to some far-flung place like the Seychelles. She could take a trip to the city and buy designer boots for a thousand euros if she felt like it. The very thought of that sort of extravagance made her feel queasy all the same. She inevitably came to the conclusion that she was as happy here as she could be. The problem wasn't with her location or indeed the boots she was wearing. It was with her heart. That heartache would follow her no matter where she ended up. So staying at home was the best answer. To Nell's mind, there was a lot to be said for familiarity.

Today, as she watched the storm gathering outside, she felt a sudden urge to cry, one that was so gut-wrenching she had a physical desire to curl into a foetal position on the floor. Instead she sat cross-legged on the rug in front of the two-bar heater. Although it was supposed to be summer, Nell felt oddly cold. Lighting fires was forbidden as the smoke could cause the search light to be blurred, so the next best thing was her little electric heater. As she stared at the long orangey bars, tears coursed down her cheeks. Her body convulsed uncontrollably as she let go and gave in to her feelings of desperation.

Unaware of the time, she eventually unplugged the heater and made her way to her bedroom. Kicking off her shoes, she crawled under the duvet fully clothed. The warmth and darkness soothed her burning eyes as she fell into a tumultuous sleep. In her dreams, Laura was walking toward her. She was on the grassy track that led to the lighthouse. Her gait was sprightly and her face beamed. She seemed excited and eager to get to her, almost as if she had some incredible news to share. When they were only a few feet apart, just as she was about to embrace her, Laura disappeared.

She'd had similar dreams a thousand times before, but for some reason this one offered more comfort than previous ones. Laura's face had never been so vividly clear. She looked older, too. Not the age she'd been last time Nell had seen her. More the age she should be now . . .

Shifting her position in the bed, Nell snuggled down and fell into a deep sleep.

At first light, she stretched and got out of bed, walking slightly mechanically and wishing she'd had the foresight to remove her clothes. She felt dishevelled and grimy as she made her way to the observatory to take the readings. The wind had died down somewhat, but not as much as she'd anticipated. It looked as if it was going to be a horrid day ahead.

She showered and put on fresh clothes and knew she'd feel better after something to eat and a cup of creamy coffee.

A scraping and banging noise from under the lighthouse alerted her. Either the outside wooden door that led to the electric control panel had blown open or a wild animal had forced it open to crawl in to take shelter. Knowing it would only irritate her and spoil her breakfast, she ventured down the spiral staircase to the front door and pulled on her boots.

She made her way to the door. Sure enough, it was flapping on its hinges. Just as she was about to slam it shut and secure the large bolt, she spotted a pair of eyes staring up at her.

'Hello?' she called out. The eyes blinked, but there was no response.

'Who's there?' she shouted again. 'Come out, for crying out loud.'

The figure moved suddenly and as it came out of the shadows, she screamed. The figure screamed back and pulled a hood down, covering the terrified eyes.

'It's OK,' Nell said. 'I won't hurt you.' She ventured a step forward. 'Please, it's too dangerous to be down here. I need to lock this door. Come inside. It's only me here. I won't hurt you, I promise.'

The figure moved forward cautiously and for the first time Nell got a proper look. The girl looked barely more than a child. Her eyes were round with fright and she was spattered with mud and shaking.

'Come on. Come with me. I'll help you.'

Nodding, the girl came out from behind the control panel and out of the boiler room into the wind and rain and waited while Nell bolted the door shut once again.

The wind herded them around the side of the lighthouse and she managed to pull the front door open and usher the girl inside.

'Well that's some nasty weather out there. The west of Ireland is rarely what we'd call tropical, but that's unseasonably awful, even for here,' she said, kicking off her boots.

'Take your shoes off, please. I don't do vacuuming and my helper isn't coming for another few days. You can hang your coat on the hook,' she said pointing to the narrow coat rack. She looked at the girl again and realised she wasn't wearing a coat. All she had was a zip-up hoody that was nowhere near warm enough for the day that was in it. She stood motionless, with her eyes cast to the floor. Nell beckoned for her to follow her up the staircase to the kitchen.

'So what brings you to me?' Nell asked. The girl stared at her in silence. Her elfin features, round chestnut eyes and stringy, matted hair made her look like a little woodland creature. Her skin was sallow and the dark circles under her eyes made her look wretched.

'Do you speak English?' she asked, suddenly thinking she could be foreign. The girl nodded.

'Tea?' Nell asked. 'Toast? Scrambled eggs and bacon?' The girl nodded again. 'Sit down there and make yourself comfortable,' she said, pretending she didn't notice the awkwardness.

The pot walloping was a welcome icebreaker as Nell worked swiftly. She glanced over quickly and realised the girl was shivering. Nell grabbed one of her well-loved cashmere throws and draped it gently around the girl's shoulders. She flinched and moved only a fraction away from her touch.

'I'm not going to do anything to you,' Nell said. 'You're the one who landed on my doorstep, don't forget.'

There was still no response so Nell made a pot of tea.

'You're lucky I hadn't eaten yet. I hate cooking, so you mightn't have been quite so lucky if you'd turned up later.'

She held out a full plate of eggs. The girl didn't look up or even acknowledge her.

'Hey, wakey-wakey,' she said. A grubby hand and stringy arm reached out and took the plate. The hollow eyes looked up and she tossed her head back ever so slightly in thanks.

'I'm not the world's best chef. But I'm guessing after a night out in that weather, anything would be pretty darn delicious right now.'

The girl nodded again. She picked up her knife and fork and ate hungrily. She was clearly starving but well able to use cutlery and although she was obviously thirsty, she didn't slurp her tea either.

As soon as the plate was cleared, she rested the knife and fork together.

'Thanks,' she whispered.

'Where are you from?' Nell asked. The girl shrugged. 'I won't tell on you. I just need to know if someone is missing you. Maybe there's someone you should phone?'

She shook her head again and looked tortured.

'Surely somebody would like to know where you are?'

She shook her head. The look of utter desolation on her face was like looking in a mirror many years ago.

'Do you have a name?' The girl looked directly at Nell. She was about to speak but instead dropped her gaze and looked at the table.

'Are you in some kind of trouble?' Nell asked.

She shook her head emphatically.

'So you're not on the run or anything like that?' She shook her head again. 'Do you have parents?' She raised one shoulder. 'Well either you do or you don't,' Nell said. 'I'm not a patient person. This blood out of a stone style of conversation doesn't bode well with me. Tell me a few things and I'll stop asking. If we can't be straight with each other, I'll have to send you on your way. I have a good set-up here. I don't need a little string of misery like you landing in and messing it all up.'

'Ma's died. Da and the brothers won't miss me,' she said in a thick Dublin accent.

Nell inhaled deeply. She hadn't heard that inner-city accent for so many years.

'Dublin northside, I take it?' Nell said. Her eyes flicked up in shock. Nell put her hand out and laid it gently on the table close to the girl's small grimy one. 'It's OK, I recognise your accent, that's all. I ran from the same place a long time ago. I lived in The Fairways. Do you know it?'

Tears flowed silently down the girl's cheeks as she bit her bottom lip and nodded.

'It's OK,' Nell said. 'There's life after the flats.'

The girl managed to compose herself while Nell cleared the dishes. She flicked on the radio for a bit of diversion. The sound of deep growling thunder outside brought Nell to the window.

'I've to go upstairs to the observatory. Part of my job is to report on the weather. Although you'd need to be deranged to not know there's a storm ripping in this direction.'

The girl still didn't move or speak. 'I'll be up there. Follow if you want. Would you like to take a shower and I'll find you something clean and dry to put on?'

She nodded.

'Right, follow me so. Don't rob anything or I'll track you down and you'll be sorry, you hear?'

Nell walked toward her room and the girl followed.

'These clothes aren't what you'd call high fashion,' she explained as she found a cotton turtleneck, a pair of leggings and a long cardigan with buttons up the front. 'I've no bras to fit you, but these pants and socks will do for now. They're clean and dry, which is more than can be said for your own.'

She left the pile of clothes on the windowsill in the bathroom and handed the girl a towel.

'Take your time. There's plenty of hot water. I won't call anyone and I won't do anything to get you into trouble. If you feel like talking when you come out, that's up to you. If you want to leave, that's fine too. Just let me know if you're going so I can bolt the door. If you want your clothes washed, bring them out when you're changed, right?'

'Thanks.'

'No worries. I'll be up there as I said.'

Nell heard the gentle murmur of the shower pump a few moments later. Even though they looked nothing like one another, this little waif reminded her of her young self. She hoped the girl hadn't been abused or mistreated, and most of all she wondered how on earth she had ended up in her boiler house. She half expected her to steal the clothes and run. Thinking it might help, Nell found two twenty euro notes and left them on the small hall table inside the front door. If she planned to run off again, the girl would need food.

Nell clambered back up the stairs and continued with her work while wondering what would happen next.

Chapter 10

IT WAS A WEEK SINCE MR GRACE'S ANNOUNCE-ment. Róisín hated starting a day exhausted, but that, unfortunately, was how she felt today.

The best solution she'd come up with was the possibility of making Mr Grace an offer to buy the building outright. She'd toyed with that plan in her own head a number of times before. She had been reluctant to spend any serious cash on aesthetics seeing as it wasn't her building. So this way, it could all work out for the best. She remembered her mother's words in the letter: *Seize every moment . . . Let your passions soar . . .* That was it exactly – she just needed to take her courage in her hands and give it her best shot. Nourriture was her passion and her life. She needed to stand up and fight for it now.

Feeling brighter, she decided she'd put in a call to the bank and make an appointment. Surely if she could dangle a cash carrot for the landlord, he'd snap it up? Of course, she didn't know what the other buyer was offering, but . . .

There was no time for pondering on it now. The local primary schools were having a fund-raising day and the entire village were getting involved. The money would go toward expanding the community centre.

Róisín was going to be setting up a food tent. She'd

rolled out the concept at several festivals last summer and it had made more money than she'd ever imagined. This time, she'd invested in two hotplates so she could make fresh crepes to attract the children as well as the more foodie adults. She forced herself to concentrate on the here and now and checked off the list of cured meats, sundried tomatoes, olives, cheeses, breads and pastries that would line the tent.

'Are the quiches out of the oven yet, Brigid?' she called into the kitchen.

'Just this minute,' she said. 'The fruit crumbles and tarts are about five minutes from being done too.'

'You're a superstar,' she said with a smile. 'I'll go on over with the foods that are ready.'

'Most of it is already in place,' Brigid said. 'I sent the strapping young lads on a mission. You'll probably need to go and make sure they haven't drop-kicked it all from the door of the tent. They're great work horses, but most of them wouldn't notice if the quiches were upside down or if the Westphalia ham was draped over a chocolate cake.'

Róisín laughed as she scooped up a neatly stacked pyramid of cupcakes on a wide board.

'There are another sixty cupcakes on the way,' Brigid said, reading her mind.

'Thank you. I love you. You know that, don't you?'

'Uh-huh,' Brigid said, smiling at her. 'See you in a few.'

Róisín couldn't bear the thought of having to tell her incredible staff that they mightn't have jobs any longer. Brigid was meant to start work at eight each morning, but it wasn't unusual for her to be there by seven, especially on a day like today. She never moaned and was always enthusiastic about trying new ingredients. She'd instantly come on board with the section for special dietary requirements when Róisín suggested it.

'There's a gluten- and dairy-free baking two-day course up in Dublin. Would you consider letting me go?' she'd asked. Róisín booked her on and within two weeks of the suggestion they had a new table of special breads on offer, alongside the usual ones.

A knock at the back door to the kitchen revealed a deliveryman who Róisín didn't recognise.

'I'm from the organic fruit company,' he said. 'I have two large juice machines with attachments for smoothies. We were meant to be here last week but the machines were delayed. Our overseas suppliers let us down.'

'Oh brilliant, I totally forgot you were coming!' she said. 'Come on in. Things are a bit hectic today, but that's fine.'

'The machines are quite large, so where do you want me to set them up?' he asked.

'I wanted to make the juice bar over here,' she explained. 'I like the idea that this section can be seen from the road. I'm hoping to entice some of the many cyclists who visit.'

'I get you,' he said. 'Good idea. I'll get started on setting them up.'

Róisín thanked him, then headed off across the road with the cupcakes.

'Guys,' she called out to the two students who were helping erect the tent, 'sorry about this but I need all hands on deck in the café for fifteen minutes.' She checked the time. 'We have an hour before the punters will even begin to trickle in here. I promise I'll get you a tonne of help over here once the new juice bar is sorted. I need all eyes on the demonstration too.'

The lads downed tools and munching on warm cupcakes followed her across the road. Ballyshore was the type of place that still operated on an honesty policy, so Róisín was fairly confident that nobody would disturb the goods.

With a bit of shifting and shouting and lots of jibing, Róisín and the staff managed to install the new juicing section. The demonstration from the supplier was quick and to the point. By the time he left, everybody had managed to take a turn and they were ready to sell juices.

'I'll write up one of the big blackboards later on this evening,' Róisín said. 'It's better to have a few juices on each day. We'll rotate them depending on what's in season. That way they'll be cheaper to produce and we'll maximise on taste.'

Knowing she needed to concentrate on the festival tent, she kept to her word and dispersed all but one member of staff across the road.

'Let's blitz this and once it's ready to go, Eoin and Steve can take the walkie-talkies for when they're running low on supplies.'

Everyone seemed happy and the two lads, who were enthusiastic and there to make cash for the summer, took charge of the foodie tent. She made sure the walkie-talkies were working before stationing herself at the new crepe station.

Mercifully, the storm and incessant rain of the previous couple of days seemed to have abated and already families were appearing on the street. She had a bird's-eye view of the shop from where she was cooking, so Róisín was happy she could cope with even the busiest day. Jill had promised to come for the afternoon, so they'd have some fresh blood to keep everyone going.

The rest of the morning flew as she tossed pancakes and filled them with chocolate and strawberries. Although she had some delicious savoury ideas, the children were her main customer base and all they wanted was sweet stuff.

'Hello love,' Keeley said appearing by her side. 'The village is buzzing. I think there are twice as many people as last year!'

'I know, I've been flat out and I know the lads have been messaging across to Nourriture to restock the tent all day.'

'Good for you,' she said. 'I'm not staying long. I wanted to bring Billy and Jess for a few minutes. Liv is up to her tonsils in preparations. Her students are arriving tomorrow.'

'God help them,' Róisín said with a grin. 'Knowing Liv, she'll have them cooking and cleaning while she takes to her bed. Why are you taking the kids again?'

'Ah they love it at our house. Your father is putting the finishing touches to their bunk-beds.'

'Did you do a paint job on them?' Róisín asked as she continued to toss crepes.

'I certainly did. I got different duvet covers for them, too. It's very sweet really. The top part looks like Gotham City and the bottom is like the palace from *Frozen*! It's a clever way of dividing a small room and making both children feel as if they have their own area.'

'Well done, Mum,' Róisín said as she gave a customer change.

She cooked one each for the children and wrapped them in the special cardboard cones she'd ordered.

'Now you two must let me know if these are any good,' Róisín said. 'You're my official testers.'

The silence, followed by the chocolaty cheeks and wide smiles were all the praise she required.

'Will you have one, Mum?'

'No thanks. I need to watch my waistline!'

'You haven't a pick on you,' Róisín said swatting her. 'Is the B&B full?'

'Booked solid for the foreseeable future, which is a great compliment. Many of the guests are returning too . . .' She sighed. 'Your father's not much help, though. He's having the life of Reilly. He's taken to his retirement like a duck to water. Well, to be exact he's spending most of his time on the water.'

'With Jimmy in the boat?' Róisín asked as she continued to serve customers.

Before Keeley could answer, a gaggle of children burst into the tent along with Jill. The noise level rose and Róisín waved goodbye to her mum and Billy and Jess.

She needed to have a word with Liv. While she knew their mother adored Billy and Jess, she was also extremely busy. Leaving her with them so often wasn't fair.

Róisín felt as if her face was becoming crispy from the heat of the hotplates, so she asked Jill to take over for a bit.

'Deadly,' she said grabbing the wooden tool for spreading the batter. 'Wait until you see me in action. Roll up and get your crepes!' she yelled. It was clear she had a great connection with the little ones and she was like the Pied Piper as they flocked to her and formed an orderly queue. Róisín laughed as 'work Jill' shone through.

After a while longer of serving at the tent shop, she walked over to Nourriture.

Much to her delight, the shop had been having a bumper day's business.

'My God, I figured we were stealing all the custom in the tent,' she said to Brigid.

'Not at all! I've had to put on another batch of sourdough. The cupcakes, croissants and cream puffs all sold out too. There are lots of fresh things coming from the oven shortly, though, so there's no need to panic.'

'Great stuff. Thanks, Brigid. I'm going to fly up to the office for ten minutes if anyone needs me. I need to do a bit of paperwork and besides, Jill is cracking her teacher whip out in the tent.'

Taking the stairs two at a time, Róisín felt this was exactly the right time to ask for a loan. Fair enough, today was an exception to the rule, but the fact that Nourriture had the potential to sell this amount of food was heartening. In her mind she was jumping two steps ahead and envisaging a mobile shop that could be sent out to all the music and arts festivals. Lads like Steve and Eoin were tailormade for sending off as salesmen.

Her optimism was bolstered further by the enthusiastic lady on the other end of the phone at the bank up in Galway city. Apparently they were eager to lend and were open to discussion with anyone who had ideas.

'Can I make an appointment to come and see you?' she asked.

'I'm free tomorrow morning at eleven or Tuesday of next week,' said chirpy Sandra.

'Tomorrow morning would be great,' Róisín said. Sandra explained what the bank looked for and how many months' paperwork she needed to bring along.

'Right, I have it all written down. I have all those things in my office. I own and run Nourriture so I know the answers to all the potential questions.'

'That's great,' said Sandra. 'You must bring any business partners along too.'

'Oh no, it's just me,' she said.

It was as if a weight had been lifted off her shoulders. Róisín was almost high with excitement, but forced herself to stay calm. It was too early to say anything to anybody else, but then she thought of calling her dad. He'd been steady and level when she'd needed advice in the past.

'Hi love,' he said, answering instantly. 'I'm here with your sister having a nice cup of tea and we're looking at the fabulous beds I made. How are things?'

'All good,' she said. 'I was just calling to let you know that Mum should be there any second with the children.' She didn't want to talk about money or business while things were difficult financially for Liv and Martin.

'They've just pulled up in the drive,' Doug said. 'Wait until you hear their reaction.'

Róisín laughed as she listened to the delighted squeals in the background.

She hung up, feeling more positive than she had in ages. Liv would have a whole new lease of life when the new venture with the students took off. Her dad would have a nice little routine going once he settled into retirement. Her mum would be fine once her summer season was in full flight. And as for her? She could feel it in her bones that her food empire was only getting started. Perhaps she could finally shed the negativity of her life with Jacques, and how it ended. It had been such a dark time for her, all that happened between them, but she couldn't keep living in darkness. Her mother's letter was so right – to live fully, to smell the flowers – it was how Róisín wanted to live, but the heartache of Jacques had stolen that from her, made her forget herself. She resolved to be more positive from now on, more open. And it would start right now: she'd snatch a bottle of bubbly from the wine shop and bring it home to Jill that evening to celebrate a good day's work.

Chapter 11

IT WAS LATE IN THE AFTERNOON BY THE TIME Keeley got home from Liv's house. The children were so delighted with the beds, it had made all the effort worthwhile.

As she took the sheets off the clothesline and brought in some fresh flowers for two of the bedrooms, Keeley thought about Doug. For over four decades he'd worked in carpentry, making everything from furniture to kitchens, six days a week, never complaining. She knew he wasn't really fulfilled by it, but he had a family to provide for so he got up every day and worked hard and ensured they had everything they needed. She had always appreciated that commitment. So she really did feel he was entitled to enjoy his retirement. She honestly didn't begrudge him that. But she couldn't help feeling as if he were almost retiring from her as well as from his job. Once he threw off the shackles of the job, he changed. It had only been three months since his retirement party, but it was like he was going through a second teenagehood. Liv and Róisín slagged him about his 'bromance' with Jimmy, and it was true that they were spending every minute they could together. Partners in crime and all that, but where did that leave her and her idea that his retirement would mean more quality time for them? Doug wasn't old. In fact,

Keeley mused, at sixty-five he seemed quite young to her as she was hurtling toward her sixtieth birthday. But she was aware that they were lucky to have their health. They ought to be enjoying this time in their lives together.

When she'd returned from her dinner at the castle with Claus the other night, Doug wasn't even home. She'd sorted the breakfast things and changed into her nightdress before he appeared.

'Where were you?' she asked.

'Out with Jimmy,' he said. 'What's with the third degree?' He smelled of booze, so she guessed he was tipsy.

'I don't mind you going off with Jimmy,' she said evenly. 'But I was trying to call you all afternoon and couldn't get you. I get worried. Especially when you're out in a boat.'

'Ah I was fine. I'm big enough and bold enough to look after myself,' he said.

Keeley turned off her bedside light. As long as he was alright, then that's all that matters, she thought. He climbed in beside her moments later and fell immediately into a snoring sleep.

She didn't bother telling him about her dinner with Claus. There didn't seem much point and besides, he didn't ask what she'd done with her day and evening. He never really did, now that she came to think about it. The following morning he'd disappeared to buy fishing supplies, leaving no opportunity to chat.

Once a couple more days passed, there didn't seem any point in talking about her unexpected dinner date. Clearly, Marie at the castle hadn't managed to spread the news that she'd been there.

Today looked to be a slightly easier day on paper. Luckily the guests she had in the rooms were all staying a further night, so she didn't need to change the beds. Once they were all fed and watered and sent on their merry way for the day, she sat down to do a bit of work for the upcoming fundraiser she was involved with.

Every year since the children were little, Keeley had organised a sponsored walk for the paediatric unit at Galway hospital. She'd started the first one when Olivia and Róisín were very small.

She'd pressed ahead that first year, unsure of herself but determined to try and make a difference. She'd been overwhelmed by the support she'd received.

It became an annual event and one that all the locals looked forward to. Each year there was a theme and that determined how the fundraising campaign should run. The local newspapers and radio stations were a marvellous support and Keeley had gotten to know so many lovely people. The first time she had to go on live radio, she'd thought she'd die of fright. Now it was second nature and she actually enjoyed the banter with the DJ.

All the major plans were set and it was tying in with the festival at Ballyshore this year. The starting point was at the edge of the village and the route went right out toward the lighthouse and looped back to the beach. In all it was just over five kilometres, which Keeley felt was doable for most abilities. And Róisín had rowed in with the offer of setting up tables with juices and healthy snacks, so that would be a welcome addition.

Keeley needed her file so she could make some last-minute calls. She went to her art room and pulled open the top drawer of her small filing cabinet. She found the folder with the fundraising information and pulled it out. Her hand brushed off the file labelled with Róisín's name.

Hesitating, she set the fund-raising file on the floor and plucked out Róisín's. It was a long time since she'd looked through it. Instantly, tears sprang to her eyes as she thumbed through the contents. Her own writing was barely recognisable on the copies of the adoption papers from the convent. She'd trembled so much that day, it was a wonder she'd managed to write anything legible at all. It had all been fairly discreet. The nuns had been kind, but there was no information given verbally and Keeley had been terrified to ask. She'd wanted to take Róisín and run before anyone changed their mind. As she studied the papers, the memories came flooding back.

'The child's mother is deceased,' the nun had said. 'It states that on the birth cert., as you can see.'

Keeley looked at the yellowing page containing all of Róisín's details. She'd shown this page to Róisín many years ago. When she was ten. She'd thought it best to share the information she had, although it had made her physically ill afterwards. The emotions she'd felt the day she finally got her baby had all come rushing back as she'd sat with Róisín.

'What does this line mean?' Róisín asked, as she looked at the adoption form.

'*Not permitted to retain familial information due to deceased mother* means that the people who gave you to Dad and me were not allowed to tell us anything about your birth mother's family.'

'Why?'

'When someone dies, it can be the wishes of her family that nobody contacts them afterwards.'

'But didn't they want to know about me?' Róisín asked with tears in her eyes.

Keeley had felt her heart breaking as she hugged Róisín and stroked her face and told her that all things happen for a reason. That the nuns and her poor dead mother must've known that she and Doug were going to love her and mind her and never leave her.

'So that's why my birth mother's family let me go? They were giving me to you and Dad?'

'Yes, pet. You were the most precious gift imaginable. But it's just the same as giving someone a birthday present. You don't call to their house the next day and ask for the gift back, now do you?'

'I wanted those skates back that I gave Jill when she was five.'

'I know you did. I remember,' Keeley said, forcing a smile. 'But I explained that once we gift something to another person, the gift is theirs to keep.'

'Even if the gift is a person . . .' Róisín said quietly.

Keeley couldn't believe that twenty years had passed since that conversation. Of course Róisín had a copy of her birth cert. as she'd needed it to get her passport. But they'd never talked about it since that day twenty years ago.

Keeley turned the page and studied Róisín's birth cert. There was very little extra information there. The father was down as unknown. Apart from one time when she was very young, Róisín had never questioned this, but it had plagued Keeley for years. How had her darling girl come about? She prayed it wasn't in violent circumstances.

Róisín was born in Galway University Hospital and it seemed she was taken from there to the convent. Doug had asked a couple of questions when they signed the adoption papers.

'The baby wasn't born here in this building, was she?' he'd asked.

'No, as it states on the birth cert., she was born in the hospital in Galway, twenty minutes' drive from here,' the nun said. 'She came to us yesterday. She's three weeks and two days old. You can see it marked clearly on the birth cert. when and where she was born.'

Of course, the adoption was all perfectly legal, but Doug had told Keeley on several occasions how lucky they were to get Róisín.

'Someone was watching over us that we got her. We could've been on the register for years without any luck. It was all a blessing that the adoption register put those nuns in touch with us. They could've called anyone and they chose us.'

Keeley knew she'd be grateful until her dying day that Róisín had come to them. She'd told her that a thousand times. When they looked at the documents and her birth cert. twenty years ago, she'd told Róisín what she believed to be true.

'I've no proof, love, but I've always believed that your birth mother sent you to us. That she was and always will be watching over you.'

'So she's like my guardian angel in heaven?'

'Yes love, she is. Yours and mine. She made me happier than you will ever know.'

The file had remained at the house all this time. Róisín had never asked for it and Keeley had never offered it. It was a strange arrangement now that she thought about it. But, Keeley mused, Róisín never showed her the letter that arrived on her birthday this year. She was consumed with curiosity about it. Róisín hadn't thrown herself on the floor and sobbed, so surely it couldn't be anything awful or harrowing. Keeley bit her lip. The elephant in the room was beginning to take over.

A thought struck Keeley. The nuns hadn't mentioned the birthday cards that Róisín received each year. It was such an unusual thing to do and yet they never acknowledged it. And the letter . . . did they know of its existence? All the postmarks were Galway, but did that definitely mean the convent? Who exactly had kept the cards and letter all this time and was diligent enough to remember to send them on the correct day every year?

She couldn't discuss her worries with Doug. As far as he was concerned, everything was just as it should be. Even the day they'd signed the papers and taken Róisín home, he'd been as calm as a millpond.

'It's OK, love,' Doug had said, resting his hand on her arm. 'Take your time. Sign the papers in your own time. It's all going to be fine now.' His calm and confident smile that day had eased her addled mind. He'd countersigned and they'd handed the precious pages back to the head nun.

They'd been given a single black-and-white photograph of Róisín, which they'd both studied incessantly for the week before they met her. They'd had many copies made since, but the original one still made her heart leap. She picked it out of the file now and stroked it lovingly. Nothing could have prepared Keeley for the emotions that almost knocked her from standing as a young nun had brought the baby to meet them for the first time that day.

'Hello there, little lady,' Doug had said, walking over to offer his finger for the baby to clutch. Instinctively, she'd curled her tiny hand around his finger.

'From this moment on you're my girl,' Doug said, turning

to grin at Keeley. She was rooted to the spot. Every fibre of her body wanted to scoop the baby from the young woman's arms and snuggle her closely, but she was terrified to even touch her in case somebody rushed in and said there'd been a dreadful mistake and took her away.

That feeling of unease had stayed with Keeley. In fact, it never left her. All these years later, she still felt the deep-rooted fear in her heart that Róisín could be snatched away from them.

If she was honest with herself, she knew the real reason she was so fearful. The secret she'd held all these years had never stopped haunting her. She knew she would take it to her grave, however. Talking about it or telling another person, even Doug, could jeopardise everything. She'd decided long ago that keeping it inside was the price she had to pay in exchange for having Róisín. Most of the time she managed to quash the fears and feelings of guilt. But every now and again, like today, when she saw something from the past, it jolted her.

Every year, an envelope arrived like clockwork on Róisín's birthday, addressed to 'baby Daly'. In the early years, each card depicted the age Róisín had reached. Keeley was grateful because the numerical images were easier to take than ones with *Daughter* emblazoned on the front might have been. The messages weren't very long in most of them, but they were heartfelt.

She had so many emotions racing through her as she imagined Róisín's biological mother writing the messages. How difficult must it have been for the poor woman? Her inscriptions made it very clear that she knew she was dying. What must have been going through her head as she wrote each one?

Keeley had known the torture of longing for a child and thinking it would never come to pass. But how would any woman cope with knowing she was about to give birth and she wouldn't be alive to raise her own baby?

'Did my birth mum really write these?' Róisín had asked in astonishment, way back when she was only five or six years old.

'Yes, love. She wanted you to have a card from her on your birthday each year,' Keeley had replied.

'If she wanted to do that, why didn't she just come and give them to me?' Róisín had asked.

'She died soon after you were born, sweetheart,' Doug had explained. 'That's why Mum and I were allowed to be your parents.'

'But didn't I have any daddy?' she had asked in confusion.

Keeley had looked at Doug for guidance. He'd been amazing while Róisín was standing there and looking into his eyes. After all, she was a child, so she hadn't meant to hurt his feelings. She was merely asking a relevant question.

'No pet, your dad lived somewhere very far away and he couldn't take care of you.' That part of the story was a total fabrication but until she was old enough to understand, Keeley and Doug felt it was kindest to offer the child some sort of explanation.

She'd accepted this answer and had rarely brought it up again. For their part, Keeley and Doug had cried together after that conversation, hoping their daughter would find their love to be enough as she grew up.

'My heart dropped like a stone when she asked if she had a daddy,' Doug had said, wiping his eyes. 'How stupid am I, sobbing like a baby over the innocent remarks of a child?'

'You're not stupid, love,' Keeley said. 'But you know she didn't mean to hurt you. She adores you and no matter who her father is or was, he couldn't have loved her more than you do.'

'No,' Doug had sighed. 'You're right.'

Keeley was envious of the inner peace that little episode seemed to afford Doug. He'd never cried like that again, nor had he questioned his role in Róisín's life. It was as if he'd laid his fears to rest that day and moved on.

The adoption had been of its time, but things would be so different today, Keeley thought as she looked over the papers. There was no way it would be so casual now. At the time, the nuns were so happy that Róisín was going to a good and loving home and that it was clear how much she was wanted. Keeley knew they wouldn't be so lucky now. Things were done in a different way thirty years ago, which was why they had so little information to go on. She felt the familiar pull of guilt as she thought about the part Doug didn't know. Then she shook it off. It was a secret that would stay kept, that was for sure.

'Hello?'

Startled back to the present, Keeley shoved the file back into the drawer and went into the hallway.

'Ida! How are you?'

'Yes, good thanks, Keeley. So we are ready to leave. We can pay the bill now, please?'

'Of course, come with me and we'll sort it out in the office.'

Keeley led Ida into her office and offered her a seat.

'I hope you've enjoyed your stay,' she said. 'It's such a pity you weren't well the other night.'

'I used to suffer with seasickness as a child, but I figured at my age I would be finished with that. It seems not. You have a lovely home here, Keeley. I am so taken with the area and all the Irish people. But we were so fortunate to find you. Thank you for taking Claus out on his birthday. It was wonderful that he didn't have to be alone. I worry about him, you know?'

'It was my pleasure,' she said. 'He's a lovely gentleman.'

'I think it's because I never married, but he's always been like my protector. Maybe that's why I never managed to find a man. I compared everyone I met to Claus of course. None even came close, so I thought it best to step away.'

'He's a good man by all accounts,' Keeley said. 'It's lovely that he minds you so well too. But I think you are a great comfort and companion to him as well. It's not all one sided.'

'I was in love once,' Ida said, suddenly. 'With a man I couldn't have. He was married and had a small child. We met quite by chance through work. We didn't spend the night together. I couldn't do that to another woman. But we were soulmates. It broke my heart that I couldn't have him. He offered to leave his wife, but I couldn't have it on my conscience that I would take that little girl's father away from her. Our father left when we were little, you see. So I knew what that felt like. I wasn't going to be the one to shatter that child's life.'

'How sad,' Keeley said. 'For all of you. But for the record I think what you did was very selfless. Have you seen him since?'

'No,' she said wiping her eyes. 'Goodness, I have no idea why I told you this, Keeley. I apologise. All you want is for me to pay my bill and go. You didn't have a sign on your gate saying that you do counselling also!'

'Oh please, I'm honoured that you feel you can talk to me,' she said, reaching out and patting her hand.

'Could I ask you a silly favour?' Ida asked.

'Sure,' Keeley smiled.

'The brown bread you serve at breakfast. Do you make it yourself?'

'Yes, would you like the recipe?'

'Thank you, but what I am wondering is whether you might consider showing me how to make it next time we come? I'd love to see how you do it.'

'I'd be honoured. It's a deal.'

'Thank you, Keeley. You are a dear. Now let's pay you.'

Ida counted out the money and handed it to Keeley. As she stood to leave, Claus walked in.

'Ah there you are, ladies.'

'So we are all ready to go,' Ida said. She hugged Keeley and whispered thank you in her ear. Keeley hugged her back and wished them a pleasant journey.

'We have had the most wonderful time,' Claus said. 'I cannot thank you enough.'

'My pleasure.' Keeley smiled warmly.

'And I hope your husband will not be angry with me for borrowing you and taking you to dinner,' Claus said. 'Please tell him I thank him too. He's a lucky man.'

'Don't worry about Doug,' Keeley said flapping her hand. 'He wouldn't notice if I went to Mars for the evening!'

'Really?' Claus laughed. 'Well if I was married to you, Keeley, I would know every step you took.'

Keeley blushed and walked on ahead of them to the front door.

'We plan to travel for another two months,' Ida said. 'Do you think we could come back at the end of August or beginning of September? Would you take us?'

'Of course!' Keeley said. 'I'd be thrilled. Call me. Wait, I'll fetch a card.'

'No need!' Claus said. 'I already have one.'

They both waved as they drove away. They were such lovely people and even though she'd only just met Ida, she'd felt a wonderful connection with her. Her story of unrequited love was so sad. Keeley knew she was lucky in so many ways. But she couldn't help feeling a little bit giddy at Claus's words. He was a real romantic!

Chapter 12

ROB WALSH WAS IN TURMOIL AS HE STOOD AT THE counter of Blake's jewellery store in Limerick city. Theresa was a nice girl. Well, she was incredibly hot and hung on his every word. All his mates were in awe of her and kept telling him he was a lucky bloke to have a girl like that on his arm.

He'd found her fun in the beginning and there was no doubting she was gorgeous, with her long legs and perfect blonde waves, and yet he kept thinking there was something missing. Some sort of feeling he felt he should be having. He could never tell any of the lads that, though. They'd laugh him out of the pub. But as he looked at the small photo of his parents that he kept in his wallet, he couldn't help being envious of the way they were looking into one another's eyes. His father was always asking him when he'd give him some grandchildren, and the pressure had increased tenfold since his brother's announcement.

'I don't mind that your brother is gay and I'm happy he's happy, but the onus is on you to produce the next generation, Robert.'

'Right, Da. I'll start to sow my wild oats all over the county, then. How many children would you like by the end of the year?'

'Don't be smart, son,' Melvin Walsh said. 'But what's

the point in me building my bank balance and ending up as the richest man in the graveyard? I understand that you wanted to get your craft beer business started and established. But you're doing surprisingly well now. Do yourself a favour and settle down. Don't let the window of opportunity pass you by, son.'

Rob had incredible respect for his old man. He'd taken his inheritance from his own parents and turned it into a relative goldmine by investing wisely and selling off parts of the land at the right time. It seemed that anything Melvin Walsh touched turned to cash.

The increasing fortunes over the years hadn't saved Rob's mother, who had died after a heart attack. Rob could still remember the day they'd all walked behind his mam's coffin as they laid her to rest in the local cemetery. Although he was fifteen at the time, his father was always terrified he and his brother would somehow forget Ellen. So he spoke of her often, and at times Rob feared that he hadn't actually accepted she was gone.

There were photos of Ellen all over the house and Melvin had never so much as looked at another woman. He'd dedicated his life to his boys and the business. Now, as he was growing older, he made no bones about the fact that he wanted to see out his days surrounded by grandchildren.

'What about Theresa?' he'd asked Rob last night as he was headed out the door to meet her. 'Are you going to make an honest woman of her?'

Rob had stopped and sighed. He knew it was time to move out from the comfortable bachelor pad he and his dad shared. He also knew Melvin was probably right. He should be thinking about his future.

'I don't know,' he'd replied honestly.

While Rob couldn't think of a reason why he shouldn't marry Theresa, neither could he say that he was busting a gut to spend the rest of his life with her. They'd gone for dinner and Rob had felt totally paranoid as she'd sat staring with doe eyes at him. It seemed that she was pleading silently for him to pop the question. If everyone he met thought it was a good plan and almost inevitable, perhaps he was the one misjudging the situation?

So he'd caved. He'd come to Limerick city and picked out a stop-'em-dead diamond ring. The enthusiastic shop assistant was chatting animatedly and assuring him they would resize the ring within two days should it need it.

'She's one lucky lady,' she beamed. 'Good luck with the proposal. Have you something romantic in mind?'

'Not really,' he said as he accepted the package. 'I'm sure I'll think of something.'

He felt claustrophobic by the time he sat in the van. He had some deliveries to make, so there was no reason to fret about the ring right this second, he reasoned.

Looking at his schedule, he smiled when he saw Nourriture on his list. Róisín was always flying about and coming up with new ideas. A trip to Ballyshore was just what he needed to settle his nerves. The place was what he'd consider to be a total backwater, but it was serene and beautiful. There was a great vibe to the place too, mainly thanks to Nourriture, which was quite simply fantastic. Róisín had managed to use every inch of space to pack in an amazing array of products. She usually asked him to haul shelves or even parts of counters into a different section, but he didn't mind.

Turning up the music, he tried not to think about the

ring or Theresa. He would put the box into the safe at his father's house and bide his time. The shop assistant was right, he needed to come up with something romantic to make the whole thing more special. That way, it would probably sit better with him. Besides, the photo of his parents in his wallet was taken at their sixteenth wedding anniversary. He was guessing it took time and a lot of hard work to reach a point where you seemed almost at one with another human being.

Ballyshore came into view and the shimmering water looked so inviting he actually wanted to pull off his clothes and jump in. Instead, he parked in the loading bay outside Nourriture and grabbed his delivery dockets. Finding the one for Róisín, he walked inside to see if one of the lads could give him a hand.

'Rob!' Róisín waved from the kitchen behind the counter. 'Just the man I wanted to see. Did you think of bringing me that second driftwood shelf?'

'Ah blast,' he said knocking his forehead with the heel of his hand. 'I totally forgot.' He made the display shelves at a workshop back at the farm. Only certain retailers were offered them, and Róisín had fallen in love with the design. He'd promised her a second one and given her his word that he'd bring it next time he was passing.

'Did you remember the beer?' she teased.

'The day I go on a delivery without my craft beer I'll check myself into the local nuthouse,' he said with a grin.

She dispensed one of the young lads to help carry the bottles into the off licence section. Once it was all stacked to his liking, with the labels facing the right way and the Grolsch-type tops in a neat row, he waited for Róisín to come and sign the delivery docket.

'I'll be with you in a jiffy,' she called over. 'Will you have a bite to eat and a smoothie? I got a new machine and it makes drinks that are almost as good as your Celtic Beer.'

He smiled and nodded, saying he'd order a plate of food. He was almost finished when Róisín sat down at his table.

'How's it going?' Rob asked.

She sighed. 'It's seriously busy in here. Not that I'm complaining,' she assured him. 'I've a lot going on though.' She crossed her legs and hit off his brief case, knocking it to the floor.

'Oh no!' she said diving to grab it. As she did, the ring-box rolled out. 'Hey, hey, hey!' she said with a wide grin. 'Have you some news on the way?'

'No,' he said, sounding a lot crankier than he'd intended.

She sat back and said nothing.

'Listen, I'm a bit all over the place right now,' he admitted. 'I'm with this girl Theresa and my old man is constantly telling me I need to settle down. He thinks she's good for me. My friends all think she's a dolly. The business is starting to do really well and so I guess it's time . . .'

Róisín folded her arms and didn't flinch.

'What?' he said.

'Listen, I'm certainly not an oracle on relationships, believe me, the only big one I had went royally wrong. So please don't think I'm preaching or even attempting to sound like a wise owl . . .'

'But?'

'But, you don't seem that excited about any of this. I know you're a man, so that means you're emotionally crippled.'

'Hey, less of that, thank you very much,' he said, grinning.

'But seriously? Shouldn't you be even a teensy bit happy at the thought of proposing to your beloved?'

'Ah, I am. It'll be grand. I'm probably a bit nervous. I've never done this kind of thing before.'

'Grand,' she said sarcastically. 'Diamond rings and wedding dresses and celebrations shouldn't be organised around *grand*.'

'So I should expect fireworks and bluebirds and roses then? Does the Disney dream really exist?'

'Nah,' Róisín said thoughtfully. 'I don't suppose it does. But I'm a bit sad for you that you're not more upbeat about it all. But hey, it's none of my business.'

Rob nodded and turned his head to follow Róisín's gaze. Her eyes had dulled and her smile was gone.

'Excuse me a moment,' she said patting him on the shoulder. He watched as she walked over to talk to an elderly man, not dissimilar to his own father. The conversation was brief. Róisín walked back toward him, looking ashen faced.

'You OK?'

She shrugged her shoulders and pursed her lips. 'Sorry Rob, something's come up. I need to go up to my office. It was nice chatting to you. Good luck with the ring and all that.'

Before he could answer, she dashed from the shop and through a door at the rear near the kitchen. Not sure if he should run after her, he shuffled to the counter to pay.

'Róisín said it's on the house,' Brigid said.

'She'll have to stop doing that,' he said, smiling. 'Tell her thanks. I'll have the shelf for her in the next couple of days. I'll deliver it myself.'

'OK cool. I'll let her know. See you then, Rob.'

As he drove from Ballyshore, Rob couldn't help worrying about Róisín. She was an unusual character. Stunningly beautiful with her coal-black hair and piercing blue eyes, he'd been a little nervous of her in the beginning. She was very self-assured but not overly friendly. She'd thawed hugely over the past year as he'd gotten to know her. She believed in his product too, which had clearly gained him some form of acceptance in her eyes.

The first time he'd spoken to her at any length was back in January. The shop was quiet and he'd asked if he could join her to drink his coffee before he set off again.

She was telling him about a new company that was producing raw food products and how she wanted to give them some shop space.

'You're so passionate about what you do,' he said.

'Well there's no point in running a business unless you believe in what you're selling.'

'True,' he said. 'My father was a bit upset with me and my brother that we didn't want to take over his farm. But thankfully he had the foresight to see that we both had good ideas of our own.'

'My parents are very supportive too,' she said.

The next time he'd called to Nourriture, Róisín had asked him to join her for a coffee and now it was routine.

He eyeballed the bag containing the ring and sighed. Was Róisín right? Was he doing the wrong thing while attempting to do the right thing?

She'd said she was sad for him. That resonated with him. Nobody should be sad when they're about to get engaged, surely?

The phone rang and his mind was drawn to a frazzled

customer who needed extra stock immediately. Grateful for the distraction, Rob decided to put all thought of rings and celebrations to one side. He'd give himself a month, he decided. He'd pretend in his own head that he and Theresa were engaged and he'd see how it made him feel. One month, then he'd know for sure.

Chapter 13

IT WAS THREE DAYS SINCE NELL HAD DISCOVERED the young girl crouched in her boiler-house.

She still hadn't talked at any length. After the initial information about her mother dying and how she'd come from Dublin, it was as if she'd shut down. Nell wasn't too bothered. In fact, it suited her. She wasn't exactly in the market for a lodger and it most certainly wasn't her wish, at seventy-four, to become the guardian of a troubled teen.

But so far she hadn't actually annoyed her and she didn't get in the way or cause a fuss. Her long, limp, brown hair and bloodshot chestnut eyes weren't helped by her frail pointy face and sticky out ears. She looked like a little string of misery, God help her.

'Have you a name?' Nell eventually asked that morning, when she found her sitting in front of the lighthouse staring out at the water.

The girl simply perched on the edge of the bank and refused to speak. Nell sighed.

'Listen girly,' she said. 'I'm not asking you to tell me stuff. Believe me, I don't need to know. I'm not one of those sorts. I keep myself to myself so you needn't think I'm a gossip-monger. But if you're going to hang around here for a while I do need to know a thing or two . . . starting with what I should call you.'

The girl looked up at her and hesitated. Nell thought she was going to say something, but then she didn't.

'You're as quiet as a mouse,' she said folding her arms. 'So unless you have any objections, that'll be your name.' She shrugged and didn't look too upset by this. 'Mouse it is. Are you in trouble? As in, are you running from the law or anything like that?' Mouse shook her head. 'So nobody's going to screech up to my door in a squad car and accuse me of harbouring a master criminal?'

'Nope,' she said.

'Do you want to make a call to anybody?'

'Nope.'

'Fair enough. Are you hungry?' Nell ventured. She nodded vehemently. For such a skinny little slip of a thing, she ate a lot. 'I'll make us some breakfast. Follow me inside in a few minutes.'

Nell made eggs with beans and a pile of toast once again. Laura had loved that type of food too. They used to sit and listen to the radio together, especially on weekends or if Laura wasn't well enough to go to school.

Willing herself to stop thinking about Laura, she got on with making breakfast. She was about to call Mouse when she appeared. She banged the two plates onto the table and waited for her to say something.

'Manners are free. If you're staying here, I expect you to use them. If you've never done it before, learn.'

Mouse looked over and seemed unperturbed by her tone. 'Thanks.'

'Welcome,' she said, sitting opposite her. 'As you can see, everything is geared toward one person in this place. The table isn't ideal. But that hasn't been an issue before now.' Nell bought the table in one of those furniture warehouses and it had enough room for a single plate, cutlery and side-plate at a push.

Mouse polished off the food in record time, just as she'd done over the last couple of days.

'Hey, slow down or you'll have beans coming out your nose,' Nell said. The girl placed the cutlery down ever so gently and kept her gaze on the table.

'You probably think I sound like a grumpy old woman. I don't get many visitors around here. Especially not kids. I'm out of practice.'

She didn't quite smile, but Nell was pretty sure the corners of her mouth had at least twitched a little.

'I need to send a couple of e-mails,' she said. 'Can I leave you to clean up the breakfast things?' Mouse nodded and looked quite happy.

Nell nearly collapsed when Mouse followed her up into the observatory and started talking.

'Thanks for being so kind to me. I know it's a total pain in the ass to have a little scrubber like me turn up. I promise I won't stay much longer.'

Nell nodded.

'Thanks for not pushing me to talk.'

'Yeah, whatever,' Nell said. She turned back to the laptop and finished what she was doing. Mouse perched at the window and stared out.

'Take the binoculars. You'll see all sorts of stuff with them,' Nell said.

Mouse did as she suggested and spent the next hour engrossed in that.

'Right,' Nell said, stretching. 'I'm going to make a pot of soup. That's what I do on Thursdays. It's for John-Joe. Come and watch if you want. Or you can join in?'

Mouse followed her back to the kitchen where Nell began to peel and roughly chop potatoes and onions. 'I'm not what you'd call a chef. But I like the idea of tossing a load of ingredients into a big pot, whizzing it up and producing something comforting.'

'You must like this John-Jo if you make him soup,' Mouse ventured. 'Is he your fella?'

Nell harrumphed. 'I actually think he's one of the greatest idiots I've ever had the misfortune of meeting. He's married to my long-term housekeeper. She's a gem of a woman. It makes her life easier when her good-for-nothing husband is kept happy.'

'Fair enough,' Mouse said, nodding.

Nell continued with the job in hand. She didn't ask Mouse any of the questions that were racing through her brain. But if the truth was told, Nell was as curious as a monkey to know the ins and outs of how Mouse had ended up in Ballyshore at her lighthouse. But she was the queen of keeping secrets, so she wasn't going to engage in double standards.

'Want to chop carrots?' she asked.

Mouse nodded. 'Is there a certain way to do it?'

'It's a carrot. What can you possibly do to it that will change that?'

Mouse grinned.

They continued in a comfortable silence until Mouse stopped chopping and tipped the carrots into the pot of bubbling stock.

'So I already told you I'm from Dublin,' she said.

'All the best girls are.'

'Yeah, I guess.' Mouse smiled briefly. Nell was utterly winded for a second. The difference in the young girl's face when she actually smiled was astonishing. For a moment . . . just a fleeting second . . . she reminded her of Laura.

'I had to get away,' Mouse said. 'Ma went into hospital over a year ago. She was meant to dry out and come home. But it seems she'd already done too much damage. She died in the place that was supposed to cure her. Great, yeah?'

'Not really,' Nell said. 'Life's a bitch at times.'

'I'm the youngest so I think the social workers assumed the brothers would mind me,' Mouse said.

'And they didn't?'

'Nah, between them and Da they were too busy planning the next job. By job I don't mean legal employment . . .'

'I know exactly what you mean,' Nell said.

'I don't know where the stuff came from, but some days the flat would be stuffed with all sorts, from tellies and jewellery to fancy bags and God knows what . . . They won't miss me. At least, I doubt they will. Have I been on *Crime Call* yet?' She grinned. 'Or is there an SOS on Facebook with a picture of me in a communion dress looking cute?'

'I don't watch much television,' Nell said. 'Never did. I'm not on Facebook either. Mo is . . . she'll be in tomorrow. You can ask her.'

'Why did you come out here?' Mouse asked.

'Why did you?' she shot back.

Mouse shrugged her shoulders. 'I think I wanted to get as far away from the grime and buildings and cars and crap . . . I didn't use sat nav or nothing,' Mouse said. 'I just got on trains and landed in different towns and walked and hung out. It's amazing how you can become invisible.'

'I know,' Nell said. 'It's worked nicely for me for a long time.'

Mouse looked at her. 'Who showed you how to make soup?'

'Nobody. I started doing stuff like this out of necessity. I looked after someone who needed to be on a special diet. So I had to learn. It's therapeutic, though. Makes my head feel less clogged. Then I perform my weekly act of kindness by giving some to Mo. That makes me feel better in here,' she said thumping her chest. 'Then she gives it to her lazy assed husband John-Joe. By all accounts, it makes him happy. Everybody wins.'

'Why is he a lazy ass? Why do you dislike him so much?'

'He's never bothered to find work. He allows Mo to clean for people and it hasn't occurred to him to even feel guilty.'

'Do you know that for a fact?'

'No, but I've come to that conclusion and nobody has ever argued with me. I've never actually told anyone, mind you . . . That's the beauty of not having to answer to anybody.' She stirred the pot and slapped a lid on.

'Are all men a waste of space?' Mouse asked.

'Why on earth do you think I'd know the answer to that question?' Nell asked.

'You're old, aren't you?' she said matter-of-factly.

'Charming.'

'Well, your hair is white and you don't look my age.'

'I'm seventy-four,' Nell stated.

'Yup, that's old,' Mouse confirmed.

Instead of feeling remotely insulted, Nell laughed. 'Back to the men question,' she said as she leaned against the counter. 'I've yet to meet a man who didn't disappoint me.'

'Janey Mac, I think I'll just jump into the sea and be done with it,' Mouse said, sighing dramatically. 'The only fella I think I could love is Superman. Not the new one. I don't know him. The real one. The one who died, Christopher Reeve. I used to watch *Superman* with Ma when we had a video-player. One of the big old black ones that took enormous tapes.'

'They're the only ones I remember,' Nell said.

'We used to sit and watch Superman flying with his jocks outside his tights and his gammy red boots and I wished with all my heart that he was mine. The way he spun the world backwards . . . He was a legend.'

'Don't hold your breath waiting for a man in tights to move your world,' Nell warned. Mouse sat up on the counter and stared into Nell's eyes.

'Have you ever been in love, Nell?'

'A long time ago, yes,' she admitted. 'Once was enough. I gave him my heart and he didn't appreciate it. I won't do that again.'

'Are you happy living out here by the sea?'

'I'd hardly be here if I wasn't. Nobody can let me down and nobody expects anything of me. In short, nobody gets hurt.'

'Isn't it better to feel something though? Even if it's pain?' Mouse asked. She held her head to the side and stared intently at Nell. For the first time in years, Nell felt an emotional connection. This girl was clearly damaged, but she was endearing.

'For a little whipper-snapper who lulled me into a false sense of security where I thought you were quiet and shy, you ask a lot of strange questions,' Nell said.

'Sorry,' she said, holding her hands up in apology. 'You're

the first person I've ever spoken to like this. You're easy to chat to. You don't make me feel as if I'm in the wrong purely because I exist.'

'Ah go on out of that,' Nell said turning to stir the soup as she felt oddly misty-eyed. Nell wasn't going to tell Mouse, but that was the nicest thing anyone had said to her in a long time.

'Can I come out and do your garden with you today? I watched you yesterday. You know loads about growing stuff, don't you?'

Nell glanced at her watch and looked up at the sky. 'There's more rain on the way. Let's go out and I'll show you a couple of things while the soup is cooking.'

'Deadly,' Mouse said as a wide smile lit her eyes to a sparkle.

Nell marched off in search of a coat and hat for Mouse as she struggled to hide her delight. Knowing Mouse wasn't going to stay long, she reminded herself not to get accustomed to this. Still, she mused as she fished a stripy hat out of a drawer, it was kind of nice while it lasted.

Chapter 14

RÓISÍN FELT QUIETLY CONFIDENT AS SHE SAT IN the waiting area of the bank. She fingered the card she'd stowed carefully in her bag. It was one of her birthday cards from her birth mother. She somehow felt that if she brought it along, it would bring her luck; that her mother would be here with her. It was stupid, really, but it still gave her a sense of comfort.

She pulled it out of her bag and read it quickly. She knew most of them off by heart at this point, but the words still touched her.

Darling girl,
How does it feel being two? I hope you're not too terrible! In fact a small part of me hopes you are. Why? Because I hear I was. I like to think I was spirited. That's a much nicer word than terrible, isn't it?
I hope you have cake and balloons and that you're learning how to blow out your candles and do clap-handies afterwards. When I was two I had wispy hair that barely covered my head. By the time I was three I had the smallest ponytail on the top of my head. Mam used to call me Pebbles after the baby in The Flintstones. *I was ever so proud of that ponytail and pointed it out to anyone who showed even a passing interest in me.*
I wish I could be there to hold you and dress you in a little

*party outfit and tell you how much I love you. But I know your
mother will do a great job.*

*I am smiling and waving and I hope you are happy as can
be. Be who you want to be, little lady. I hope all your dreams
come true today!*

With love and light,
Mam

Róisín smiled as she folded the card and put it back in
her bag. I hope all my dreams come true today too, she
thought, closing her eyes and taking a deep breath.

She'd had her meeting with the loans and mortgage
specialist two days previously and this was the moment
of truth. She'd told Jill all about it and her friend had
hugged her and assured her she was on the cusp of something amazing.

'I just know it. You're so amazing, Ro-Ro. Just imagine,
you could end up getting tickets to all the best festivals
and become the proud owner of the first Michelin-starred
restaurant in this part of the country! If anyone can do it,
you will.'

Jill was there to hug her and wish her well as she drove
off toward the bank this morning, and she really appreciated that.

'Róisín?' said Sandra, the bank official. 'This way.'

She followed her into the small office where they had
met the other day.

'So I have some great news for you,' Sandra said. 'I
won't keep you in suspense, the bank is happy to approve
a loan in principle. Obviously this is subject to agreement
on a price from your landlord. We also took the sum of
twenty thousand euros that you asked for separately into

account for expanding your mobile food emporium for festivals, and we're happy to fund this initiative too.'

'Really?' Róisín said, unable to hide her delight. 'Oh my goodness, I'm thrilled, Sandra.'

'It's a great idea and as I said to you the last day, once we see a business that's turning over a good profit, it's a no-brainer.'

'And people say the banks don't want to lend money!'

They shook hands and Róisín filled out another pile of forms. She was astonished by just how much paperwork was involved, but right at this moment in time, she would have filled out a thousand forms if it meant she'd get her money.

'So the next step for you,' Sandra explained, 'is to hire a quantity surveyor to give a full report on the building. You'll need a reputable estate agent, and I would recommend using a couple, to establish a current market value too.'

'OK,' Róisín said as she scribbled notes down. 'I know that Mr Grace is being put under pressure by his sons. So I'm banking on them seeing this as an opportunity to get a bag of cash each.'

'Money matters among families are always a mess,' Sandra said as Róisín stood up to leave. 'But considering the premises was going to rack and ruin before you moved in and took over, I'd say they'd be foolish to pass you up on your offer.'

Róisín felt like leaping in the air and dancing, but she opted for a frothy latte and a bar of chocolate instead to toast her big moment.

As she sipped her drink in a nearby café, she pulled out her smartphone and looked up the local estate agencies.

Dialling the first one, she explained her plan to an engaging woman called Sue.

'So I need your discretion until I have a price that I can present to Mr Grace,' she said.

'Of course,' Sue said. 'I'll come over to the property myself and I promise you the utmost discretion.'

Róisín got a good feeling from Sue and would happily go with her on instinct alone, but she remembered Sandra's advice to look for a few prices to compare. So she dialled two more numbers and made appointments for each company to send a representative, asking them to ensure they only spoke to her.

Finding a quantity surveyor seemed like a more daunting task and she hadn't the foggiest idea how to go about it, so Róisín phoned her dad.

'Hello love,' he said sounding as if he were down a drain.

'Hi Dad,' she said. 'Where are you?'

'Jimmy and I are on the ferry. We're going to France for two days to buy cheap wine. I've brought the car and everything.'

'Really?' she said unable to hide her surprise. 'I didn't realise you were going to France. I would've given you some ideas of great places to eat.'

'Ah no, we're not going for a gastro tour,' he said. 'It's literally to stock our own cellars and have a bit of fun.'

'I see,' Róisín said with a smirk. Her dad's 'cellar' consisted of a cheap thirty-six-bottle wine rack that was tacked to the wall under the stairs. He enjoyed the odd glass of wine, but wasn't exactly what one would call a connoisseur. There were never more than three or four bottles on the rack and they were all gifts from her shop.

'This retirement lark is the business,' he said happily. 'I should've done it years ago.'

'Yes, except you probably couldn't have afforded it,' she pointed out, rubbing her temples.

'What's up? Did you need me for something in particular?'

'I sort of did. But I'll speak to you when you return,' Róisín said.

'Shoot! What is it?'

'I need a quantity surveyor to check out the shop. I'm hoping to make an offer on the place.'

'Really?' he said. 'That's great, love. I didn't realise old Mr Grace was selling up. It's a great opportunity.'

'Maybe. It's all up in the air at the moment, so keep it under your hat just now. I'm just gathering information so I can make him a fair offer. I'm hoping he'll like the idea of a lump sum and run with it.'

There was an almighty crashing noise in the background.

'Dad?'

'Sorry about that, love,' he said as he burst out laughing. 'Jimmy and I are in the mini casino on the ferry. There's a one-armed bandit machine and we've just hit the jackpot! Woo-hoo!'

'You go on, Dad,' she said, not wanting to ruin his fun. 'I'll talk to you when you get back.'

She hung up, shaking her head and smiling. Her dad was like a naughty teenager with Jimmy lately. But still, he was right to have a bit of fun! As she was about to leave the café a text came through from Doug with the name and phone number of a lady called Yvonne, who Jimmy said was a fantastic quantity surveyor.

She left the café and dialled the number immediately.

Yvonne was based in Galway city but said she had business in a nearby town and could meet Róisín at Nourriture within the hour.

'Are you sure?' Róisín asked.

'Absolutely, I'd only have to make a return trip another day and I have all my equipment in the car, so it makes sense.'

Róisín gave Yvonne directions and rushed back to her car. Jill called as she was almost back at Nourriture.

'Well?'

'It went brilliantly,' she said. 'Even better than I'd hoped. I've to get a current valuation and I'm meeting a quantity surveyor right now. Once I get all the paperwork in order, I'll be able to make an offer.'

'Excellent! I knew you could do it. Do you need me to help at the shop while you're doing your meeting?'

'No, I think it'll be fine. But thanks for the offer.'

'No problem. Listen, I hope you don't mind but I've invited a few friends over to ours for a barbecue tonight.'

'Yeah, sure,' she said. 'Sounds great. It's a lovely evening.'

'Great, I'll get beers and can you swipe a couple of bottles of Prosecco? I got burgers and sausages. That'll do for food.'

'I'll bring some other more edible stuff as well,' Róisín said pointedly. It never ceased to amaze her how much junk Jill put in her body yet her skin was beautiful and she had a figure to die for.

'See you later on then,' Jill said hanging up. Not wanting to attract attention to the quantity surveyor, Róisín told Brigid she was having a meeting upstairs in the office and that she needed privacy.

'No problem,' she said. 'The juice bar is flying, by the way. We put up that offer of a juice and a muffin and it went down a bomb. We'll need to add to the order going forward.'

'That's great Brigid, and to think I was worried about spending the money on the machines!'

She dashed upstairs and put on a pot of coffee, just in time for Brigid to shout up the stairs that someone called Yvonne was there to see her.

The meeting was swift as Yvonne took down the details and asked if she could work away at surveying the place.

'The main thing is that this must be kept quiet for now,' Róisín reiterated.

'That's fine by me. You're hiring me, Róisín, so it's nobody else's business what I report. I'll get started and if I need anything, I'll let you know.'

The shop was super busy, so Róisín went behind the counter to help out. A short while later Keeley arrived with Billy and Jess.

'Hi guys,' she said. 'Are you here for a little snack?'

Róisín led the children to a table and took their order. 'Coffee, Mum?' she asked. Keeley nodded, looking truly exhausted. Róisín brought it over and hugged her mum. 'How are you doing?'

'I'm fine, love. I'm just feeling a bit of pressure. Your father went away on an impromptu holiday with Jimmy and the B&B is full. Liv is finding the students a bit much so I'm trying to help out with these two munchkins.' Róisín brought her mother a slice of lemon cake and sat with her for a moment. She was just about to work out how she could be of help to her when Yvonne appeared.

'Sorry Mum, I'll be back to you in two minutes.'

As it turned out, Yvonne had a pile of questions to ask so they had to go back up to the office for privacy.

'I won't be long,' she called over to Keeley.

'I might have to go,' she said. 'If I miss you, we can chat on the phone later.'

Róisín ended up spending the guts of an hour with Yvonne, but it was all very productive. By the time she had any sort of breathing space, Róisín needed to round off on the till for the day and help Brigid to look over the orders for the following morning.

Steve and Eoin had heard of a music festival and a horse show, both of which were taking place over the course of the next few weekends.

'We could pitch a tent and bring some stuff to sell,' they said. 'We're thinking of going to the music one anyway.'

Róisín struck a deal with the guys that she'd pay for their festival tickets and throw them some pocket money if they manned the food tent for a set number of hours each day. They were delighted. Grinning, she realised yet again how lucky she was to have such easy-going staff.

Róisín had never felt more on top of things. She felt a shiver of anticipation as she allowed herself to imagine the potential of Nourriture. Once she had all the ducks in a row, and assuming Mr Grace accepted her offer, who knew where she'd be in a few years' time. The future was looking very bright.

Brigid called up to say goodbye and handed her the post from that morning.

'See you tomorrow,' she said.

'See you bright and early,' Brigid called back.

Most of the letters contained bills. But one stopped her in her tracks. It was an airmail envelope and the postmark was Bordeaux. She stared at it for a few moments, then ripped it open, her heart beating madly.

Dear Róisín,

It is with deep sadness that I write to inform you of Jacques' death.

We are all still in shock. He was out on a boat with friends and fell overboard and drowned.

I know it is almost five years since you have seen him, but he told me recently that you were the love of his life.

I never knew why you left France, but I suspect it was due to Jacques' inability to commit.

Our hearts are broken. I thought you would like to know what has happened.

Yours truly,

Vivienne Augustine

Chapter 15

THE MENTAL IMAGE OF JACQUES WITH HIS TANNED and toned body and his pale green eyes and floppy, caramel-coloured hair made her long for him with such intensity, she felt physical pain. Róisín felt as if she would vomit. In spite of everything, it tugged at her soul to know that he'd told his mother, Vivienne, that she'd been the love of his life.

Leaving him had been the hardest thing she'd ever done. She'd loved him completely, but she knew she couldn't allow him to treat her the way he had. His actions had left her with no option but to walk away. But that didn't mean it was easy.

The first time she'd met Jacques she was sitting outside a café, rooting in her bag for change to buy an iced coffee. He approached, wearing the customary pristine white apron folded over and tied to perfection. It was only when he stood in front of her and spun around and proceeded to spin the small round tray on one finger that she realised he was wearing shorts.

'*Oui*?' he said, pulling a pen from behind his ear.

'Uh, *je voudrais . . .*' she knew the French for *can you bring me an iced coffee*, but right at that moment she was dumbstruck. He bounced down onto his hunkers and it was as if a force had whooshed through the gap between them.

'*Je voudrais un café frappé, s'il vous plaît,*' she managed.

'Uh?' he answered. His expression couldn't have been any more goonish than her own, but it made her giggle. He laughed too. Standing upright again he shot off and returned with two iced coffees.

'May I?' he asked, gesturing to the chair beside her.

'*Mai oui!*' she answered with a smile.

He explained that he was new to the whole waiting tables thing and that he wasn't sure it was for him. After a few moments of quick-fire questions, they established that he was studying in the same university where she was training.

'So you're earning some spare cash? To help with your fees?' she asked in French.

'*Non!*' he said, flicking his hair and sitting back in his chair with one leg thrown up on the other. 'It's to keep me away from ze trouble.'

'Why?' she laughed. 'Do you get into a lot of trouble?'

'I am a bad boy, RooSheen,' he said. The way he pronounced her name made her weak. 'I don't look for ze trouble, but she always find me.' He shrugged and threw his hands to heaven.

As soon as the iced coffees were gone, so too were Róisín and Jacques. He peeled off his apron, folded it neatly and they walked away. It didn't seem in the slightest bit odd when he took her hand and they strolled like that. He pointed out lots of cool buildings and told her what happened inside each one.

'How do you know all this?' she asked.

'I don't,' he said with a wicked grin. 'Zis is my favourite game. I love to guess what will happen inside all zes beautiful buildings.'

When he kissed her, it felt as if it were always meant to happen. Yes, her heart skipped a beat, she felt butterflies in her tummy and all the sparks flew. But most of all it felt right. She didn't jump backwards nor did she want him to stop.

Their romance flourished at the same pace as their friendship. It never felt forced and it was always mutual – without the need for words. Their eyes did all the talking and he knew instinctively what she wanted and vice versa.

'Come and live wis me, Roo-Sheen,' Jacques said after a year together. 'I want to spend the rest of my life raising our babies.'

'Our what?' Róisín nearly keeled over. 'Are you saying that you want us to have children together?' She was so happy she felt as if she were floating on air. Although she was still only twenty-three, Róisín had finished college and thought she was mature and ready to commit. Besides, she'd known from the first second Jacques had dropped to his hunkers and stared into her eyes that he was her one. Their relationship had been so smooth. No pretence, no game-playing, no lies. Now he wanted to have babies with her! It was all too good to be true.

'We will need to have IVF, *chérie*.' Jacques took her hands and explained how a childhood illness had left him unable to conceive naturally. Instead of causing a rift in their relationship, it cemented things. Although they were young, they were making a conscious decision together, to start a family. Róisín felt as if she were floating on a cloud of love.

The only downside to their relationship was the guilt she felt every time she called home.

'You sound like you're still having a lovely time,' Keeley

said. Róisín had cradled the phone and longed to tell her mother that she and Jacques had just taken an apartment together. That they had soft buttery leather sofas and a state-of-the-art kitchen. That their bedroom suite was like something from an old French movie: stressed wood with calico fabric cushioning between ornate frames. His parents had insisted on decorating and providing anything they needed.

'He is our only child and we cannot take the money when we die. Live, love and enjoy every second,' was Vivienne's philosophy.

Róisín brought Jacques home to Ireland for St Patrick's Day the following month. He was astounded by the parades and the celebrations. Her parents were more than hospitable and welcomed him the same way they would any guest. But they wanted him in a guest room, alone.

'He seems like a lovely person,' Keeley said with tears in her eyes. 'Does this mean you're never coming home?'

'We've no concrete plans, Mum,' she lied.

'You're very pale, love. Is everything OK? Are you eating? Does Jacques look after you?'

Róisín longed to tell her parents and Liv and Jill that she was looking peaky because she and Jacques were in the middle of IVF treatment. But she was feeling so hormonal that she couldn't risk having to deal with her mother sobbing and making her feel like a selfish cow for going back to France.

The IVF took more out of them than either of them had anticipated. Jacques insisted he couldn't tell his parents if Róisín wasn't telling her parents.

'I know my mother,' he said, shaking his head. 'She will be crazy with excitement. I cannot say to her zat we cannot talk about ze babies.'

The first embryos were implanted successfully.

'Jacques, can you believe we're having twins?' she said hugging him and sobbing through her giggles. 'Let's wait until my twelve-week scan and then we'll tell our parents, OK?'

He nodded and held her gaze. '*Je t'aime, ma* RooSheen,' he said. '*Je t'aime.*'

He treated her like a princess, insisting she didn't do too much.

'I'm pregnant, not ill, Jacques!'

'Ah but you are growing babies. Es such an important job. Sit, *ma chérie.*'

The day she was ten weeks pregnant, Jacques took her for lunch. They sat in the sunshine and watched people going by. The pains came from nowhere. She began to sweat profusely. He panicked and called an ambulance, which she tried to say was ridiculous. By the time they reached the hospital and a monitor was connected an hour later, there were no heartbeats.

Jacques wanted to tell Vivienne.

'She can 'elp you. She is woman, she know 'ow woman feel. Let me tell her.'

Róisín was adamant that nobody should know what had happened. At night, once he was asleep, she would curl in a ball and sob. Thoughts of her own mother, who she'd never known, danced in her mind. Thoughts of Keeley and the lonely years when she'd longed for a baby added to her misery.

No wonder her parents didn't want her living in France. She'd only known for ten weeks what it felt like to be a mother, but it was enough to show her just how strong the bond could be. It was immaterial that Keeley hadn't given birth to her. She was still her daughter. She knew how it felt to have a child and suddenly have it taken away.

As it turned out, all the silence and hiding took its toll. By the time their remaining embryos were ready to be implanted, Róisín had noticed a distance between them. They made the decision to keep the embryos on ice. They'd fully intended using them within a year. But once they began to talk about the cracks in their relationship, things went from bad to worse.

'Your parents didn't want me zere,' he argued. 'Zey look at me like I am a murderer and zat I steal zeir daughter. Why you let zem be zis way, RooSheen?'

The hurt in his eyes almost killed her. He was right. She hadn't fought for him. She hadn't told her parents the truth about the IVF or indeed just how deep their love really was. She wasn't strong enough to tell her parents that she was choosing him over them, because she knew that's the way her mother would see it.

'My parents adore you. Zey do anysing to make you 'appy. But it's like I am some sort of dirty secret for you.'

'That's not true,' she wailed. 'You don't understand. My parents adopted me. They adore me too and I can't bear to hurt them.'

'But it's OK to hurt me?'

'I'll make it up to you,' she said, kissing him and stroking his face.

'Prove it. Tell your parents you will stay en France. Zat we will have a family, but you will raise zem here, with me.'

Róisín hesitated. Only for a second, but her eyes said it all. Just as they had done from the first second she'd met him. Jacques gave her no opportunity to respond. He packed his bag and walked away.

She stayed in the apartment for two days without moving. She sobbed her heart out and tried to think of a compromise. Perhaps they could have a holiday home in the west of Ireland and divide their time?

After a week she called him. He was cold and straight to the point. Either she gave him her all or he wasn't interested.

'True love 'ave no compromise, Roo-Sheen. I thought what we 'ad was pure and nobody would ever touch it. *Au revoir* my love.'

She knew it was over when she saw him kissing another girl under the archway in Bordeaux city centre. The breath stopped in her body and she began to shake uncontrollably. She was engulfed by a storm of emotions. Three days later, she packed her belongings and returned to the delighted embrace of her family.

Almost as soon as he'd arrived, Jacques was gone. It still made her heart ache that he hadn't loved her nearly as much as she'd loved him. She honestly believed he did. But although he was perfectly happy to live with her and allow his parents to throw money at their relationship, he wasn't willing to compromise in any way to make her happy.

The pain in her heart, after she returned to Ireland, was so deep and raw that she simply couldn't begin to put it into words. At first she was numb and by the time she felt she might like to tell someone, she'd been smiling and hiding her feelings for too long. The moment had passed. It was too late. She'd made her bed and had to lie in it.

Róisín read and re-read Vivienne's words, trying to take

in the idea of Jacques gone from the world. It was surreal. She felt a tightening in her chest as she thought about the embryos they had created, which were still stored at the clinic in Bordeaux. Should she destroy them? The legal document they'd compiled stated that both parties must be in agreement in order for them to be used. But should she fight for them? Knowing what it was like growing up with a parent who had died, she honestly didn't think she wanted to inflict that on a child. But perhaps she owed it to them, to Jacques' memory, to continue what had been started?

She looked around her office in a daze. It seemed like a lifetime had passed since Brigid had handed her the envelope. The future she had seen beckoning to her clouded over once again. Just when she thought she was free, Jacques had dragged her back into the past again. And now, she had to make a decision that she never thought she'd have to face in her life.

Chapter 16

THE FOLLOWING MORNING KEELEY HAD JUST switched off the vacuum cleaner and wound the flex away when she heard a car screeching to a halt on the gravel outside.

Puzzled, she opened the front door and met an extremely flustered Liv.

'Mum,' she said. 'I need you to mind these two. I am run ragged making packed lunches, washing sheets and driving other people's children from A to B. Martin has to stay on in the States for an indefinite bloody period.'

'What do you mean?' Keeley said. 'What's happening?'

'Nothing bar the usual scenario where I'm left to do absolutely everything while he swans off into the sunset.'

'He has to work, love. You can't really blame him for that.'

'Yes, take his side, why don't you?' Liv said angrily.

'Ah Liv, that's not fair,' Keeley said.

'Look,' Liv said, her voice high with fury. 'The house-work and ferrying about never stops! I need some time for *me*.' Yanking Jess by the arm, she extracted her from the car seat and set her down on the gravel as she ushered Billy out too. 'Be good for your granny and I'll see you later.'

'I'll drop them home by six thirty! I have to taxi some guests to the castle this evening, OK?'

She was back in the car and gone, kicking a cloud of dust behind her, before Keeley could even argue.

'Mum is sick of her bloody life,' Billy said, his eyes wide. 'She didn't sign up for this. We have endless weeks of school holidays and she isn't an entertainer.'

'Did she say that to you?' Keeley asked as she crouched down to pull the children closer to her. Billy nodded as he took Jess's hand. Keeley stood up and watched as he led his little sister into the house. Normally they were arguing and squabbling with one another, but clearly they'd been subjected to one too many of Liv's loud rants so they'd joined forces for a change. Keeley felt a stab of pure anger at her daughter, allowing herself to say such things in front of her children. It was totally irresponsible and unfair.

'I think your mum is just finding it very busy with all the other children in your house,' Keeley said as she sat them at the table and fished two cupcakes out of the freezer. 'We'll have a little snack and things will seem so much better.'

'The new girls are really fun,' Billy said. 'And they brought us sweets.'

'They speak funny,' Jess said with a grin.

'They do,' Billy agreed. 'They come from Spainland and Franceland and they smell nice.'

'They smell nice?' Keeley asked in awe.

'Yes, they use baby cologne,' Billy said. 'All the kids in Spainland where they live have it.'

'I see, and do they like talking to both of you?' Keeley asked. 'Because you should make an effort to chat to them, you know. They're trying to learn English.'

'But they know how to talk,' Jess said.

'Yes, but they know their own language better,' Keeley said.

'Why can't people all talk the same way?' Billy asked with a sigh. 'It would be much easier.'

'The girls from Franceland are very good at cleaning as well,' Jess said earnestly. 'They do all the carpets and the dishwasher and the brown girl from Spainland puts the clothes on the line. Last night she runned out to find the things when the rain came.'

Keeley could barely believe her ears. What was Liv playing at?

'And they are all very good at not fighting over the iron. We have ironing time after they clean the dinner pots.'

'And we had a special dinner last night,' Billy said. 'It was called tortilla and we liked it, didn't we Jess?' Jess nodded emphatically. 'Mum was very cranky though and said that the girls are ungrateful hussies because they turn their noses at her chicken nuggets. What does that mean, granny? How do you turn your nose at a nugget?'

'The phrase is actually to turn your nose *up* at something. It means you don't really like it that much . . . Oh I think your mum was a bit jealous of how well the girls can cook so she was making a joke.'

Both children looked greatly relieved.

'We don't want the girls to go back to Franceland and Spainland,' Jess said. 'They play with us and they even do my hair. They know how to do plaits and put bows in.'

Keeley hadn't planned on having the children today and she needed to do a large grocery shop. It was fine because she could bring them along, but she was really starting to get fed-up with being dumped upon. She hadn't slept much last night. Not because she wasn't tired, but because she was so furious. Doug's impromptu wine-buying trip with Jimmy was still making her seethe. The B&B was booked solid, and she'd been counting on his help.

Keeley didn't want to be Mrs Killjoy, but she was starting to see a very different side to Doug. A selfish and inconsiderate man seemed to be emerging, and she didn't like it one bit. Now it looked as if Liv was taking advantage in every way, too. If she was making the foreign students do all the cooking, washing and cleaning, what on earth was she complaining about?

Knowing the children weren't at fault in all of this, she forced her own anger to the back of her mind and gathered her shopping bags. Two of the guest rooms were waiting to be cleaned, but she figured she could do all that when they returned. She'd allow the children to choose a little toy each and they could play in the garden while she did the chores.

'If the sun comes out later on, can we go to Seal's Rest Bay?' Billy asked.

'I'm afraid not, love,' she said. 'I have too many things to do today. But I promise I'll take you very soon. How about you both get a little present when we go shopping and that might cheer you up?' They were both heart-warmingly thrilled by the suggestion and ran out to get into the car. Luckily, Keeley had had the foresight to buy booster seats. It made sense, seeing as the children spent just as much time in her car as they did in Liv's.

She locked the B&B, knowing none of her guests were planning on returning any time before mid-afternoon. She had her shopping list and knew exactly what she needed to get. Keeley had always been organised. She hated being late and couldn't bear it when people said they would do something and then didn't. That was why it baffled her so much that Liv was such a scatterbrain. How had Róisín ended up being so dynamic while Liv was so reluctant to get ahead?

Thankfully, the supermarket was practically empty.

'Are we the only people not at the beach today?' Billy asked.

'It looks like it,' she said. 'How about we buy a paddling pool? We could have our very own beach out the back garden. Would that help?' The children were so excited, she actually giggled.

A fresh wave of irritation flooded her as she paid for the shopping, including a pool with some plastic coloured balls to throw in. Liv was missing out on these little dotes.

By the time she hauled the shopping out to the car, drove home, unpacked and was ready to blow up the pool, Billy and Jess were hopping from one foot to the other.

'I need to try and find a pump,' she said. 'I reckon Granddad might have one in his shed. Let's go and see.'

They opened the door and her face fell. The place was like a skip. There were wood chips everywhere and all the coffee cups she'd been missing were happily growing mould. A black sack in the corner was stinking so much, she felt it ought to be giving off green gas. Tins of varnish had been left with the lids off and rock hard paint brushes were mummified in either paint or varnish, never to be used again. Off-cuts of wood were strewn all over the place, with no attempt to even make it look tidy. There was another awful, musty smell coming from the rear of the shed. Gingerly she walked over and found an empty paint can stuffed with cigar butts.

'You silly old fool,' she said shaking her head.

'Who is a silly old fool?' Billy asked as he held his nose with his fingers. 'It stinks in here.'

'Yes, it's vile. Granddad has been smoking cigars again. They're bad for him and they certainly won't help with his dickey heart.'

'What's wrong with his dick?' Billy asked in shock.

'No, pet,' Keeley said, trying not to laugh. 'Granddad had a bit of trouble with his heart a few years ago. Cigars aren't good for anyone, but people who have problems with their health certainly shouldn't smoke. You two are never to do anything so stupid.'

'If it makes us smell like in here, we won't,' Billy said wrinkling his nose.

Luckily the electric pump was easy to root out, so she took the soiled dishes and rancid bin and shooed the children out into the sun once more.

The pool was only a tiny thing, but once it began to fill up with water, the children were as excited as if it was the beach. She'd put it right outside the window so she could easily keep an eye on them while she finished cleaning the two guest rooms.

The screams of delight and constant giggles kept her going as she vacuumed and cleaned the bathrooms.

She hadn't imagined retirement being this way. When

Doug had announced his, she'd foolishly thought he'd be around more and her load would be lightened. She pictured them working the B&B together and taking the winters off, maybe heading to the Canaries or somewhere for winter sun. But here she was, four months into his retirement, and he wasn't here and she was double-jobbing. And as for winter sun, she'd probably be fighting Jimmy for a sunbed if they ever went at all.

A firm rapping at the front door made her rush to see who was there. She called to the children to jump out of the pool.

'Just for a moment until I answer the door, then you can hop back in while I'm watching you.' They did as she asked and she smiled. They were great kids really.

She arranged her face into a smile and pulled the door open.

'Keeley!'

'Claus!' she said, mirroring his wide smile. 'What a surprise! I had no idea you were coming back to Ballyshore so soon. I thought you said you'd be travelling until August or September.'

'It's a long story,' he said. 'May I come in?'

'Of course. I'll have to ask you to sit in the back kitchen with me if you don't mind? I have the grandchildren here and they're splashing in a little pool. I can't leave them unattended.'

He followed her and waited politely until she invited him to sit.

'Would you like coffee or tea?'

'I would love coffee, if it's not too much trouble?' he said.

'None at all, I'll join you,' she said filling the kettle.

Racing to the back door, she told the children they had a guest. They grabbed the towels Keeley had left them and tiptoed to the back door. Jess was shivering, so Keeley scooped her up and cuddled her.

'This nice man was a guest here a little while ago and he's back now.' As she turned around, Keeley was surprised to see Claus making the coffee.

'Hello,' Jess said peeking out of her towel cocoon.

'Where are you from?' Billy asked. 'We have girls staying at our house and they come from Spainland and Franceland, don't they Granny?' He looked to Keeley for clarification.

'Yes, my daughter has taken in some students for the summer,' she said.

'But it's all a bit much,' said Billy gravely. 'So we had to come here and be with Granny. Kids are a lot of trouble, you know?'

Keeley felt a stab of embarrassment at his words, but Claus just nodded and smiled gently. 'Well from what I can see, you are two marvellous little helpers. And you seem to be so good for your grandmother.'

'They're the best children in Ireland, Claus,' Keeley said.

'Oh yes, I can see that,' he answered.

'I'll make that,' she said, putting Jess on a chair.

'No you will not,' he said firmly but kindly. 'You need someone to mind you too.'

Once the coffee was made, Keeley excused them for five minutes so she could dress the children.

'Is he here to help with the washing and cooking like our girls?' Billy asked as she tugged a T-shirt over his head.

'Eh, no,' Keeley said. 'Listen sweetheart, the girls in

your house aren't here to do housework either. They're students, which means they're here to learn and have fun. So we won't tell people they do all the work, OK?'

'Why not?' Jess asked looking confused. ''Cause they do.'

'Yes, well I might have a little word with Mum about that. But for now we'll remember that they are like my guests, OK?'

The children nodded and ran back into the kitchen. Keeley set up colouring for them and they scribbled away happily.

'I'm fully booked this evening, Claus,' she said. 'If I'd known you were coming, I could have tried to move things around . . .'

'Don't worry,' he said. 'I booked into a little house over at Ballyshore village. Well, I've rented it, to be exact. I've had some bad news,' he said looking stricken. 'It's Ida . . .'

'Oh no, is she OK?'

'Ida passed away the day after we left here, Keeley,' he said quietly. 'We knew she was very ill and had only a little time left. She had cancer and it was her dream to come to Ireland.'

'Oh Claus,' Keeley said covering her mouth with her hand. She felt winded. 'I had no idea.'

'She didn't want to make a fuss and she knew she wouldn't be able to enjoy herself quite as freely if people knew she was so sick.'

'I'm so sorry,' she whispered. 'She was such a lovely lady. I thoroughly enjoyed chatting to her. I was looking forward to seeing her when you returned. I was going to show her how to make brown bread. I offered her the recipe but she said she'd prefer to see me doing it instead . . .'

'She told me that you had made a wonderful connection. I'm not sure what she meant and she didn't elaborate, so I didn't push it. But Ida said that you helped her to shed light on a matter that she had been harbouring for many years. She said you gave her comfort as she spoke about it with you . . .' He got quite choked up. 'So thank you for helping her, Keeley.'

'Oh Claus,' she said, hugging him and sobbing. 'She was far too young to die.'

'She was only fifty-eight. I know it's not exactly young, but she will always be my little sister.'

They sat in silence for a few minutes, each trying to compose themselves.

'We never know the time or place we will leave this world, do we?' Keeley said.

'No,' he said with a sigh. 'I feel as if I need to rethink my time. Life is precious and it's very short. I intend to make the best of mine. I've rented the house for six months. I don't want to go home just yet. So I suppose you could say we are almost neighbours now.'

'Good for you,' she said. 'What a lovely idea. Well, you won't be lonely. Ballyshore is a hive of activity at this time of the year. There's lots going on, starting with my sponsored walk on Sunday.'

'Really? Can I join or is it too late?'

'Ah, I have an in with the organiser. I think I can organise for you to be a part of it. We do it every June bank holiday and it promises to be a fantastic day out.'

'Where is Doug?' he asked suddenly. 'Is he out in his shed? I could pop out and say hello.'

'No, he's not there—' she began.

'Granddad has gone on a boat with his friend Jimmy. They're having the best fun,' Billy said. 'When I'm a grown up, I'm going to do things with my friends all day just the way he does.'

She knew she was being disloyal, but Keeley couldn't help passing a comment. 'Doug has retired from his entire previous life. He's having the time of his life, which is lovely.' As soon as she said the words she regretted them. 'Sorry,' she said to Claus. 'I'm very cranky today.'

'You're stressed out and overworked Keeley, that's all. And now I bring you bad news. Why don't you try to take a break?'

'It's almost high season. I absolutely cannot afford to do that now. Besides, what on earth would I do? Sit and stare out at the garden on my own?'

'I'd welcome your company any time,' he said looking incredibly sad.

'Yes,' she sighed and bit her lip. 'Of course you would. That was utterly insensitive of me. My apologies.'

He patted her hand for a moment and stood up. 'I'll go. It was good to see a friendly face. If you happen to be passing, I'm staying in one of the town houses along the main street.'

She nodded. 'Which number?'

'Two,' he said.

She waved him off and felt oddly empty as he disappeared out of sight. Knowing she mightn't even manage to make contact, she dialled Doug's number. The foreign ringtone sounded. Fully expecting it to go to voicemail, she prepared herself to sound chipper.

'Hello?' The noise in the background was deafening.

'Doug?' she said.

'Hello?'

'Can you hear me?'

'We're at a street festival,' he shouted. 'It's the best craic ever. You would love it here. There's food and beer and loads of street performers. It's lovely and warm too. Not like Ballyshore where you feel like your skin will be whipped off in the wind.'

'It sounds great,' she said weakly.

'Ah listen I can't hear you. I'll give you a shout tomorrow. Love you.'

There was a click and he was gone. Keeley glanced at the kitchen clock and realised she had just enough time to drop the children home before returning for the guests. Some needed to shower before they went out and she'd promised to give four guests a lift to the castle.

It was genuinely lovely to see Claus just now. She felt desperately sorry for him, and for poor Ida. The tragedy of the woman's death had really made her think. There were no second chances at life. There was one shot at it and then it was curtains. Why, then, was she spending her days feeling put-upon and frazzled? What was happening that she always felt as if she'd drawn the short straw? Life was too short. She needed to contemplate what it was that she wanted. She'd spent long enough being the only one to compromise all the time. Her head hurt when she thought about Ida. It was all so unfair.

Still, at least she was still here and tomorrow was another day and it would be a very busy one, too, as she put the finishing touches to the sponsored walk. It was a pity

Doug wouldn't be here to share it. But there was nothing she could do to change that. As she gathered the children into the car, Keeley forced herself to smile and count her blessings.

Chapter 17

NELL WAS TRYING TO DECIDE WHETHER SHE WAS put out or rather pleased. It wasn't yet Monday, but she hadn't a morsel in the house.

'I'm like Old Mother Hubbard,' she said to Mouse. 'I've shopped once a week for as long as I can remember. I've never needed to go more often and now all of a sudden you've turned up and my routine is inside out.'

'Sorry,' said Mouse.

'You look anything but,' Nell said. 'I ought to be very cross with you. I don't take kindly to having my routine altered.'

'Ah you'll get over it,' Mouse said as she stood on a chair and stared out the observatory window with the binoculars jammed to her eyes. 'Jay-sus,' she said. 'I can see right across the water. It's mad how this place is only a few hours from the flats and yet it's like a different planet.'

'I know. I still appreciate it,' Nell said. 'For months, even years after I came here, I used to smile every time I looked out that window. I don't think the locals appreciate quite how incredible the scenery is.'

'Nah,' Mouse agreed. 'But how could they? Unless you've spent most of your life living in a concrete bunker, this would seem normal.'

'Right,' Nell said. 'I'm going to the village to get some supplies. Are you coming?'

'Do I have to?' Mouse looked suspicious.

'No,' Nell said evenly. 'But I thought you would like a change of scene.'

'OK then.'

'Don't do me any favours. Stay if you want.'

'Would you honestly trust me here without you?'

'Why, what are you planning on doing? Setting fire to the place?'

Mouse laughed loudly. 'You're as mad as I am. I think we could be related and we don't know it. Ma used to yell and shout at me because I annoyed her so much. We sparked off each other.' She looked painfully sad all of a sudden. 'I miss her. The feeling is so strong sometimes that it makes me feel like I'll be sick.'

'I know that feeling,' Nell said with all harshness gone from her tone momentarily. 'It gets better, but it never really goes away.'

Mouse shrugged and nodded.

'So are you coming then?'

'Yeah.' Mouse stopped dead. 'There's a bright yellow car coming along the road,' she said pointing.

'That's Mo. My housekeeper I told you about.'

'Ah the one with the goon of a husband.'

'Yes, but that's strictly between us, remember? Don't hang me out to dry now.'

'I won't.' She climbed down off the chair and scurried over to sit down beside Nell.

'Mo is lovely. You'll like her,' Nell said. 'Everybody likes Mo. Even if she has a mouth like a jackhammer. She never stops talking.'

'What will we tell her?' Mouse looked terrified. 'I don't want her asking a load of questions. I won't answer if she does . . .'

'Hey,' Nell said. 'It'll be fine. Leave it to me. You just agree.'

Mo bustled in the door and called out.

'Up here,' Nell said. 'Come up and meet my new lodger,' she said.

'Ooh, I don't remember you telling me you were getting a lodger,' Mo said as she climbed the stairs. 'Hello there, pet,' she said with a wide grin.

'Hiya,' Mouse said, swallowing hard. Nell noticed the colour had drained from her face and she was all hunched over.

'This is Mo,' Nell said. 'Mo, this is Mouse. She came here by chance, long story that I'll tell you some time. Another time and not now,' she said firmly. 'But right this minute we're headed for Ballyshore.'

'Ballyshore? Today?' Mo asked. 'Is everything all right with you, Nell?'

'Everything is just fine thanks, Mo. My routine is diversifying. Stranger things have happened.'

Nell couldn't help smiling as she and Mouse bundled into her little car a short time later.

'God bless Mo, I'd say I'll need to hire a cherry-picker to remove her jaw from the floor. In fairness to her, this is the first time in years that I've had anybody here.'

'Why?' Mouse asked as they bumbled along the country lane toward the main road. 'Why don't you ever have people over? Your place is slick. I'd have parties and all sorts of fun if I owned the lighthouse.'

'I don't own it,' Nell stated.

'Yeah but you've lived in it for ever, haven't you?'

'Pretty much,' Nell said. 'I chose to live the way I do. It suits me. I'm happy. Nobody can annoy me, hurt me or disappoint me.'

'Wow,' Mouse whistled. 'You're weird. I know I'm hardly in a position to judge . . . but I'm only hiding out with you for the moment. I don't see it as a long-term solution.'

'Good, because I won't be harbouring you indefinitely,' she spat back.

Mouse looked out the window in silence. She didn't speak another word until they pulled up at the small supermarket in Ballyshore village.

'Sorry,' Nell said gruffly. 'I didn't mean to bark. You can stay as long as you like. I won't have you thinking I'd turf you out on the street. I'm not like that.'

'Cheers,' Mouse said, seeming to have completely forgiven her already. 'Hey look at that place! What's going on here?' she said pointing.

'There's a festival happening. I totally forgot it's the June bank holiday weekend. There's a sponsored walk this weekend. They do it every year.'

'Are you joining in?'

'No,' she scoffed. 'I don't do crowds and shoving and pushing. I couldn't think of anything worse.'

'What's the cause? Who are they walking for?'

'The children's hospital,' Nell said and she looked stricken for a brief moment. 'I'll make an anonymous donation like I do every year. I've no issue with raising funds for the hospital. It's the hordes of people and unnecessary fussing I abhor.'

'I think it sounds like a bit of craic,' Mouse said.

'Then you should go. But for now I need to get in and out of this place quickly. Let's go,' she said. Nell groaned inwardly as Joseph, the nosey parker from the Thatch pub, appeared.

'Hello Nell,' Joseph said. Without even drawing breath he zoned in on Mouse. 'Who might you be? We haven't seen you around these parts before.'

'She's staying with me,' Nell said and kept walking.

'I'm from Dublin, just like Nell. They call me Mouse.'

'Do they indeed?' Joseph said. 'Well welcome to Ballyshore, Miss Mouse.'

'Mouse will do fine,' she said with a grin.

'Bye, Joseph. Mind how you go now,' Nell said before walking into the supermarket.

She found a basket and began to fill it with food. Mouse stood at the door with her arms folded. By the time she made it to the till and put all the things in bags, Mouse was gone.

Juggling the bags as best she could Nell walked out, ready to give the girl a piece of her mind. Much to her dismay, Mouse was posing outside the festival tents holding an oversized loaf of bread as a local photographer took pictures.

Nell dumped the groceries in the car and called out to her that she was leaving.

'I'm coming now,' Mouse waved.

Nell started the car and sat gripping the steering-wheel. Her knuckles were white with rage by the time Mouse jumped in beside her.

'That was fun,' Mouse said sitting in. 'Your man says I'll be in the local paper next time. That's funny. I lived in Dublin for ages and never got in a paper and I'm here five minutes and I'm a star already, eh?' She nudged Nell and laughed.

Nell didn't even answer, she was so furious with Mouse for being such a show-off. She was going to draw attention to them. She didn't want all the villagers feeling they could start asking questions or trying to befriend her. If she'd known what a liability Mouse was going to be, she'd never have brought her to the village.

'Why are you so gruff with people?' Mouse asked as they drove back toward the lighthouse. 'I mean . . . you're OK with me, but you don't seem to like people in general.'

'I don't have much interest in them and the feeling is mutual.'

'Why?'

'Why didn't you come and help me with the groceries?' Nell shot back.

'I don't have any money so I didn't want to be in the way,' she said nibbling the side of her finger.

Nell drove on home and as soon as she stopped the car Mouse grabbed all the shopping bags and bundled them into the house. She emptied the food roughly onto the worktop and began to open and slam cupboard doors, putting it all away. She was practically tossing the groceries into the fridges and cupboards.

'Thank you for your help,' Nell said, figuring it would be wise to ignore the violence with which the task was being carried out. Nell knew she needed to make an attempt at tolerance. Mouse was young and enthusiastic. She clearly hadn't meant any harm just now. It wasn't the girl's fault she didn't like unnecessary contact with the outside world.

Mo was ready for her coffee and appeared looking as

eager as a puppy. Nell was utterly exhausted. She'd become accustomed to being on her own most of the time. All the chatter and movement was unnerving. Her head was pounding and she longed for some silence.

'I'll put the kettle on,' Mo said. 'Oh before I forget John-Joe loved the soup you made last week. Now, I probably shouldn't say this . . . but, what the heck . . . he still thinks your carrot and coriander is the best, especially when you throw in a bit of runny cream. There, I said it.' She looked so relieved Nell had to stifle a smile.

'It's hardly earth-shattering news,' Nell said. 'But you can breathe easy. I made the carrot soup yesterday and I have a carton of runny cream here. I'll have it there for you to bring home.'

'You did not!' Mo burst out laughing and swatted her arm as she walked over.

'I helped,' Mouse said. 'Nell tells me your fella is spoiled rotten and she makes soup for him non-stop. I'd watch her, if I were you. She could be trying to swipe him from under your nose.'

'I beg your pardon,' Nell said looking furious.

Mouse roared laughing. 'See, guilty! Watch that one, Mo. I'm telling you . . .'

Mo laughed, but Nell could see that the other woman was having a long, hard think about it.

'Don't mind her,' Nell said shooting Mouse a cross look. 'Believe me, Mo, your John-Joe is a one-woman man. I don't think there's another woman alive who would mind him the way you do. So don't fret. I've absolutely no intention of taking him away from you and he wouldn't want to go either.'

'Ah, I do my best and I'm lucky to have him. He's the

light of my life, you know?' Mo said proudly. 'So tell me all about yourself, Mouse.' She sat at the small round kitchen table and stared over at Mouse, clearly waiting for the low-down.

'I used to live in Dublin.' She tucked a strand of brown hair behind her ear. 'My ma died and I left soon after.' She faltered and looked over at Nell with beseeching eyes.

'Things were difficult for Mouse so she came here. It's much simpler living here. It's all still very raw and she's not able to discuss it. So she's seeing how she goes. There's no concrete plan in place. Other than that, there's nothing to tell. Fair enough?' Nell stood with her hands on her hips and looked straight at Mo.

'Yeah, we're kind of winging it for the moment,' Mouse said, picking up on Nell's story.

'How did your ma die?' Mo asked, dabbing at her eye with her sleeve for effect.

'Like Nell says, I'm not good at talking about it. Can we take a rain-check?'

'Mo, this isn't up for discussion. I can't say it any plainer than that,' Nell reiterated.

Mo opened her mouth and closed it again. It was clear she wasn't used to being given short shrift.

'Now,' Nell said loudly hoping to dispel with the awkward moment as she produced the container of soup.

Nell had known Mo long enough to realise that the interrogation was only over until she got another opportunity, one where she wasn't in the room and Mo felt she could corner the young girl. She was very fond of Mo, but she couldn't bear that she thrived on gossip. Although Mo often tried to fill her in on the goings-on in Ballyshore, Nell never encouraged her.

They finished their coffee and Mo went upstairs to carry on with her work. By the time she was finished, Mouse had joined her up at the observatory and, annoyingly, began poking the equipment.

'Don't alter any of the devices,' Nell warned. 'I have everything set in a certain way for a valid reason.'

'Fair enough,' Mouse said.

'I'm off then,' Mo said appearing at the staircase.

'OK. Thank you as usual,' Nell said. 'The soup is on the kitchen counter.'

'Thank you, dear. He'll be over the moon with that.' She hesitated. 'I left your newspapers on the hall table . . .'

'We'll have to make sure we get the local one this week,' Mouse piped up. 'I'm going to be in it,' she said. 'When we were at the village for the shopping, a photographer was there and took my picture.'

'Did he really? Why was that then?' Mo asked.

'I was standing at the food tent thingy and they're doing a piece on the festival. There'll be a load of pictures according to the man.'

'Ah yes, the festival and the sponsored walk are great for the locals. Brings people together and sure what's bad about that?'

'I think it all sounds like fun,' Mouse said. 'I might even go and do the walk. Are you going, Mo?'

'Oh yes, dear. I go every year. Even if you're not the fittest flea on the planet it's a great event. Raises money for sick children too. Would you like me to collect you?' Mo asked. 'We could go together if you want?'

'That won't be necessary,' Nell interjected. 'If Mouse wants to go, I'll run her into the village. Enjoy your weekend, Mo. Bye now, off you go.'

'I'll keep an eye out for you in the papers this week,' Mo said. 'I'll bring you an extra copy next Friday, if you like?'

'I'd love that, thanks.'

Mo turned and left and there was silence for a few minutes after she slammed the front door.

Mouse dragged a chair over to one of the large curved windows and stood on it, leaning her forehead against the glass so she could watch Mo's bright yellow car drive off.

'It's like a little yellow jellybean snaking off down the road,' Mouse said. 'She's a nice auld one, isn't she?'

'She's harmless,' Nell conceded.

'Nice of her to bring you those bundles of papers, isn't it? Does she do that a lot?'

'Every week,' Nell confirmed.

'Fair play to her. Not that they'd interest me a whole lot.'

'Don't you read papers?'

'I don't read full stop. To be more exact, I can't,' she said with a shrug. 'It used to make me feel stupid. But I'm used to it now. I get to know the words on the stuff I need. The rest of the time I learn things off by heart.'

Nell was astonished. She hadn't thought it would be possible to be an illiterate teenager in this day and age.

'How old exactly are you, Mouse?'

'Eighteen since last month,' she said, jutting her jaw out proudly.

Nell wanted to lie on the floor and wail. She was only a baby. God bless her, off roaming the world at such a young age. She didn't want Mouse thinking she thought of her as a lost cause, so she pulled herself together and tried to act as if the whole situation was quite normal. 'I could show you how to read, if you want?'

'For what?'

'Reading has all sorts of advantages. You can see what's going on in the world or find new stories that interest you. It would help you to get a job some day.'

'I'd like a job,' she said nodding enthusiastically.

'Well, you're not going to find one if you can't read or write.'

'Who told you I can't write either?' she asked suspiciously.

'It kind of figures,' Nell said. 'One works well with the other.'

Mouse nodded and chewed her fingernails again. For the first time in years, Nell wanted to cross the room and take the girl in her arms. It was so long since she'd hugged anybody, let alone a young girl.

'I'm actually shocked at how young you are, Mouse.'

'Why, how old did you think I was?'

'I must've thought you were older for some reason . . .'

'I'm younger than the girl in the photo downstairs. Is she your daughter?'

The room took on an eerie atmosphere all of a sudden. Nell knew she could bark at Mouse and tell her that photo was none of her business. But she didn't.

'She was my daughter. Her name was Laura. She died.'

'I figured.'

'Why, because I'm here alone?'

'Nah, there are none of her things lying around. No clothes or toothbrush or bits of make-up. If she were alive, there'd be some trace of her. You don't talk about her either. So I guessed she'd passed away.'

Nell nodded. They both seemed lost in their own thoughts until Nell spoke again. 'Aren't you going to ask me how she died?'

'I figured you'd say if you want to. I'd like to know. But I'm not pushing you to tell. I haven't exactly told you much about me. So I understand.'

Nell smiled. 'She was ill for a long time. She had type one diabetes. The type you're born with. Hers was particularly severe. From the beginning she had issues with her heart and kidneys. That's part and parcel of diabetes with a lot of patients. It involved lots of tests and monitoring. It wasn't easy. That's why her father decided to leave me standing like a fool at the altar on our wedding day. He thought it was too much to take on. Laura was two and he thought it best to opt out of a lifetime of hassle with a sick child and her mother.'

'Useless prick.'

'Yes, he was,' Nell nodded. 'I'm not overly fond of bad language . . .'

'But sometimes it fits?'

She tried not to smile. 'He was the one who missed out in the end. He didn't get to raise his funny, beautiful, clever and unbelievably brave daughter.'

'Stupid prick then,' Mouse deadpanned.

'He was pretty stupid,' Nell agreed. 'Not that I thought that the day I stood in a cheap lace dress trussed up like a prize turkey waiting for a man who was already on a plane to Australia.'

'No way,' Mouse said shaking her head.

'He left a note,' she said with a sigh.

'Oh well that's all just dandy then, isn't it?' Mouse said. 'You must've been mortified. I'd have hunted him down and beaten him to death with a baseball bat,' she said.

'I was so in love with him,' Nell said sadly. 'I was so taken in by him and believed all his lies.'

'Did he know Laura well at that stage? Were you living together?'

'Oh yes. He stayed over a lot and he saw Laura every day. But we were living at my ma's. I thought we'd be together for ever.'

'How could he just walk out when he knew his little girl needed him?' Mouse asked.

'I don't know. I couldn't do it.'

'I suppose it's not that different to my da. I know I'm the one who ran away. But he hasn't exactly issued a red alert to find me, has he?' Mouse looked pained. 'Some men shouldn't be das. They're not mature enough.'

Nell nodded.

'Where is he now?'

'Still in Australia,' Nell said. 'Festering down there somewhere.'

'Did he never get in contact again?'

Nell felt overcome with grief all of a sudden. 'Can we talk about something else now? I actually can't handle . . .'

'Ah sorry,' Mouse said lurching forward and hugging her awkwardly. 'You're a decent old doll. He was and still is a prick. My own da is in the same category. Let's leave it at that, yeah?'

Nell nodded. 'I'll tell you more another day if you like?' she said.

'Sure.' Mouse lifted her arms and carefully pulled Nell into a two-way embrace. The young girl's hair smelled of the shampoo from the bathroom and Nell was surprised by how incredibly comforting it was to hug her.

'Thanks, Mouse,' she said sounding choked.

'For what?'

'Understanding and not insisting I talk more.'

'I'm not the best at feelings and all that stuff. So you needn't worry that I want to be all emotional and all that . . .'

'You can stay as long as you like,' Nell said as she cleared her throat.

Much to her surprise, Nell could feel Mouse's body shaking with sobs.

'Hey, are you OK?'

'Yeah,' she said pulling back and staring up at her. 'You're the best. Nobody has ever been this nice to me unless they're either pissed or a social worker. You're not even getting paid to do this.'

'I don't want to pry,' Nell said. 'But shouldn't you call your da or one of your brothers and let them know you're OK?'

Mouse shrugged. Nell decided to leave the idea with her. Maybe she'd decide to call in a few days. 'Look, the phone is there. Use it any time you want.'

'Cheers.'

Nell could sense that Mouse needed to stop all the chatter. She looked pale and tired.

'I've a few bits to do on the computer. Do you want to watch a movie or something?'

'Sure,' she said wandering toward the television.

Nell instantly searched the Internet for some books and letter cards to teach Mouse how to read. She'd never done anything like this before, but felt enthusiastic about the challenge. She guessed Mouse was a very bright girl but simply hadn't had the opportunity to learn. Even if her young guest wasn't planning on staying for long, Nell figured the best gift she could give her was the ability to read and write. She couldn't predict how long she might have with this girl, but for now, Nell was enjoying this new lease of life being breathed into her lighthouse.

Chapter 18

IT WAS SUNDAY MORNING OF THE JUNE BANK holiday and Róisín was attempting to wake Jill.

'Ugh, go away Ro-Ro. My mouth is as dry as Gandhi's flip-flop and I honestly think I could pass away at any moment. I'm gravely ill.'

'I'm not surprised,' she said dryly. 'You were knocking back bottles of that blue goo like nobody's business last night.'

'In my defence,' she said as she staggered to the small living-room looking like she'd been backcombed, 'it was a great idea at the time.'

'This place is vile. We need to do a quick blitz and get up to the village for the charity race.'

'Oh listen,' her housemate said turning an even paler shade of green, 'I won't be doing any race. I'll barf all over the road. We can't have people wheeling buggies through vomit. It wouldn't be right. You go on ahead and I'll go back to bed. I'll see you later.'

'Don't you dare try and bail on me, Jill,' Róisín said sternly. 'You do this every year and never get away with it. This year is no exception. Get your ass into the shower and I'll continue cleaning up.'

'You're so mean,' she said. 'I'll wake Gordon and get him to come too.'

'Ah don't. He doesn't really like this sort of thing. Leave him be,' Róisín said, avoiding eye contact.

'Oh so it's fine for me to be dragged out while I'm at death's door but Gordon can sleep! Charming,' she said poking her tongue out. 'Well I know where your loyalties lie,' she laughed. 'I don't blame you having a soft spot for Gordon. He's pretty amazing!'

Even though she knew her mother would appreciate as much help as she could get, Róisín also knew Gordon would be surplus to requirements. Mercifully, Jill had never asked directly so Róisín had never told her, but she couldn't abide Gordon. He spent more time looking in the mirror than her and Jill combined and he seriously believed he was God's gift to womankind. Gordon worked at the local gym, where he was meant to be an instructor. He'd managed to sidle out of teaching swimming lessons by spoofing and saying he had a chlorine allergy. Róisín had once asked him why he didn't want to give lessons.

'The hot air at the pool is so bad for my skin and hair. It's better if I stick to the weights room and do the odd class.'

She had stared at him in shock when she realised he wasn't joking.

When Jill had started going out with Gordon last year, Róisín had seriously thought she was taking the mick.

'Where did you find this guy?' she asked after a couple of glasses of wine. 'He's hilarious!'

'I know, right?' Jill said. 'I really fancy him too. I know he's not my usual type, but he makes me feel good.'

It was at the tip of her tongue to say that was because he had the brain of an ostrich, so clearly she felt like Einstein beside him. But much to her astonishment, Róisín realised that Jill was being serious. She really did fancy this shallow numbskull. Figuring the relationship wouldn't last spitting time, she'd kept her opinions to herself. Jill kept saying he was a temporary decoration to her life. So now it was far too late for Róisín to pass comments or share her thoughts. Instead, she simply avoided being in his company whenever possible.

By the time she'd finished cleaning the cottage and picking up abandoned wine glasses, Róisín was losing patience.

'Jill, where are you? We need to go.'

'Coming,' she shouted from the bedroom. 'Ah I'm not feeling that much better. Are you sure you need me?' she asked. Her eyes were so bloodshot she looked as if she'd been punched.

'Take some paracetamol and follow me,' she barked at her.

After a couple of minutes, Jill fell into step with her. By the time they reached the village, which was less than a ten minute walk away, the atmosphere and excitement took over.

'Look at the turnout!' Róisín said in delight. 'Mum will be thrilled.'

They spotted Keeley and went directly to her so they could get their instructions. Jill decided she'd be happy to sit at one of the water stops, which was at a crossroads.

'Make sure you point people in the right direction or they'll end up at a dead-end,' Keeley said. 'There are bottles of water that Joseph donated from the pub, so hand those out and be as cheerful as you can!'

'Aye, aye, captain,' Jill said as she headed toward her station.

'I'll check in with Nourriture and come back to help you, Mum,' Róisín said. Before she could get there, she bumped into Liv with the children. It was the first time she'd met the foreign students, so she introduced herself. The four girls seemed very sweet and they were clearly delighted with the festival and fun.

'Hey, you two,' she said happily to Billy and Jess. 'Are you ready for the walk?'

'I'm going to sit out this year,' Liv said. 'I'll help Mum while the girls do the walk with the children.'

Róisín glanced over at Liv with a furrowed brow.

'What's up with you, Liv? You're turning into a right lazy lump. Since when is a five kilometre walk too much for you? If Billy can do it, surely you can too?'

'I don't see you doing it,' she spat back.

'I'm working. I can't.'

'Your excuse for everything,' she said rolling her eyes. 'The big career woman.'

'Hey,' Róisín said, reaching out to touch her arm. 'Don't bite my head off. I don't want to fight with you, Liv. I was only teasing. What's up?'

'I'm fine,' she said, tossing her head and making it clear she was really cross. 'You'd better get on with running your empire.'

Liv hoisted her picnic basket by the handles and made to leave.

'Liv, please,' Róisín said and her sister looked at her. 'Come on, do you guys need anything else for your picnic today?' she said, nodding at the basket. 'Help yourself in the shop if you like.'

'It's fine,' Liv snapped.

'Let me see what you have, it's no hassle. I'd like to

give you something. If I can't feed my own family, what kind of a person am I?' She laughed lightly as she pulled open the basket lid and peered inside. She only caught a glimpse of the wine bottle with the cork rammed back inside, but it seemed to have quite a bit missing. Perhaps it was one left over from the night before, Róisín thought. But another voice in her head was telling her that she knew her sister better than most, and she'd been drinking.

Liv closed the lid with a snap. 'I said we're fine,' she said coldly. 'Come on, kids.' She marched off, followed by Billy, Jess and the four students, all of them looking far from happy.

'Hi love,' said Keeley coming over with her clipboard. 'What's up? You look dreadfully worried.'

'Oh . . . no . . . I'm fine, Mum. Just multitasking in my head as usual,' she lied. Now wasn't the moment to tell their mother that she suspected Liv was not sober and it was only nine thirty in the morning.

Accepting a list of jobs from Keeley, Róisín jumped into action.

It was a full hour before she came across Liv again. She was sitting on the wall opposite Nourriture looking utterly miserable. She was about to approach her when a voice came booming out of the overhead PA announcing the start of the walk.

There was a rush of people, prams and even small children on scooters to the starting-point. There was a loud bang as the starter-gun sounded amidst applause and laughter and the walk got underway.

It was a good ten minutes before all the participants were on the road.

'Wow, Mum, this must be a record turnout,' Róisín said.

'This seems to get bigger and better every year. Well done. You should be so proud of yourself.'

'It's all for a wonderful cause,' she said.

'Oh hello there,' Róisín said. 'It's Claus, isn't it?'

'Yes, hello there,' he said. 'I don't know if your mother told you, but I have taken a little house here at Ballyshore for a few months.'

'No, I didn't realise,' Róisín said.

'Poor Claus has suffered a bereavement,' Keeley said. 'His sister Ida, who you met before . . . she passed away.' Keeley wiped her eyes with her hand, and it was obvious she was very upset.

'I'm so very sorry to hear that,' Róisín said.

'It's all been a nightmare,' Claus replied smiling sadly, 'but your mother has been wonderfully kind to me.'

'Well, if I can ever do anything for you, please let me know. Drop by any time. I'm here most days, or failing that my manager Brigid is a true gem.'

'You seem to have a wonderful business going here,' he said, nodding toward Nourriture.

'It's a work-in-progress,' Róisín smiled. 'But I adore it. It gets better all the time and I'm constantly adding new and exciting products and initiatives. I'd be delighted to look after you anytime.'

'How about you two do a guided tour another time,' Keeley said. 'I've got a couple of thousand people marching their way right back to us shortly and all of them need a medal and a care package, so get to your stations!' she said with a grin.

'Quite the taskmaster your mother,' he said smiling.

Róisín went to her assigned area and glanced around for Liv. She was gone from the wall and she couldn't see her. Some of the people taking part in the walk would be back shortly so she'd have to wait before she could get her sister on her own and talk to her properly. She just hoped Billy and Jess were alright – it would be an easy day to lose a child in the crowd.

The rest of the morning flew by as the participants trickled back into the village. The atmosphere was wonderful and the sun actually shone, which made a nice change.

Róisín was back in the shop, behind the counter when Rob walked in.

'I said I'd drop the shelf down,' he said. 'I totally forgot about the fund-raiser today.'

'It's a bit bananas here at the moment,' she said, taking a payment and filling a small tub with pâté.

'I can give you a hand if you want?' Rob said.

'Really? You wouldn't mind?'

'Of course not. Looks like fun, in fact. I'd be delighted to give you an extra pair of hands; you definitely need it.'

'That'd be great,' she said, smiling gratefully at him.

'Will I work the off licence? Needless to say I'll be pushing my own product the most,' he said, winking.

'Sure, and if you've any plastic shot glasses, you could do tastings of Celtic Beer if you want?'

'Yeah, perfect!' he said looking thrilled.

Several times over the next few hours Róisín laughed out loud as she heard Rob selling to the customers.

'What do you mean you don't drink beer? You haven't lived until you've tried Celtic Beer.'

She had no idea how much he was selling, but the customers were all delighted with him.

By the time the shop closed, Róisín was tired but

completely wound up. Brigid and the other staff left and Rob stayed back to assemble the shelf.

'That was great fun,' he said. 'I think there are several tipsy tourists knocking about now, mind you.'

'You could sell sand to the Arabs once you get going. I was having a real giggle at you earlier on telling that French woman that Celtic Beer is good for the complexion because the ingredients are grown in Ireland!'

'And she bought eight bottles, so where's the harm in that? I'm sure by the time she's finished drinking them all, she'll think she looks stunning.'

Róisín shook her head and laughed. 'Would you like a bowl of soup? It's Thai chicken and butternut squash. It's pretty delicious with a wedge of sourdough on the side.'

'I'm sold,' he said gratefully. 'I'd love a glass of wine as well,' he said. 'But I'm supposed to be going back to Limerick tonight. My father will be expecting me.'

'There are usually spare rooms at the Thatch pub if you want to check.'

'I thought of that earlier but it's fully booked. The whole village is, thanks to the bank holiday and the walk.'

'You can kip on our sofa,' she said. 'Jill won't mind. In fact, she'll throw a party in your honour if I know her!'

'Are you sure?' he asked. 'Do you know, I'd love that. Thank you. There's a lot going on at home and I'd actually love a bit of space.'

'Well, there's nowhere better to exhale than Ballyshore. I take it you haven't made proposals then?'

'No.' He looked uncomfortable. 'Not yet at least . . .'

She stared at him. He looked kind of lost. As if he was genuinely torn.

'I'll step outside and give my dad a shout.'

Róisín liked the way Rob talked about his dad and clearly he was an important part of his life. Family was so important, but not everyone actually got that.

She loved being in the shop when everyone was gone. It felt so different when it fell quiet. She set the table and selected a bottle of Chardonnay. She thought it was totally weird that he was thinking of getting engaged to Theresa when he was so unsure. Still, she was hardly one for giving advice on relationships considering her own track record. She swallowed hard as an image of Jacques flitted into her mind's eye. It was difficult keeping a handle on her feelings since reading Vivienne's letter, but once she kept busy she could manage it. She just had to keep moving.

By the time Rob returned she had the soup ready along with a selection of cured meats, cheeses and dips.

'It's what my father calls picky food,' she said. 'But it'll be tasty.'

She poured two generous glasses of wine and they clinked glasses.

'Thanks for your help today,' she said. 'It was a great day business-wise. I'm thrilled.'

'You've a little goldmine going here,' he said. 'The atmosphere is brilliant, too. That's what sets you apart from anywhere else in the village.'

'That and my products,' she said. 'Don't get me wrong, I'm very fond of Joseph at the Thatch pub, but his food is very outdated and most of it comes from either the freezer or a packet.'

They enjoyed the food and before she knew it, Róisín was holding up an empty bottle.

'Will we open another? Would you drink another glass?' she asked.

He nodded. 'I'm on holiday after all!'

'So who designed the Celtic Beer product? I love the bottles,' she said. 'Those old Grolsch-type flip lids are really great. And the amber-coloured glass is stunning against the label.'

Rob explained that he'd designed the label himself. 'It's recycled glass and we've tried to make it look like a top quality product.'

'Well it worked,' she said genuinely.

A text from Jill let her know there was a gang congregating at their house again. She said she'd be there shortly and that Rob would be with her.

'Wooo!' Jill texted back. 'Fresh blood. Can't wait to have a gawk at him.'

Róisín rolled her eyes and put the phone away.

A bang at the door made Róisín groan. 'I really don't want to have to open the tills again,' she said. 'I'd better see in case it's a starving tourist who needs some supplies.'

It was Liv and the children.

'Hi guys,' she said to the children. 'Come in! Look at your face painting you two, you look great! And where have you been, Liv?' she said, looking hard at her sister. 'I've sent you about five texts and you didn't answer.'

'I'm not staying,' Liv said crossly. 'I've had it up to here with all the crowds and hanging about. We're getting a lift home. Can you slip me a bottle of wine? I'm heading home with the car stuffed with kids and I need a glass of wine. I'd like to salvage even an hour of this miserable day.'

'Why was it miserable?' Róisín asked. 'Didn't the students enjoy the race?'

'Oh they did,' Liv said. 'In fact, it seems everyone had

a whale of a time except me . . .' She bustled toward the wine section. 'Oh!' She stopped dead. 'I didn't realise you had company.'

'This is Rob,' Róisín said.

'I won't stay. I'm the married with children boring as hell sister. Don't worry, I won't wreck your buzz. I'll swipe some wine and get out of here.'

'You're welcome to join us if you like?' Rob said standing up and looking uncomfortable.

'Oh believe me Rob, you don't need me here. I'm like the old woman who lived in the shoe. I've kids and teenagers coming out of every orifice. Thanks Ro-Ro,' she said snatching the wine and herding the children out.

Róisín followed her, feeling really concerned.

'Liv, are you OK?'

'No!' she said. 'I've just told you. I've had a crap day and I want to get home and unwind unless that's against the law now?'

'No,' Róisín said evenly. 'It's not against the law. I'm just concerned because you're so stressed and I know you're on your own. Will I drop over later on? We could have a catch-up?'

'As if you want to swap a night with a divine-looking man for a space on my vile sofa with half the nations of the world represented in every bedroom. Do yourself a favour and enjoy your life before you end up like me.'

Róisín was shocked by the tone of her voice. She'd never heard Liv talk like this before, or look so angry before. Then she wondered, is this Liv talking, or is it the wine talking?

'Honey, why don't you come and sit for a bit?' Róisín leaned forward slightly, trying to catch sight of the wine bottle from earlier without giving herself away.

'What the hell are you doing?' Liv demanded.

'Em . . . I was just checking if you needed anything for supper.'

'Liar. You were looking to see if I'm drunk, weren't you?' she said, her eyes blazing. 'Well here!' She yanked the bottle from the basket and thrust it at Róisín. 'It's empty, which is why I blatantly asked you for another one. I'm not some sort of secret drinker. I met one of the mums from Billy's class and we shared the half bottle I had. Is that OK, Miss Drinks Police?'

'Hey,' she said gently, resting a hand on her sister's shoulder. 'I'm not here to judge or make you feel bad. I want to help you.'

'By practically accusing me of being an alcoholic?' Liv shouted, then she burst into heaving sobs.

'Liv, please, please talk to me,' Róisín said, feeling as if she wanted to cry too. 'You're not yourself lately. You always seem stressed and in bad form and, well . . . I feel like we've drifted.'

'So you thought you'd get me to drift back by accusing me of being a boozer?'

'I didn't . . . Jesus, help me out here. I know you were drinking earlier, and you were the same the night of my birthday too. I'm worried you're overdoing it.'

'Quite the little detective, aren't we?' Liv sneered before squaring her shoulders, wiping her tears and taking a big breath. 'I am absolutely fine, not that you give a toss.'

'Liv,' she said, with warning in her voice now. 'Stop being a cow and take this conversation at face value. I'm worried about you. End of. I'm not stalking you or trying to catch you out or make you feel bad. I'm worried, that's all. I love you. You're my favourite sister in the whole world,' she said, nudging her and doing an exaggerated pout.

The fight seemed to go out of Liv. She looked deflated all of a sudden and her shoulders sagged. 'Look, don't worry, Róisín. And thanks. I guess I just needed someone to tell me they love me. I feel better now, honestly. Say goodbye to Auntie Róisín,' she encouraged the children. A quick hug and she was gone before Róisín could say another word.

Róisín had never known Liv to act so oddly. As she shut the door and walked back to where Rob was sitting, she felt a sense of dread in the pit of her stomach. Something was going on with Liv, but why didn't her sister feel she could talk to her about it? Róisín wondered if she was too focused on her job and her own problems – was Liv right and she was prioritising all the wrong things at the expense of the people she loved?

Chapter 19

BY THE TIME THEY'D FINISHED A BOTTLE OF WINE, Róisín was more than ready to get out of Nourriture. The wine took the edge off her mood, but she was still anxious about Liv. So much was happening lately – Jacques, Mr Grace, Liv – she felt a real need to let off some steam.

'I love this place, but it's still work,' she said. 'Will we head to the cottage? It's only ten minutes' walk.'

'Sure,' he said, following her and helping her lock up. 'It must be really handy living and working within walking distance. Up until now I've spent most of my week in the van.'

'Yeah it is. I did that on purpose. I was living back with my parents after some time in France and even though their place is only ten minutes in the car, it's still not really walkable at night. The road is so narrow and the cars zoom around that bay road as if it's a race-track.'

They walked in companionable silence until the cottage came into view.

'I'll warn you now, Jill is a hoot but her boyfriend is an acquired taste. Don't freak out. I'll mind you!'

They stepped into the cottage. In true Jill style there was a mess from the front door to the back. The music was pumping and a few people were dancing while Jill was flitting from one person to the other.

'Ro-Ro!' Jill yelled. 'How's it going? So who's this, then?' she asked, winking obviously.

'This is Rob – my friend,' she said.

'Alright Rob!' she said. 'How's it going so far? Are you enjoying downtown Ballyshore? Can you handle the craziness of it? We're not far off a scene in *Father Ted*, are we?'

'I wouldn't say that, Mrs Doyle,' Rob quipped. 'I think it's pretty fantastic around here. Hey Alan! How's it going?' he said waving. 'Excuse me for a moment, ladies. I haven't seen this lad for years.'

'He's sweet,' said Jill as soon as he walked away. 'Where on earth have you been hiding him? He's not a dork but not a jock and he seems to be able to string a sentence together. Result, my friend, result.'

'He's a supplier,' Róisín said rolling her eyes.

'Yeeees,' Jill said. 'A supplier of romance and lurve . . .'

Róisín made her way to her bedroom and kicked off her shoes. She changed into a pair of pink and black leopard print leggings with an oversized T-shirt and pulled her hair out of its tight bun. She instantly felt more relaxed.

Rob seemed well able to mingle and work the room, so she didn't follow him or act as if she was trying to mind him. Instead she went over to chat to a few of the girls she hadn't seen for ages. They had been interrailing in Europe and were full of stories about their escapades.

They were having a great giggle, with Naomi telling them about her disastrous date with a fireman who thought he was Patrick Swayze, when Gordon appeared.

'Who's for tequila slammers? I've got the salt and lemon, come on birdies what's holding you back? Roll up, roll up, let's get the chicks all tanked up!' he yelled. 'Anyone, anyone? Bueller?'

'Where did you find him?' Naomi asked.

'He's Jill's fella.'

'Feck off,' Naomi said. 'Has she lost her mind while we've been gone? He's a nightmare.'

'Ah, he's OK when you get to know him,' Róisín said in a lame attempt to sound loyal.

'Don't worry, Ro. I'm hardly going to tell Jill we were all agreeing that her boyfriend is a moron.'

One of the girls decided to have a tequila, which made Gordon ecstatic. Just as he was about to search for another victim Jill bopped over.

'Jilly-Nilly-Milly-Moo!' he said tweaking her cheek. 'Tequila for you, my sweet?'

'For sure,' she said kissing him and beaming over at Róisín and waving.

'What on earth does she see in him?' said a voice from behind.

Róisín turned to find Rob there.

'Lord only knows,' Róisín said. 'I just don't get it . . . what am I missing?'

'Eh, if you find out maybe you'd tell me.'

'Ah hey there! What's your name?' Gordon shouted, pointing at Rob.

'Hi I'm Rob.'

'G'day!' he said in a terrible attempt at an Australian accent. 'Tequila coming up. And don't you dare say no! We've only just met and you wouldn't want us to get off on the wrong foot now, would ya mate?'

'Ha,' Rob said. 'Good man there, Gordon, but I'll pass on the old tequila if it's all the same to you. Can't bear the stuff. I'll only end up puking and nobody needs that.'

'Deadly! Nothing like a good puke to know you've had a good night out. Here's a large one. Don't thank me now, thank me later when all the birds in the room are looking hot. Some of them are a bit munterish at the minute, but help is at hand,' he said far too loudly. Jill laughed hysterically while most of the other girls turned and walked to the other side of the room.

'Stick with me Rob, mate. I'm a real ladies' man. I'll sort you, yeah? Here.' Gordon was shoving a tumbler of tequila at Rob.

'He said no, Gordon,' Róisín said. 'OK?'

'Whatever, Róisín,' he said, shrugging. 'Just because you couldn't drink it. You're so cool with your shop that sells all home-made stuff that nobody normal eats. You're like some sort of granny with your pancake machine.'

'Don't be rude,' Jill said, looking shocked for a second.

'Aaaaah!' Gordon touched his nose with his finger and pointed at Róisín and kept repeating the movement. 'Got ya, didn't I? Róisín, your face, ya mad yoke! You thought I was really being a shite, didn't ya? Go on, admit it, I got ya fair and square, right?'

Róisín had never wanted to punch another person so much. In fact, she couldn't remember ever having such a burning desire to cause another human being pain. So instead of resorting to violence, she snatched the tumbler of tequila, downed it in one gulp and walked away to a chorus of wolf whistles and cheers.

'Deadly buzz!' Gordon shouted. 'Good girl yourself, Róisín. Sure you're a little firecracker in there. You're a bit bloody scary, but you're a firecracker.' He snorted. 'Round of applause for Róisín, folks!'

'You're terrible, Róisín. I'm a bit shocked, but it doesn't

change how I feel about you overall,' said Colm, suddenly at her elbow.

'Colm!' she said. 'I didn't realise you were even here.'

'I've been watching you from the far corner, Róisín. You're looking lovely. You always do. But I think the summer weather makes your eyes shine that bit more. Mabel loves the summer. She cheeps all the more in her cage. Mammy and me often smile for no reason because of Mabel.'

'Ah that's lovely,' Róisín said. 'It's nice to have, eh, pets . . . nothing like a bird singing to lift the spirits. So how are things with you, Colm? Any holidays planned?'

'Oh yes. We'll go on a bus tour as usual. They're great craic. The sing-songs on the bus are mighty and the entertainment at the hotels is second to none. Some day, God willing, you'd come too?' He looked so earnest and hopeful Róisín hadn't the heart to be cutting.

'Do you know, my business is so twenty-four/seven that it simply doesn't leave time for bus tours. But I hope you have a great time.'

'Mabel doesn't know we're going. She's minded very well by Mr Stokes when we go. We bring him back a box of chocolates by way of thanks, but she's never the same when we're gone.'

'No,' Róisín said shaking her head. 'She wouldn't be. She'd be pining.' Róisín had to stifle a giggle as the famous *Monty Python* parrot sketch came to her mind.

'Will we take a romantic stroll outside, Róisín?' he asked, licking his lips.

'Ah, thanks Colm but I'm happy here in the thick of things.'

'Will you dance so?'

'I'm not so much in a dancing mood just at the moment.'

'Will we sit in the corner and have a drink in that case? That'd be nice, wouldn't it, Róisín? I think so at least, Róisín . . .'

'Colm, I don't want to be rude. Honestly I don't. You're a lovely man and you'll make a great partner for some lucky girl. But that girl isn't me I'm afraid.'

'Oh. I see, Róisín,' he said, looking at his brown laced shoes. 'Right then.'

'I'll see you around, yeah?'

She managed to extract herself from Colm and chat to Rob for a bit. Another hour slipped by.

By then most of the partygoers were feeling kind of over the whole Gordon shouting thing and they all began to do what Róisín was doing: avoiding eye contact with him. It didn't exactly deter him as he continued to stagger about with the tequila, looking for takers.

Mercifully, he passed out face-down on a beanbag in the corner. Jill was oblivious to the general feeling of relief when the shouting and annoyance stopped.

An hour later the cottage was empty. Gordon was helped to bed by a couple of lads on their way out. Jill followed, leaving Róisín and Rob in the living room.

'I think I'll chuck another log on the fire. I know it's meant to be summer, but I'm freezing.'

'It could have something to do with the fact it's half two in the morning as well,' he said.

'If you want to crash, I'll grab you the sleeping bag.'

'No, I'm happy to sit and chat for a while if you are?' he said.

'Deadly buzz,' she said and laughed.

'So what's the deal with you and your sister?' he asked.

'She seemed really stressed out earlier on. Mind you, I know what it's like with siblings. I've a brother and we fight like dogs at times.'

'No, we're really close. We usually get on pretty well . . . although she's not actually my blood relation at all.'

'No?'

She found a bottle of wine and held it up, offering him some. He nodded.

'I was adopted when I was just over three weeks old.'

'And do you have any contact with your birth mother?'

'No.' She screwed up her face for a moment. 'Hey, it's not your problem, I won't bore you . . .'

'You're not boring me, this is intriguing. Have you tried to find your mother or what's the story?'

She told him what she knew and even though she hadn't discussed it with another soul, she even told him about the cards and how the letter had come on her birthday.

'I think that's lovely,' he said. 'My mum died when I was a kid and I would give anything to get cards or letters from her or anyone who knew her. I think about her a lot and wonder if she's still with me in spirit. Do you believe in spirits?'

'I think I do,' she said. 'But I can't say I've ever seen a ghost or anything.'

'Me neither,' he said. They sat in silence.

'What's upsetting Liv, do you think?' Rob asked.

'Her husband, Martin, works away a lot. So she's left with the kiddies. She used to be fine with the whole thing, but in recent times she seems to have changed. She's really quick to get angry and has zero patience. She wasn't like that before.'

'Sounds like she's not entirely happy . . .'

'And Martin used to be a real dote. Salt-of-the-earth kind of guy, who'd do anything for Liv and the kids. Sure, that's how he ended up doing this job that takes him abroad so often. He wasn't making much money in his previous job so he changed. But he's not the same either. Last time he was home he was less relaxed and he made a few snide remarks about Liv and the kids.'

'It's not easy, all this relationship stuff,' he said. 'It always seems to be a balancing act. One week it's all fine and the next things can go totally pear-shaped.'

'Tell me about it,' Róisín said. 'I make a mess of everything when it comes to men. I think I'll give up and decide to be a mad old spinster with a house full of cats.'

'You don't seem like the cat-woman type,' he said with a grin.

'So how are things with Theresa?'

'I'm really not sure,' he said. 'From her perspective we're right on track, but I really don't know how I feel.'

'There's nothing worse than those niggling doubts,' she said.

'We don't talk much. We've never sat together and chatted like we're doing now, for instance.' He pulled his fingers through his hair. 'Sorry, you must think I'm a right bitch sitting here moaning about my girlfriend. I feel very disloyal. She doesn't deserve that.'

Róisín stifled a yawn and, as if it were contagious, Rob did the same.

'Right, I'm off to bed,' she said. She grabbed a sleeping bag and pillow and made sure he was comfortable. As she fell into bed, Róisín felt happier and more relaxed than she'd felt in a long time.

Chapter 20

A BUNDLE OF SMALL PARCELS BROUGHT A SMILE to Nell's face as she accepted them from the postman.

'It's a long time since I've been up to the door of this place,' he said. 'It's usually just the odd bill dropped into the postbox down the lane.'

'That's right,' Nell said, giving him no information.

'I hear you have a new lodger. That must be nice for you,' he said, nodding eagerly.

'Your ears are clearly pricked at all times.'

A wave of irritation swept over Nell. Obviously Mo had been shooting her mouth off around the village again. She'd had numerous conversations with that woman over the years about this very problem. Mo didn't seem to take it on board that Nell didn't want anybody knowing her business.

'It's nice to see you and talk to you for a change,' the man said smiling.

'Right,' Nell said. 'I'm a private person and that's the way I prefer it.'

'Ah getting to know people and listening to them when they feel like talking comes with the job. I love to get to know folks. I enjoy it no end.'

'Good for you,' she said. 'It seems you have the right job in that case. Now if you wouldn't mind letting me have my goods, I have a lot of things to do.'

Nell took the clipboard with the delivery note on it and signed for the parcels and held her hands out. He shoved the parcels forward slightly and she took them, then stepped back and slammed the front door.

'That was a bit harsh,' Mouse said from her perch halfway up the staircase.

'Why were you crouched there, spying?'

'I wasn't spying. It's not exactly Buckingham Palace here. Not many people call to the door so of course I was going to be curious. What did you get? Or is that none of my business either?'

'Yes, it's completely your business as a matter of fact,' Nell said. 'It's none of Postman Pat's or whatever he calls himself business, however. Which is why I wasn't going to be made to feel obliged to discuss anything with a stranger. Nosey idiot. It's his job to deliver post and packages, not pry into everyone's business. I never understood that mentality.'

'He was only chatting.'

'Well let him do it someplace else. Now, enough talk about him. Come and I'll show you what I have.'

They went to the kitchen, where Nell tossed a package at Mouse without warning. She managed to react quickly enough and catch it before it smashed into her chest.

'Bloody hell!' she complained. 'What was that?'

'Just checking you're awake. You have decent reflexes. So you should at your age. Go ahead then,' she coaxed. 'Open it.'

Nell ripped open the other parcel and pulled out a box that contained brightly coloured cards with letters and numbers printed on them.

'It's an alphabet and numbers box,' she said. 'We're

going to use them to teach you how to read and do some basic sums.'

Mouse swallowed. She placed the other package on the table unopened. She shoved it away. Her movement was only slight, but Nell clocked it all the same.

'Don't be scared, Mouse. I know it's strange and you probably feel as if you'll never learn. But I promise I won't be impatient. I've no affiliation to Postman Pat or any of the curious fools at the village, so I don't have a lot of time for them. But you're my friend. I may not be many things, but I'm very loyal. I want to help you. You'll allow me to try, won't you?' Nell wished her voice sounded less harsh. But she wasn't good at being gooey, so it probably didn't come out as heartfelt as she hoped.

Mouse clicked her knuckles and eyeballed the cards before nodding.

'Good girl. Now be a dear and open that other package. Even if you're not interested, I am. I paid good money for it so I need to check the company have sent the correct things.'

Mouse tore it open and several thin books slid out.

'Smell them,' Nell ordered. Mouse looked wary. 'Pick one up and flick through the pages while holding it beneath your nose,' she insisted.

Mouse did it and a smile spread across her face.

'Nice, isn't it?'

Mouse nodded.

'If you can learn your letters and how to recognise them in words, you can read all sorts of books. You can get that lovely smell whenever you like.'

Mouse picked up each of the books and sniffed them in turn.

'Touch the covers,' Nell said, spreading them out on the table. 'Look at how shiny they are. Which colour do you like the best?'

Mouse pointed to a bright yellow one. 'It's like Mo's car only it looks better on the book.'

'Well let's make a pact to try and get you reading a page from the yellow book by this time next month.'

'I dunno,' Mouse said, shoving it away again. 'Maybe we'll just see how we go. I'm probably too thick to learn it. So I wouldn't want to disappoint you or anything.'

'We'll see.'

Knowing she could balk and refuse to comply, Nell grabbed the letters box and took out the vowels. All the other letters were blue and the vowels were red. She'd done as much research as she could online and had a vague idea of how to get started.

'These five lads are called vowels,' she said. 'They're like the lead singers of the band. And the others are called consonants, and they're the backing singers and the instruments. But we need all of them to make a hit.'

'Huh?' Mouse said, looking confused.

'OK, what band or singer do you like?'

'Don't tell anyone,' she said looking over her shoulder. Nell smiled. 'Who on earth am I going to tell? The kettle?'

'Ah, yeah. Sorry,' she laughed. 'OK then, Da and the brothers would've slagged the knickers off me. But I kind of like 1D.'

'Me too,' said Nell with a sniff.

'You know what 1D is?' Mouse said.

'I live in a lighthouse, not at the bottom of the sea, Mouse.' The young girl grinned. 'So we'll pretend the vowels are the lads from 1D. This is Harry, then Louis, then Niall and so on.' She laid the five vowels on the table. 'So when we use the lads with the rest of the letters . . .'

'They can be the fans,' she said happily.

'Right then, when we mix the lads with the fans, it makes words.'

'Got ya,' she said with a grin.

The special writing copies she'd ordered reminded Nell so much of Laura it made her want to weep. Laura had loved to sit and make rows of perfect letters in between the red and blue ruled lines.

Handing Mouse a pencil, she sat opposite her with a copy of her own and demonstrated what she wanted her to do.

'The first letter we're going to try and draw is "c". But when you're learning to read we call it "cuh",' she said, pronouncing it phonetically. 'As in cuh-ah-tuh, cat!' She found the letter and made the word on the table.

She fully expected Mouse to stare at her as if she'd lost her mind. Instead she strained her neck like a little baby bird and darted her eyes back to her own page and made a 'c'. She did another one beside that and continued until she'd filled three lines.

'Cuh for cat,' she said. 'Next, how do I write the "a"?'

Nell was flabbergasted by the speed and enthusiasm with which Mouse was learning. Almost two hours passed before she felt her back beginning to ache and her neck getting stiff.

'That's more than enough for today. You did good. Better than that, you're a star. You should feel very proud.'

'I feel buzzed,' Mouse said as she balanced on the two back legs of her chair. 'The only time I spent in school was a disaster. I had no idea what the teacher was doing so I didn't even try to understand. But this is mega. If I can already read a few words and it's only the first day, I really can imagine being able to know how to do a page of that yellow book. It's happening, isn't it, Nell? I'm learning!'

'Yes, Mouse, you are.' A little tear escaped from her eye as Nell accepted a hug from Mouse.

'I'm going up to look at the water with the binoculars. Coming?' Mouse said.

'I'll follow you in a few minutes,' Nell said. She gathered the books and pencils and put them to one side. It both saddened and astonished her that a bright little one like Mouse could end up being so overlooked. Life really wasn't fair, she mused. Why had Mouse had such a tough time? Why did Laura have to die? There were rapists and murderers who had no regard for human life walking around without so much as a backwards glance, and yet in her limited experience of other humans she had come into contact with, two wonderful women who had been given a damned raw deal.

This was why she'd shunned the world. What had it to offer but disappointment and unfairness? Swallowing the large lump in her throat, Nell sighed. She was more convinced than ever that living out here was the best place for her. But she was wise enough to realise that Mouse had been sent to her for a reason. Perhaps Laura had guided her here? So she would stand by her and help her in any way possible. She would take pride in giving this young woman as many tools as she could to pave the way to making her future brighter. And as soon as she was ready to go, Nell would set her free and go back to the comfort of her own company.

Even though so many years had passed by, Nell was

acutely aware that none of the pain and heartache she carried had been eradicated.

Still, she mused, she ought to know by now that life wasn't meant to be plain sailing. If there was a God, which Nell wasn't certain she believed at all, what was the line of thinking?

She was muttering to herself and giving out when Mouse shouted up to her.

'Nell, there's a boat out on the water. It looks like a dinghy and it's being washed down towards us at mega speed.'

Nell ran up the stairs and there in the distance was an orange and black rubber dinghy. On closer inspection, she could make out several figures.

'Is that allowed?' Mouse asked.

'Well it's not safe, that's for sure,' she said. The boat came into clearer view and with the help of the binoculars Nell could see there was an adult male flailing and laughing with a set of plastic oars as the three younger guys with him joined in.

'They should be fine,' Nell said handing the binoculars back to Mouse, who stood on a chair and stared at them until they'd gone by and out of sight. She sighed and jumped down off the stool looking quite dissatisfied.

'So how did you live here with a kid for so long? Was she as weird as you, being locked away out here like Rapunzel?'

'No, she wasn't,' Nell said. 'Laura went to school the same as all the other girls. At least, she did when she was well enough. During the holidays she was happy here with me. She was quiet and arty. She loved to paint and draw and read.'

'They're all things that you do by yourself,' Mouse pointed out. 'Didn't she go to ballet or Irish dancing or play sports?'

'She couldn't.'

'Why, because she was too odd?'

'No, because she had type one diabetes and was frail. We spent a lot of time at the children's hospital, as a matter of fact. The treatments weren't as good as they are now.'

'Did she have many friends?'

'A few,' Nell said. She'd tried to block out those anguished tears that used to soak Laura's cheeks.

'Why can't I be normal like everyone else, Ma?'

'Most of her friends were from school. We didn't get many visitors up here. In the beginning some of the mothers came with their children, but it was clearly out of curiosity more than a real desire to play with Laura.'

'Well you have to admit not many people live in a lighthouse. So you can hardly blame people for wanting to have a good look.'

'No, and of course I don't blame them for that. But it was incredible how quickly they all tossed my beautiful girl aside. Her limitations made her invisible. Her sickness made her an outcast.'

'That's crap,' Mouse said. 'They sound like a shower of losers.'

'That's exactly what I thought,' Nell said. 'I knew they weren't worth her tears and we had enough love right here with just the two of us.'

Mouse still didn't look convinced.

'Laura had major surgeries, Mouse. She had her right foot amputated when she was fourteen.'

'Christ! Why?'

'Some diabetic patients suffer with ulcers. Toes are often affected, too. Laura got a particularly nasty ulcer. She was given all the treatments possible, but it didn't heal. Instead it spread and caused her such hideous suffering she actually begged the doctors to remove her foot.'

'That's terrible,' Mouse said in a voice barely above a whisper.

'We went to London to the children's hospital for that.' Nell sighed. 'We made the best of it. Once she was out of danger we took an apartment for a couple of weeks. We saw all the sights and had a wonderful time. By the end of it she was like a formula one driver in that wheelchair!'

'Why didn't you think of moving to London then? Wouldn't it have been better to be in with people?'

'No. Both of us were relieved to get home.'

Mouse narrowed her eyes and Nell guessed she was trying to fathom the scenario.

'I know it sounds totally messed up. But you would've needed to know Laura to understand our relationship. We were like two peas in a pod. As I said, all we needed was right here.'

'Hey, I'm not judging you,' Mouse said holding both hands up in surrender.

'Yes, you are,' Nell said. Her voice wasn't angry, however. 'It would be impossible for you not to, Mouse. But every case of every sickness is different. From the word go, Laura's diabetes seemed to be determined to try and curb her life.'

'Really?'

'That's why her father ran off to Australia. He couldn't take the prospect of a life with a sick child. It wasn't what he wanted apparently.'

'And you did of course,' Mouse said sarcastically. 'What a low-life he was.'

'Well, that was the start of diabetes attempting to stamp us down,' she said sadly. 'Laura was so brave. She never complained and even though I used to hear her sobbing at night sometimes, she didn't act as if she was down in the dumps when we were together.'

'Do you think she put on a happy front to please you?'

Nell nodded. 'I didn't realise it for years, but that's exactly what she was doing. Guilt was the worst emotion back then. I felt guilty that she'd been born with this horrible weakness in her body. I blamed myself and used to sit and try to rack my brains for what I'd eaten or drunk that could've caused it while I was pregnant.'

'Why, is that how you get diabetes? If your ma eats a bucket of snails while you're in her belly? Or drinks a litre of gin a day? Although if that were the case, I'd be well and truly fu—'

'No,' Nell interrupted. 'It's not about that. In fact there's no known cause for type one diabetes.'

'Well there you go then!' Mouse said. 'If the bloody doctors don't even know how it gets there, then you can't be to blame.'

'I know that sounds logical, Mouse. But when you see a tiny child struggling with a life-limiting disease and you're her mother, it's hard not to shoulder the blame. That's what mothers do.'

'Huh,' she said in disgust. 'Not mine.'

'It sounds as if your mother wasn't well.'

'That's putting it mildly,' she said. All of a sudden the bravado vanished and Mouse's shoulders shook.

'Hey,' said Nell. 'I'm sorry . . . I . . .'

'Ah it's not your fault,' Mouse said waving her hand. 'She did her best. She was tortured by demons in her head. She had an abusive father growing up and he messed her up. She drank to escape. But when she was sober and when she was being herself, she was great.'

'Do you miss her?'

Mouse nodded.

'I miss Laura. I'll never stop missing her, but I've come to terms with the fact that I did everything I could for her. It may not have been conventional and it wouldn't suit everyone, but we were happy, you know?'

Mouse nodded again. 'I can see why she was happy here.'

'Thanks,' Nell said. 'I've a few things to do so I'll be at my desk.'

'I'm going to watch a movie, if that's OK?'

'Knock yourself out.'

Nell listened to make sure Mouse was engrossed in her movie before she began a search through the newspapers. She was behind with her usual chores but she didn't really mind.

Flicking through the pile of papers Mo had left, she found nothing of interest until the very back page. A tiny article caught her eye. She snipped it out with the scissors and pasted it into her scrapbook.

As she replaced the scrapbook in the drawer, Nell wondered how different her life would have been if Laura had survived. If she'd lasted even a year longer, nothing would be the way it now was.

'Thank you for sending me Mouse,' she whispered, because Nell now honestly believed that Laura had guided her here.

Chapter 21

KEELEY HAD JUST FINISHED HER CHORES FOR THE morning when Doug pitched up in the car with Jimmy.

'Hello,' she said with a smile.

'How's it going, love?' he asked pulling her into a bear hug. 'Ah it's great to be back. We're starving, mind you. The food on the boat wasn't the best and we've had a long drive.'

'I'll do you a fry up,' Keeley said. 'And you can tell me all about your adventures.'

'That'd be smashing,' Doug said as she dragged his bag into the kitchen with Jimmy in tow, laden down with wine boxes.

'How much wine did you buy?' Keeley asked.

'That's it, just a few cases. It was so cheap and it's very drinkable.'

It was all deposited on the kitchen floor alongside the bag.

As they ate their food the men were talking like two teenagers. It seemed they'd had a great bonding session and were delighted to announce that they would go back in the next few weeks.

Keeley wished she could smile and feel delighted for Doug, but she actually wanted to grab him and shake him.

'So how did your fund-raiser go then?' Doug asked.

'We had a huge turnout and people were incredibly generous. I'm exhausted today, but it was well worth it. We've no final figure yet, but I'm hoping we beat last year.'

'Good on ya,' Jimmy said. 'I'll be off. Better try and get my haul into the house and all that.'

Doug went out to wave him off as Keeley cleared the plates and wiped the table down.

He came bounding back in the kitchen door and immediately started rooting in his bag, tossing clothes all over the floor while he was at it.

'I bought you a pressie,' he said. 'It's in here somewhere . . .' He stood up and scratched his head. 'Ah no, I think I put it into one of the wine boxes for safekeeping.' He pulled one open and found the gift. Wrapped in white tissue paper, it looked like a holy figurine. He handed it to her looking sheepish.

As she unwrapped it, Keeley wasn't sure whether to laugh or cry. It was a bad plastic replica of the Madonna, filled with water.

'It's got vodka inside. I think it's one of those gifts you can use as a statue afterwards. Two gifts in one.'

'I don't drink vodka,' was all she could manage. Looking down at the mess on the kitchen floor, she honestly wanted to cry. 'Can you please lift the wine boxes out of here?'

'Absolutely,' he said, scooping them up. Sighing, she stuffed the dirty clothes back into the bag and dragged it out to the small utility room where her oversized washing-machine and dryer stood. Everything in the bag was either worn or covered in dirty clothes, so the whole lot needed doing.

She was about to call Róisín to say hello when the landline rang.

'Mum?'

'Hi Liv, how are you today?' she asked wearily. She knew it was uncharitable of her, but she hoped the children weren't about to arrive for the day.

'Mum, I'm up at the doctor's. But it seems I need to go to the hospital.'

'Why?' Keeley felt her blood go cold as guilt washed over her. 'Are you OK, love?'

'Doctor Murphy says I need to get the burn on my arm dressed properly at the hospital.' Liv started crying.

'Don't cry, love, where are the children? What burn?' Keeley asked in confusion.

'The children are here with me,' she said. 'Can you come and take them? And the students will be back from their language school. I've no shopping done and they won't have any dinner.'

'I'll do it all,' Keeley said. 'I'll be there in five minutes. Dad is home so he can help too. Who is taking you to the hospital?'

'I can go in a taxi. It's on the way.'

'What happened to your arm, love?' she asked.

'I was making waffles for breakfast and I managed to scald the top of my arm as I was taking a tray from the oven.'

'Gosh, that sounds very sore.'

'It's agony,' she said. 'I'd better go. Dr Murphy is saying I need to get this sorted quickly or I'll risk infection and a possible skin graft.'

'OK, we're on the way.'

Keeley hung up and called Doug.

'Huh?' he answered groggily.

'Liv needs help,' she said with growing irritation as she

found him stretched out and half asleep. 'Get your shoes off the sofa and I need you to either take the children or do the shopping for Liv. You choose.' She explained what Dr Murphy had said and ran to grab a light coat as it looked like it might rain.

'I'll take the children,' he said. 'We'll go to the playground and have a snack at Nourriture.'

'OK great,' she said. 'Let's lock up here and go in together so I can drive Liv's car home from the doctor's surgery. I'll post a note on the door in case any of the guests arrive early. They're not due to check in until late evening but you never know.'

'It'll be fine, love,' he said.

Sighing, she grabbed her bag and her car keys.

'Keeley?'

'Yeah?' She stopped and looked at Doug.

'I really missed you while I was away. It was fun with Jimmy and all that, but it's not the same as being with my girl.' He leaned over and kissed her. 'Liv will be fine. As you used to say when she was tiny, everything is as it should be, Mum and Dad are here now.' She smiled at him, grateful for his support. He drove her bats at times, but Keeley loved him just as much as she did when they first met.

'Granddad!' Billy shouted when he spotted them coming through the door of the surgery. He ran to meet them. 'Mum is feeling yucky, the oven tried to cook her arm so the doctor has to fix her.'

'I heard,' Doug said going down onto his hunkers to hug him and a very pleased-looking Jess. 'While Mum's arm is being made better, why don't we go and see how the playground is doing? Then we could go to see Auntie Róisín. I heard she has chocolate cake in that shop of hers.'

Doug hugged Liv and told her he'd stay with the kids for as long as she needed. 'You just concentrate on getting your poor arm fixed.'

'Thanks, Dad,' she said.

Keeley's heart went out to Liv. She looked terrified.

'Why don't I come with you, pet?' Keeley said.

'No, thanks Mum, but I'm happier on my own. There's no point in us both sitting in A&E for hours. Besides, I need you to help out with the house and all that.'

'Have you phoned Martin? Is he on his way?'

'No and no,' Liv said. 'There's no point, he has to work and it'll be the middle of the night where he is. Leave him out of it.'

'Well, OK then . . . sure maybe you can drop him a text. He'll want to know, love. I'll do some shopping and go over to your house,' Keeley said. 'I'll stay with the students and your dad will bring the children over once I'm sorted. I'll do their dinner and make sure they have what they need for tomorrow. Take your time.'

They hugged and Liv assured her she would call or text as soon as she had any news.

As Keeley drove Liv's car toward the supermarket, she couldn't quite believe how filthy it was. There were packets and juice cartons and used paper cups strewn all over the floor. The seats were stained with food and the smell was far too like a dustbin for her liking. She could barely see out the window because the outside was so dirty, and a light on the dash told her there was no diesel.

Pulling into the nearest garage, she filled the tank and paid for a car wash. There was a queue for the brush wash so she used the time to gather all the rubbish into a plastic bag. She knew Liv wasn't exactly in the running for house-wife of year award, but she'd never been slovenly like this. Clearly things were getting on top of her. Maybe the burn on her arm was a blessing in disguise. She needed to get a bit more organised and try to sort things so she wasn't chasing her tail quite so much.

If she thought the car was shocking, it had nothing on the actual house. Keeley was stunned as she walked through the front door, laden down with bags of groceries. The hall floor was covered in grass and mud that was so dried-in, it could've been there for a decade. The kitchen was a sight, with dishes stacked in the sink and every worktop sticky and cluttered. There were empty wine and beer bottles crammed onto the draining board and the place smelled like a pub.

The dishwasher was full and, mercifully, the crockery in there was clean. Rolling up her sleeves, Keeley set to work. Once she had dinner on and the table set, she moved into the lounge. It looked like a student flat after several parties. Just like the car, the sofa was littered with so many crisp and biscuit packets that Keeley suspected this was where the children had been eating. More worryingly, it appeared they'd been helping themselves to junk food instead of proper dinners. She grabbed a black sack and cleaned the room, wiping the sofas with a damp cloth and dusting everywhere. Once it was vacuumed, the place looked completely different. She opened the window to air the room before moving to the bedrooms and bath-rooms. Each room was worse than the next until she reached the two bedrooms where the students were staying. Those rooms were neat and tidy. The newly refurbished box room with the bunk-beds was deplorable. It was blatantly clear that nothing had been cleaned or even tended to since she'd been there weeks before. Ashamed of her own daughter, Keeley stripped the beds and found clean sheets in the hot press.

Aware that she was probably stepping over a line, but unable to help herself, Keeley ventured into the master bedroom. It was like a rat's nest. Clothes and damp towels were strewn on the floor and soiled plates and glasses were stacked on the bedside lockers. She flung the windows open and set to work. The en suite was as neglected as the other rooms and Keeley felt like crying when she saw the state of the shower. Clogged with hair and decorated with shampoo that had dribbled out of the bottle and down the wall before cementing itself on the tray, it was utterly disgusting.

She was sweating and red in the face with her hair stuck to her forehead by the time she heard voices in the kitchen.

'Hello girls,' she called out. Pulling off the rubber gloves as she approached, she smiled and introduced herself to the students.

'I saw you all at the race last weekend, but we didn't officially meet,' Keeley said. They looked pleasantly surprised to meet her as they stared in awe at the difference in the house.

'You clean!' one said, pointing out the obvious before clapping a hand on her mouth and blushing.

Keeley smiled and explained that Liv was in hospital with a burn on her arm and she would be there for the next while to look after them. The girls looked at one another and hesitated before showing her a couple of plastic bags they were carrying. Inside were chicken breasts and vegetables, which they said they intended cooking for dinner.

'We no like toast for the dinner,' one girl said.

'No, of course not,' Keeley said, trying to act relaxed. 'Tonight you are having a nice dish called Shepherd's Pie. It's one of my favourites and I hope you will enjoy it.'

Thankfully, Doug arrived then with the children, who ran straight into the open arms of the girls. Keeley guessed they were around fifteen or sixteen years old. They were so sweet to Jess and Billy it made her smile.

'This is Sophia, this is Amélie, this is Natalie and this girl is Juanita,' said Billy proudly. 'They're the nicest girls in the whole world.'

'And me!' Jess said.

'This is Jess's favourite thing to say,' Amélie said and laughed. Doug arrived in with the children's belongings.

'Hello all,' he called out. 'I'm Doug.'

The girls were lovely and so appreciative of all the work Keeley had done. They ate every bit of their dinner and immediately stood up and put their plates and cutlery in the dishwasher. Before she could even blink, they were wiping the table and sweeping the floor.

'You're very helpful girls,' Keeley said.

'Ah we learn,' Natalie said. 'It's too much for Liv. She is too tired after her day job so we must help.'

Keeley glanced over at Doug who shook his head briefly, indicating she shouldn't say anything.

'Well, you're great girls and your mothers should be very proud of you,' Doug interjected. 'Are you going to watch television or what do you normally do after you eat?'

'Eh, no . . .' Juanita said. 'Liv no like it if we are in her air space so we go to outside for walk or we go to the bedroom and chat.'

'For the entire evening?' Keeley said in astonishment. The girls nodded.

'Well, we're not watching anything so you're more than welcome to go into the living room,' Keeley said. They thanked her and went to their rooms.

The children wanted to watch a DVD, so Doug put one on and joined Keeley in the kitchen.

'What on earth has been going on here?' he asked.

'I don't know, Doug, but Liv has behaved appallingly. They came back with ingredients in a bag to make their dinner. The house was like a tenement when I got here and they've clearly been treated like the unpaid help.'

A knock at the front door made the children spill from the living room with Doug in hot pursuit. He pulled the door open with a wide smile on his face.

'Mr Clear?' the man in a suit said, with no return smile.

'Eh no, that's my son-in-law and he's not here right now.'

'I see,' the man coughed. 'Well, I'm from the language school and I'm here to collect the four students.'

'Oh, no problem. I didn't know they were going out this evening. I'll give them a shout, come in.'

'Eh they're not going out. They're leaving.'

'You'd better come in,' Doug said moving aside. 'Come in and meet my wife, Keeley. It's our daughter Liv's house, but she's actually at the hospital.'

'I'm sorry to hear that your daughter isn't well,' said the man as he looked around. 'It's really not as bad as the girls were saying,' he said looking puzzled. 'I've been sent by the agency to remove them and place them in alternative accommodation.' He held his hands up. 'I know how teenagers can exaggerate, but the girls have been lodging complaints from the moment they arrived in Ireland. They said they're given no proper food and that the house is desperately dirty. Now, clearly there have been some grave exaggerations here . . .'

'Eh . . .' Keeley said squeezing her eyes shut for a moment, '. . . I hate to drop my daughter in hot water here, but I'm afraid the girls are telling the truth.' She explained how awful the house was when she arrived earlier and apologised on Liv's behalf. 'All I can say is that our daughter is clearly very unwell. It's not like her to let things get so bad. I should have come over more to check that she was coping, but I figured she was managing. Her husband works abroad a lot of the time and I didn't realise how much she's been struggling.'

They decided it was in everyone's best interest if the girls were relocated.

'We'll be in touch with the paperwork. Obviously the weekly payments will be stopped with immediate effect and we won't be in a position to send students here again.'

A while later the students gathered in the sitting room with their belongings hastily packed into bags.

'Hey,' Billy said. 'Where are the girls going?'

'Are you going back to Franceland and Spainland?' Jess asked looking sad. 'Is the fun time over?'

'We need to go now,' said Natalie kindly. 'It was good to meet you both.'

The children waved and Keeley felt it was best not to say too much to them. They didn't need to know the real reason they were leaving.

Keeley's cheeks burned with shame as the girls waved and looked so pleased it was as if they were being released from prison.

'I'm mortified,' Keeley said as she closed the front door. 'How could Liv treat other people's children so shabbily?'

'I'm speechless,' Doug said. 'I actually cannot fathom what was going on in her head.'

The phone beeped and Keeley grabbed it.

'It's from Liv,' she said sighing deeply. 'Oh dear Lord,' she said as her hands began to shake.

'What is it?' Doug took her phone and read the text.

Not great news this end. I'm going 2 need 2 stay in for a couple of days. Seems I need special burns dressing. Will update later. Liv.

'It sounds bad,' Keeley said.

'Well, burns are nasty. The risk of infection is high and if it's on the soft skin on the inside of her arm, that's pretty bad I'm reckoning.'

'She's in the best place I suppose,' Keeley said hopefully. 'Let's not tell her about all this fuss with the students. She'll find out soon enough. But right now, we'll just have to pull together.'

'I agree,' said Doug. 'Do you need to get back to the B&B? I can hold the fort here.'

'Yes but I'll call Róisín and let her know what's happening and ask her to drop over to me when she's finished work.'

'Good plan,' Doug agreed.

'The kids can stay on camp-beds in our room,' Keeley said.

She went to their room to find pyjamas and their toothbrushes. She couldn't believe the mess inside the narrow wardrobe. All the clothes were shoved in a ball and it was difficult to find anything, let alone two matching pairs of pyjamas. Grabbing a black sack from the kitchen, Keeley stuffed the majority of the clothes inside and bundled it into the car along with the dirty sheets from the beds.

She was baffled by how Liv's house had gotten so bad so quickly. She'd been here a few weeks before and it wasn't anything like this. As soon as Liv was out of hospital and feeling better, Keeley was going to sit her down and try to get to the bottom of it all. Things couldn't continue like this. It wasn't good for the children, and it certainly wasn't good for Liv.

Chapter 22

RÓISÍN WAS PULLING THE SHUTTERS DOWN ON Nourriture for the night when her mobile phone rang. As soon as she answered, her mother took off on a breathy ramble about Liv and hospital and students and children.

'Hey Mum, slow down,' she said rubbing her temples. She'd planned on going for a long walk on the beach to get some air and think about the next steps for her business and what she should do about matters in France.

She had a final meeting scheduled with the bank for tomorrow, when she hoped they would give her approval for her loan now that she had all the reports and surveys in order. Then she'd be in a position to make Mr Grace an offer. She wanted to be ready with as many answers as possible. She'd also had an hour-and-a-half of being trailed by Claus the German man. While he seemed like a nice fellow, she didn't really need a lost sheep roaming in to chat about the world when she was so busy. Still, she knew he was grieving and lonely and no matter how hassled she was, she couldn't bring herself to dismiss him.

She walked toward the cottage and listened as her mum explained about Liv.

'That's awful. I hope she doesn't have to go for that skin-grafting process. It's meant to be dreadfully painful.'

'Yes, so I believe. She needs to sort herself out though.

If you could've seen the mess at the house . . . and the way she was treating those foreign students. She needs a stern talking-to. I know she's in pain right now, but I've never been so embarrassed. She wasn't raised to treat people so shabbily. I could kill her.'

'You need to calm down, Mum,' Róisín said. 'I'm sure there's a perfectly reasonable explanation for it all. It's probably just too much for her. She was saying yesterday that she's exhausted all the time. Now she's being clumsy.' Roisin paused. 'Listen, I hope I'm not speaking out of turn here. But I'm actually worried about Liv's drinking.'

'Really? Well . . . I did notice she's been getting into a bit of a state lately. She never used to get so drunk.'

'I know and I tried to speak to her about it, but she got so aggressive and said I was accusing her of being an alcoholic.'

'Oh dear,' said Keeley. 'Do you think it would be a good idea if I phoned Martin? I'm not sure what he knows and what he doesn't know at this point.'

'Yeah.' Róisín hesitated. 'Mum, I think there's something not right with Liv and Martin over the last few months. Martin has changed since he's working away. He's snappier with Liv and the children. I hope I'm wrong, but I'm beginning to suspect there're a few cracks in their marriage.'

Keeley sighed deeply. 'I agree.'

'You do?' Róisín was a bit shocked.

'I've noticed it too. I think poor Liv might be using the drink as a sort of emotional crutch. Which isn't going to get her anywhere. This is such a mess. I feel awful for not moving more swiftly on my hunch.'

'Look, we'll both be there for Liv.'

'Yes, we will,' Keeley said. 'You're a wonderful sister, Róisín. Liv is so lucky to have you. We all are.'

'Thanks Mum,' she said, smiling. 'I'd better go. I'll call over later.'

'OK love, but do you think I should call Martin?'

'I don't know, Mum. He mightn't like the interference and it could really annoy Liv if she finds out. She's tetchy enough and if she thinks we're going behind her back she could lash out and tell us both to sod off.'

'Hmm. Maybe you're right. Will we keep a close eye and see what pans out. After all, we're only speculating here. We could be totally wrong.'

'Yeah, let's be there for Liv and see where we all stand in a few days. I've to fly here.'

'Bye love. See you later.'

As Róisín ended the call with her mother, she arrived at the cottage and opened the front door with her key.

'Hello?' she called out. There was no sign of Jill so she assumed she was out. As she toasted a pita bread to have with the hummus she'd swiped from the shop, she heard giggling coming from the bedroom. Sighing, she realised Jill had company – again.

'Hey,' Jill said staggering into the kitchen, looking like she'd been dragged through a bush backwards.

'Nice look,' Róisín said with a grin. 'In the movies it looks cute when a girl wears her fella's clothes, but an AC/DC T-shirt with holes doesn't quite cut it.'

'Ah who cares,' Jill said. 'Guess what?'

'What?'

'Gordon's moving in. Officially. As in we're going to be a proper grown-up couple instead of just shag buddies.'

'No way!' Róisín said, rushing to hug her while trying

to hide her dismay. 'Oh my God, that's such exciting news. Congratulations!'

'We decided officially just a while ago. We've been consummating our decision,' she said with a wink.

'Super. A little too much info, mind you. Aw, I'm thrilled for you.'

'Really?' she said.

'Of course you goon, why wouldn't I be?'

'Yeah, it's totally great . . . But . . .'

'But what?'

'Oh Ro-Ro, I don't know how to say this without sounding like a cow . . .'

'Try me,' she said, feeling suddenly nervous.

'Well, you know the way I was renting here for a few months before you joined me?'

'Yeah.'

'Me and Gordon have been chatting and we kind of . . . well, we think we'd like to live on our own for a bit.'

'Oh sure,' she said swallowing. 'Of course. So when are you thinking of moving out?' This wasn't a great time to try and find a new flatmate and she really didn't want to take on paying all the rent herself.

'Well, that's kind of the thing . . . we were wondering if . . . you could move out?'

'Oh. I see. Oh, right. I'll find some place else. When was Gordon thinking of moving in?'

'Done deed, Rosie-Posie-Ro-Ro,' he said appearing in his rather unattractive y-fronts. His dark furry paunch and fairly impressive man-boobs weren't helping – at all. Resisting the urge to cover her eyes with her hands, she turned to the kitchen sink for refuge.

'Gordon,' Jill giggled. 'Put away your moobs. Poor Róisín

doesn't know where to look. Besides,' she sidled over to him, 'you're mine now, so you can't go flaunting your bits at other women.'

'Oh don't you worry. I wouldn't dream of infringing on your territory, Jill.'

'Especially when you have lover boy Rob at your beck and call,' Jill said with a wink. 'I know you're keeping your cards close to your chest as usual Ro-Ro, but I know you too well. Maybe you could get a little love nest with him?'

'I think you're putting two and two together and coming up with five,' Róisín said. 'Rob is a nice guy but he's not my type, and he's in a serious relationship.'

'Could've fooled me,' Jill snorted. 'The two of you were as thick as thieves the other night.'

'He was giving me some business advice, that's all. He has a few issues at the moment too, so we were kind of venting at one another.'

'Is that what they call it now?' Gordon said, pinching Jill's bottom. 'We do lots of venting at each other too, don't we Jilly-Nilly-Milly-Moo?'

'Right, so, that's fine then,' Róisín said, hoping she was hiding her hurt. She knew it was all perfectly reasonable and it was a great thing if Jill wanted to live with this ape. But she was feeling so vulnerable in so many ways just at the minute. Having no home on top of it all was really not what she'd have opted for.

'I knew you'd understand,' Jill said. 'So we're still pals? And there's totally no hassle with you staying until you find a place.'

'Yeah, don't think we're kicking you out. We don't want any homeless friends. Ugh, not cool,' Gordon said, bursting out laughing. Róisín yet again felt that surge of violence. It confirmed what she already knew: she had to get out of here, and fast.

'We've told our folks and they're all stoked for us, so we're meeting at the Thatch pub at eight thirty. You'll come, won't you?' Jill asked.

'Yup, a moo-ving in party,' he said making cow noises and laughing.

'I'll be there, but I'm not sure what time,' Róisín said as she explained about Liv.

'Oh no!' Jill looked genuinely concerned. 'Poor Liv. That's awful. I feel really guilty now. You're trying to deal with this and I'm here bouncing around like a Jack-in-the-box on speed. No wonder I detected an odd vibe from you.' Jill pulled her into a massive hug and kissed her on the head. 'You take your time and we'll see you whenever you can.'

All thoughts of Gordon and his moobs were well and truly put to the back of her mind as Róisín pulled up at the B&B. The children were playing with a small kite in the front garden and came rushing to greet her.

'We're having a sleepover here,' Billy reported. 'Our girls went back to Franceland and Spainland and Mum is at the hop-it-al. Daddy is still in America and he's not coming home yet.'

'Well I'm sure Mum will be fine again soon,' Róisín said. The children didn't seem to understand that their mum was unwell, so she kept smiling and told them she'd come out and help with the kite in a while.

'Granddad is helping us to get it into the sky. But he said it needs a new bit of wire on a part,' Billy said. 'He's in the shed finding a fixing bit.'

'Excellent. Granddad is the right man for the job,' Róisín said making her way inside. The mood in the kitchen was sombre as Keeley cleared away the dinner things.

'Any further contact from Liv?' Róisín asked.

'No, love. Last we heard they were doing all sorts of swabbing and dressing and they have her on a drip for antibiotics and another for fluids.'

'Poor Liv. Still, she's in the right hands now.'

'True,' Keeley said, sighing heavily. 'The children ate a good dinner and they seem happy enough, don't they?'

'They're delighted with life,' Róisín said. 'Dad will play with them so they'll be fine.

'Well, I rang Martin earlier to fill him in – with Liv's blessing. I thought about what you said and decided it would be wrong to go behind her back, so I texted and asked her first.'

'Right, what did he say? Did he know Liv had even burned herself?'

'No, as it happens. I could be wrong, but I'm not sure they've spoken in quite a few days. I think your hunch is right, Róisín. I'm not being the interfering old mother-in-law here, but if things don't improve soon, I don't know what I'll do.'

'If Martin isn't looking after Liv and the kids, I'll have something to say to him,' Róisín said getting suddenly angry. 'I feel like phoning him now myself.'

'Don't, love. You said it yourself, we can't go jumping in with brute force. Liv is our concern, but her marriage is not really our business at the end of the day. Leave it for now and let's see what pans out. I think I'm getting old,' Keeley said. 'I'm exhausted after today. I'm not able for all this stress, you know?'

'In that case I must be older than I thought. I'm wrecked too.'

'Things will improve. Swings and roundabouts and all that,' Keeley said. 'That's life, isn't it love?'

'Speaking of getting old and life and all that,' Róisín said. 'We still need to organise your sixtieth birthday bash. Don't think you're getting away scot-free. We'll talk about it once Liv is home and settled again.'

'Ah, it's the least of our priorities at the moment, love.'

'It is not,' Róisín scoffed. 'Oh, good news! Jill and Gordon are moving in together.'

'Really?' Keeley looked pained. 'Is she really happy with him?'

'Delirious,' Róisín said. 'Which is the main thing.'

'He's an awful eejit, though,' Keeley said. 'I know that's most unkind of me. But I don't know what she sees in him. Really I don't. She's a fabulous girl and full of spark. He's a lucky fellow is all I can say.'

'I agree with you wholeheartedly, Mum,' Róisín admitted. As they had a chat, Róisín was relieved to be able to vent her reservations about Jill's chosen man. 'I often thought I should say it to her, but you know it's not actually my business to tell her what I think. I'm not moving in with the guy and hey, love is blind so they say.'

'So they say,' Keeley said. 'And how are things with you?' she asked.

'There are no men, blind or otherwise on the scene if that's what you're digging at,' she said with a smile. 'I do have some news I'd like to share though.' Róisín filled Keeley in on the idea she had, to buy Mr Grace's building.

'Why didn't you tell us, love?' Keeley said. 'That's a

dreadful burden for you to carry. You mustn't keep things to yourself like that.'

'I know I probably should have said something,' she agreed. 'But I needed to get my head around it all. Besides, I think this was the best thing that could've happened. It gave me the incentive to get up off my ass and do something proactive.'

'I suppose that's one way of looking at it,' Keeley said. 'But we're your parents and you should share your woes as well as your joys with us. You should know that by now.'

'I do, Mum,' she said. Róisín dropped her gaze. She couldn't allow her mother to see her face. Keeley was good at reading her mind. It had been so difficult keeping everything from her when she'd returned from France.

'Between Liv living in squalor and not coping and you worrying about your business and not telling me, I'm beginning to wonder what kind of a mother I really am!'

'Don't say that,' Róisín said. 'You're a brilliant mother, and grandmother. You know you are,' she said giving her a stern look. 'But I suppose Liv and I feel we're not kids any longer. We need to shoulder our own burdens at times too, you know?'

'Ah listen, don't mind me,' Keeley said. 'I think I'm just feeling a little bit hard done by at the moment. Your father is having some sort of a second wind. He's like a teenager again. He's off having a whale of a time with Jimmy and I think I'm feeling like a bit of a washed-up old housemaid. Ida's death was tough, too.'

'All the more reason to start planning something nice,' Róisín said.

'You're right,' Keeley said. 'I will. Let's plan a really special night!'

'That's more like it,' Róisín smiled. 'Oh, by the way, since Jill and Gordon are now living together as of this afternoon, I'll be moving out of the cottage. I'm thinking of giving the tenant notice in the flat above the café once I buy the building. I often thought I wouldn't like to live above Nourriture, but if it's actually my place, I think it would work out nicely.'

'Well if you're looking for somewhere in the meantime, you can always stay here.'

'Thanks Mum,' she said. Róisín knew it was a genuine offer, but she also knew the B&B was booked solidly for the next few months. So it wouldn't be an option really. Think positively, she told herself, you'll be a building owner and living above the shop shortly! 'Would you mind if I have a quick shower?'

'Of course not,' Keeley said hugging her. 'Take as long as you wish.'

Róisín showered and wrapped herself in a towel. She Googled an address in France. Hitting the e-mail button, she sent an image of the homepage to herself. Scrolling down, she found the contact address and clicked on it. She filled out a query form and asked to be contacted with advice on her options at this point. Even writing the French words brought a lump to her throat. She'd loved everything about living there and learning to converse fluently.

Images of the long and heartfelt conversations she'd had with Jacques assailed her. She didn't realise how hard she was crying until she hit Send on the e-mail and heard her mother's footsteps. She wiped her face with the towel.

'I'll set up two lovely beds for you in our room,' Keeley was saying to the children. Their chirpy voices tugged at her heart.

Dashing back into the en suite for privacy, she managed to grab her clothes and shut the door before they came into the room.

'I won't be long,' she called out, hoping she didn't sound as strangled as she felt.

'No problem, love. We're just getting some beds organised for Billy and Jess.'

Róisín had gathered her thoughts by the time she was dressed. She smoothed on a bit of BB cream and a quick slick of mascara.

'Feeling better?' Keeley asked.

'Yes, thanks. I think I'll fly over to the hospital and visit Liv. Put her mind at rest about these two monkeys,' she said, hugging Billy and scooping Jess into her arms.

'Great, I have an overnight bag for her. Will you tell her that I'll see her tomorrow.'

'OK you two, pose for a picture for your mum with big goofy smiles. I need you to do your best faces to cheer her up.' The two were delighted to perform. They were so funny that Róisín took a quick video on her phone. 'Good job you two, Mum will love that!' Doug joined in and sent Liv a little message too.

'Phones are great, aren't they? She'll be delighted now,' he said looking pleased.

As Róisín drove on the way to the hospital, passing the mountains on her left and the patchwork of fields sewn together with higgledy-piggledy stone walls, she was struck, once again, by the beauty of her surroundings.

The hospital was busy and it took her a few minutes to find a parking space. By the time she got to Liv's ward she was hot and hassled.

'Hey Liv,' she said, huffing and throwing the overnight

bag on the floor. 'I brought you some things and I was meant to be delivering a large smile too, but I'm mildly possessed after navigating that awful car park.'

'Try sitting in this crunching bed with your arm wrapped up like a paw. And all of it because of your own stupidity.'

'Aw, poor you. Is it really sore? It looks impressive if nothing else,' she said with a smile.

'I can't wait to get out of here. It's a hell-hole. The nurses are lovely but the place is like a train station. I don't know how anyone stays in here.'

'I don't think anyone is here because they're bored,' Róisín said. 'So Mum was chatting to Martin earlier.'

'Right,' she said and looked away. 'Well at least he knows now.'

There was a silence that Róisín chose not to fill. She waited.

Liv turned to look at her, her face devoid of expression.

'Is everything OK with you and Martin?' Róisín whispered.

'Why are you whispering at me as if I'm dying?' Liv snapped.

'I didn't realise I was.'

'Martin is miles away working. He's busy. There was no point in telling him. What can he do from America? It's only a burn and he's far too busy.'

Róisín didn't answer. Liv picked at the bedclothes and kept her gaze downward. 'I texted him last night,' she said. 'He hasn't answered.'

'Oh. Maybe his phone is out of range or it could be the time difference. I'm sure he'll be on to you in the morning some time.'

'But he was able to talk to Mum and now knows I'm

in here and he hasn't bothered his ass to even answer my text.' Liv looked straight ahead.

'What's happening between you two, Liv?'

'I don't want to talk about it right now. I've enough on my mind. I need to get speaking to the specialist first thing tomorrow and get the hell out of here before I go insane.'

Róisín couldn't read her sister's thoughts. Normally they were so in tune with one another. But lately, Róisín felt Liv was in some distant place that she couldn't reach.

'So the kids are fine,' Róisín said.

'Great,' Liv said dryly.

'I asked them to pose for a picture for you. They were the cutest. They were doing such funny dances and making hilarious expressions so I did this little video too. Hang on, let me find it now . . .' By the time she clicked it on, Liv was looking in the other direction. 'Here you go,' she said holding the phone out. 'Eh, there's a message from Dad too,' she grinned, 'he's as bad as the kids when it comes to acting the maggot!'

Liv didn't take it but instead stared at the screen without moving a muscle.

'Well, I thought they were cute,' Róisín said raising her eyebrows. 'Mum and Dad are having Billy and Jess to stay over tonight, and I'm going to help out with them tomorrow, so all angles are covered.' Liv nodded. No word of thanks and no apparent concern for anyone. Róisín swallowed. She knew her sister didn't want to discuss anything but at the same time, her mood was totally out of character.

'Jill and Gordon are moving in together.'

'Great. I wish them well,' Liv deadpanned.

'I'll be moving out. They need their space and besides,

I can't abide him. I don't know what she sees in him. Just the other night, we had a few people over and . . .'

'I don't care, Ro. I'm not interested,' Liv said quietly and calmly. 'I couldn't give a fiddlers if Jill moves Jack-the-ripper into her cottage. Good for her. Whatever. Just because you don't fancy Gordon doesn't mean he's a tool. You're not the goddess of love now, are you?'

Róisín pushed her chair back. 'Your night things are in the bag. I'll tell Billy and Jess you send your love. I hope you get some sleep and feel better in the morning.'

She rushed out before she exploded. Tears of frustration burned her eyes. Under any other circumstances Róisín would've yelled at Liv and called her a selfish little wench. But she wasn't going to disgrace herself in public and it wasn't the right time to go hammer and tongs at Liv. But her patience and making allowances time was swiftly running out. Liv needed to cop on – fast.

Her phone rang as she reached the hospital exit doors.

'Hi Mum,' she said trying to hide her anger. 'Everything OK with you?'

'All fine, love. How's poor Liv?'

'Poor Liv seems to think that all the woes of the world are resting on her shoulders. She'll come out of it, but I'd let her sleep tonight and talk to her in the morning.'

'Oh dear. Is she in terrible pain? I'd say she's miserable without the children and with Martin so far away. God love her. It's not what I'd wish for her. I'll go in first thing in the morning. A bit of TLC is what she needs. Poor little love.'

Róisín said she'd call her mother in the morning and hung up. How was her mum so kind and thoughtful all the time? She did nothing but think of her family. She worried, forgave, minded and encouraged all the time without faltering. That, Róisín mused, is what being a mother is all about.

Clicking onto the hospital's Wi-Fi, she typed an e-mail to the fertility clinic in France.

'Thanks Mum,' she whispered as she pushed through the revolving door. 'You've helped me make up my mind.'

Chapter 23

THE FOLLOWING MORNING RÓISÍN PREPARED FOR her meeting at the bank and set off nervously.

But there was no need to worry. As it turned out, the meeting was all she'd hoped it would be. Róisín could barely contain herself as she drove back to Ballyshore. She rang her parents to give them the good news.

'Hold on and I'll put your father on,' Keeley said excitedly. 'He's dying to know how you got on.'

Doug was full of encouragement. 'Get your pieces of paper in order before you approach Mr Grace. Take your quote from the estate agent and all your reports from the QS along with your offer letter and deliver it by hand,' he advised. 'It's essential to be official and businesslike with your paperwork, but a bit of personality is always the icing on the cake.'

'Thanks Dad,' she said. 'Any news from Liv?'

'Not a thing our end. Your mother went into the hospital earlier, but Liv was fast asleep and she didn't want to wake her. The children are fine though. We're going to build a nice wooden sand-box. It'll give us all a little project. I'll take them to the builder's suppliers for wood and the bags of sand. '

'Ah they'll love that,' Róisín grinned, knowing it was Granddad who'd enjoy it the most.

Róisín arrived back in Ballyshore and checked in with

Brigid to make sure everything was running smoothly before she climbed the stairs to her office. She'd already drafted a letter of offer to Mr Grace, which she printed out.

Satisfied she had all her documents in order, she walked purposefully to his house at the edge of the village. Luckily, he was in the garden doing a bit of weeding.

'Hello there, Róisín dear.'

'Hi Mr Grace,' she said. 'Sorry to disturb you, but I was wondering if I might have a few moments of your time?'

'Yes,' he said. 'As a matter of fact you've saved me a trip. I was planning to drop over to you today.'

'Oh good,' she said. They sat on a rickety old bench in his garden and Róisín took a deep breath.

'You know the letter you delivered a short while back? Well, it got me thinking. I would like to make you an offer to buy the building.'

'Oh,' he said looking surprised. 'I see.'

'Before you say anything, I've done my homework.'

'You have?'

'Yes,' Róisín said. 'I've had the place valued and I've gone to the bank and had a loan approved. I know you are under pressure to provide for your family, so I thought this would be the best-case scenario for both of us.' She held out the large envelope with the documents. 'Would you consider my offer?' she asked, feeling suddenly vulnerable.

'OK,' he said slowly. He opened the envelope and slid out her carefully prepared pages. He glanced down at the bottom line and sighed. 'I'm really sorry, Róisín, I truly am, but I'm afraid it's nowhere near what the other investor is offering. As I said, this other offer blew me out of the water. I'd be an old fool to turn it down.'

'But what about Nourriture?' she asked weakly. 'What about . . . me . . .'

'I'm so sorry. But what would you do in my position?'

'Yes, I guess you're right,' she said feeling ill. 'I'll go now Mr Grace, if you don't mind. I was so sure it would work out for both of us . . . I'm sorry for wasting your time . . . When do I need to be out?'

'You have another two months of your lease.'

Róisín nodded weakly and walked away. The footpath blurred as she tried to control her emotions.

On autopilot, she arrived at Nourriture. Standing a few yards from the door, she looked at the tables in the tiny space across the road, under the old tree. She stared at the building, with its lovingly tended hanging baskets with bright flowers. She really loved this place.

She went into the shop behind a family who hurried to the smoothie counter. The smell of fresh baking embraced. Looking around the shop as if for the first time, she put her hand on one of the beautifully crafted wooden tables and walked on into the off licence section. She'd had a vision in her head, nurtured it and it had come to fruition. This place was her baby. The nearest thing she could muster to a baby. It was more than her livelihood, this place was her very own creation. Numbly she answered Brigid's questions and then walked up the back stairs to her tiny office. She felt so alone. Without really thinking, she took her box of cards from the shelf and pulled out the one that had arrived on her sixteenth birthday, searching for inspiration.

My darling girl
Sixteen is one of those ages I remember clearly. I didn't know which end was up. I hated anyone who treated me like a baby,

but deep down inside, I was petrified of being a grown-up too.

I didn't know it at the time, but the most important person in my life when I was your age was my mother. I fought with her, rolled my eyes at most things she said and genuinely treated her like a fool, most of the time. When I think about it, it makes me blush. She was doing what all good mothers do, you see. She was loving me unconditionally. She still had my back and still adored me, even if I was thoroughly dislikeable! Why? Because that's what mothers do. That's what family is all about. Your people are the ones who will stick by you through thick and thin. They're the ones who will always come back for more: whether it's love or a shouting match! They're the ones who can truly forgive and forget.

I don't want to sound all preachy and square because I'm actually asking you to do what I didn't do at your age. But my excuse is that I didn't have someone cool to put me straight. Yes, I am cool. I have dyed hair, a nose ring and far too many piercings in my ears. I wear too much liquid eyeliner and I can't fathom going out in public without some sort of nail polish! Share your worries with someone you trust. I wish I'd opened up more. Knowing how I feel about you, my beautiful girl, there is nothing you could say or do that would make me think you are anything but amazing. I can't be there to hold you or advise you or help you when you're struggling, but I'll tell you a secret: a mother's love is always there. Mine will never die. I may not be there physically, but I'll be there somehow.

Happy 16th birthday darling. Make a wish and blow it on the breeze. I'll do my best to catch it.

I love you.

Mam

Although Róisín had read these cards so many times, she felt that many of them were only beginning to make sense to her now. *Share your worries*. Her mother was right. She really couldn't do it alone, that's what she had to accept.

She grabbed her car keys, ran down the stairs and drove like a bat out of hell towards the B&B. She needed to talk to her parents about France, about Nourriture and about all the thoughts that were tumbling around in her mind.

Her heart stopped when she pulled up and saw her mother. She was leaning against the outside wall of the house, crying openly.

'Mum!' she said rushing to hug her. 'What's happened?'

'Liv just phoned,' she said. 'She was crying uncontrollably and said she wishes she was dead.'

'What?' Róisín was in shock. 'What's going on? Do you think she's suffering with depression or something?'

'I asked her that,' Keeley said. 'But she assured me it's nothing like that. She said she didn't want to discuss it while she's in hospital.'

'Do you believe her?' Róisín asked. 'It would make sense in a way . . . her house is a tip and she's not managing with the children . . . maybe that's the reason.'

'She's adamant that's not it. Don't say it to your father,' Keeley said, 'I didn't want to worry him. But Liv wasn't asleep when I went in to visit her this morning.'

'Oh?'

'She was awake, but she barely spoke to me, Róisín. She was so low. Nothing I said seemed to be helping so I asked if she'd prefer to be left alone. She nodded, so I gave her a kiss and left. She never asked about the children or anything.' Keeley sighed. 'I'm so worried about her. I feel so helpless. I wish I could wave a magic wand and make it all better for her.'

'Come on, Mum,' she said gently. 'Let's go inside and have some tea and figure it out.'

She knew now was not the time to off-load on her poor parents, no matter how badly she needed their help and guidance.

Chapter 24

ROB WAS PACKING THE VAN TO GO ON A DELIVERY when Theresa arrived unannounced.

'Hello sweetie!' She sidled over to him in sky-high heels, trussed in a tight bandage dress. Her blonde hair was styled in perfect waves and she battled to keep it from blowing in the breeze.

'Hi,' he said fixing a smile on his face. 'How's it going? I was about to head off.'

'I was wondering if you'd managed to get tickets to the lunch in the Hilton hotel for Friday?' she asked. 'I really want to go.'

'Oh,' he said, clicking his fingers. 'I totally forgot. To be honest, I can't afford to spend the guts of a day fluting about in a hotel. Why don't you get some of the girls to go?'

'They are,' she pouted. 'But they all have their hunky fiancés and husbands escorting them.' She stared at him beseechingly as she said the word fiancé.

'Let me look at my schedule and I'll let you know,' he said.

'OK cool. I'll wait here,' she said.

'Do you need me to do it this second?'

'Well yes,' she said looking astonished. 'This is a big deal, Rob. Everyone who is anyone will be at this. We need to keep in with the right crowd.'

It was at the tip of his tongue to say that he didn't give a toss about impressing anyone. He had no issue with donating to a charity, but he couldn't bear the thought of drinking all afternoon at a table of show-offs. That's what all the men were like in Theresa's gang. Each one was more mouthy than the next. They were more along the lines of Gordon, he thought suddenly. Róisín came into his mind. With her quirky tutu skirts and her pretty dark hair and those flashing blue eyes . . . she was effortlessly stylish and totally unique, whereas Theresa and her 'girls' were like clones of one another. Guilt washed over him as he looked up at her. She was standing clutching her stupidly expensive handbag, blinking at him hopefully.

He grabbed his appointment book and riffled through the pages. 'I have a few things on. But I suppose I could move them,' he said.

'You're so funny with your big clumpy book,' she said. 'You need to start using your smartphone properly and get rid of paper. It's so ten years ago.'

'I find this the most efficient way of planning my appointments,' he said. 'Once it's written there in black and white, I can work best.'

'So you'll come?' she asked, making it clear she had no interest in his work.

'I guess.'

'Great stuff.' She rose onto her tippy-toes to kiss him. 'And are you planning on treating me to the ticket?'

'Eh, yeah. Sure . . . how much?'

'They're one hundred and eighty euros each,' she said. 'But they're in short supply so I was lucky to reserve them.'

He grabbed his cheque book and scribbled out the amount. She took it gleefully and stashed it in her handbag with a smile. Not too against paper when it's in the form of a cheque, he thought crossly.

After Theresa left, Rob found himself comparing her to Róisín in every way. In his wildest dreams he couldn't imagine Róisín sitting at one of those lunches for the afternoon. Nor would she be interested in the babble that went with it. Clearly she and her family were on board with fund-raising and helping others, but they did it in a far less pretentious way. In Rob's opinion they did it in a more inclusive manner – and in the right way.

He wasn't due to go to Ballyshore for another few weeks. That was a shame. He'd thoroughly enjoyed the other night. Róisín had made him laugh so much when she'd described some of the things Gordon came out with.

At the same time, there was something guarded and a little bit sad about Róisín, too. She was dynamic and full of business ideas, but she was one of those girls who seemed to prefer being single. She certainly didn't suffer with a lack of male attention, that was for sure. Several guys, including a poor fella called Colm, had made fairly obvious advances at the party. But she gave them all short shrift.

'None of these are your type, then?' he'd teased her as yet another suitor walked away empty-handed. 'So what is your type?'

'At this stage, I don't actually know,' she'd replied thoughtfully. 'I used to think I knew. But I was so wrong it's astonishing. So I'm concentrating on the part of my life that I seem to be slightly better at. That's work, in case you don't know . . .'

'I can see that you're very good at that,' he'd said. 'But it's a shame that a gorgeous girl like you doesn't have someone to go home to at night.'

'Ah cheers,' she'd said. 'You're kind. Theresa is a lucky girl!'

He couldn't get that comment out of his head. Had she meant Theresa was lucky because she sort of liked him too, or just that Theresa was lucky because he was kind?

He was realising that Róisín was everything he was looking for in a woman. She was savvy, smart, independent and beautiful. He felt he could tell her anything. They were on the same wavelength . . . that was it. He and Theresa were on two different planets. All the things she adored seemed silly to him and he knew his interests bored her senseless. How could he propose to a girl he couldn't connect with?

He walked back toward the van and saw his dad coming towards him, his old dog shadowing him as usual.

'Are you off now, son?'

'I've a few deliveries to make. I won't be away overnight though.'

'No worries at all. I have my bridge club coming. I'll give them a bit of dinner too, so if you're home you're welcome to join us?'

'Thanks for that Dad, but I might leave you to it. You're all a bit rowdy for me!'

His dad chuckled and shook his head. 'You'd think it was a nice civilised idea for an evening, but it nearly always turns into a loud affair.'

'No harm done,' Rob said. 'I'll see you later on.'

'Was that Theresa I saw you chatting to just now?' Melvin asked.

'Yup,' Rob said. 'She's getting us tickets for the big luncheon on Friday. It'll be a great day by all accounts.'

'Is it me or yourself you're trying to convince?'

'How do you mean?'

'I've been watching you,' Melvin said. 'I don't think I was being fair when I tried to bamboozle you into getting engaged.'

'Really?'

'I want to see you happy and settled. I'm hanging out for grandchildren but the more I sit back and observe you, the more I wonder about you and Theresa. She's a lovely young one, no doubt about it, but you don't light up when you see her.'

Later Rob thought about his father's words. His thoughts were slowly beginning to join up. When he'd believed the rest of the world thought he and Theresa were a match made in heaven, it felt as if he might be able to convince himself some day too. But now that he'd had this revelation about Róisín and his dad had changed his mind about Theresa as well, Rob felt as if he'd been tossed a life-ring.

Now that he thought it through, his mates had never actually said they thought he and Theresa were suited either. Sure, they made lurid comments about her and clapped him on the back, saying he was a stud, but that was all superficial stuff. She was a babe and there was no denying that, but Róisín was more beautiful in his eyes. Anyway, he thought with irritation, looks had nothing to do with it. It was how people connected that really mattered, right?

Did girls think the same way as guys, though? Would Róisín be knocked off her feet if he looked more like Jamie Dornan? Rob wished he had a female he could talk to. Not for the first time, he wished his mother was here. He didn't have a woman's perspective on things and it made him miss her with fresh grief.

Chapter 25

NELL COULDN'T QUITE BELIEVE HOW MUCH MOUSE
had come on in the space of a few days.

'Well it's not as if I have much else to do,' she said. 'I
can do twelve hours a day of reading and writing if I want.'

'I understand that,' Nell said. 'But you're really grasping
it all so well. That's no easy feat, you know? You're a very
bright girl.'

'Cheers!'

'Can you show me the writing you've just finished?'
Nell asked. She felt a lump in her throat as she stared at
the work. The first few pages of the book were certainly
in the drunk spider camp. But the latest piece of work
was quite frankly brilliant.

'It looks like it was written by a different person,' Nell
said. 'Look at the difference.'

They were busy sounding out a longer word, as Nell
nodded in encouragement, when the front door opened.

'Only me!' Mo shouted. 'Hello girls?'

'In the kitchen,' Nell shouted.

'I have the most exciting thing,' Mo said as she bustled
in. 'Look, Mouse! You're in the *Ballyshore People*!'

Nell thought the young girl would explode with excitement.

'Look at what the stupid eejit called me!' she said as

she traced her finger along the words. 'I recognise the second word because it's my name. But the first one says muh,' she sounded it out. 'Ha!' she giggled. 'It's says I'm called Mini Mouse!'

'They didn't really print that, did they?' Nell said looking over her shoulder.

'They certainly did,' Mo said. 'Good for you, love. No matter what your name is, you're now famous!'

'Deadly,' she said. 'Can I keep this?' she asked Mo.

'Yes, love. That copy is for you. The other one is for Nell.'

'Thank you. I'll look at it later,' Nell muttered, making it quite clear she wasn't going to sit and go through every page of the local paper with them.

Excusing herself, she pulled on her boots and ventured outside. Her garden was looking particularly cheerful as she stooped to pull some weeds. A thought had struck her last night. She needed to encourage Mouse to get out a bit and integrate herself with the locals. There was nothing wrong with her as such. She wasn't ill like poor Laura had been. It wasn't right that she should sit out here and have no friends.

She put in a good hour's work in the garden then went inside the empty kitchen and called up the stairs, 'Mouse, can you come here for a minute?'

'Yeah?' she appeared looking intrigued.

'Grab your anorak. We're going into town. As in Galway city.'

'Huh?' she said. 'For what?'

'You need clothes and more than that, you need to start getting out.'

'Deadly,' she said. 'I love shopping.'

Nell pulled off her gardening clobber and found a pair of linen trousers and a white oversized shirt. Releasing her hair from the tightly scraped-back bun she shook it out and teased it into a slightly less severe-looking chignon. Leaning into the mirror, she wondered if she ought to put on make-up or even some sort of cream. All she had was a tub of generic moisturiser from the supermarket so she slathered some on.

Mouse was outside waiting. Through the window she gazed at the young girl. She was a funny little creature. In a way she was as wild as a boar and in others she was totally refined and ladylike. She was easily pleased and didn't expect anything at all.

'Mo, we're going up to Galway city. If we don't see you later, I suppose we'll see you next week.'

Nell almost laughed at the gobsmacked look on Mo's face.

She started the car and Mouse jumped in.

'The last time I got clothes I robbed them,' she admitted. 'It was only a polo-neck and a pair of leggings, but I'd no money.'

'If you'd no money, then you shouldn't have gotten them,' Nell barked. 'Stealing is wrong. What about the poor shop owner you swiped from?'

'Ah it was Penney's. They don't care. They have about a thousand pairs of leggings anyhow.'

'That's not the point. You shouldn't do it.'

'I suppose not,' Mouse said yawning.

Nell stifled a grin. The girl had no remorse and clearly didn't feel she'd done anything wrong.

'Now, stealing a car and every bit of jewellery some toff-nosed lady owns, that's bad form,' Mouse said.

'Leggings and a top are low grade in the greater scheme of things.'

'In the greater scheme of things it's best not to nick anything at all.'

'In an ideal world,' Mouse corrected.

'Well, let there be no stealing today. I don't have a king's ransom to spend on you, but we'll deck you out and all of it will be paid for.'

'What do you normally spend your money on?' Mouse asked.

'I save,' she said.

'For what?' She laughed. 'Can't be a rainy day because there've been so many of them it's a joke. Are you going to break out some day and buy a mansion and a Rolls Royce?'

'I doubt it,' said Nell. 'But who knows?'

It was such a long time since she'd had a day like this. The fact it was a spur of the moment thing was probably better, Nell mused.

They found a multi-storey car park that she swore wasn't there the last time she'd visited Galway. It was like a maze as they tried to find a way out.

'This is like a bleedin' rabbit warren,' Mouse said. 'They don't make it easy to get out. Do we need to answer questions and find clues to get to a street?'

'Here we go,' Nell said spotting an exit. They found themselves on the edge of a bustling street with Eyre Square in the centre.

'This place is deadly. It's like a mixture of a fairground and a city.'

'Galway is a really cultural place,' Nell said. 'Laura used to love coming here. We'd go to the hospital and once she was well enough, we'd come and wander around Shop Street and see the street performers.'

'You said she was all into art and stuff. Did she do any paintings that you kept?'

'Yes, a few,' Nell said. 'But they're stored safely in the back of a wardrobe.'

'Why on earth would you do that? If they were mine I'd have them in pride of place so the whole world could see them. Well, in your case that'd be you and Mo and now me.'

'I'll take your thoughts into consideration. Maybe I'll put them up on the walls.'

'Hey,' Mouse held her hands aloft. 'No grief from me. It's totally up to you.' Her attention was drawn immediately from the conversation as she was distracted by something. 'No way!' she said shooting forward, causing Nell to quicken her pace. 'Look at the shops. They have everything from Dublin with some extra weird ones that I don't know.'

Nell trailed behind Mouse for a bit, lost in her own memories. The street seemed to be echoing with Laura's laughter. In her mind's eye she could see her daughter pointing at things of interest while tugging at her sleeve.

'Nell? Cock-a-doodle-do?' Mouse said waving at her. 'Earth to Nell, come in Nell!'

'What?' she barked.

'I'm going in here, that's all.' Mouse stomped away looking hurt.

Nell charged after her and grabbed her by the shoulder. 'Don't mind me. I wasn't being gruff with you, Mouse. I was reminiscing and it made me sad. I'm sorry.'

'Hey, it's cool,' Mouse said looking instantly fine. Nell

marvelled once again at how resilient the young girl was. She really knew how to let things roll off her without taking anything to heart. She was a tough little cookie in many ways.

A different side of her emerged over the next few minutes, however. They found a massive store with three floors of thumping music and a huge array of colourful and fun clothes. Glancing at some of the price tags, Nell was pleasantly surprised.

'This place is from the States,' Mouse said knowingly. 'It's pure class, isn't it? I want every single thing in here! If you told me I could have one of each thing, I would grab it and run until I got to the moon!'

Nell giggled and said, 'Thank you, Mouse.'

'Janey Mac, I think you've gone loo-lah,' said Mouse. 'Why are you saying thank you to me?'

'Because your enthusiasm is infectious. I can't get you one of everything but here are a few euros. Go on and knock yourself out.' She handed Mouse a wad of twenty euro notes.

'I can't take that,' she said eyeballing the money and chewing the inside of her lip.

'You can and you will. You'll offend me if you don't.'

'Grand. Fair enough, you've convinced me,' she said and nearly took Nell's hand off grabbing it.

Nell didn't hold back and burst out laughing. 'Now that's what I like to see! A girl who knows what she ought to do.'

Mouse ran off and then appeared a few minutes later. 'There you are,' she said, sounding slightly out of breath. 'Come on. You're missing stuff by standing there all misty-eyed.'

'Laura would've been in heaven in here,' Nell said.

'Well please God she's here with us now and seeing as she is actually in heaven, that's a good thing, right?' Mouse cocked her head to the side and looked into Nell's eyes. Yet again the older woman couldn't help smiling. Mouse was so direct and said it as she felt it, but she wasn't offensive. That was a true gift.

'Let's try on some things then,' Nell said, deciding to make the most of the day and enjoy the moment.

'Are you buying a glittery tube mini-skirt?' Mouse asked. 'Ooh you'd be a right sight strutting around the supermarket in Ballyshore in that! Give the auld fishermen something to make them choke on their dentures.'

Nell thoroughly enjoyed the fashion show that followed. She sat comfortably on a pretty armchair while Mouse danced in and out of a changing cubicle in various outfits.

'Sick, right?' she said appearing in a pink jumpsuit.

'No, I like it,' Nell said.

'Sick means good,' Mouse deadpanned.

'OK, sick then.'

The next dress, a white shimmery number with a leg slit so high Nell feared she might see Mouse's rib cage, got the thumbs down.

'Not your best so far,' Nell said.

'Rancid more like it.'

By the time Mouse had a neat pile of 'sick' items, Nell was ready for some food. They paid for the clothes and joined the queue at the in-house coffee shop. Nell chose and paid for two ham and cheese toasties, a coffee for her and a frappé for Mouse, who'd disappeared off to the ladies.

By the time she came back, Nell was at the top of the

queue so Mouse scanned the busy seating area and said she'd find them somewhere.

'Does your daughter want cream on the frappé?' the man behind the counter asked. It was at the tip of Nell's tongue to correct him when a warm feeling came over her.

'Yes,' she answered. 'She loves cream. I do too. Can I have a squirt in my coffee?'

'Like Mammy, like daughter eh?' the man said. 'Here you go. Enjoy your day out. Nothing like it.'

'No there isn't,' Nell said.

As she balanced the tray and found Mouse, she realised it was the first time in years she'd actually spoken to a stranger. She hadn't seen the point for so long. She hadn't anything to say. She'd nothing to share apart from misery so she'd come to the conclusion that it was easier not to bother.

Mouse chattered about a pair of shoes she'd spotted and said she was going to go back and get them. She placed her hand over Nell's on the table. Nell regarded it. She was utterly tiny. Petite was the politically correct adjective. But her fingernails were like those of a small child. Her wrist bones were so delicate and fragile looking, it made her want to protect her all the more.

'Thanks, Nell. You've been nicer to me than anyone I've ever met. I don't know why you've taken me in. But I'll never stop being grateful.'

'What a lovely thing to say,' she said. 'If I'm honest, I would never have dreamed of having anyone come and live with me. I was happy. At least I thought I was . . .'

'And now?'

'You've opened my eyes to the world again, Mouse.

More than that, you've opened my heart once more. It was frozen in time, you know?'

'I kind of figured. If I overstay my welcome, tell me, yeah? I don't have a whole lot of cop-on. So don't be shy. Say what you think and if you want me out, I'll be gone.'

'You're welcome to stay as long as you like,' Nell said, sounding choked. 'You're a breath of fresh air, Mouse. One that I needed badly.'

Mouse grinned and held her gaze for a split-second before she returned to her food. She gobbled her lunch and was like a hen on a hot griddle, waiting for Nell to hurry up.

'Why don't you go over there and try the tracksuit top? I'll follow when I'm finished my coffee.'

'How did you know?'

'Ah sometimes I think I'm a bit psychic,' she teased. The joke was lost on Mouse, who sprang up and shot across the store.

It was more than Nell could bear when she spied a young woman in a wheelchair. She instantly made her think of Laura. The girl seemed quite upbeat and was happily manoeuvring herself around the store. She was pointing to a vest top and her friend was lifting it down. She shook her head and stuck her tongue out and they both giggled.

As Nell watched her interacting with a shop assistant and two other girls, she wondered whether or not Laura might have been more outgoing if she wasn't so ill. Or, she mused, if she hadn't kept her locked away. The image of Rapunzel that Mouse had put her finger on had been bothering her. Had she made Laura's short life more miserable than necessary? Had she added to the anguish by encouraging her to spend time with her at the lighthouse? As the years rolled by and Laura's condition worsened, their visits to the city or anywhere else were less frequent. Until eventually, the doctors delivered their most brutal blow.

'There's not a lot else we can do for Laura if her condition deteriorates any further. Her heart is weak. We can prescribe a higher dose of medication and that will give her a boost for a bit. It will help in the short term with the diabetes, but we need to realise that it will be dangerous to her heart. And once that either stops being effective, or it affects her heart, that's it. We've run out of options.'

Laura had cried. In fact, she'd sobbed uncontrollably and thumped the desk and then the walls of the hospital corridor.

'Why have I been cursed with this bastard disease?'

Nell did all she could to comfort her, but for the first time it wasn't enough.

Things stabilised after that for a few weeks. Laura was calmer than she'd ever been. Then she dropped the bomb Nell hadn't been expecting.

'I'm going on a trip,' she said. 'On my own.'

'I beg your pardon?' Nell said in astonishment. 'You can't go too far, love. You're not well . . . I know you're feeling better right now because of the drugs, but the doctors said that won't last.'

'I'm well aware of the fact I'm ill, Ma. It's dictated every move I've ever made. Every day of my life has been ruled by diabetes. So I've made a decision. Call it my bucket list moment, but I'm going to Australia.'

'Australia?' Nell blanched. 'But it's so far. Laura, it's such a long journey. I don't even know if the doctors will allow you to fly.'

'I'm a step ahead of you,' Laura said. 'I have consent. Besides, I'm being met by my father at the other end.' Nell could still remember so vividly how she'd felt at that moment. It was as if a bag of wet sand had been dumped on her head from a height. Her breath caught and she honestly wanted to scream, except no noise came out.

'What do you mean your father?' she eventually managed.

'I found some stuff in a drawer,' she said, displaying a newfound determination. 'I contacted him and told him that I'm sick.'

'Laura!' Nell said in shock.

'I told him I'm dying,' she repeated. 'And that I want to meet him before that happens.'

'But why?'

'Because he's my father and I've always wondered about him.'

Nell had never thought she could be put in such a heart-wrenching situation. How could she stand in her dying daughter's way? She'd had no choice but to let her go.

Seeing Mouse bustling toward her with a grin from ear to ear forced Nell to stop reminiscing. She didn't want to spoil Mouse's fun, so she shoved her chair back, took a deep breath and forced herself to shut down on the pain that was threatening to bubble out of her like a dormant volcano.

'What have you bought now?' she asked.

'Shoes. I love love love them. They're so sick they're in danger of totally dying!' Nell smiled.

'Good for you, Mouse.'

They left the store and spent a further hour browsing before Mouse looked bushed.

'Will we go back to the lighthouse, Rapunzel?' she asked Nell.

'Come on then, you cheeky mare,' Nell said.

As Mouse babbled about the difference between shopping with money as opposed to plotting to steal things, she couldn't help being amused. Mouse was nothing like Laura really. But she was refreshing and open and incredibly likeable. Nell knew she needed to be grateful for small mercies. As they scrunched the bags of things into the compact boot of the car, Nell made a conscious decision to try and give life in general another chance.

Chapter 26

IT WAS A FULL WEEK SINCE LIV HAD GONE INTO hospital. Keeley had a good routine going with the children. They were as good as gold really and she couldn't fault them.

They had killed two birds with one stone by agreeing that Róisín would move into Liv's house for the time being. She needed to get out of Jill's sex den, as she called the cottage.

'They're at it like rabbits,' she told Keeley.

'Well all of that aside, I'm glad you've agreed because it's so much easier for me to be at the B&B during the night. Your father isn't great at the really early morning starts and I suspect he's leaving guests to their own devices any time I'm not there. One couple left without paying the other morning and he didn't even notice.'

'Don't worry, Mum,' Róisín assured her. 'I've nothing else to do, so I may as well step into Liv's shoes for the evenings and nights. It's a pleasure to mind the children anyhow.'

'Well, you've more than enough going on, love,' Keeley said. 'I wasn't insinuating you didn't. I'm simply trying to say I'm grateful that you're helping me and your sister so much.'

Róisín arrived every morning with Billy and Jess

and handed them over to Keeley while she went to Nourriture.

'Here we are,' she called out cheerfully this morning and they all landed into the kitchen.

'Good morning, darlings,' Keeley called out.

She watched Róisín carefully these days, noting her tired eyes that suggested something was coming between her and her sleep. Keeley knew she needed to sit down with Róisín and see how she was in general. She hadn't spoken to her properly since Liv was taken into hospital. Nobody knew Róisín better than Keeley did. She was well aware that her daughter was a deep thinker who didn't talk about her feelings willingly. But there was something serious going on inside that pretty head of hers. Keeley knew she wasn't being paranoid this time. There was a conversation lurking and she needed to have it. Just as Róisín was saying goodbye to the children before rushing off to work, the landline rang.

Things had gone from bad to worse at the hospital. Liv had gone against all advice and sat in a bath, soaking the dressing and ending up with an infection. She needed more antibiotics and it now looked likely she'd need the skin-graft operation.

When Keeley picked up the receiver, she heard Liv sobbing like a baby.

'Can you come in? I need you to tell the doctors that it's time for me to get out of here. I'm going off my rocker.'

'Liv, I'm guessing you have to stay until you finish the antibiotics,' Keeley said. 'But I understand you're upset at being stuck in there. Why don't I bring the children in for a little visit?'

'OK, thanks Mum.'

'I'm on my way.'

'I'll come with you,' Róisín said. 'Let me just call Brigid and we can head off.'

When they arrived the doctor was talking to Liv. Keeley and Róisín introduced themselves and he explained what would happen.

'We will have to do a skin graft on Olivia's arm. But the infection needs to clear first.'

'Is this skin-graft operation a big one?' Keeley asked.

'Well, the one we'll do is called a split-level thickness graft. We will remove some skin from your thigh,' he said turning to Liv. 'Or failing that we'll go to your hip area and transplant it to your lower arm area. It means you'll come back into hospital for a few days more.'

'Will she be knocked out for it?' Keeley asked.

'Yes it's a general anaesthetic and as I say, we'll need to keep you here for three or four days following the procedure. We need to ensure the graft takes. In other words, we need to make sure the new piece of skin develops blood vessels and attaches to the surrounding skin properly. This usually takes thirty-six hours.'

Liv nodded, trying to look brave. Keeley felt as if her heart would break as she saw her daughter's usual iron will crumbling, leaving her looking as vulnerable as she had the first day she started school aged four.

'You're a feisty little madam,' Keeley said, rubbing her shoulder. 'And now is the time for you to channel that. You'll be fine, love.' Keeley took her daughter's face in her hands and stared into her eyes. 'You can do this,' she whispered, nodding emphatically. In spite of her tears and obvious terror, Liv nodded too.

'You'll be a better girl soon, won't you Mum?' Billy asked.

'I'll let you sleep in my Princess Elsa bed,' Jess said.

'I'll be OK, you guys,' she said. 'It's only a bit of a burn.'

'Atta girl,' Keeley whispered, winking at her.

'Mum will be all better in no time,' Róisín added with a smile.

'I'll leave you for now,' said Dr Young. 'We'll schedule the surgery for three weeks' time. You'll finish the antibiotics, have a rest and come back in to see me. OK? Unless there's a problem, I'll see you then.'

'So does that mean I can go home?' she asked hopefully.

'Once you have support and help and promise to keep that dressing dry, I don't see why not.'

'We'll mind her,' Keeley said.

'Absolutely,' Róisín chimed in.

'OK then. You're out of here,' said Dr Young before walking out of the ward.

They packed her things and made their way to the car.

'Have you updated Martin?' Róisín asked.

'Nope,' Liv said.

'Why don't you call him?' Keeley said. 'Here, you can use my phone if yours isn't charged.'

'I'm not calling him,' Liv said through gritted teeth.

'But he'll want to know,' Róisín said, looking at Keeley and back at Liv.

'Don't cause a scene in front of the children,' Liv hissed. 'I want to get home. End of. Would you both mind if we get into the car and out of this God-forsaken kip?'

'I'll get a taxi,' Róisín said. 'I need to get to work so I'll go back to the B&B and get my car. You guys go on ahead to Liv's.'

'If you're sure, love?' Keeley said.

'It'd be simpler. I think Liv's had enough stress for now.'

'Finally someone is thinking straight,' Liv said as she bustled toward her mother's car.

As they were on the road home, Keeley broke the news of the students' departure.

'What?' she yelled. 'How dare they imply they'd been treated badly. They were living in the lap of luxury with a stunning view and not a care in the world.'

'Liv,' Keeley said using her warning voice. 'Not in front of the children. The girls needed to go,' she added cheerfully and loudly.

'They went back to Franceland and Spainland,' Billy said. 'We were sad for a minute, but Granny 'splained that they missed their mum, just the way we miss you when you have to be in the hospital.'

'Yeah, we miss you when you go away,' Jess said. ''Cause you and Daddy did go away and we only got Auntie Ro-Ro. But she brings us cake from her shop so it's OK. But we'll be much more happy with you back!' They both clapped from the back seat and Liv dissolved into tears.

Keeley glanced over and tried to concentrate on the road, but it was extremely hard.

'Hey,' she said patting her daughter's leg. 'Take it easy, love. I know you must be so emotional after being away from the children. But it'll all be better now.'

'Yeah,' Liv said bitterly. 'It'll all be fabulous.'

Keeley couldn't talk in front of the children so she drove on until they got home.

'Oh I almost forgot to tell you,' she said. 'Róisín said she'd come and stay at yours for a bit, until you're back on your feet.'

'Really?' Liv said. 'Why?'

'I think she genuinely wants to help out,' Keeley said.

'But she also wants to get out of the love nest she's living in. She says Jill needs the space to be with her man. She was giving out yards about it earlier on.'

'Ah stop!' Liv said. 'It's lovely for Jill. I'm surprised at Róisín being so cranky about it.'

'I don't think she means any harm,' Keeley said. 'But it's more a case of three's a crowd and all that.'

'Well I think it sounds as if she's being a jealous little cow. I hope she doesn't expect people to be excited for her if she ever manages to get a man,' Liv snapped. 'Mind you, the way she's going I don't think there's any danger of that.'

Keeley was about to reprimand Liv and tell her that she was the one being cranky but figured it wasn't the right moment. Liv was stressed and she needed to make allowances for her right now.

Doug was at Liv's house when they pulled up. He waved and jumped up and down like a small child.

'What is he like?' Liv grinned. 'Where on earth did you find him, Mum?'

'He's one of a kind, I'll give him that,' Keeley said with a smile.

They had lunch and for once the sun decided to make an appearance, so Doug and Keeley pottered in the garden with the children while Liv made a bed on the sofa and watched television.

Keeley made dinner for them all.

'This is lovely,' Liv said. 'Thanks, Mum and Dad, it was such a relief to be out of that hospital and back in my own place. Your cooking is slightly better than the muck they serve in there.'

'I should hope so too!' Keeley laughed.

'Did you clean up?' Liv asked.

'We all helped,' Keeley said. 'I think you've been getting a bit behind with things lately.'

'But she'll be grand again now, won't you, love?' Doug said.

Keeley looked over at Liv and wasn't quite as optimistic.

By the time they'd cleared away after dinner and put the children in bed, Róisín reappeared.

'Hey sis. Good to see you looking more like your old self,' she said. 'Is it OK if I crash here for a bit? Did Mum tell you the cottage has become a love shack?'

'So I hear,' Liv said looking cross. 'I believe you're being a right nark about poor Jill's happiness.'

'No . . . not at all . . . I was only saying it's . . .'

'I know what you were saying,' Liv snapped. 'You need to think outside of yourself sometimes, Róisín. Life isn't perfect for anyone. So, enough of the pity-party. You're a successful businesswoman. So if you want to stay here, that's fine. But don't think you can sit around looking like your world is ending. If you can be helpful and pleasant, you're welcome. If not, sling your hook.'

Liv walked into her bedroom and slammed the door. Róisín, Keeley and Doug stood staring at one another open-mouthed.

'Did I miss something?' Róisín asked.

'If you did, I missed it too, love,' Doug said.

'I'll go and have a word with her,' Keeley said.

'I'll put the kettle on,' Róisín said, looking ashen-faced.

Doug got a call from Jimmy and said he'd slip away. 'I'll leave you girls to it,' he said.

Keeley went into the sitting room and sat down. She

was glad there were no new guests checking in at the B&B. They were all away at a wedding so she knew there was no rush for her to get back just yet.

Róisín made a pot of tea and they sat in the living room and tried to take stock of things.

'Tell me about your day,' said Keeley. 'I could do with some good news. Any more excitement with your new business plans?'

'Afraid not. It seems Mr Grace's other offer is substantial, much more than mine.'

'So will he give the building to you, seeing as you've been so loyal in the past?' she asked.

'Sadly not,' Róisín said. 'Who can blame him? He's only looking after his sons' best interests. My little emporium clearly only means something to me.'

Keeley sighed. 'I wish we could do something to help you financially, love. What are you thinking of doing?'

'I honestly don't know, Mum,' she said. 'But I've decided on one thing. I'm not letting go of Nourriture without a fight.'

'Good on you, love,' Keeley said. She stared at Róisín. 'What else is bothering you?'

Róisín swallowed hard. She sighed deeply and dropped her chin to her chest.

'There's an unresolved issue . . . One I thought could be kept on the back-burner. But I need to deal with it sooner rather than later.'

'Go on.'

'Mum, Jacques is dead.'

'Oh dear . . . I had no idea . . . what happened?'

'It was a boating accident,' Róisín said. 'I got a letter from his mother, Vivienne, a while ago.'

'And you never mentioned it?'

'No, I didn't want to talk about him.'

'Hi.'

Keeley and Róisín turned to see Liv standing there looking sheepish.

'Hey Liv,' Róisín said. 'How are you feeling?'

'Like the biggest thundering bitch in the universe. I'm so sorry I've been so vile. Especially to you, Ro. I'm so proud of everything you've achieved. I don't deserve you and I'm so, so, so sorry.'

'You are a horrible cow,' Róisín said standing up to hug her. 'But you're also my sister. So no matter what you do, you're stuck with me.'

'Can you forgive me?' Liv asked.

'I'll see,' Róisín said with a smile. 'Of course, you goon. Come and sit.'

'Sorry, Mum,' she said as Keeley smiled.

'Come and sit with us. Róisín is just about to tell me something important. Go on . . . what happened with you and Jacques, love?'

'We had our lives all planned out,' Róisín said. 'But he bailed on me. I couldn't think of what to do, so I fled.'

'Did he go off with another woman?'

'No Mum,' she said as tears coursed down her cheeks. 'He wanted a family,' she continued. 'He longed for children and I was all on for it too. But things weren't simple. He had mumps as a child. It left him practically sterile.'

'What do you mean practically?' Keeley asked.

'He was told that the only way he would father a child was with the help of IVF.'

Keeley nodded and took Róisín's hand.

Róisín explained to Keeley and Liv what had happened.

How she'd known the joy of being a mother for those ten short weeks and how Jacques had distanced himself from her when she needed him most. How they'd argued about her not wanting to commit to living in France and telling her family her plans.

'Oh Róisín,' Keeley said, as she too began to cry.

'That's just heartbreaking,' Liv said, reaching out to hold Róisín's hand.

'We figured the most sensible thing would be to freeze the embryos. So that's what happened. Our relationship took a nose-dive, I saw him kissing another woman, so I ran home.'

'Oh darling, I wish you'd told me,' Keeley said looking stricken.

'How could you come back here and not tell us?' Liv asked in astonishment. 'You must've been hurting so much. I'm so sorry I wasn't there for you.'

'I couldn't say it out loud . . . I couldn't begin to talk about it. I figured if I kept it all inside that I would heal more quickly. That it would be the same as any ordinary break-up . . .'

'But when you heard he'd died, you knew you needed to make a decision about the embryos . . .' Keeley finished.

She nodded. 'Vivienne doesn't know anything,' Róisín was quick to add. 'The letter was purely to let me know what had happened.'

'What are you thinking of doing?' Liv asked.

'Well, we both signed an agreement to say that the embryos couldn't be used unless both parties were in agreement. Now that he's dead, I'm guessing I can't have them implanted.'

'Is that what you want?' Keeley asked.

Róisín shrugged. 'I've thought of it non-stop since getting Vivienne's letter. But how could I even consider being a mother when I've no home and possibly no job?'

'You're still very young, love,' Keeley reminded her. 'You have so many years ahead to think about starting a family.'

'I need to meet someone first,' she said dryly. 'Unless I try to get those embryos implanted.'

'I'd think long and hard before you go rushing off to get pregnant on your own,' Liv said. 'It's no picnic.'

'It's not easy,' Keeley was quick to agree. 'But it's also the most rewarding and wonderful thing in the world. If you decide to try and have a baby, I'll always be here for you. You know that, don't you?'

'Thanks Mum,' she said as she began to cry.

'Wait a minute,' Liv said. 'Don't think being a mum is all smiles and cuteness. Look at how much you put into Nourriture. I'm guessing you give it no less than 100 per cent, am I right?'

Róisín nodded.

'Well try continuing that and adding a baby into the equation. You'll have to find another 100 per cent from thin air to put into the baby. Don't get me wrong,' she held her good arm aloft. 'I adore my kids. But being a mother is probably the most difficult job any woman can ever have.'

Róisín looked at her sister. Sitting there, she looked tired, hunched, stressed and – much as she hated to even think it – miserable. She certainly wasn't an advert for motherhood in her current state.

Liv actually looked haunted. Róisín's heart went out to her. How had the two of them ended up in such turmoil? They were both a mess. There wasn't much joy in their lives right now. Sighing, Róisín guessed that no matter what she decided, at least one thing was for sure: a change, any change in her life right now would be most welcome.

Chapter 27

THE TWO SPARE BEDROOMS WERE STILL UNOCCU-
pied since the students' departure, so Róisín had chosen
the one with a view of the ocean. She'd finally gone to
the cottage and packed all her stuff into boxes and was
using Liv's car to move it all. Much as she loved her own
Fiat 500, she knew it wasn't suited to being a removal
van. To make it easier to move her stuff inside, she drove
to the rear of the house and let herself in the back door.

There was no sign of the children and Liv was on the
phone. She seemed to be having an argument.

Róisín didn't want her sister thinking she was ear-
wigging so she walked into the kitchen and waved. By
the time she'd finished unpacking the car, Liv was off the
phone.

She was red eyed but seemed to be making a concerted
effort to smile so Róisín decided not to push her to talk.

'Glass of wine?' she offered.

'Eh, maybe not just yet. Where are the children?'

'Ever the worrier,' she said. 'They're having a sleepover
with Martin's sister. It's hardly a crime to want a glass of
wine while I have a free evening for a change. You need
to loosen out a bit. No wonder you're single.'

Róisín walked toward her bedroom. Liv followed her.

'Hey, I'm sorry, Ro. That was bitchy. I'm not in good

form right now, that's all. Lately I've lost a lot of my human-ness. I knew the house was turning into a skip and I wasn't able to care. I wasn't even able for the kids,' she said. 'I feel so ashamed. I've been the worst mother and wife.'

'No you weren't,' Róisín said. 'It's hard for you being here alone so much. And besides, the children are so small they won't remember. I mean, it's not as if you left them locked in a room with a bar of chocolate while you went off to the pub.'

'I know,' she said. 'I'll make it up to them once I start to feel better. Oh when I think of those foreign students . . . Ugh, the shame of it . . .'

'Listen, I can draft up a letter that we can send to the agency to explain. I'm sure they'd pass on your apologies to the girls. I know this is dreadful of me, but you'll never see them again, so put it out of your mind. You can't fix every misdemeanour in your life, so there's no point in beating yourself up.'

'Thanks Róisín,' Liv said. 'So how was it, collecting your stuff from the cottage?'

'Strangely enough, Jill was really emotional! Odd seeing as I'm the one moving out. She was funny, though, her main worry is that she won't have anyone to watch *My Big Fat Gypsy Wedding* with. Apparently Gordon doesn't get it.'

'Aw poor Jill! Tell her to come here and she can watch whatever she likes with us.' They were flicking through the channels when Róisín's mobile rang.

'Hello?'

'Hi Róisín, it's Rob here.'

'Ah hi Rob,' she said. 'How are you? Sorry, can you hold on for one second?'

She covered the phone with her hand and mouthed to Liv that it was a supplier and she needed to talk to him about an order. She rushed to her bedroom and shut the door.

'Sorry about that, Rob. So how are you?'

'Not too bad, thanks. Yourself?'

'Yeah, OK. I'm actually in the process of moving house. I'm staying with my sister for a while as it happens.'

'Oh right. Listen it's really short notice, but I need to go to Galway for a couple of days and I was going to leave now and come straight to Ballyshore on my way. I got a room in a guesthouse in the village so if it suited, maybe we could meet up for a drink? No pressure at all . . . it probably doesn't suit if you're in the middle of moving.'

'Let me just clear it with my sister. She's not feeling great at the moment so I might need to stick around with her.'

As she made her way back to the living room, Róisín heard voices and was surprised to see Liv laughing and joking with her old school friends Mags and Sheena.

'The girls have dropped by,' she said, stating the obvious. Gone was the forlorn look of earlier and it was clear Liv was preparing for a girly night of giggles and tipples.

'You OK if I head out for a bit?' Róisín asked while waving at the others.

'Sure. You going on a hot date?' Liv teased.

'Nothing like that,' Róisín said. 'Just meeting a supplier for a bit.'

The girls continued chatting and Róisín went back to Rob as she walked back to her bedroom.

'I'd love to get out for a bit. Give me a shout when you're near the village.'

'Perfect,' he said. 'See you then. Bye.' He hung up before she could respond.

Róisín finished her unpacking and had a quick shower. Not wanting to drink and drive, she accepted the offer of a glass of wine with the girls and planned to order a taxi to take her to the Thatch.

'Ooh it's a date so?' Liv said with a grin, when she said who she was meeting.

'Hardly,' she replied. 'He's a nice guy, but he's more like my brother, you know?'

'Yeah. Millions might believe you, sister dear, but I know you too well. You're counting down the minutes until you meet him. I can see it in your eyes.'

'I am not!' she giggled.

Thankfully the conversation turned to Keeley's birthday, and Róisín asked the girls to come up with fun ideas for it. Rob texted to say he was five minutes away so she called a taxi and grabbed a denim jacket and her bag.

'See you later,' she said.

'Don't do anything we wouldn't do,' Liv yelled back as the others giggled. 'Which gives you plenty of scope!'

Rob was already sitting at a table in the Thatch when she walked in.

'Hi, how are you?' he asked smiling warmly. 'Hope I didn't interrupt your evening?'

'Not at all, I was actually glad to get out! It's like a witches' coven at Liv's place. Her children are off being minded, her husband is working away and her school friends are there. They'll be swinging out of the lights before long! I love a bit of craic, but they're kind of on a different level to me.'

'How so?' he asked as he ordered her a drink.

'Ah, they're all married with kids and their nights together are filled with chats about husbands and how hard it is being a mother. They're lovely, but I guess they're on another wavelength.'

'I know what you mean,' he said. 'All my friends are either engaged or married with kids at this stage, too.'

'Have you thought any more about popping the question?' she asked.

He pulled a face. 'That's kind of why I've run away for a couple of days. My dad and I had a chat and he's said he doesn't want me marrying Theresa unless it's what I truly want.'

'And is it?' Róisín asked.

'I was convinced I was being pressurised into it. I was happily blaming it all on my father. But now that he's taken his foot off my head, I'm a bit lost.'

'I see,' Róisín nodded. 'Listen, you've probably chosen the wrong person to ask for advice on marriage.'

'Have you ever had a long-term relationship?' he asked.

Róisín regarded him. He was a supplier. A work associate. Yet, she found him so easy to chat to. Pushing that fact aside, she decided to order them another drink and answer the question.

'I was with a man in France . . .' she said and proceeded to tell him all about Jacques. She looked at the table when it came to the part about the IVF.

'I got a letter recently,' she said and told him what had happened. It actually felt good to talk it over, and she let the whole story spill out.

'Wow,' he said whistling. 'I'm so sorry to hear that. You must be heartbroken.'

'I'm really sad that Jacques died. Of course I am. But we weren't right for one another. There was never a chance we would get back together. But I've been left with a decision. I contacted the fertility clinic to ask them what my options are.'

'What did they say?'

'Nothing. I've had no response yet.'

'Would you like to . . . implant them?' he asked.

'I don't know . . .' There was the truth. That's what was really bothering her. 'What if those frozen embryos are my only chance of having a family of my own?'

'Why would it be?' he asked. 'I'm not trying to be smart here, but who's to say you won't meet someone and have a baby?'

'I'm thirty. We had problems conceiving which was why we did the IVF. There's nobody on the horizon. I live in Ballyshore and work in a small business. What are the odds?'

'Lots of people come in and out of your life each and every day,' Rob argued. 'You never know when the man of your dreams might waltz in and order a tub of pâté!' She grinned. But it was only fleeting.

'I'm not very good at this,' she admitted.

'What? Making decisions?'

'No, talking about my innermost thoughts . . .'

'Me neither,' he said.

'God, you could've fooled me. You're really open and chatty,' said Róisín.

'It depends who I'm talking to,' he said sheepishly. 'I'm going to have to make a choice and stick to it. I've given myself a deadline. I'll decide by the end of the summer. By the end of August I'll either be engaged or a free agent.' He shuffled his feet on the floor. 'I wish I had my mother to advise me actually. It's times like these when I need her more than ever.'

He sat back and sighed. 'Nothing is simple, is it?' he said. 'If I ever have children, I really hope I'll be a good father and that their mother is there too. That's the ideal, isn't it? Some people dream of winning the Lottery, I'd settle for a complete family where everyone looks out for one another.'

Róisín felt like sobbing. He was the most lovely guy she'd met in a long time. They were both deep in thought for a while until he broke the silence.

'You know what I think you should do? I think you should sit down with your parents and ask them all the questions you've been suppressing. Go for it. They love you and want you to be happy. They know you love them. Do it.'

'And you need to make a decision as to whether you want to settle for a woman you don't really love or set yourself free and allow your heart to find what you truly deserve.'

There was a moment when their eyes met. She could barely breathe. She wanted to say that she didn't mean he should find someone like her . . . that he should find someone he was comfortable with, someone who made him laugh . . . instead of digging herself in deeper, she just stayed quiet.

'Let's have another drink and talk about something mundane like the weather,' he said. 'We always seem to end up having very deep chats!'

They stuck to their guns and talked about everything from their favourite cocktail to what they'd do if they did win the Lottery – this time Rob talked about fast cars and luxurious cruises rather than a wife and children.

Róisín couldn't believe it when Joseph came over and told them it was an hour past closing time.

'I left you to chat while I cleaned up, but I'll be prosecuted if the police catch you here at this time.'

They thanked him and walked out onto the street. Róisín dialled for a taxi, knowing it would take at least fifteen minutes. They sat on the wall overlooking the sea and listened to the water lapping against the rocks. There was still a good bit of brightness in the sky.

'I love this time of night,' she said. 'It's as if the world is holding onto the day by its fingernails. Not wanting to let go.'

'Which is kind of ironic seeing as it will all begin again in a few hours,' he said.

They sat in companionable silence until the lights from the taxi invaded the inkiness of the air.

'I hope you find the answers you need,' she said as she stood up to leave.

'I will,' he said. 'I have a deadline now. I've said it out loud so it's legally binding!'

'Sleep well, and pop in for some breakfast or lunch if you feel like it,' she said. He waved and then clearly thought better of it and walked over and kissed her on the cheek. She inhaled his musky scent and had to stop herself closing her eyes. Turning around she rushed to the taxi and waved as she departed.

She opened the front door gently and crept in the door, not wanting to disturb Liv. As she walked to the living room, the sight that met her made her gasp. The girls were gone and Liv was passed out on the floor with a half bottle of port beside her.

'Oh Liv, bad choice, lovie. Your head will feel that in the morning.'

Being careful not to bang her burnt and bandaged arm, Róisín managed to pull her sister into her room. Removing her jeans, she tucked her into bed and left the door open in case she needed her. She put a glass of water and paracetamol on the bedside locker.

As she lay in her own bed a few moments later, all thoughts of Rob were tossed aside as she worried about Liv and how she seemed to be coming apart at the seams.

Chapter 28

NELL HAD ALWAYS ENJOYED HER EARLY MORNING cup of tea. This morning, as Mouse was sleeping in after their expedition to the city, she savoured the now rare silence.

She'd been longing to look at the newspapers properly. She grabbed the local one first and pored over the stories of interest in the area. Apparently Ballyshore was experiencing a huge increase in tourism. The newly finished playground was partially to thank, along with the annual food festival.

She smiled as she stared at the photo of Mouse, posing with one hand on her hip and one leg bent. The wind had caught her caramel-coloured hair and was blowing it prettily to one side.

There were six full pages of pictures of people taking part in the race, people eating pancakes, people pushing prams and lots of beaming faces as they sat in the sun drinking cool beer. The village had come a long way over the years. She cut out some of the photos and stuck them into her book.

As always, she wondered what might have become of Laura if she'd lived. Would she still be here or would she have stayed away?

'Hey,' Mouse said appearing in bare feet and startling her.

'Hi,' Nell said. 'You're up early.'

'Yeah, I've got a plan. I'd like to do something,' she said looking shy.

'What's that?'

'I want to try and read the first page of the yellow book.'

'OK,' Nell said rushing to find it. 'Now take your time and don't be disappointed if you find it difficult at first.'

Mouse put it onto the table and peeled back the cover. She leaned forward and inhaled the fresh smell.

At first she faltered and used her finger to trace each word. Her voice became stronger and less hesitant as she progressed. In what seemed like seconds later she was finished. She looked up at Nell.

'What are you crying for?' she asked.

'I'm so proud of you. You're some girl, do you know that?' Nell said shaking her head in awe. 'If I had a brass band in the cupboard, I'd bring them out now! You are brilliant.'

'Thanks,' Mouse said. 'I can't believe I did it, Nell.'

'Do you realise there's no stopping you now? If you can learn to read that whole page, with a little more time you will read every single word you see!'

Mouse gripped the book and looked as if she was deep in thought.

'What's going on in that head of yours?' Nell asked.

'Do you think I could try for a job?'

'Well,' Nell hesitated. She didn't want to dash the girl's hopes, but she hadn't any qualifications so it might be difficult just at the moment.

'You see I saw an advert. The last time we were at the village. In the window of the pub, I sounded it out and I'm sure it said Help Wanted.'

'Well it would be worth a try,' said Nell, 'but they might want to know if you've any experience.'

'I spent most of my childhood in pubs or outside of them, does that count?' she asked with a grin.

'You never know,' Nell said. 'Go and make yourself look neat and tidy and I'll take you to the village in the car.'

Nell made toast and fresh tea for them to share and by the time Mouse reappeared it was ready.

'I don't want anything,' Mouse said looking terrified.

'Have a little bit and then you won't fall over in fear.'

There wasn't much chat in the car and Nell figured it was best to leave Mouse to gather her thoughts.

'Will you come in with me?' Mouse asked. Nell wanted to say no, but the pleading in the young girl's eyes softened her.

'I don't think I'll exactly help your cause, but I'll stay at the door if that makes you feel better.'

They knocked on the locked door and waited. After a few minutes the door was flung open.

'What can I do for you, ladies?' Joseph asked. 'We don't open for another little while.'

'I'm here to ask about a job,' Mouse said. 'I'd like to try and do it if you'd give me a shot.'

'I see, Miss Mouse, and have you a CV with you?' he asked.

'A what?'

'A CV, with the details of what you've done before and all your information.'

'Any information I need is in here,' Mouse said knocking on her own head. 'As for the experience, that's easy because I have none. But I'd do whatever you need. I've never actually had a job before. But I really want one. I'm starting a new life, you see. I was in Dublin and it was shi— terrible. Ma died and I came here to be with Nell.'

'She's living with me up at the lighthouse,' Nell confirmed.

'I heard as much,' said Joseph. He scratched his chin and looked at Mouse. 'Would you serve the food and do what the chef tells you? He can be a bit of a nark. Would you be able for him?'

'I grew up in the flats with two brothers who would've happily stamped me into the dirt and I never let them. So I'm sure your chef will be a pussy cat in comparison.'

'I'll give you a trial for a week,' he said.

'No way!' Mouse said, looking from him to Nell. Nell smiled and winked at her.

'Thanks so much, Joseph. I won't let you down. I don't rob and I won't curse at the customers.'

'Well, that's all good,' he said.

'When will I start?'

He looked at his watch and over at Nell. She nodded at him.

'Now?'

'Deadly,' she said. 'I'd nothing on this afternoon apart from practising my reading. I'm only learning, but I'm doing well and I try really hard.'

He looked at Mouse and Nell noticed a flash of sympathy.

'You sound like you're making all sorts of great changes in your life, Mouse. I'd say your mother is watching over you and proud as punch.'

Mouse beamed.

'Does she need something specific to wear?' Nell asked.

'I have Aertex tops with the pub name on them,' he

said. 'I'll give her a couple and the jeans she has on are perfect.'

'What time will I collect her later?' Nell asked.

'Four o'clock, if that suits?' Joseph said. 'We'll see how we go today and if we're both happy, we'll fill out a form later on. Is that fair?'

Mouse nodded.

Nell thanked Joseph and quickly scribbled her phone number on a piece of paper then wandered back outside with Mouse in tow.

'Can you believe it?' she said with her eyes shining. 'I have a real job, Nell!'

'You're a superstar,' Nell said. 'I am so proud. Now take your time and listen to what you're being asked to do. I'll see you at four. If you have any issues, call me.'

Nell couldn't stop smiling as she drove back to the light-house. By the time she'd finished a cup of coffee and done her usual morning checks, she felt mildly bereft. Looking around, she realised how accustomed she'd become to Mouse's company. This pain was nothing like the all-consuming horror after Laura's death, but it was a sad reminder all the same.

A wave of dread swept over Nell. She'd let Mouse in. Not just into the lighthouse, but into her heart. She'd vowed she wasn't ever going to do that with another person after Laura. She hadn't meant to become attached to her, but now that Mouse was here, Nell couldn't imagine being on her own again.

The hours dragged until it was time to collect Mouse. Nell hated herself for clock-watching but she couldn't help it.

There was a parking space close to the Thatch, so Nell

pulled in and waited nervously, hoping it hadn't gone disastrously wrong. Just after four o'clock Mouse appeared and looked around. She beeped the horn and waved. Mouse's face lit up and she ran to the car and jumped in.

'Well?' Nell asked cagily.

'I rocked it,' Mouse said looking as if she'd burst with excitement. 'Joseph is dead-on. He's really good at explaining stuff and he told me that if I keep going the way I was today, I'll have a permanent job!'

'That's amazing,' Nell said. 'Not that I had any doubts about you.'

'I got the form to fill out. Will you help me when we get home?'

Nell's eyes misted over as she nodded and turned on the car. Mouse had called the lighthouse home.

'I missed you today,' Nell said out of the blue as they drove along the narrow road approaching the lighthouse. 'I've become used to having you around. I'm not a fluffy person, as you may have gathered. But I believe some things happen for a reason. After so many years of bitterness and heartache, I think you were guided to me. Probably by your mother and my Laura. We're both a bit broken and I guess it works. Who knows, maybe we'll fix each other a little bit.'

They arrived at the lighthouse and as they walked past the photograph on the hall table just inside the front door, Mouse paused.

'I'd love to know the end of the story,' she said quietly, 'when you're ready to tell it.'

Nell went and sat at the kitchen table. 'After Australia, you mean?'

Mouse nodded and came and sat down next to her.

Nell took a deep breath. 'When Laura told me about going to see her father, we had the most horrific fight. I told her she was forbidden to leave me. She fought back like a caged tiger and lashed out, telling me I was the worst mother and the worst person on the planet. That I'd ruined her life and she hated me.'

'Oh Nell,' Mouse said. 'Poor you.'

'Ah I've mulled it over in my head. For years I've mulled it over,' she said. 'And I know Laura was partially right. I held her back in lots of ways. I used her sickness so I could withdraw from the world.'

'That's not true,' Mouse said emphatically.

'Why do you say that?'

'Because Laura has been gone a long time and you're still here living in your lighthouse, hiding. So you didn't actually use her as an excuse. You just brought her with you.'

'I never thought of it that way,' Nell said. 'Anyway, there's no point in looking back. What's done is done. My Laura is gone and nothing would ever have changed that outcome, unfortunately.'

'Did she die in Australia?' Mouse asked.

Nell shook her head. She sat in total silence for quite a while. Lost in the memories that clearly still caused so much pain.

'She was gone for almost a year. Eleven months to be exact.'

'Did you talk regularly?'

Nell shook her head. 'Only once. She phoned to say that she'd arrived safely and her father had collected her at the airport. She sounded so happy and said it was amazing there.'

'What a bitch,' Mouse said before clapping her hand over her mouth. 'Oh I'm sorry,' she said. 'I didn't mean . . .'

'Don't worry, Mouse, I had the very same reaction. I told her she was a traitor, that she was an ungrateful little witch, that I'd dedicated my life to her and she'd turned her back on me.'

'But she knew you didn't mean it, right?'

'Oh I meant every word of it,' Nell said. 'I was so hurt and so consumed with jealousy at hearing about the fine house and the swimming pool and the four half-siblings, three girls and a boy, who had welcomed her with open arms . . . the glamorous Australian wife called Daisy who cried when she hugged my Laura . . . it was all too much of a smack in the face.'

'I'd say you felt like getting on a flight and finding that smug family and beating them to a pulp.'

Nell laughed. 'That's kind of a violent example of what I felt like doing, but yes . . . ashamed as I am to admit it, I was devastated. I think what hurt me the most was the way that Laura seemed able to forgive her father for leaving us. I mean, I was the one who was left holding the baby and yet I ended up on my own.'

'There's nothing fair about that. Did your ex make any contact with you while Laura was living with him?'

'No,' she said. 'Not for a long time. He probably didn't really feel there was much point, and he had his own thing going on. Whatever about Laura, I was surplus to requirements.'

'That sucks,' Mouse said. 'It was as if they tossed you aside . . . as if you were worthless . . . that's not right.'

'That was how I viewed it, too. But actually they were just a normal family. Daisy had no idea Laura even existed until she turned up at their house. His four kids were just as surprised, but they instantly embraced her and treated her like one of them.'

'Didn't a tiny part of you hope that she'd have a terrible time and come home with her tail between her legs?'

'Of course, Mouse. I wouldn't be human if I didn't feel that way. But hindsight is a great thing and knowing that they were so kind to Laura has given me great comfort and peace of mind since she passed away. I'm glad she lived her final days in happiness.'

'So she died in Australia?' Mouse asked again.

Nell didn't really want to get into that part. But felt she had to give the girl an answer.

'No, she came back here. She realised she was truly at the end of the road and when push came to shove, she chose to be with me in the end.'

'I'm glad you were with her,' Mouse said. 'At least you got to say goodbye.'

'We had six weeks together. We talked incessantly. We tried to squash our whole lives into that time. I savoured each and every conversation, and I know Laura did too.'

Mouse got up and hugged her. 'Thanks for telling me. I'm going to take a shower, if that's OK? Could we fill out the form afterwards?'

Nell nodded and Mouse left the room. Nell looked to the ceiling.

'Thank you, darling,' she whispered. 'I don't know if I deserve a second chance after what I did . . . I couldn't cope after you died. I wish I had done things differently. I won't mess up this time.'

Chapter 29

DOUG WAS TAKING BILLY AND JESS OUT ON THE boat for the day. Keeley had packed a picnic and waved them off. She needed a few essentials, so she drove around the bay and stopped by Nourriture to say hello to Róisín on her way to the supermarket. She was shocked by her daughter's appearance.

'What happened you?' she said, looking at her pale complexion and panda eyes.

'I didn't get much sleep,' she admitted.

'She was panned out on the chair up at her desk when I came in to make the breads this morning,' Brigid said as she breezed by. 'And the smell of alcohol was so strong, I was nervous about lighting the gas ovens!'

'Is everything alright, love?' Keeley asked.

'I'm fine Mum, I need today to be over and done with and I'll go to bed and wake up feeling normal tomorrow. Either that or I'll keel over and die at any moment.'

'Where were you? Did Jill drag you out celebrating?'

'Something like that,' Róisín said brushing over it. She was about to tell her mother that the real reason she was so under the weather was that she'd been lying awake waiting for Liv to start choking on her own vomit, but the shop was too busy to get into it. Besides, her mum seemed to be in such good form she didn't want to upset her.

As she waited for her coffee, Keeley was delighted to see Claus arrive.

'Hello!' she said cheerfully. 'How are you today?'

'Not too bad,' he said. 'I'm feeling better every day, in fact. I think the Irish air is good for my soul.'

'Will you join me for a coffee?' Keeley said. 'I've been abandoned. Doug has taken the grandchildren out for a day of boating. They're headed to one of the little islands for a picnic and I've got a few free hours.'

'I'd love that,' he said, taking his wallet from his pocket to pay.

'They're on me,' Róisín said waving his money away. 'Family friends get special treatment. If you'll excuse me, I've to go up to my office and try not to die.'

'See you later, love,' Keeley said, shaking her head and smiling. 'I don't think I've seen Róisín so hung-over in years. It'll do her good, mind you,' Keeley confided. 'She works so hard and never takes time to herself.'

'She's very pleased with her shop, isn't she?' Claus said.

'It's not just a shop, Claus,' Keeley said. 'She does all sorts of foodie events and she absolutely eats, sleeps and breathes her trade. She built this place from nothing.'

'What was here before Nourriture?'

'It was vacant for a long time and Róisín took it on to see if she could make it work. Lots of the locals thought she was mad. The pub at the end of the village was the only place to eat and it was and still is very busy. But nobody thought there'd be a calling for a food emporium like this.'

'And the supermarket isn't great,' said Claus. 'Now that I'm actually living here, I'm realising how limited it is. I guess from living in Germany, I have become accustomed to having a large and varied supermarket on my doorstep.'

'When you live in the country it's not a big deal to drive and find shops. This village is all about the scenery and the beauty. Nourriture and the thatched roof of the pub and the fact that the supermarket is almost apologising for its existence means the place isn't destroyed. Besides, as you well know, it's a hub of activity so I don't think the tourists and locals object to the way it is now.'

They finished their coffee and Claus suggested a walk. 'If you're busy, I understand. I don't want you thinking I'm some poor widower who needs you to mind me.'

'I don't,' she said with a smile. 'I'd love a walk along the beach.'

As they fell into step with one another, Keeley took a deep cleansing breath. She adored her surroundings and couldn't imagine living any place else, but it made her feel a little sad that she had to share these precious moments with a veritable stranger. As if reading her mind, Claus spoke.

'I miss Heidi. I always thought she would accompany me at this point in our lives. It's so peaceful and beautiful here. I wish she could've seen it.'

'Well,' Keeley confided, 'my husband is still alive but I never seem to see him. I too thought I'd have more time so Doug and I could do things together. I'd made a pact with myself that this would be the last summer for the B&B. It's all too much and I'm too tied to it. But I've been realising that I might be very much out on a limb if I don't keep it going.'

'Doug seems like a very nice fellow,' Claus said. 'But if I had you, I would cherish you. You're right to want a slower pace and more of the enjoyable things than work.'

'I'll be sixty soon,' she said. 'Róisín wants to organise a big party for me.'

'That's a nice idea,' he said. 'You more than deserve it. I hope you will agree.'

'A part of me would love it and another part of me just longs to do something low-key that would involve all the people I love. Since Liv's accident and Róisín's present upheaval, it's put things in perspective.'

'How is Liv doing?' he asked.

'She's in much better form and we've worked out a good rota so that she's being helped out in a constructive way. But she's different. I can't put my finger on it. I've tried talking to her so many times, but it seems the more I push, the more irritated she becomes. I'm just hoping she gets over this hump soon.'

'Correct me if I'm wrong here,' Claus said, 'but Liv seems to be the more needy one? Róisín is the one who can manage with most things, yes?'

'That's pretty fair to say.' Keeley sighed.

'Róisín's very like her mother,' Claus said with a smile.

'That's the amazing part,' Keeley said. 'She's adopted and Liv isn't.'

'Oh, I had no idea.'

'We were told we'd never have children, so we adopted Róisín. Then Liv came along three years later by some incredible miracle. But it's always amazed me that I see so much of myself in Róisín.'

'It proves that children pick up a lot of their personality traits and values from their parents, whether biological or not.'

'I know. She's having a tough time right now as well, but she's coping with such strength.'

'What's wrong with Róisín?' he asked.

Keeley hesitated. She wasn't used to discussing her family with strangers. She usually had Doug for that. It seemed a little disloyal.

'She's having a spot of bother with her business. But it's nothing she can't sort out,' Keeley said.

Claus stopped walking. 'You can trust me, Keeley,' he said. 'I promise you I won't judge your girls or you. If you need to talk, I'm here and more than happy to listen.'

'Thank you,' she said, but chose not to continue the conversation. Claus seemed to respect that and Keeley was grateful. They finished their walk and he invited her to see his rental property.

'It's actually lovely inside,' she said in awe. 'Much brighter and airier than I'd expected.'

'It's great,' he said. 'I love the sea view and the proximity to the village.'

'It's probably a nice change from your own home too. Is it easier to be here rather than at home without Heidi?'

'Very much so,' he said. 'I haven't decided how long I will stay. As long as I need, I guess.'

Keeley knew she needed to get home, so she thanked Claus for his company and said she'd see him again soon. As she drove up to the B&B several minutes later, Keeley turned off the engine and sat motionlessly staring at the house. This place had been her saviour once upon a time. It had given her a livelihood and a sense of purpose. She could enter the *Guinness Book of Records* for the amount of sheets changed in one decade . . . but now, she mused, life was about far more than perfect corners on bedsheets, dust-free skirting boards and fresh scones. Keeley realised she'd been living her life through an invisible microscope for years. She'd zoned in on every little problem and tried to solve it. She'd spent long enough in a downward stare, she needed to lift her head and look up and enjoy the view.

Ida's face flashed before her. The poor woman was younger than she was now and her life had ended . . . and as for Róisín's birth mother, she'd missed out on raising, loving and knowing her incredible girl. Lives could be extinguished so swiftly and unexpectedly, without warning. She had no right to waste the time she'd been given. It was up to her to make the most of the precious life she was living, right here, right now.

As she opened the car door and stood out, she turned to look at the water across the road. The small inlet seemed to be opening its arms and welcoming the infinite expanse of the sea. There were so many opportunities open to her. She shouldn't feel shackled or bogged down. She should embrace life and rejoice in all it had to offer.

Feeling as if a weight had been lifted from her, she walked purposefully into the house. Her mind was made up. She wasn't taking any more bookings. She needed more time for herself and more than that, she was sick of working like a slave. The B&B had more than served its purpose, so why should she continue with it now?

Feeling rejuvenated and relieved, Keeley began to plan her birthday party in her head. She would use the evening to make her announcement that she too was about to retire. Perhaps if she was a woman of leisure, she and Doug could plan a holiday. After that, the world was their oyster.

Chapter 30

RÓISÍN WANTED TO CRY WHEN BRIGID SHOUTED up the stairs that there was someone there to see her. Staggering down the steps, she stopped short when she saw Rob.

'Hey,' he said. 'How's it going?'

'I've been better,' she said. 'A lot better, in fact.'

'All self-inflicted,' he said. 'I accept no responsibility. I didn't rugby tackle you to the floor and pour drink down your neck.'

'No,' she said with a grin. 'But you weren't exactly a good example.'

'I never said I was a role model,' he said.

'Coffee?' she asked.

He nodded. She walked to the machine and made two cappuccinos and joined him at the window seat, where he was gazing out at the view, his chin on his hands. She put his cup down along with a glass of water and two painkillers.

'Thanks,' he said, grabbing the tablets and swallowing them. 'So much for clearing my head,' he said. 'I might go for a walk on the beach. I don't suppose you'd like to come?'

'I would love nothing more,' she said. 'But I have so much to do here it's not funny. I got practically no sleep.

My sister was worse for wear when I got back and I ended up sleeping with one eye open in case she died in her sleep.'

Claus walked in the door, and Róisín waved.

'Back again?' she said.

He nodded and wandered into the wine shop to have a browse.

'Who's your man?' Rob said stroking his beard. 'He looks familiar.'

'He's a German tourist who stayed at my parents' B&B a while back. He was here with his sister and the poor woman was dying of cancer.'

'So what's he doing back?'

'He lost his wife five years ago and then his sister recently, as I said. This was the last place they were together so he's here to grieve.'

Rob stared in at Claus. 'I could've sworn I've seen him somewhere before.'

'He looks like a typical tourist,' Róisín said. 'The smart clothes and tanned skin and immaculate hair . . . he looks like he even has manicures.'

'I suppose,' Rob said looking puzzled. 'They're a certain look, that's for sure. Not like me and my family! We look like we've just been pulled from a barn and thrown into our clothes. None of that polished look about us.'

'The long hair, shaggy beard and jeans with a T-shirt look is a far cry from Claus and his perfect designer gear for sure,' she smiled. 'That's odd,' she said, peering out the window. 'Claus is gone out the other door from the wine shop without saying goodbye.'

'Is he normally friendly?' he asked.

'Yeah. To be honest, he can be a little bit of a sticky

plaster. I hate saying that because it sounds really mean, but he has a tendency to hang about and look for company. I don't mind a lot of the time, but if I'm super busy it can be a strain.'

'I know what you mean. But I guess he's lonely . . . I can't get it out of my head that I know his face . . . anyway, I'll go and leave you to it. If you can escape, I'll be on the beach gulping in fresh air and trying not to keel over!'

'Enjoy!' she said. 'Hey, are you staying at the guesthouse tonight?'

'Yeah, I'll head off early in the morning, but I think I need one more night off from my life.'

'No pressure, but I'd be happy to give you dinner if you want to drop by after I close? Say, seven? It won't be a late one because I'll need to get back to Liv. But I would love a quiet meal where there aren't ructions with little ones. I adore my niece and nephew, but my delicate head would be a lot better if I'm not hungry when I get home. Besides, Liv's idea of cooking doesn't stretch much past chicken nuggets and tinned pasta hoops.'

'Sounds like an offer I cannot refuse!' he said. 'See you later.'

Nourriture was really busy, spurred on by the clear blue skies and crisp sunlight. All the picnic food sold out and they did a brisk trade on smoothies and ice creams. By the time the shop closed and she filled out the orders for the following day, Róisín could barely stay awake.

She prepared two plates of food and made a jug of refreshing juice with home-made elderflower cordial and sparkling water.

A gentle rap on the door let her know Rob was there.

'How's it going?' she said letting him in. 'How was your afternoon?'

'Nice, thanks,' he said. 'How was yours? There were loads of people on the beach with your signature paper bags, so I'm guessing it was busy.'

'Yeah, I can't complain. It's my own fault coming to work after a skin-full of drink. I never normally do that. You're a terrible influence,' she laughed. 'So did you do some thinking?' she asked as they sat to eat.

'I did, but I'm no clearer,' he said. 'I miss my mother. I know she'd have some simple solution to my worries. And how about you? I know you've been busy all day, but have you had any more thoughts on what you'll do about the clinic?'

'I'd love to be a mother,' she said, only realising how much as she spoke the words. 'More than I think I've allowed myself to believe. But I don't know if I could bear to do it alone. When you said last night that your one wish would be to have a "proper" family, it resonated so strongly with me. When a couple have a baby, each of them is hoping they'll make a good mother or father, right?'

'Sure.'

'But in this case, I'd be entering into the whole thing knowing this baby has a heartbreaking past before it's even born. Is that fair?'

She didn't even feel the tears coming on, but as soon as they started she couldn't stop. He put his hand across the table and took hers. He looked at her with such tenderness, it made her sob even louder.

'Why couldn't I have met someone like you?' she said. There was a silence.

Róisín mentally kicked herself for her outburst. She took

back her hand and wiped her eyes roughly. She took a deep breath to compose herself. 'Thanks for letting me talk,' she said.

'Hey, I could say the same to you. I really appreciate your honesty.'

'Let's talk about you again,' she said with a weak smile. 'Do you know what you're going to do about getting engaged?'

'I think I do,' he said. 'I think the time is almost right. I know where my dad is coming from and I agree with him.'

'Great,' she said, sounding as upbeat as possible.

They hugged and Rob left. As she cleared away the plates and turned the lights off, Róisín was even more confused than ever.

In the car on the way to Liv's house she started to cry again. Bashing the steering-wheel with the heel of her hand, she hated herself for sobbing yet again.

'You bloody fool,' she shouted at herself.

This time Róisín knew exactly why she was crying. She was falling in love with Rob. He was the sweetest and most easy to chat to man she'd ever met. And he was marrying another woman.

Chapter 31

IT WAS SIX IN THE MORNING AND KEELEY WAS WIDE awake. Doug had just left with Jimmy. He'd come home last night looking as if he'd hit the Jackpot.

'I have great news,' he said. 'Jimmy's daughter, Tara, has invited us to her place in Spain. She's going away for a couple of weeks and said she'd be happy for us to take her house.'

'I see,' she said, as anger bubbled through her. 'And what about me? Or Liv? Or Róisín?'

'Liv is on the mend,' he said. 'Róisín is wrapped up in Nourriture and you're busy with the B&B. It makes sense and it'll get me out of your hair.'

Keeley hadn't the energy to argue and felt there was little or no point attempting to tell Doug that she felt tossed aside. So she'd waved him off, fuming on the inside. Not only had he left their wardrobe in a shambles from his high-speed packing, but he'd woken all the guests shouting and frolicking out the front this morning.

The only positive thing was that she was done and dusted with breakfasts nice and early. She decided she needed to do something for herself. So she drove to Ballyshore. She knocked on Claus's door and was relieved to see he was there.

'Doug has gone for two weeks. He and Jimmy are having a bromance and I'm not included. Fancy a coffee?'

'Sure,' he said. 'Why don't you come in and I'll make us one? I never get to do that seeing as I don't have visitors.'

She walked in, feeling as if she was playing hooky from life in general.

'I'm sorry you are feeling so hurt,' Claus said. 'I'm sure Doug is a very nice man but if you don't mind me saying, he's a fool.'

She smiled. 'Thanks and for the record, I agree. In fact, I think he's worse than that. I think he's a selfish idiot who doesn't give a damn about me. He wasn't this self-centred as a young man. Maybe he's having some sort of a crisis.'

'Who knows?' Claus said. 'But I think he should stop and see what he is doing, before it's too late.'

'How do you mean too late?' Keeley asked.

'Well, some other man might see what an incredible woman you are and steal you away from him. That way he can have all the time in the world with this Jimmy.'

'I doubt that would ever happen!' Keeley said with a chuckle. 'For a start, I know all the eligible bachelors for a ten-mile radius and believe me, there's a reason why they're single! Secondly, I think I'm well past the point of attracting a new man. I wouldn't have the inclination or the energy.'

'What if you've already done that without even trying?' Claus said. He looked at the floor. 'I'm sorry. I've said too much . . .'

'Claus?' She looked over at him. 'Are you saying . . .?'

'Forget I said anything,' he said, looking embarrassed.

'I'm even more of a silly old fool than your husband. I am lonely without Heidi and you are the first woman I have found so attractive.'

'You do? You find me attractive?' she asked. Realising she was gaping like a goldfish, Keeley tried to act nonchalant.

'I'm sure you are used to this sort of compliment,' he continued. 'You must have lots of men at your establishment over the years telling you that they would give anything to swap places with Doug?'

'Eh, not really,' Keeley said, not wanting to admit that Claus was the first.

He put a perfect cappuccino down in front of her. 'Please, have your drink and we can pretend I didn't say anything. I don't want to scare you away. I would much rather we are friends that nothing at all. Don't run away now that I have been so foolish.'

Claus sat opposite her and stared at the table. He didn't touch his own cup of coffee and looked utterly tortured.

'Hey,' Keeley said with a sigh. 'Thank you.'

'Pardon?'

'Thank you for making me feel alive again. I've forgotten what it's like to be desired. Even if it's only with words. I was starting to believe that Doug's lack of interest was my fault. As I told you, I'll be sixty soon and I was dreading it.'

'Why so?'

'Well, sixty sounds ancient, doesn't it? When I was younger, I thought sixty-year-olds were life's leftovers!'

'Not any longer,' he said. 'People live for many more years. Sixty is only a number, it's not a bad one either. Especially if you are healthy . . .'

Keeley looked at Claus. He was incredibly polished and attractive with his immaculate hair, his impeccably pressed short-sleeved linen shirt and chino shorts. His skin had a lovely olive tone to it and although his eyes were surrounded by deep crevices, it added a distinguished element that no young man could boast. He was nothing like Doug to look at or speak to. She was ashamed to admit that she found him very appealing.

'I'm feeling very emotional and hard done by, Claus. You're very attractive and you're being ever so nice to me. That's a recipe for disaster.'

She pushed back her chair and walked toward the front door. Claus didn't move.

'Do you have to go, Keeley?' he asked. 'You and I could be so good together. I think you suspect it too. Why did you come to me today? When Doug left, you turned to me first. Why?'

'I . . .' She was at a loss. 'I don't know. I wanted to see you, that's all. But I never meant us to be anything other than friends, Claus. I know Doug is being a fool right now, but we've been married for so long . . .'

'I understand that,' Claus said. 'But sometimes, just because somebody is with you for years, it doesn't mean they should always be there. Love can last a lifetime and sometimes it fades. People change. Situations change. That isn't necessarily a bad thing, you know?'

'I don't think I can take this on board right now, Claus. My daughters are both having troubles . . . It's July, I'm in the middle of the busiest time of the year . . . I can't add to my load . . .'

'Will you come and visit again? Or could we share a walk again? Perhaps when you can feel less uncomfortable?

I enjoy your company and as I said, I would like to have you in my life.'

'I don't know, Claus . . .'

He stood and walked over to her. She flinched.

'I won't hurt you,' he said simply. 'I would look after you and make you as happy as I could. You deserve to be cherished, Keeley. I often wonder how it is that incredible women like you are not made to feel more special.'

She looked at his face. He was so sincere. A massive part of her wanted to throw caution to the wind and tell him that she'd give it a go. Tell him that she'd leave the B&B and come and live with him. Imagine what it would be like having a man like Claus . . .

'We could travel the world,' he said, adding fuel to the embers in her mind. 'We could see the sights and dine in sumptuous restaurants. I would never leave you alone and expect you to work and look after everything. If you would come away with me, Keeley, I know you wouldn't regret it.'

She reached up and stroked his face. A tiny gasp escaped her lips as she turned and ran from the house.

Knowing she needed to gather her thoughts, she climbed into her car and drove home. The B&B was the same as it always had been. The washing she'd hung on the clothesline was flapping away as if waving her off.

A pair of Doug's shoes lay forgotten and discarded in their bedroom. Where was he now? Was he even thinking of her or was he so convinced this time in his life was purely for himself that she didn't figure whatsoever? Would she ever figure again? Should she cut her losses and go with Claus?

An image of her girls flashed through her mind. How

on earth would she even begin to tell them that she was leaving their father and skipping off with her new boyfriend? She giggled uncontrollably as she savoured that word over in her head . . . boyfriend. Well, Claus was hardly a boy! It was wrong of her to even consider the offer. The phone rang, making her jump.

'I'm phoning to make a booking,' said the voice.

'I'm terribly sorry,' she said. 'But I am winding down and closing shortly so I'm not in a position to help you. I can give you phone numbers of other accommodation close by though?' She read out the numbers and hung up.

A tingly feeling washed over her. She realised it was excitement. Once the B&B was closed, she'd be faced with a very real conundrum. What would she do all day? Who would she do it with? She wasn't interested in spending her final years mopping up and cooking for Doug and Jimmy. She was far too old to feel like a hanger-on or some sort of aging groupie with the two men. How wonderful would it be to walk onto a cruise ship on Claus's arm? Or have him take her to dinner and pull out her chair while offering her a glass of wine? Was she losing her marbles?

Her ringtone sang out from her handbag, interrupting her thoughts.

'Hello?' she said.

'Hi, love.'

'Hi, Doug,' she said guardedly. 'How are things?'

'Great. This place is just perfect. I think we should sell the house and buy something out here. There are loads of couples our age. The men all hang out and the women meet for coffee. You should see it, there's a—'

Keeley hung up.

She knew Doug was probably staring at the phone thinking they'd been cut off. She smiled when he called back and let it go to voicemail. She couldn't bear the thought of sitting on plastic seats at a café, gas-bagging with a load of other abandoned wives while Doug played with his friends in some backwater of Spain. Why would she want to do that when she could be travelling the world in style?

She walked to the bedroom and pulled a suitcase from the top of the wardrobe and began to pack. Her clothes weren't exactly glamorous, she thought as doubt washed over her. Then she thought back to the dinner she and Claus had shared at the castle. She'd worn her ten-year-old linen trouser suit and he'd called her elegant.

Feeling a spurt of determination, she continued folding clothes and putting them into the case. But then she was hit by a flood of guilt so bad, it winded her. What would happen to the girls if she left? Liv was all over the place right now. Róisín was worried sick about her business and needed her support. Zipping the case shut, she shoved it under the bed and sat down. Was this really what she wanted?

A tiny voice in the back of her mind told her it actually was . . . For the first time in years, Keeley was putting herself first.

Chapter 32

NELL KNEW SHE WAS PUSHING MOUSE, BUT SHE felt it was for her own good.

'I'm wrecked. I don't want to do any more reading tonight.' She'd just returned from her shift at the pub and they were going through the words on the menu.

'I know what all the food looks like when I take the orders. I'm good at learning things off, so it's fine,' she argued.

'But you're going to get caught out,' Nell said. 'If you can't remember or if it's really busy and you have to write lots of order tickets, you're doomed.'

'I can write most of the stuff now and the chef hasn't even noticed.'

'Great, let's keep it that way. If you can stay in that job for a while, it will stand to you. You can build up your experience and who knows where you'll end up!'

They were also planning another new venture.

'I've filled out this form too,' Nell said waving it in front of Mouse. 'You need to add in your proper name and sign it.'

Mouse took it and physically shuddered.

'Whatever about writing words like soup and fish, I can't do this ever.'

'There's no such word as can't. I've told you. Besides,

you're brilliant at learning stuff off, you just said so your-self. So the study part will be easy as pie.' Nell was going to teach Mouse how to drive. The test required her to be able to write some answers along with a practical driving test.

'Will you help me read the book so I can learn it all?'

'Of course I will,' Nell agreed. Mouse filled in the remainder of the form and sighed deeply.

'Hey,' Nell said. 'I know this is all really difficult. I get that. But you'll thank me once you're an independent woman who can drive and hold down a good job.'

Mouse's eyes lit up. 'Do you really think I could get to that point?'

'There's no reason why you can't,' Nell said. 'So move. We're going to have a go in the car.'

'What if I drive us both into the sea?'

'Then we'll drown and none of it will matter any longer.'

'Fair enough,' Mouse said with a shrug.

Nell sat in the passenger seat and instructed Mouse as clearly as she could. She named all the pedals and explained about acceleration and stopping. She pointed out the pattern on the gear-stick.

'So it's like a little map that tells me where the different positions are?' Mouse said. 'That's a deadly idea. Very clear, even for a thick person like me.'

Nell scowled. 'You're not thick, Mouse. You never got shown before. That's a different thing. If you'd been having lessons for twenty years and you still couldn't turn on the car, then I'd worry about your level of intelligence.'

Nell was pleasantly surprised by how calm she felt. Mouse was very quick on the up-take. So much so, Nell was suspicious.

'Have you driven before?'

'Nah, I was never allowed behind the wheel, but I've been in tonnes of cars that my brothers were robbing. They weren't the best drivers at first. They used to grind the gears and make the car conk out. So I guess I've had lots of examples of what not to do.'

Nell smiled. The education Mouse had managed to absorb was certainly different from that of most young girls, but she was very adaptable. They got off to a flying start and she managed to move the car into second gear and then slow down and stop.

'I'm so impressed,' Nell said. 'Once you can master going up and down this lane and your provisional licence arrives, we can move onto the road.'

'What about insurance?' Mouse asked. 'Should we get me some?'

'Eh, yes!' Nell said shaking her head. 'Of course.'

'Right,' Mouse nodded. 'Of course. It's just that Da and the brothers never bothered with that sort of thing. But I know you're meant to have it though,' she added. 'Is it expensive? I could give you my wages?'

'It can be a little bit expensive,' Nell said. 'But it'll be my present to you.'

'For what?'

'Because I can and I want to.'

Mouse nodded and bit her lip. Nell found it incredibly endearing that she didn't just snatch everything that was offered to her. Nor did she pretend that it was all happening for free with no regard for who paid.

'I'll pay you back some day,' Mouse vowed. 'It might take a few years to make good money. But I'll never forget you for this and I will pay you back.'

'You just paid me there,' Nell said. 'Payment doesn't always have to be with money, Mouse. Sometimes it's worth so much more to give someone your time. In our case, you give me hope and a sense of purpose. I get up in the mornings and I feel more alive than I have in years.'

'Really?'

'I enjoy my day and I look forward to hearing about your work. The stories you tell and the little snippets of village life are fantastic.'

'Why don't you start to go out more if you like it so much?' Mouse asked.

'I don't want to go out more. I'm content where I am most of the time. But I love hearing it all through your eyes. You don't dress it up, you don't make it all sound any more or less than it truly is. I love that.'

'So I don't owe you a pile of dosh?' Mouse said with a grin.

'No, you don't owe me anything.'

They finished the driving lesson and Mouse went off to have a shower and get her things ready for the following day.

Nell gazed out at the view. Not a day passed that she didn't think of Laura. But for some reason she was beginning to feel a sense of urgency inside. Perhaps her time was running out, although she didn't feel weak or unwell. But there was a definite shift in her psyche. For the first time in many years, Nell thought deeply about what she'd done.

Until now, she was sure she had made the right choice. She hadn't felt the need to interfere or make contact or anything. She felt content that things had worked out for the best. Now, though, for some reason she couldn't even name, she was questioning whether or not it was right. She couldn't get it out of her head. She was starting to feel as if she should try to set things straight, before she went and snuffed it. The thing was, she had no idea how to go about that, or if any good would come of her making a confession after all this time.

Nell had always made decisions in her life by gut instinct, and so far that method had never let her down. She'd migrated from such a different start in Dublin's inner-city to her current rural existence. She couldn't imagine being anywhere else and she adored her home, but she was also aware that she didn't want to go to her grave with things unsaid and undone. Now, all she needed was the courage and strength to do things in a way that would be beneficial to all concerned. After all, there was no point in destroying the wall of silence unless she was certain it would achieve some good.

Chapter 33

ROB KNEW IT WAS MAKE OR BREAK TIME. HE WAS fed up of dithering and wanted to make a decision. A quick chat with his brother, who'd pretty much told him to grow a pair, hadn't helped. Róisín had got under his skin. He'd had the most fantastic night with her. He'd never had so much fun with a girl, in fact. He'd never spoken to Theresa the way he had with Róisín. Theresa knew nothing about him actually. Their conversations were empty nothings. All she wanted was to be seen in the right place with the people she considered to be trendy.

As he drove away yesterday, he was already trying to think of a reason to go back to Ballyshore. Róisín was some woman, with her dark glossy hair and perfect body and her quirky way of dressing. The ballet tutu, T-shirt and glittery shoes combo she'd been wearing when he'd called to the shop wasn't exactly the usual uniform for a boss. Most women he'd come across with looks like hers were full of themselves. But Róisín had a sense of shyness that was truly endearing.

He assumed that she had zero interest in him, so he was on the back-foot and would need to start from scratch in attempting to woo her. It dawned on him that he hadn't felt like this ever before. His family were known to be wealthy. The local girls had always been more than willing to try and hook up with him. Much as he hated to admit it, he was probably seen as a good catch in Limerick. Trying to get Róisín to like him would be a whole new adventure.

He chastised himself. Róisín wasn't an adventure. She was the realest person he'd ever encountered and he couldn't get enough of it. Theresa and her crew seemed like stuffed dolls by comparison. The problem was this mess in France. He had been knocked for six when she'd explained about Jacques, but he felt that if she let go of Jacques and her past with him, they could have an amazing future together. He just knew it in his bones. But how could he make her see this, especially when he was up against the deadline for her decision? He reckoned his father might be just the person to ask.

He drove to the office and hurtled in the door, calling out to his dad. When he received no answer, he strode towards the office at the back. The door was shut and he could hear voices, so he busied himself with some paperwork while he waited for the meeting to finish. After a while, the door was flung open and a man stalked out, looking very annoyed. Rob stared in surprise as he recognised him: it was the man Róisín had introduced him to in Nourriture. The German didn't look left or right, he just strode quickly out of the building.

Rob walked into the office. 'Hi Dad, who was that?'

Melvin smiled at his son. 'Someone I said no to, so he no doubt hates me right now. His name is Claus Schmidt.'

'I've seen him before, out at Nourriture. What was his business with you?'

Rob listened with interest as his father explained that Claus was looking for a large piece of land to build a price-cutting supermarket. He'd no interest in employing local workmen and Melvin simply disliked his ethics. He'd made a substantial offer, but Melvin was having none of it.

'Not if we were living on the breadline and running on empty would I sell my land to a cowboy like him. So what's your plan for the day, son? Are you off selling?'

'I am, but I need to stop by and talk to Theresa first.'

'Are you finally asking that girl to marry you?'

'No Dad, I'm actually thinking of ending it. She's not the one I see myself growing old with.'

'I see.' Melvin looked disappointed.

'I think I know who is, though.'

'Really?' he said, brightening considerably.

'She's from Ballyshore, but we're only friends right now.'

'And what makes you think this other lassie is the one for you?'

'I've never been able to relax with anyone the way I do with Róisín. She's beautiful and smart and has so many ideas and opinions.'

'How would you feel if you never saw Róisín again?'

'Oh wow, I'd die . . . she makes me feel alive. I left Ballyshore earlier and all I can think about is how I'm going to find an excuse to go back there . . .' Rob stopped short. For the first time he heard his own thoughts as he told his father about Róisín.

'I think you may have answered your own conundrum there, son. And for the record,' he added, 'your mother made me feel the same way. If she were here now, I know she'd say what I'm about to say: be yourself, let this girl see exactly who you are and if she doesn't love you, then she's not the one.'

'She's the first person I've been able to be me while I'm

with her. When I'm with Theresa and her friends, I feel like a square peg trying to fit into a round hole. I don't fit in.'

'Let Theresa down gently. Just because she's not right for you doesn't mean she's a bad person.'

'I know, Dad. I will.'

As he stood to leave, Melvin put his hand on Rob's arm. 'Your mother would be so proud of you.'

Rob walked to his car. He hated the thought of upsetting Theresa, but he figured it was better to be honest now. There was no point in chasing a relationship that wasn't going to last. She just wasn't the right one for him. He hoped, in time, that she'd find someone who made her feel the way Róisín made him feel.

Chapter 34

RÓISÍN WAS FINDING IT EXTREMELY DIFFICULT TO keep her chin up. She'd called the estate agent and gone online looking for suitable alternative premises, but it only showed her that Nourriture was perfect where it was, with the beach and all the charm of the village on her side. If she moved to the local larger town or even to a city, the charm would be gone.

Even though things were getting her down, she was very glad that she had made one decision. After her talk with Rob, and particularly after her tears in the car, she'd finally admitted to herself that she didn't want to bring Jacques' child into the world – even if it meant that she risked never having a baby. It wasn't just that the child would be fatherless, it was more than that. She had changed. The business, her family, the miscarriages, and now what she felt for Rob, it was all churning up a storm inside her and she needed time to just be herself and live her own life. It would be totally wrong to bring a child into the equation, it simply wouldn't work. It wasn't with the right person. Jacques was truly gone and that part of her life was gone with him. She would have to trust in the future and whatever that held for her.

Now that she'd finally made that decision, it gave her time to mull over the other things pressing in on her at the moment: the future of Nourriture, and her sister's future. She was really worried about her. Liv had promised she'd change her ways after she'd found her passed out the other night. She'd vowed to be sensible and not get into such a state again. For the first time in their lives, Róisín didn't know if she trusted her sister's words.

It was early in the morning and as Róisín finished her coffee, she glanced at the clock yet again: 8.12 a.m. and still no sign of Liv. She'd called her twice already and she really had to get to the shop.

'Liv?' she called out. 'I have to go. I'm late as it is and I can't leave Brigid on her own.'

There was no answer. Sighing, Róisín went to her sister's bedroom. The tray she'd brought in with tea and toast and a bowl of porridge lay there on Martin's side of the bed, untouched.

'Ah Liv! Seriously! I woke you and told you I needed to go.'

'Huh?' she said. 'I fell back asleep.'

'Yes,' she sighed. 'I can see that.' The smell of stale booze in the room was awful. Róisín pulled back the curtains and opened the window. 'Listen, I need you to make a bit of an effort. I need to get to Nourriture now.'

'I can't do the kids today. Will you drop them off at Mum and Dad's?' She turned over and pulled the duvet over her head.

'Liv!' Róisín barked. 'This isn't fair. Mum is up to her tonsils with guests at this time of the morning. Dad is still away with Jimmy. She can't keep an eye on the children while she's cooking and serving. I can't have them at the shop. You have to wake up.'

'Just get out!' Liv shouted. 'Leave me alone. Stop going

on at me constantly. I told you I can't cope with those two today. They do my head in and I can't be held responsible for what I'll do if they start moaning and telling me they're bored.'

Róisín bit her lip. She hated when Liv talked about Billy and Jess like this.

'Liv,' she said gently, dropping onto the bed. 'Help me out here, sweetie. They're your children. You're the adult here. Can't you drag yourself up and out? Take them to the playground or the beach. Bring a ball and they'll be happy. You don't need a picnic even. Drop into me and I'll happily feed you all.'

'I can't go near sand with my arm. I can't do anything. So you take over. After all, you're better at everything than I am.'

'What are you on about?' Róisín said.

'Oh you are,' Liv said. 'You're the golden girl, Róisín. Everything I touch turns to shit. So save my kids and take them away from me.'

'Liv, please, stop this talk. You're a great mum. You're a brilliant wife and we all love you.'

'Get out!' she yelled. 'Take the kids or you'll be sorry.'

She pulled the duvet right up and over her face and lay there like a corpse.

'Liv. What's going on? Do you want me to call someone? Like the doctor? Are you really depressed?'

In one swift action Liv jumped out of the bed and threw her arms in the air. 'Now, I'm up! Happy?'

'Please Liv . . .' Róisín felt tears burning her eyes. 'I'm only trying to help . . .'

'Well don't,' Liv said through gritted teeth. 'All those things you just said . . . bullshit. I'm a dreadful mother and an even worse wife. Why else do you think Martin's been shagging someone else for the last year? Why do you think he spends more time in America than here?'

'What?' Róisín's heart nearly stopped. She stared at her sister. 'Martin adores you.'

'Did. He's a great actor when it suits him. But it turns out he's had this younger, prettier and wealthier version putting out for him. Who can blame him?' she said as her face crumpled.

'Oh honey, why didn't you tell us?' Róisín asked.

Liv put her face in her hands. 'I thought we'd get through it. He said he'd leave her. He said he wanted to be with us. But it turns out, he wants the kids but not me.'

'The bastard,' Róisín said as fury boiled inside her.

Liv fell heavily onto the bed, her shoulders drooping. 'It's not his fault,' she whispered. 'Look at the state of me. Everything I do is a mess.'

'Is this why you've been drinking?' Róisín asked.

Liv nodded miserably. 'I don't think I'm an alcoholic,' she said. 'In fact, I'm even crap at drinking. I get awful hangovers and I feel sick most of the time. I just wanted to numb the pain.'

Róisín sat down beside her, took Liv in her arms and stroked her hair.

'I'll help you any way I can. We'll get through this together, OK?'

'I feel like such a failure,' she said sadly. 'All I have going for me is that I'm a wife and mother. I'm not like you. I don't have ambition or a business brain. I'm a total washout.'

'Don't you ever say that,' Róisín said, holding her face

gently. 'You're a wonderful person. You're just a bit banjaxed at the moment. But you'll bounce back. I know you will.'

'Why can't I be more like you, Róisín? You have it all worked out. I see the way Mum and Dad look at you and talk about you. They're so proud. What have I ever done? Get married and have kids. And now I've messed up both royally.'

'Liv, you don't know the half of it,' Róisín said. 'I'm not the golden girl you think I am. Besides, I'm probably going to lose my business and end up homeless, plus I couldn't find love if it was standing in front of me decorated with a neon sign.'

They hugged each other tightly.

'We'll get out of the hole we're in,' Róisín said. 'Let's do it together, yeah?'

Liv nodded.

Róisín looked at her watch. 'I'm sorry, but I have to get to the shop. I'll bring the children with me. Why don't you have a shower and follow me when you're ready?'

Liv nodded and she stroked her cheek. 'You're a superstar, and don't ever let anyone make you feel anything less, you hear?'

The children were happily watching cartoons when Róisín swooped in and announced they were coming to work for a bit.

'Why are we going to your work?' Billy asked.

'Because I need help,' she lied. 'I think you two would be perfect. If you do lots of super jobs I'll give you some ice cream.'

'At breakfast time?' Jess asked hopefully.

'Uh-huh,' Róisín said amidst cheers.

She careered into the shop ten minutes later with Jess in her arms and Billy bouncing alongside her.

'Sorry I'm so late,' she said to an astonished Brigid. 'I brought some fantastic helpers,' she said brightly.

'Our mum is in her bed hiding,' Billy stated. 'We do her head in,' he added sadly.

A knowing look passed between Róisín and Brigid as the other woman sized things up instantly.

'Oh darling,' Brigid said dropping to her hunkers. 'I'm sure you don't. You're such a great little man. I'd say your mum has a headache or a sick tummy.'

'She cooked her arm,' Jess said.

'I heard,' Brigid said. 'That really hurts, so that's probably why she's a bit muddled up right now. But it's lucky you guys arrived when you did. I have a major problem.'

'What is it?' Billy looked anxious.

'I have all these cupcakes and I need help putting little crystallised flowers on top.'

'We could help, and then Auntie Róisín said we can have ice cream.'

'I think that sounds like a good deal,' Brigid said. She lifted each of them onto a chair and stood them at a corner of her workbench and handed them a few buns each.

'Thanks. I'll get Mum to come ASAP,' Róisín whispered.

'No bother,' Brigid said. 'I obviously can't sell cakes that have been decorated by licked fingers, so say goodbye to that little bit of profit!'

'Just what I need to kickstart my day, a loss before we even open the doors,' Róisín said with a wry smile.

She was totally distracted as she turned the sign to Open and unlocked the main door. The last person she expected to see on the other side of it was Rob Walsh.

'Good morning,' she said in surprise. 'What brings you to Ballyshore at eight thirty in the morning?'

'Eh, I don't suppose you'd believe I was just passing?' he said with one eyebrow raised. She pulled the door open fully and beckoned him in.

'Coffee?' she asked.

'Thanks.'

She made him a cappuccino and called across to Billy and Jess that she was looking forward to seeing the finished cakes.

'What's the story with the slave labour?' Rob asked.

'My sister's kids. She's not feeling good today, so they've come to help out until she's feeling better.'

'Are you guys icing all those buns?' he asked.

'We're putting sweets and flowers and stuff on them too,' Billy said.

'Can I buy them when you're ready?' Rob asked.

'We'll have to ask Auntie Róisín,' Jess said with a very serious expression.

'How about I go and sit over there and you could bring me the buns when they're finished? You won't sell them to anyone else, will you? I was here first.'

'That's OK,' Billy said, making a swift management decision. 'It'll cost you ten euros for them though.'

'That's a deal,' Rob said. 'Am I allowed to wait over there?' He pointed at the window seat.

'I think that's a good plan. Are you in a hurry for them?' Billy asked, looking a bit worried.

'Yes,' Róisín interrupted. 'He is.'

'Quick, Billy,' Jess said. 'Don't lick any more of those sweets. We need to put them all on now so the man will pay Auntie Róisín all his money.'

Róisín tried to keep a straight face as Rob played a blinder.

'Do I pay you now or when the cakes are done?'

'Now,' they shouted in unison.

'Well trained,' Rob whispered. He handed Róisín a ten euro note.

'Go on with that,' she said. 'I'm not taking your money.'

He insisted and left it on the counter as he took his seat. 'I'm looking forward to my cakes now,' he said loudly. 'I'm so glad I came here early. Someone else might have walked in and taken them.'

The children loved the banter and squealed with laughter.

Róisín continued with her usual early morning drill as the children began to deposit the cakes on Rob's table. She was intrigued by Jess's reaction to him. She was normally very quiet and almost a suspicious little thing. Yet, she was happily trotting across the shop and back again with cakes for Rob.

Jill walked in and said hello to the children and Rob. She walked up to the counter and made a face. 'They look like they're having a pretty good time with your boyfriend. Are you role-playing at being *The Waltons* here?'

'Shush, will you?' Róisín hissed. 'He'll hear you. He's not my boyfriend, as you well know. I have to admit he's great with the kids, though.'

'He might be good husband material yet,' Jill said, winking at her.

'So what brings you here at this hour of the day?' Róisín teased her. 'I was normally hoovering around you at this time.'

Jill shrugged. 'Just missing you, really.'

The two friends smiled at each other.

'Are you busy?' Róisín asked.

'Nope,' Jill said. 'What do you need?'

'Can you take the two children to the beach for a bit? Liv is having a hard time.'

'Sure.'

The sun was shining and the village was starting to get busy already. Róisín glanced over at Rob, who was sharing a juice with the children. The deli counter was really busy so she dashed over to him.

'Rob, thanks so much for minding these two little monkeys. My friend Jill is going to take them to the beach for a bit.'

The kids cheered as they spotted Jill filling a bag of goodies.

'That's cool. We're having a great chat here. I'm hearing all about the snoring noises their dad makes. Apparently he sounds like a big pig!'

The two children giggled and Rob laughed.

'If Jill doesn't mind, I might go to the beach with them for a bit. I could do with a bit of fresh air.'

'Yeah, no bother,' Jill said patting him on the back. 'I know about the teacher thing, but this will be a good trial run at what it might feel like to have a husband and children on a day out. I might have to hen-peck you, though. Are you cool with that?'

'As long as there's no physical violence in front of the children I think we'll do nicely,' he said with a grin. 'Do I refer to you as Mummy or are you happy to stick with your name?'

'I think Jill is OK for the moment. What about you?'

'I'd prefer if you could call me precious or darling very

loudly so the other beach-goers can hear,' he said, keeping a straight face.

'No bother,' she said saluting. 'You kiddies ready? What about you, DARLING?' she shouted.

Róisín shook her head and smiled as the unlikely four-some bundled out the door. She was mildly nervous of how Jill would fare with Rob. She realised that she really wanted her best friend to like him.

As Brigid helped her to clear the backlog at the sandwich counter, they started to discuss Keeley's birthday party.

'I'm thinking of doing a barbecue with a pig on a spit,' Róisín said. 'We could easily hire the community centre and do it up nicely. I can get some of the part-timers to come and help create a festival-type atmosphere.'

'A live band would be good too,' Brigid said.

'The guys who played at the food festival were fantastic,' Róisín agreed. 'Mum is not overly keen on the whole party plan. She keeps coming up with more excuses every time I mention it.'

'Why don't you do it as a surprise then?' Brigid said.

'Good plan,' Róisín said thoughtfully. 'I can give everyone a little job to do and it would take the pressure off Mum. You know what she's like. She ends up taking on the lion's share of everything and knowing her, she'd be too exhausted to even enjoy it. But I'd better get a move on, there's only three weeks to the big day now and there'll be so much to do.'

Róisín was delighted with the idea of a surprise. It would give them all something positive to focus on. If Liv was right about Martin and he did want out, things were going to get a lot worse before they got better. She'd get Liv involved and it would be the perfect way for all of them to show their mum just how much she meant to them. She had so many favours she could call in, so it wouldn't need to cost the earth either. The idea of spending a pile of cash right now wasn't feasible. But she knew Keeley would appreciate the gesture.

Róisín made sure the staff were organised before she ran up to the office. She wanted to make notes on the party idea. As she sat scribbling at her desk, she realised she'd left her box of cards out on the table. She picked it up to put it back on the shelf, then stopped and opened it. She reached in and picked out a card at random.

Darling girl

Now that you have left your teens behind and entered your twenties, I hope you are beginning to dream big. The world is an exciting place with so much to discover. But don't forget one thing. Nothing is more precious than the love of your family. No matter where life takes you and who you meet along the way, love is the answer.

Roam the globe if that's what your heart desires, but always keep those you love close to your heart. Be honest and truthful with your family because they won't judge you. Have faith in the people who invested their time and energy in your wellbeing.

Take people as you find them, not as others tell you. Everyone has something to say and often it's a little nugget of information you've never heard before. Getting out and taking chances teaches you so much more than sitting at home alone.

Do things that scare you. You'll be glad you did.

Love and light

Mam x

Róisín smiled to herself. She could think of a few things that scared her – should she follow her mother's advice and go for it?

She suddenly heard Keeley's voice downstairs and called down to Brigid to let her know she was on the way. She ran down the stairs and hugged her so tightly, Keeley coughed.

'Hi,' she said. 'I thought you were busy so I didn't call. I've sent the kids off with Jill. Liv is having a dreadful morning.'

'I know. I've just been with her.' Keeley looked stricken. 'I could kill Martin. But more than that, I'm so devastated that Liv felt she couldn't tell any of us what was going on.'

'I know,' Róisín agreed. There was something about Keeley that made her look closely at her. She seemed distracted in some way.

'Is everything OK, Mum?'

Keeley sighed deeply. 'Not really. Liv isn't the only one who's been having marital issues,' she said. 'I'm not exactly happy at the moment either.'

Róisín listened as her mother told her how invisible she'd begun to feel. How pushed aside and surplus to requirements she felt.

'But Mum, we would all be lost without you.'

'Thanks, pet,' she said. 'It's not you girls, of course. It's your father. I'm wondering if we'd be better apart.'

Róisín stared at her in utter shock, but before she could answer the children came zooming over.

'Hi you guys,' Róisín said, forcing a fake smile onto her face. 'You're back!'

Her head was reeling with what her mother had just

suggested, but she couldn't give Billy and Jess any more emotions to deal with at the moment. She had to push it aside for now and then tackle Keeley later, in private.

'We had the best time ever. Jill and Rob were pretending to be our mum and dad. They are the worst at it!' Billy laughed.

'They buried each other in the sand,' Jess said clapping. 'They're so funny.'

'Hi Keeley,' Jill said, planting a kiss on her cheek.

'Hello Jill love,' she said. 'So it sounds as if you were being a bit crazy?'

'We had a blast,' Jill said as Rob approached.

'Hi there,' he said to Keeley. 'Robert Walsh is my name. I sell Irish craft beers to Róisín. I dropped by earlier on and was lucky enough to be able to buy some special hand-made cakes. Then Billy and Jess minded me at the beach.'

'We licked all the sweets and stuck them on the tops of the cakes,' Billy said proudly. 'And Rob was supposed to mind us. But he's the craziest man in the universe!'

'It sounds as if Rob and Jill were lucky to have you two there to sort them out,' Róisín said.

Billy and Jess nodded.

'Well, I'd better get going,' Keeley said. 'Would you two like to come with me?' They nodded. 'What do you say to Rob?'

'Thank you,' they chorused.

'It was great to hang out. Maybe we can do it again another day?' he said. 'I might be back again soon and I think I need you two to keep me on the straight and narrow. Bye guys,' Rob said holding his hand up to do high-fives.

The children waved happily as Keeley took them out to her car.

'I need to run to the ladies,' Jill said and raced across the shop.

'Hey, thanks so much for doing that,' Róisín said.

'They're great,' Rob said.

'You're very good with children.'

'I think I'm just on the same wavelength as them.' As he stood with his hands in his dark denim jeans pockets, she could see the outline of his muscles through his pale blue T-shirt.

'So how's your day going so far?' he asked.

'Things are a little precarious for me just at the moment.'

'Why?' he asked.

Róisín looked over at Steve who was engrossed in a conversation with the people at the neighbouring table.

'There's a bit of a problem, but I can't discuss it here.'

'Want to sit for a quick coffee?' he asked. 'I've been running around nonstop since I got here.'

'Oh how rude of me,' she said flushing. 'Do you want to come up to my office?' she asked.

He nodded, and Róisín felt instantly calmer.

They bumped into Jill on her way out of the loos.

'I've got to split,' she said. 'Nice to meet you, Rob. Chat to you later, babes?' she said to Róisín.

'Chat then, and thanks a million.'

'She's great craic,' Rob said as he followed Róisín up to the office.

'I know, she's the best. We've been like sisters for years. So,' she said hesitating. 'I'm in a bit of a bind.' Rob sat opposite her. 'I don't want you to think I won't pay for the beer because I absolutely will,' she said.

'OK,' he said holding his hands up. 'Go on.'

'Well, I put in an offer to buy this building, thinking I

would have no hassle. But it turns out my landlord received an offer from an investor. One I can't even attempt to match.'

'So what's the situation?'

'I'm waiting for official written confirmation, but I'm pretty sure Nourriture is going to be bulldozed and I'll be out of a job.'

'Who's the investor?'

'I've no idea. I didn't ask.'

'Why not?' Rob asked.

'Well . . . I didn't think that was any of my business.'

'Of course it is. If you know who it is, maybe you can negotiate. Who knows, maybe whoever is buying the property will continue to rent it to you?'

'From what Mr Grace, my landlord, said, this investor wants to knock the place down and start from scratch.'

'Don't lose hope, Róisín,' Rob said. 'My father is a dab hand when it comes to investments and buying and selling properties. Would you like me to ask him for his take on this?'

'If you think that you or your father can possibly help me to hold onto Nourriture, I'll take your hand off. I really want to keep it all going and keep building on what I've started. So any help you can give me will be very gratefully received.'

'I understand,' he said. 'Let me do some homework and I'll get back to you. Where does your landlord live, by the way? How do I get hold of him?'

Róisín explained and watched in amazement as Rob jumped up and set off down the stairs.

'Where are you going?' she called.

'I'll see you soon,' he shouted back.

He saw his opportunity to prove his worth to Róisín, and he was going to grab it with both hands. He wouldn't leave a stone unturned in his research on Nourriture and the new investor.

Chapter 35

NELL WAS IMMENSELY PROUD OF MOUSE. SHE WAS coming on in leaps and bounds with her driving. They'd made it as far as the outskirts of the village before the young woman pulled over.

'Why did you stop?' Nell asked.

'I can't drive into the village. It's too narrow and there'll be cars parked on the side of the road. I'll end up clipping a pile of wing mirrors.'

Nell tutted and muttered, but she let Mouse move to the passenger seat as she slid over and took the wheel.

'Why don't you come and pick me up and we could have something to eat this evening?' Mouse suggested.

'No thanks,' Nell said.

'Why? The food at the pub is good. Or we could go to Nourriture. The woman who runs it is really decent. I've been slipping out during my break to buy the chocolate éclairs in there. They bake everything in the back of the shop.'

'I'd prefer the pub,' Nell said gruffly.

'OK, so will we go there then?'

'Maybe.'

'Ah please, Nell, I'll pay. It'd be my treat. I'd be so happy to bring you.'

Nell smiled. 'OK then. We'll do it.'

Mouse ran into work looking so delighted with herself, it made Nell chuckle. She'd never come across another person who was so easily pleased.

As she drove home to the lighthouse, Nell knew what she wanted to do. The sun was shining on her front garden and the scent of sweet pea filled the air. Grabbing her scrapbooks, she made a mug of coffee and perched on her deck-chair. She thumbed through the pages, gazing at each article and photograph in turn. For the first time, she confronted the question of broaching the subject she'd avoided for decades, turning it over in her mind and looking at it from every angle. Fear gripped her heart as she tried to imagine how the scene could play out. What was the right thing to do?

She went back into the lighthouse and opened the top drawer of her desk. Sliding the large black cassette out of the box, she found the long-forgotten VHS machine at the bottom of the large cupboard in Laura's old room. It was still connected to the box-shaped portable television set. With shaking hands, she slid the tape into the machine and held her breath until it whirred into action.

Using the black handle on the top of the TV set, she lifted it out and set it on the floor. The snowy screen changed to black before a picture appeared.

Tears soaked her face as she watched Laura blowing kisses and waving.

The message she'd recorded so long ago seemed all the more relevant today. Nell mouthed the words along with her daughter. Each one was emblazoned on her brain, never forgotten but all the same, never delivered to the rightful recipient.

'You'll pass it on, won't you, Mum?' Laura begged.

'Of course I will,' she'd promised. 'Of course I will.'

Nell curled into a ball on the floor and pressed the Rewind button. As soon as she pressed Play, she rested her head on the carpet and pretended Laura was still with her. It was so long since she'd allowed herself to do this. So long since she'd dared to let her imagination take over in this way.

This very practice had given her comfort for a long time. It had been enough to fool her poor battered heart into believing Laura wasn't gone. But the passage of time had eventually worn her down. She'd convinced herself she didn't deserve to hear Laura's voice or see her sparkling mischievous eyes as she chattered at the camera. So she'd locked the tape away, along with her own emotions, and learned to exist rather than live.

It had worked quite nicely until recently. Mouse had broken the spell. The hope in her eyes and her hunger to find a better life had shaken Nell out of the cocoon of misery that had bound her both physically and mentally for far too long.

Exhausted from emotion, Nell slept on the floor, only waking when she heard the sound of the phone. She scrambled to her feet and tried to focus. The incessant ringing let her know that she needed to answer in order to make it stop.

'Hello?'

'Nell,' said Mouse. 'Where are you? Did you forget our plan? Did you?'

'Oh Mouse,' she said. 'I was asleep. I'm sorry. I'll come now this minute. See you there in ten minutes.'

'OK, but bit of a change. I'm outside Nourriture. They've

put some tables outside, so we can watch the village go by. I'm having hummus and olives and a selection of breads, do you want the same?'

Nell felt her heart beating madly in her chest. There was no way she could go there. She never went there. And especially not today, dear God.

'Nell? You OK? Please say you'll come still.'

Nell pictured Mouse sitting waiting for her.

'I'm on my way,' she said.

Nell had vaguely thought of fishing a nice-looking sundress out of her wardrobe so as not to embarrass Mouse, but all that went by the wayside as she drove at high speed to the village.

Mercifully, a car pulled out, providing a perfect parking spot. She climbed out and spotted a happily waving Mouse. She took a deep breath to compose herself. 'Steady, you stupid old fool,' she whispered to herself.

'This is pretty,' she said, joining Mouse. 'I like the job they've done on this area.'

'Isn't it gorgeous?' Mouse said. 'Whoever owns this place has a serious eye for design.'

The tiny area was paved with rustic tiles and the four small round tables were all dotted around the thick gnarled trunk of a single tree. Simple cotton bunting was just enough of an addition to pick up the pink and yellow flowers of the oilcloths on each table. The metal fold-out chairs were warmed up by pretty cushions tied on with ribbons.

'Wait until you taste the hummus. I don't know what's in it, but it's gorgeous,' said Mouse.

They enjoyed the light and zingy dip, mopped up with a variety of delicious home-baked breads. The tangy lemonade with freshly grated lime zest peppered through for extra texture was the perfect sunny afternoon tipple.

Mouse stood triumphantly and snatched the bill. 'I said I'd pay,' she said, walking off with her nose pointed so high in the sky, it made Nell laugh. She sat and watched as the staff raced around expertly, attending to the diners who arrived and left regularly all the while. It was a thriving business, obviously. Nell smiled, delighted by how things had turned out.

Mouse was gone for so long that Nell briefly considered going in to fetch her. Just as she stood up, Mouse appeared, waving to her enthusiastically. Nell waved back in mild confusion. She didn't have to wait long to find out why Mouse was so excited.

'I've been offered a new job,' Mouse said breathlessly as they walked to the car. 'Not only did we get a free lunch, but I have a proposition from the owner. Her name is Róisín. I served her and her fella over at the pub the other night and she said she was impressed by me.'

'Was she now?' Nell said, raising an eyebrow.

'Róisín has all sorts of ideas for selling food in different ways. She's doing a new thing where she's going to do parties.'

'Outside catering?' Nell said.

'Yeah, but more than that. She has a band and a DJ on board and she'll do pig on a spit or barbecue or buffet and provide the tent and everything.'

'And where do you come in?'

'She'd like me to be part of the team for that business. She says I'd be working with some other younger fellas and we'll start off doing festivals and all that kind of thing.'

'Will you have a regular wage?'

'Yeah, I asked all that and she's going to pay me regularly.'

Nell put her arm around Mouse. 'You've been head-hunted,' she said. 'That doesn't happen to many people. You should be so proud. But wouldn't you rather stay at the Thatch? Maybe get to know your trade a bit more and then think about moving on? Maybe to somewhere bigger, like the city?'

'Why? I love it here,' Mouse said.

'I think you're being a bit rash, that's all. If you ask me, you should stay where you are. If it's not broken, don't fix it.'

'Why are you being so weird about this, Nell? Aren't you happy I'm movin' and shakin'?' Mouse grinned and looked at Nell. Her expression was odd. 'Come on then. Spit it out. What don't you like about this place?'

'Nothing at all,' Nell said. 'If you want to move here, you do that.'

'What'll I tell Joseph? He's been so good to me. If it wasn't for him, I wouldn't have anything. Is it wrong of me to take a new job and leave him in the lurch? It's bad karma to dump people just because something better has come along, isn't it?'

'I'm sure he'll understand, if you explain it to him.'

'Will you come with me?' she asked. 'I'd like to talk to him now and tell him I'm trying to make up my mind.'

Nell nodded and walked beside Mouse as they headed to the Thatch. As it turned out, Joseph was outside chatting to a German man.

'Back again, Mouse?' he asked and nodded at Nell to say hello. She nodded back and stood to the side.

'Can I have a word?' Mouse asked.

'No problem.' Joseph turned to the man. 'I'll go, and thanks for coming to chat. Sorry I can't help you,' he said, making it clear he didn't want to talk to the man any longer.

'Sorry if I interrupted,' Mouse said as the man walked away.

'No, you saved me,' he said. 'That man doesn't take no for an answer and I'm beginning to get fed-up with him.'

'Tell him to sod off then,' Mouse said simply.

'I kind of did. Not quite in those words, but I think he's getting the message. So what can I do for you, Miss Mouse?'

'I've a problem,' she said. 'Well, it's more of a brain-melting type of thing and I don't want to burn my bridges,' she said.

'OK, tell me what's happened.'

She explained about Róisín and her offer and how she'd like to take it, but she didn't want to upset him.

'Aren't you very honest?' he said. 'How about I make this easy and fire you?' He smiled.

'What?' She looked horrified. 'I don't want to be fired. That'd be a bad thing on my CV.'

He laughed out loud. 'Well, put it this way . . . I only have another few weeks of busy days. After the summer sun fades, I don't do food. The kitchen only operates in the summer. So I won't be able to keep you on full-time. It'd only be weekend work really.'

'Jaysus, I think I'll take it all back now.' She grinned. 'You were going to toss me out on my ear anyway?'

'Not quite, but I think this is a great opportunity for you.'

He pulled her into a hug and winked over at Nell. 'You

go and show all those festival and party people that you can be the hostess with the mostest.'

'Thanks Joseph,' she said sincerely. 'You're a lovely man. You gave me a chance when loads of people wouldn't have touched me. I'll never forget you for it.'

'If you become a millionaire like Richard Branson or Bill Gates, will you give me a few euros?'

'Of course I will,' she said nodding seriously.

'I'll still be here for a long while,' Joseph said. 'So drop in and visit the odd time, won't you?'

'Try and stop me. Nobody else can make a rock shandy like you can. So I'll be back for a pint of that,' she said, nudging him and smiling.

Nell did the drive home because Mouse said she was too worked up to concentrate on not crashing.

'I'm all jittery. I don't know if my nerves will stand all this,' she admitted. 'This is like a dream come true, Nell.'

As they arrived back at the lighthouse, Nell suddenly knew she wanted to share the video with Mouse. Nervously, she asked her to come into Laura's old bedroom. 'There's something I'd like to show you, Mouse.'

Chapter 36

KEELEY HADN'T PAINTED FOR QUITE A WHILE. Normally her artwork was her saviour, calming her and allowing her to switch off. Lately, there'd been so much going on she hadn't taken the time to enjoy her art. Now, she made her way to the little front room. The smell of paint and turpentine always made her relax. Her easel was poised in such a way that she could see directly across to the bay. Of course she'd painted many different versions of this view over the years, but each season meant a change in light and vista. She was focusing on a stunningly beautifully shaped tree that framed the side of the front garden. She was enjoying mixing her palette of oils and was carefully building the colour so she could do justice to the incredible silver- and mushroom-toned branches.

She'd been to classes in the local adult education centre to learn as much as she could about painting. But she knew that her best pieces came from her heart. Many of her finished pictures adorned the walls of their home. She was more proud of some than others, but each one told a story that only she could read.

She looked at the trio of pictures on the wall to her left. Funnily enough, Liv had said several times how creepy they were. They depicted the same fictional cottage in different stages of dilapidation. Little did her daughter know that they'd been painted during a very tumultuous time in Keeley's life. Those months after her fourth miscarriage were incredibly bleak. She'd never told anyone how scared she was at that time. She'd particularly hidden it from Doug. She hadn't wanted him to think he'd been saddled with a lunatic, so she'd poured all her feelings into her art instead.

She sighed as she thought of him. He'd been her rock and her best friend for so many years. She'd fallen in love with him the second they'd met, forty years ago. He was far more in touch with his emotions than she was in those days. He'd cried like a baby when Olivia was born. Then he'd held her in his arms and laughed like a hyena. He was the one who'd expressed sadness, dismay and an aching sense of loss when the doctor told them Keeley couldn't have more children.

'I wish it could be different for you. You deserve to have as many babies as your heart desires. It's not fair,' he'd said. 'There are plenty of women who pop out children and barely mind them. Why are we being punished?'

'I don't see it as being punished, love,' she'd said, in an attempt to calm him down. 'We're blessed to have Róisín and now we have Olivia too. There were so many complications. One or both of us could've died. We should be happy with our lot.'

'Sod that,' he'd raged. 'I think it's so unfair.'

It seemed fitting that she took on the role of the person who was outwardly stronger emotionally. And so this stoic and unbendable exterior was born. She became accustomed to behaving that way and realised she was very good at it.

She didn't hide all her feelings from Doug. She did talk

and express herself from time to time, but on the whole her true fears were on the walls of their home.

Liv had asked her to do some paintings for her house and had been very specific: 'None of your weird stuff now, keep it to paintings that won't give us all nightmares.'

She'd laughed at that and promised to stick to a summery palette, with flowers in bloom in every one. Astute as she was, Liv had never passed comment on the lone figure that appeared in many of her works. The only one who had noticed her was Róisín.

'Who's that little girl?' she'd asked one day when she was about four years old.

'She doesn't have a name,' Keeley said. 'I didn't even realise she was a girl. What makes you say she is?'

'Because boys don't have pretty necks like hers.'

Keeley never painted the figure's face and she was always curled up in a sitting position, with her arms wrapped around her bent knees.

It was a while since she'd included the figure in a painting, but today as she looked out at the frothy water of the bay opposite, a tsunami of feelings flooded her. Feelings of heart-wrenching guilt at holding things inside . . . thoughts that she had never shared . . . new feelings of confusion as to where her life was going now. When the guilt hit her, it came with such force that it made her shudder. Whenever she thought of the packed case under the bed, it shamed her. After all, it represented the ultimate betrayal, as far as she was concerned – and yet . . . she couldn't deny the delicious shivers of excitement it brought out in her too. Imagine walking into a room and someone noticing, someone nearly weak at the knees because you're there. It felt like a second chance at life. She felt twenty years younger once more.

But then, Doug's face floated into her mind's eye. She saw his gentle smile and imagined the familiarity of his touch. As she closed her eyes, she saw flashes of the good times they'd shared and the wave of sickening guilt washed over her again. Right now she was devastated by her son-in-law's grotesque carelessness, and yet she had the audacity to allow herself to be attracted to someone else. But then, she told herself, they were two totally different situations: she had raised her children, done her time, kept her vows, but now things were different somehow. Actually, she was different now, so maybe her feelings could be justified? Maybe it was finally her turn to live life on her terms?

Her head ached with the constant back and forth argument, and she tried to drown it out by flinging her thoughts into the canvas. Her hands worked swiftly as she sketched her treasured figure. For the first time, she was standing with her arms stretched out as if she were trying to embrace the ocean. The figure appeared to be welcoming a greater force and opening up to what lay ahead.

Keeley walked to the window and stood with her hands on her hips. It seemed crazy to contemplate splitting up after so many years. Most couples ran into difficulty when they were young and fiery. Money issues and work pressures were enough to tear even the strongest people apart. So how sad would it be if they were to fall at this late stage?

Then Keeley thought of Claus. She'd never looked at another man in all the time she'd been married. She never felt the need to. She knew deep down that Doug probably loved her in his own way. But she also knew that she'd been overlooked and treated like an afterthought. A new voice in her head was telling her that it simply wasn't good enough. She'd hate either of her daughters to be with a man who didn't give them his all, so why was she putting up with it?

Thoughts of Liv's tear-stained face yesterday filled her with anger. She could swing for Martin, knowing he'd betrayed her beautiful daughter and chosen another woman over his children. He was a lousy liar and she would give him a piece of her mind when the time came. A voice in Keeley's head reminded her that Doug hadn't cheated. As far as she knew, he was simply choosing to spend his time with another man in another country.

Anger rose and seared through her, making her hands shake.

Claus was so different from Doug and there was no way she could compare the two, but she had to admit the thought of being minded and cherished sounded like a fantastic prospect. She'd never been materialistic and might be bored silly after a week, but she knew that the main draw with Claus right now was that he was actually interested in her.

A taxi pulled up outside and Keeley stood to the side of the window and peered out. She watched Doug pulling his bags from the back seat. So the wanderer had returned, she thought. Great, he had two full bags of washing for her to contend with. No doubt he'd be exhausted, hungry and looking to put his feet on the coffee table and snore with a belly full of breakfast that she was expected to cook.

She stayed in her art room and flicked on her ancient stereo. It was a true eighties throwback in that it was covered in fire-engine-red plastic and the speakers were the size of bedside lockers. It still worked perfectly well, which was why she'd insisted on keeping it.

Turning up the music, she removed the sheet from the canvas and set about looking busy. She bit her lip. She'd never done this before. Normally she'd rush to greet Doug, even if he'd only been over at Ballyshore for the afternoon. But something was stopping her.

'Hello?' he called out.

'In here,' she said.

He walked in the door and stopped in his tracks.

'Hi,' he said, when she didn't move to hug him.

'Hi.'

'Doing a bit of art?'

'Yup,' she said.

'So I got home,' he said, stating the obvious. Into the silence he said, 'Keeley, I'm sorry. I know I've been an idiot. I don't know what got into me lately. I thought I wanted to have a second wind. But I've realised that I don't want to do any of that without you.'

She listened, and a part of her appreciated his words, but she felt distant from them. She was relieved he hadn't stopped loving her totally, but she was really fed-up with him.

'I can understand that you want to try and forge a new type of life now that you're retired. But I can't get over the cheek of you, Doug.'

'I'm sorry,' he repeated.

'I'm retiring too,' she said. 'I've had enough of working. Who knows, maybe I'll leave Ballyshore and go and live somewhere like Mexico where I'll become a beach bum and spend my days lolling in the sun.'

He stood, looking awkward.

'I've never felt let down by you in all the years we've known one another,' she said honestly. 'But I've seen a side of you that I don't appreciate. Liv's marriage has fallen apart, Róisín is under huge pressure with her business and I'm working all the time with no support . . . What have you been doing? Skipping the light fandango.'

'I know,' he said rubbing his face. 'I got caught up in being a singleton like Jimmy. I think I always admired him. He coped so well raising Tara after his Eileen died. When Tara married that Spanish fellow and moved away, I honestly thought he'd sink into a deep depression, but he did the opposite. He was out most nights, working away during the day and travelling the world like a modern version of Christopher Columbus.'

'And now you don't think he's the bee's knees?' Keeley asked with an eyebrow raised.

'I'm fond of him. He's a great man. But all he's doing is attempting to fill the lonely hours of each day and evening. He's like someone possessed,' Doug said. 'He's hyper and he only needs a wink of sleep and he's up and looking for something else to do.'

'I thought you loved his fun-loving nature,' Keeley said with a distinct lack of sympathy.

'I do. He's a force of nature, God bless him. But dear Lord, I couldn't spend another week with him, Keeley. He's turbo-charged and hasn't an ounce of common sense. He throws himself into every idea without so much as a backwards glance.'

Keeley cocked her head to the side and stared at Doug. 'So the real reason you've come home is because Jimmy is like a teenager. You can't keep up, so you thought you'd come home after all?'

'Yes, but not just that . . .'

'Do you know what, Doug? I'm not sure I like this arrangement any longer. I'd hate either of our girls to play second-fiddle to any man. I've told Liv in no uncertain terms what I think of Martin's carry-on. I try to lead by example and I can assure you, I've no intention of being treated like an afterthought.'

'What are you saying?' Doug asked.

'I think you should go and we should spend a bit of time apart. Take stock of things. Have some time out from one another.'

'Why? After all this time . . . do we really need to know if we want to be together? I think you're being a bit ridiculous, Keeley.'

'Actually I don't think I'm being the ridiculous one. Quite the opposite. I'm the one who's been slaving away and washing and cooking and cleaning like Cinderella for years. I mightn't ever get to go to a ball, but I sure as hell won't spend another day being taken for granted.'

Doug picked up his bags and dragged them outside. As she saw him speeding off in his jeep, Keeley realised she was relieved. If nothing else, she wouldn't have to do all that washing and ironing.

She fully expected to fall in a crumbling heap at any moment. She held her two hands aloft. No shakes. She walked from her art room and clicked on the kettle. The phone rang and she ignored it. The caller's voice came out over the speakerphone as it clicked to the answer machine.

She listened as they left details of when they'd like to come. As soon as the message ended, she walked to the machine and pressed the Record button.

'You've reached Keeley's B&B. I would like to thank

you for your business over the years and to let you know that I am no longer taking bookings. All previously booked rooms will be honoured, but from September first I will cease trading as I embrace retirement. Once again, I would like to thank all my patrons for their wonderful support over the years.'

Decision taken, she thought, as she made a cup of tea. She thought of the packed case under the bed. A ripple of excitement shot through her. She closed her eyes and tried to imagine what it might feel like to kiss Claus.

Keeley had no idea what she'd do next, but as far as she was concerned, she wasn't putting up with half a life for one minute longer.

Chapter 37

RÓISÍN HAD BEEN IN NOURRITURE SINCE VERY early in the morning. She couldn't sleep. There was so much going on in her head, from Liv's marriage to how she felt about Rob to her ridiculously impulsive move yesterday. She'd no idea why she'd hired Mouse. It had all come about by chance. Niamh, who'd been working with Steve and Eoin on and off, had said she was off to Spain for a year, so she'd panicked and hired Mouse. There was something enticing about the young Dublin girl. She was so enthusiastic and Róisín had never met anyone so keen to get ahead. But what on earth was she going to do if everything went belly-up?

Brigid arrived in and started baking. Steve appeared and began to set up the tables and before she knew it, the village was alive. The buzz of the new day did what it always did and gave her fresh hope.

She was busy tapping away on her calculator for what felt like the hundredth time as she tried to work out whether or not she could afford to take on the small unit at the end of the village, apply for planning and build. Her fingers kept slipping on the buttons and she ended up with ridiculous figures.

'Hello love,' Doug said.

'Dad!' she said coming around to the front of the shop. 'I thought you were away?'

'I was, and I came back.'

'So why do you look so dishevelled?'

'Do I?'

'Eh, you look like you've the worries of the world on your shoulders and you're so crumpled you could have slept in the ditch.'

'I got back from Spain on a really early flight and your mother kicked me out of the house.'

'I beg your pardon?' Róisín laughed. 'Did you waltz in while she was in the middle of serving a pile of breakfasts? Is that it? This is your roundabout way of saying you want me to feed you, I suppose?'

'No, love. Your mother asked me to go. As in, leave her alone and stay some place else.'

'Oh my God,' she said, in shock. Her conversation with Keeley here in the shop that they never got to finish flicked through her mind. 'I think you'd better come up to my office and tell me exactly what's happening.'

They went up the stairs to her office and she shut the door behind them.

'I don't know what's come over me lately,' he said. 'I knew I was being a horror and I couldn't stop. So Keeley, being Keeley, has put her foot down and told me to go for a while. Apparently we're both having a think about what we want from the future.'

Róisín felt like she was having an out-of-body experience. Yes, Keeley had talked about feeling unappreciated, but she'd honestly thought it was a phase and her mum would buck up, as usual. She really hadn't thought she'd take it this far. Was there some sort of a curse on them all? Why were their lives falling apart?

'This is insane,' she blurted. 'You two are like two peas in a pod. How has it come to this?'

'I'm actually not sure,' he said. 'It seems your mother has been very unhappy for some time. I've been acting like an idiot and it's all come to a head.'

Róisín was so torn. Her dad looked heartbroken, but she was genuinely cross with him for making her mum feel so bad.

'This is only temporary,' she stated confidently. 'You need to prove to Mum that you love her.'

'But how?' he asked, looking like a helpless child.

'You can start by helping me organise her sixtieth party. You can get cracking on the invite list. I'm doing the food and drink and entertainment. I'll speak to Liv and ask her to pitch in too. Between us, we'll show Mum just how much she means to us.'

'You're on!' Doug said, looking brighter. 'Will we tell her about the party or will we spring it on her?'

'I think she ought to know that we're doing something because I have spoken to her and suggested a night. So I don't want to add to her current delicate state of mind by letting her think we've all forgotten or can't be bothered.'

'OK.' Doug looked perplexed.

'I'll tell her the date and time and that's it. It'll be a bit like that *Don't Tell the Bride* show, where the bride has to step aside and the groom organises the wedding.'

'Do you think Keeley will go for that?' he asked, looking unsure. 'I'm not certain your mother will take kindly to us shutting her out of proceedings.'

'I actually think it's exactly what she needs right now.

She's feeling taken for granted and fed-up. She needs to slow down and start thinking of herself for a change. This is our opportunity to show her that we're not all drains on her life all the time.'

Róisín knew that her father was so flummoxed at being told to sling his hook, he'd agree to take up stilt-walking and fire-eating if it meant getting back on side with Keeley. But she'd been watching her mother lately and it was clear she was reaching the end of her tether in more ways than one.

'So are you on board with me?' Róisín asked. 'Will we show Mum how much we care?'

'Yes. Let's do that,' he said. 'Meanwhile I'm going to have to ask Liv if I can camp at her place for a bit.'

'Dear me,' Róisín said. 'Her place is really ending up as a halfway house, isn't it? I suppose you've heard that she and Martin are on the rocks?'

'I could swing for that man,' he said. 'How dare he hurt my girl like that.'

Róisín gave him a reproachful look. 'That's a bit pot and kettle, if you don't mind me saying, Dad.'

'I wasn't unfaithful to your mother. I would never do anything to intentionally hurt her . . . you've got to believe me, Róisín . . .'

'Let's just try and make things better, OK?' she said.

Doug went off to ask Liv if he could stay in the other spare room for a while. Róisín gave him full instructions of how he was to pitch the idea to her.

'Don't forget to say that you'll help with the children and maybe you could offer to do that shelving and stuff she wants in the kitchen? She has to go into the hospital for this skin-graft surgery tomorrow, so it's actually good timing. Offer your services as the manny while she's in hospital.'

'I'd be happy to do it. It'd keep my mind off the horrible stuff and I'd feel less guilty for landing in on her.'

Róisín waited for her father to drive off before she called her mum.

'I suppose he's been over to you giving out yards and saying I've lost my marbles, has he?' Keeley said.

'No, he's not angry, Mum. I'd say he's more like a puppy dog that's been beaten with a rolled-up newspaper.'

'He deserves it, Róisín,' Keeley said. 'I won't put up with being taken for granted and treated like dirt. Enough is enough, and he can go off and have a long, hard think about his behaviour.'

'I understand, Mum,' Róisín said. 'But I can't help feeling sorry for him. He's not nasty or cruel. He was acting like a total doofus. No excuses there, but there were no malicious intentions, I don't think.'

'Yes, you're probably right, love,' Keeley said evenly. 'But the result remains the same. I am the one who has been made to feel like a dogsbody. Unless I stand up for myself, I'll end up hating my life.'

'OK Mum,' Róisín said. 'Listen, I know you're not in a celebration mood right now, but we're organising a birthday bash for you. We'll let you know the date and time and that's it.'

'Really?'

Róisín smiled as she heard the cogs in her mother's brain turning in surprise.

'You deserve it and I think it will be a good way for Dad to apologise.'

'Thank you,' Keeley said.

'No problem. Mum?'

'Yes.'

'For the record, I think you're dead right. I love Dad, but he's been acting like he's young, free and single lately. It's not fair to you.'

'Thanks, love.'

'Oh and by the way, I've signed him up to mind Billy and Jess while Liv's in hospital.'

'Well done,' Keeley said. 'Not that I don't want to mind the little cherubs too. But I think the more can be dumped on him, the better. A taste of his own medicine won't go astray.'

Róisín hung up and immediately made some calls about the party. She called in every favour she had. She was completely organised less than an hour later. All she needed was to confirm some details nearer the time.

Joseph from the Thatch came into the shop and asked to speak to her.

'How are you, Joseph?' she asked, hoping he wasn't going to be the bearer of bad tidings.

'I'm well thanks, love. I just wanted to give you the heads-up on young Mouse. I believe you swiped her from me yesterday?'

'Oh I'm sorry . . .' she said, blushing.

'I'm only kidding,' he said. 'She's a great girl and I'd love to keep her on, but I won't have the volume of trade once the kids go back to school. So you did me a favour. She hasn't much experience and my place was the first time she'd ever worked.'

'She mentioned that.'

'She's learning to read and write and I can't tell you how eager she is. All I wanted to say is that if anything goes pear-shaped, will you give me the nod? I wouldn't like to see her stuck. She has incredible potential and I've a soft spot for her. She's a great little young one.'

'That's kind of you,' Róisín said. 'I'm sure she'll be honoured to know you're looking out for her.'

'Ah don't mention that I was here,' he said. 'She mightn't like that. I'd hate her to think I was checking up on her.'

'Fair enough, Joseph,' she said. 'Thanks for dropping by.'

Róisín had liked Mouse instantly, too. She was choosing to ignore the nagging voice in the back of her mind that was telling her she could possibly end up looking for a job herself if things didn't pan out. But what was the point of going on without hope?

The previously sunny skies suddenly clouded over and what seemed like an instant later, the summer rain was bouncing off the pavements, sending a horde of tourists into Nourriture. The rest of the day seemed to pass in a flash as they sold out of pretty much all of their food. She and Brigid were run off their feet, but finally it was time to pull down the shutters and count the day's takings.

She was about to lock the doors for the night when Rob appeared.

'Can I have a word in private?' he asked.

They went up to her office and sat down. He looked very serious and Róisín felt a wave of dread wash over her.

'You're not going to like this,' he said gravely.

'Try me.'

'I told you I'd dig about and try to find out the background to Nourriture and your landlord and all that, and

I've been doing just that. I've been working on it flat out, but there's a big problem.' He took a deep breath. 'You know I told you I thought I recognised the German fella who stayed at your mother's B&B?'

'Claus?' she asked. 'Yeah, but then you said it mustn't be him . . .'

'It was and is the same guy.'

'Really?'

'He's been sniffing around my father's land in Limerick and we told him we don't want to do business with him.'

'So he's an investor,' Róisín said, nodding. 'That's hardly the crime of the century.'

'Not if you're doing things legally and legitimately,' Rob said.

'But he's retired now and his wife and sister have both passed away recently,' Róisín pointed out. 'He seems very low and out of the game.'

'Or so he'd like to have you believe.'

Róisín listened in horror as Rob told her what he'd discovered. Claus, it seemed, was not the person he'd made himself out to be.

'I've had him checked out, Róisín, and the news isn't good. He's been ducking and diving for a long time and the walls are closing in on him now. He absconded from Germany several months ago and there's a warrant for his arrest.'

'Why?'

'It seems he's involved in a very complex pyramid scheme. He gets money from other business people and promises to get them a massive return on their funds. Then he uses the money to buy properties. The money he generates from rent is used to keep the original investors off his back.'

'But isn't that a vicious circle that will close in on him eventually?'

'It already has,' Rob said. 'He's in a lot of trouble and a lot of debt. But now that he's moved his operations further afield from Germany, he's bought himself time, among other things.'

'My God, so he's a total crook?'

'It's worse than that,' Rob said. 'He's a serial womaniser and has conned a lot of women out of their entire pension funds.'

'But his sister and wife . . .'

'He's never been married and the so-called sister is no blood relation. She's his sidekick. They work together at times and then split the proceeds.'

'The rotten louser,' Róisín said, shaking her head. 'We met Ida and Mum was really taken with her. She was so upset about her death. She'll be in bits when she hears it was all a fake.'

Róisín shook her head in disbelief, thinking about Keeley and how she was behaving at the moment. It made her wonder.

She looked up at Rob. 'I think he's made quite an impact on my mum, now that you mention it. I hope she hasn't given him any money. What she has is hard earned and I know she doesn't have a big pension.'

'Well, from what I can make out, this guy isn't too picky. He'll take what he can get. But you haven't heard the best of it,' Rob said. 'Claus is the one offering your Mr Grace the money to buy Nourriture.'

'What?' Róisín screamed. 'But that'll never work. He'll

kick me out of my business and I'll be left high and dry for no reason. By the sounds of it, he'll be caught soon and we'll all end up losing.'

'Precisely,' Rob said. 'So I suggest we set up a meeting with Mr Grace. I need to get some paperwork to back the story up and then I can see your deal being back on track.'

Róisín jumped up and threw her arms around Rob's neck. 'I could kiss you right now,' she said. There was a brief moment of awkwardness as she realised she had practically pinned him to a wall. The small office felt positively claustrophobic as she disentangled her arms from his neck.

'I can't begin to tell you how relieved I am,' she babbled, trying to talk away her embarrassment. 'I've been in total denial for the last while. I even hired a new staff member yesterday and then spent the entire night with one eye open worrying about how I'd manage to pay her and keep going.'

'Don't they say that believing in yourself is the way forward? There were books written about that if I'm not mistaken.'

'True, but I've never been so scared in my entire life. I've no place to live and I've been seriously scared that I'd have no job either.'

'I can't imagine you ever being in a position where you don't have a roof over your head and cash in your pocket. You're one of life's survivors, Róisín.'

'Thanks,' she said. 'Look, can I buy you a drink? It's the least I can do.'

'I'd love nothing more, but I need to get going. I've a load of orders to fill and I need to get back to my father and work out the next step properly. We had no intention of doing business with him, but this German bloke needs to be stopped in his tracks. I'd wait a couple of days until you approach Mr Grace, too. We don't want to jeopardise your chances of pulling this deal off.'

Róisín saw him out and bolted the door of Nourriture. Leaning back against the wall, she punched the air as tears of relief and gratitude ran down her cheeks. Maybe she was going to fulfil her dream after all. Was she on the verge of owning this building? As she gazed around, a feeling of sheer excitement washed over her as she looked to the heavens.

'Can you see me now, Mam? You said you'd watch over me. Now I know you did. I'm being as brave as I can be. I want this."

She knew she had no right to feel this way, but she was ridiculously disappointed that Rob hadn't stayed. An odd sensation rushed through her. Shaking her head, she realised it was jealousy. She thought of the ring Rob had bought for Theresa. He'd said the last time the subject arose that he'd made up his mind. That he knew what he wanted to do.

Róisín wished she had the guts to tell him she liked him. More than that, to tell him that she'd never met a man like him and that she thought, possibly, she was in love with him.

Chapter 38

MOUSE WAS SPEECHLESS. AS SHE SAT CROSS-LEGGED on the floor in the bedroom, the look of astonishment on her face was almost funny.

'Say something,' Nell said eventually. 'What are you thinking?'

'I don't know where to begin,' she admitted. 'Wow. Laura was gorgeous.'

'Wasn't she?' Nell said proudly.

'And so bubbly and full of life in that video. I kind of expected her to be some sort of recluse and more . . . I dunno . . . odd, on account of what had happened to her.'

'She wasn't a bit like me,' Nell said.

'I didn't mean it that way . . .'

'No, I know you didn't. But she was the light and soul of my life. Maybe now you can see why there was such a massive hole in my life when she went.'

Mouse nodded as tears spilled down her cheeks. 'Can I see her again?' she asked.

Nell rewound the tape and they both sat enthralled once more.

'She clearly didn't let any of the illness or problems she'd experienced get to her,' Mouse said. 'Was she always that upbeat or was that just for the video camera?'

'No, that was her in a nutshell,' Nell said. 'That video

was made the day before she went to Australia. She was so excited.'

'How did you cope with her joy at going?'

Nell dropped her head in her hands as her body shook with sorrow.

'Oh God, I'm sorry. I shouldn't have asked that . . .'

'I've never spoken about this with anybody,' Nell said. 'Oh I was so lonely, Mouse. She was my entire life . . . when she went I thought I would die. I wanted to die, in fact.'

'Did you consider topping yourself?' Mouse asked.

She nodded. 'I'm ashamed to say I thought about it for sure.'

'What stopped you?'

'I knew she'd come home to me at some point. I wanted to be here when she did. I knew she'd need me again and it was my duty to wait for that moment.'

'It's really hard being a mam, isn't it?' Mouse said. 'I know you said you were heartbroken when she went looking for her da. But has there ever been a moment when you felt glad she'd got to know him after all that time?'

'I've tried really hard to come around to that way of thinking. But I can't do it.'

'Why?' Mouse asked. 'Isn't it nice for her that she knew who her da was?'

'It's not that,' Nell said. She looked over at Mouse. Her eyes were still damp with tears. 'I'll tell you another time,' she said. 'But if Laura hadn't gone to Australia and wasn't away from me and all the protection I gave her, she may have lived longer.'

'Really?' Mouse's brow furrowed in confusion.

'I'll tell you another day . . . when I'm ready. Mouse, I'm not trying to shut you out. But as I just said, I've never spoken to anyone about Laura or what finally became of her . . . so I need a bit of time.'

'I'm trying to get it,' Mouse admitted. 'But it's so many years ago. I'm struggling with the idea that you still can't lay those ghosts to rest.'

'I know it's as clear as mud for you this minute . . . it'll become clear when I explain . . .' Her voice caught as a wave of pain washed over her once more.

'Hey,' Mouse said hugging her. 'It's OK, you don't have to say anything else now. Let's take a breather.'

'How about we go outside and watch the water flowing? I used to do that many moons ago and it was nice. I'd like a glass of wine. Will you have one?'

'I've never had a drink,' Mouse said. 'I saw what it did to Ma and it put me right off.'

'Fizzy orange then?'

Mouse nodded and followed Nell to the kitchen. As soon as they were settled by the flowing water the swishing and rushing, in contrast to the stillness of the vast sky above, worked its charm.

Nell desperately wanted to confide in Mouse. She wanted to pour all the pain from her heart and finally feel as if she could begin to heal. But she was so terrified of driving her away. Mouse was the closest person in her life. She wasn't a replacement for Laura by any stretch of the imagination, but she was slowly worming her way into her heart.

Sure, she'd had Mo's company and care over the years, but theirs was a more surface relationship. In spite of her outspoken manner, Mo had never delved into emotional conversations. It was all about John-Joe and how hard his life was.

Those conversations had been more than enough for the longest time. Nell hadn't wanted any further contact with the outside world. She'd been comfortable curled up in an emotional ball where nothing got in and, more to the point, nothing got out. She was perfectly happy that way . . . or so she'd thought. Since Mouse's arrival it was as if the tight bandaging that had cocooned her emotions had been loosened. She longed to set the past free, but she was terrified of several things. Was it too late? Would she destroy people? Shuddering, she drank her wine and hoped for some sort of divine intervention that would guide her in the right direction.

Mouse finished her orange and rolled onto her tummy.

'Did none of Laura's friends stay in contact with you after she died?'

'Not really,' Nell said. 'Very few of them stayed in Ballyshore, you see. In small rural villages like this one, there aren't many opportunities. So people move away to go to university or get jobs. There were a couple of girls Laura was close to. We still send one another Christmas cards, but that's about it.'

'Didn't any of them invite you for coffee or anything?'

'Yes, they did,' Nell said. 'One of the girls even invited me to her wedding. I couldn't go. I wouldn't have enjoyed it and there was no point in me wasting a space at the wedding breakfast when she could invite a good friend.'

Mouse didn't comment, but Nell could see that she was desperately trying to work out what had gone on. The walls were closing in and Nell knew she'd be ready to talk soon.

* * *

The following morning Mouse was like a cat on a hot griddle. She couldn't eat her breakfast and was even struggling to drink a mug of tea.

'Why are you so nervous?' Nell asked.

'If I make a mess of things today at Nourriture, Róisín might fire me.'

'But you were in the same predicament with Joseph at the pub and it didn't seem to faze you that much.'

'He was different,' Mouse said. 'He's such an old dote and he kept telling me I was doing great. But Róisín is a different sort. She's really businesslike and acts all grown-up and if I'm honest, she's a bit scary.'

'So why did you take the job?'

'I think it's good to do things that scare me sometimes. The most terrifying thing I ever did was run away from home. Look how well that's turned out,' she said. 'Still, it doesn't mean I'm not bricking it today.'

'You'll be fine,' Nell said. 'She wouldn't have offered you a job if she didn't have a good feeling about you.'

Mouse nodded, but didn't look that convinced.

'Mouse?' Nell asked. 'I know you don't like to mention it, but I think you should consider talking to your da. Let him know you're OK.'

'I know.' She sighed. 'I've been thinking about him and the brothers lately. They're a pile of saps, but I miss them. I never want to go back there either. But I might give them a call.'

'Good girl,' Nell said. She said no more. Mouse would have to choose her own time.

Chapter 39

DOUG CALLED KEELEY TO SEE HOW SHE WAS doing, and it was difficult to hear him over the giggles and screams.

'Sorry about the noise,' he said. 'There's all sorts of shenanigans going on here. The two kids are wired to the moon.'

She smiled, but wasn't in the mood for joining in with friendly banter.

'You've landed on your feet over there by the sounds of it,' she said as he explained that Róisín was bringing home delicious dinners from Nourriture.

'I'd prefer to be there with you,' Doug said.

Keeley wasn't having a bar of it.

'How did Liv get on with the surgery?' he asked. 'Did the surgeon think it was a success?'

'Yes,' she said evenly. 'It all seemed to go according to plan. Liv was already sitting up in the bed waiting for some tea and toast by the time I had to leave.'

'I'll pop in this evening once Róisín gets home. I could do with a break, to be honest,' he said. 'I love Billy and Jess with all my heart, but they're quite hard work.'

'Are they really?' Keeley said sarcastically. 'Funny, I noticed that while you were away and I was trying to run the B&B and mind them too.'

'Keeley, I'll tell you I'm sorry a thousand times a day if you like,' he said. 'I was a stupid old fool. When are you going to forgive me and let me come home, love?'

She was about to answer when Claus drove up.

'I have to go,' she said slamming down the phone.

She opened the front door and walked out to him.

'I'm sorry, I hope I'm not imposing,' he said. 'I was passing. I can go.'

'Oh no, come on in,' she said. 'I could do with a listening ear, if I'm honest.'

'I was fed-up being alone,' Claus said. 'So we'll help one another, yes?'

'Come in,' Keeley said. 'Actually, would you like a glass of wine?'

'I'd love one,' he said with a wide smile. 'I miss sharing a glass of wine with a pretty lady.'

She blushed and felt like a schoolgirl again. She opened a bottle of wine and found two glasses and poured a generous amount into each. They clinked glasses and she took a big gulp.

'I feel like an outsider in my own family,' she confessed. 'I thought it would be a good idea in the long run. But now that I've sent Doug packing, it's as if my family have all snuggled in together and I'm the one being punished. Am I an awful person, Claus?'

'Of course not,' he said, patting her hand. 'So, start from the beginning. Liv is still feeling sick?'

'Yes, well she had surgery today to fix the burn on her arm. It seems to have gone well and she's recovering in the hospital. She needs to stay there for two or three days.'

'And Doug is minding the children, yes?'

'Yes,' she said. 'Martin has been having an affair and heading for divorce.'

'Oh dear. She isn't having so much fun. I see now.'

'Yeah,' Keeley sighed.

'Well, at least Doug is putting his time to good use instead of running off with his friend and pretending he has no family.'

Keeley shrugged her shoulder.

'That man needs to realise what he's got. He has no idea of how lucky he is. There are so many others who would do anything to be in his shoes.' Claus looked intently at Keeley. She smiled weakly. It was actually lovely to have a cheerleader. Someone who only wanted to take her side.

'What about Róisín?' Claus asked. 'She is fine now?'

'Not really,' Keeley said. 'In fact, she just texted me to say she wants to see me this evening, something important she needs to talk to me about in person. It must be about the business, I'm afraid. She's worried sick about Nourriture. She was hoping to buy the building and set herself up for the future. But she's been priced out of the market. It looks as if she's going to lose everything she's worked so hard to create.'

'That's a shame,' Claus said. 'I wish I could take you away from all of this misery.' He clasped his hands together and closed his eyes. 'I have a proposition for you, Keeley. You don't have to answer now . . .'

'Go on,' she said.

'Why don't you cut your losses? Sell this place and come to Germany with me? I have the most magnificent home with a swimming pool, beautiful gardens and everything you could wish for. I don't want to spend the rest of my life alone . . . I never thought I would meet another woman who could come close to Heidi. But you are everything, and more . . .'

'Oh Claus,' she said. She felt faint. Was he honestly asking her to elope with him? 'I don't think I can consider running away from my family. Things aren't exactly perfect right now, but I'm not at a point where I'd turn my back on them.'

'But haven't they done that to you?' he asked.

She opened her mouth to speak and couldn't. For the first time ever, Keeley doubted her family. What if Claus was right? What if they didn't give a damn about her? Why should she stay here and be treated like dirt?

She thought of Róisín and how she had mentioned organising a party for her. Darkness clouded her mind. She'd only said that to mollify her. There'd been no talk of a party since. Doug hadn't even mentioned her birthday and it was only a matter of weeks away.

'If you sold this house and gave a part of it to Doug, you would have plenty of cash to keep you going. I would look after you, of course. But knowing you as I do, I would imagine you would feel more comfortable if you had your own funds also.'

'I've always had my own money,' she agreed.

'Precisely. Hey, I could even invest your money for you.'

'Would you really do that for me?' she asked. She swallowed hard. All of a sudden it all became too much. She dropped her head into her hands as her body was engulfed in sobs.

'I'm sorry. I never meant to talk like this about my family,' she said. 'They're not that awful. This is just a bad patch. That's all.'

Claus looked odd. Keeley couldn't put her finger on it.

'I can't begin to tell you how disappointed I am,' he said. 'I thought we were friends. In fact, I thought we were kindred spirits. Not for such a long time have I met another person who makes me feel the way you do . . .' He stood up and walked over to her. He took her hand and coaxed her out of her chair. He traced her face with gentle fingers and tilted his head to the side.

'You're such a beautiful person, Keeley. Inside and out. I know I shouldn't say this to you, but I'm in love with you. I can't walk away from here without letting you know how I feel. If there's a chance . . . even the smallest glimmer of hope for us?'

'Oh Claus . . . I wish things were simpler. There are too many people who'll be hurt . . .'

'But what about you, Keeley? Don't you matter? What about your happiness?' He stared into her eyes and she felt entranced by him. He lowered his lips to hers and only barely touched her. She gasped. He kissed her again. More fervently this time.

'Claus, I'm sorry . . .'

'Don't be sorry, my love . . .'

'No,' she said, pulling away. 'You need to leave. This is all wrong. It can't work. I won't throw away everything I've fought for and worked towards my entire life. I need to see if I can work things out with Doug. After forty years of marriage, I owe him that. I owe myself that.'

'Oh Keeley,' he said. 'I cannot express how hurt I am. I thought you were different. I will go now and I won't come back again. I will go back to Germany alone . . . I wish this could have worked out differently.' He strode toward the door.

'Claus, wait,' she said. 'I didn't mean to hurt you. I'm sorry if you thought our relationship had the potential to develop, but I'm a married woman.'

'Yes, I know. To a man who doesn't appreciate you or value your worth.'

'That's not entirely true.'

'Isn't it? And as for your daughters . . . they should be ashamed of themselves. I would have loved you and cherished you, Keeley. I'm sorry it has to end this way.'

He left and drove away and she couldn't help feeling even more confused than before. She leaned against the wall and cried.

Wiping her eyes with the back of her hand, doubt crept in. What if he could see things more clearly from the outside? She'd always thought they loved her. Yes, they could be selfish and lazy, but were they all that bad? Curling up on the sofa, she cried until her throat hurt. She'd never felt so alone.

Chapter 40

ROB AND MELVIN WERE SITTING AT THE COMPUTER together. The images that were popping up on screen made Rob's blood run cold. The more they dug, the more there was to find. It was an incredible level of fraud.

'This guy is a total crook,' he said, shaking his head.

It turned out Claus wasn't at all who he'd said he was. His real name was Wolfgang Bauer and he had left a trail of destruction behind him in Germany.

'How can people like him sleep at night?' Melvin asked. 'Surely there has to come a point in a fellow's life when he looks inside his own head and wonders if he's going to heaven or hell.'

'I doubt a fellow like him has any remorse, or conscience for that matter,' Rob said. 'So what do you think we should do?'

'I know what we are doing,' Melvin said as he reached for his phone. 'I'm calling Sidney at the police station. I was only chatting to him yesterday. I'd say he'd be delighted to put a stop to this clown's gallop.'

Rob nodded. He wanted him put away, but more than that he wanted to clear the decks so Róisín could go ahead and buy Nourriture.

'Just so you know and before you hear it on the grape-vine, it's all over with Theresa. So I'm not going behind her back with any of this,' he said waving a hand toward the computer.

'Is Theresa OK?'

'I hope she will be,' he said. 'I upset her and I'm not proud of that, but in the long run it's the right thing to do, Dad. I don't love her the way I should. It wasn't fair to her. She deserves better.'

'You're right, she does,' Melvin said. 'And so do you.'

'You think?' Rob brightened. He really thought his father was going to be disappointed with him. 'I care about young Theresa, she's a great girl. But you're my son, you're my priority and I want you to find someone special. Someone who you love the way I loved your mother.'

'Thanks,' he said sheepishly. He thought of Theresa's tear-stained face and her confusion as he tried to let her down gently. She'd been totally thrown and he knew she'd been expecting a proposal rather than a farewell. Her dismay had turned to anger and she'd flung the pile of glossy brochures she'd been carrying across the room.

She'd told him: 'I was going to suggest we go to Portugal in a villa with three other couples and spend a lovely time drinking cocktails and being seen in all the right spots.'

That had been the closure he needed. He couldn't think of anything worse than being incarcerated in a villa, having a fortnight of posing rammed down his throat. Theresa might not see it right now, but he wasn't the right guy for her. She needed a man with an even tan, bright smile, fast car and a large bank balance. She wanted a jock, and he simply wasn't that guy.

'I was thinking about your Ballyshore love,' Melvin said. 'I've a suggestion to make, if you don't mind.'

Rob shrugged. 'Sure, you haven't led me astray yet.'

Melvin looked him up and down. 'You're a grand-looking fellow, Robert. You inherited your mother's good looks, in fact. But you're a bit wild looking. Would you consider going to the barber and getting a proper shave and haircut? Seeing as you're out and about selling your beer, sprucing yourself up wouldn't do any harm, full stop. You mentioned her ex was a Frenchman, and they're fierce well groomed usually. So maybe you could give her a bit of a surprise by turning up in something other than beer-stained jeans,' he said pointedly, looking at the dark brown spots decorating Rob's loose-fitting jeans.

Rob laughed. 'You don't pull any punches, do you, Dad?'

'Well, if I can't say it to you, who can? I know you can't abide the glossy magazine types that Theresa favoured, but there's a healthy balance between scruffy and suave, and it mightn't go astray to try and strike it.'

He clapped Melvin on the back and grinned, but it made him think all the same. What if he changed his look and turned into a semi smooth-looking type in a suit and proper laced-up shoes as opposed to the trainers he currently favoured? If he looked the part, maybe Róisín would think differently about him.

'Do you know what, Da? I think you're right.'

'You do?' Melvin looked astonished.

'I'm going to take your advice. After all, you were the one who managed to get Mam to fall in love with you all those years ago.'

'She was the catch of the county,' he affirmed. 'I treated her like a princess before someone else managed to.'

Rob nodded. Treat her like a princess . . .

Melvin was busy thumbing through his old-fashioned phone book.

'I have all the important numbers in here. I know I have the police station too.'

'I'll catch you later on,' Rob said.

The drive into Limerick city was quicker than he'd anticipated. Why was the traffic non-existent and the roads totally clear when he was afraid of what lay ahead? He found a parking space easy enough, too, then walked to the most salubrious store in town and lurked in the men's department.

'Hello, sir, can I help you with anything today?' This question was put to him by a very pretty blonde lady who was dressed in a tight-fitting, but incredibly classy white trouser suit.

'Eh yeah,' he said feeling instantly self-conscious. 'I don't know how to say this . . .' She smiled politely. 'I need to change my image,' he blurted. 'I'm in love with a girl. She's gorgeous and clever and I want her to see that I've made an effort. Could you help me look more appealing?'

The lady smiled and her eyes lit up as she patted his arm. 'That's the most romantic thing I've ever heard. I'd love to help you.' She appraised him thoughtfully. 'So what are you thinking? Clothes and shoes, or are you willing to do something with your entire look?' She glanced up towards his hair.

'Is this too wild looking?' he asked pulling his fingers through his shaggy curls.

'I actually think you look great,' she said. 'Maybe a nice shave, though, and I could ask Susie in the salon to trim your hair?'

He nodded. The lady went to make a call as Rob looked

at the clothes. They had everything from three-piece suits to smart casuals. The running theme was elegance.

'Susie can take you in twenty minutes. That'll give us time to pick out a couple of looks from here,' she said.

'A couple?'

'Well you're hoping to see this girl more than once I take it?' she said raising one eyebrow.

He nodded. 'Go for it,' he said, deciding he needed to trust this woman.

'Have you a budget?' she asked.

He shook his head. 'Within reason . . . I'm not interested in paying ten grand for a pair of shoes or anything like that,' he said.

She laughed. 'That's fine. We're not quite at that level in here. I'm Fiona, by the way.'

'Rob.'

'Right then, Rob. Let's get cracking.'

She showed him rack after rack of clothes and pointed at all sorts of colours. Some he liked and others he didn't.

'OK, I have a good idea of what you're comfortable with,' said Fiona. 'Do you want to go into the dressing room and I'll pass you in a few things.'

Rob felt like he'd run a marathon by the time Fiona thought he had enough stuff.

'How do women get enjoyment from shopping?' he asked in bewilderment. 'This is torture.'

Fiona laughed. 'Keep your eyes on the prize,' she said with a wink. 'Just imagine how amazed your lady will be when she sees you.'

'You're right. This will all be worthwhile if she sees me in a different light,' he said.

'I can't see any girl not appreciating all this effort.'

By the time he'd paid Fiona, the hairdresser was on the phone.

'He's coming now,' Fiona said. 'Why don't you go on ahead and I'll pack your clothes? I'm dying to see how you look!'

'If things don't work out with Róisín, can I come back and ask you out?' he said with a sheepish grin.

'I'm not sure my husband would like that,' she said. 'But if I was single, I'd be there like a shot.'

'Cheers,' he said.

The hair salon was tiny, but very stylishly kitted out.

'Hi, what can I do for you today?' Susie asked as she shook his hand.

'I'm trying to look more attractive,' he said. 'I'm looking to win a lady's heart.'

'Fabulous!' she grinned. 'I love it. You're the last of the romantics. Hallelujah that romance isn't dead!'

'You're worse than Fiona,' he said with a grin. 'She's delighted with the whole notion. I just hope it has the desired effect on the right lady.'

Susie sat him in front of the mirror. She pulled his hair back off his face and combed it in different directions.

'I think you'd be gorgeous with a short back and sides and a bit of length left in the top. Your curls are ever so sexy and I think it would be a travesty to remove them all.'

'A travesty, eh?' he said, raising one eyebrow.

'What do you think? Are you open to having the beard removed, too? You don't have one of those faces that needs to be hidden in hair.'

Rob swallowed. It was years since he'd been clean-shaven, let alone had short hair. He'd have nothing to hide behind.

'OK, I trust you. But if I look like a munter, we'll have to glue something back on to my face,' he warned.

'I don't see that being the case,' she said. 'Sit back and relax.'

Rob did the exact opposite. He gripped the chair like his life depended on it.

'You're not on a roller-coaster,' Susie joked.

'That's what you think,' he said. 'I'm terrified. What if I look a fright and can't go near her for two months?'

'You of little faith,' she said with a smile. 'I've cut hair before, you know.'

Rob decided to pretend he was enjoying the experience and allowed his mind to wander. He hadn't managed to think to the future at all. What if Róisín was interested in him? Wouldn't that be astonishing? What would he do? Move to Ballyshore? She'd hardly want to up sticks and leave Nourriture.

How would his father feel if he wanted to leave Limerick and live in Ballyshore? As Susie finished, he couldn't help grinning at himself. What kind of a fool was he turning into? The girl hadn't even agreed to have dinner with him and he was fifteen steps ahead, practically getting a removal van organised!

'What do you think?' Susie asked. 'I'm glad you're smiling at least!'

'Hey, it's great,' he said looking in the mirror.

'You look ten years younger,' she said. 'Whoever this girl is, she'll be bowled over by your new look.'

He paid and tried not to cough at the price.

'I'll be waiting another ten years before I get a haircut,' he teased. 'No wonder your salon is so classy when you charge enough to keep a family of four in dinners for a month.'

Rob took the stairs two at a time and stood looking triumphant in the men's clothing department.

'Well, I'll be damned,' Fiona said. 'Who knew such an attractive beast lay under all that hair? You've probably preserved yourself very nicely now that I see your skin. Any woman would kill for that flawless look!'

'Forget that,' he said. 'Do I look better? Would you give me one if you weren't married?'

She threw back her head and laughed. 'I'd be like a child after an ice cream van on a sunny day if it weren't for himself at home.'

'That'll do nicely,' he said as he accepted the pile of bags from Fiona. 'Thanks for all your help.'

'If you're passing some day, pop in and tell me how you got on. I'll be dying to know.'

'You're on,' he said. 'Now which outfit will I put on? I'm going to see her now before my hair looks flat and my beard grows again!'

Fiona advised him to wear the chinos with a white T-shirt and canvas shoes. 'It's cool and summery without looking too forced.'

Rob had a spring in his step as he drove out of Limerick city. Feeling like a schoolboy, he hoped Róisín wouldn't drop-kick him across the shop when he asked her out.

Chapter 41

RÓISÍN COULDN'T CONCENTRATE ON A THING. SHE wanted to call Rob and ask him if he'd made any headway with the whole Claus issue, but he'd said he'd get in touch once he had any news. She was also peppering to talk to Keeley, but her mum was busy for the day and couldn't meet until the evening. Róisín knew that was one conversation she'd have to have face-to-face. Keeley would be so shocked to learn that both Ida and Claus had lied so cruelly to her.

Liv's arrival into the shop with Billy and Jess was enough to take her mind off everything. Liv's operation had been a great success and she looked a lot less stressed than before.

'How's it going?' she asked.

'Not too bad,' Liv said. 'Could I have a word with you upstairs for a few minutes?' she asked.

Róisín was at a loss as to what to do with the children when Mouse suddenly appeared. Róisín had liked Mouse instantly, but she also knew deep down that it would give her an extra incentive to keep Nourriture going, whether it was right here or somewhere else. The more pressure she was under and the more people who relied on her, the harder she'd try.

'Hi Mouse,' Róisín said. 'Brilliant timing! Would you

be able to look after my niece and nephew for a little bit? I know this isn't totally in your job description, but there's been a family crisis.'

Billy said, 'We won't be bold.'

'That's OK you two,' Mouse said. 'I'm really nervous because this is my first week at Nourriture. So maybe you could help me out?'

'Why are you scared?' Billy asked. 'Did you think Auntie Róisín would be mean to you and make you eat lots of vegetables?'

'I'm just scared because I'm the new girl,' Mouse said. 'But I'm much happier now I know I can hang out with you.'

'Thanks, Mouse,' Róisín said.

'Is your real name Mouse?' Jess asked in awe.

'No, it's actually Celina,' she said. 'But I prefer Mouse. That's the name my friend Nell calls me. I live at her house and she's really nice.'

'Mouse is nicer than Celina,' Jess said, and Billy nodded in agreement.

'Thanks, I think so too. Want to go out to the park and play?' Mouse asked.

They both looked so thrilled that Róisín breathed a sigh of relief.

'I promise I won't have you babysitting as a habit. I'm just stuck for today,' Róisín said, patting her on the back.

'No hassle,' Mouse said, taking both their hands. 'It's not as if I'm a qualified brain surgeon and you're insulting my experience or anything.'

Róisín laughed and waved as the trio left, chatting like old pals. Then she turned to Liv and beckoned her to follow her up the stairs. Once in the office, they sat either side of the desk.

'What's going on?'

'Martin's been on. He wants to come home. He says he's sorry and it's all over with the young one . . .'

'I see,' Róisín said, sighing. 'What do you think?'

'I don't know, Ro. I've lost all confidence and I honestly thought I was going insane. I knew there was something very odd happening and any time I brought it up with him, he made me feel as if I was the crazy one.'

'I can't tell you what to do,' Róisín said. 'Do you love him?'

'I've always loved him. In fact, I know I've always loved him more than he loves me.'

'Why do you say that?'

'I always felt uneasy. He made me feel as if I wasn't worthy of him. As if I was only hanging on to him by the skin of my teeth.'

'Oh Liv, that's awful.'

'There's someone who has been lovely to me,' Liv said, blushing.

'Oh really? Who?'

'Colm.'

'Whaat?' Róisín was about to giggle and say he was the creepiest creature when she saw the expression on Liv's face and stopped herself.

'He's been calling over. Just for a cup of tea and a chat, that sort of thing. At first he was only really dropping by to see if you were there. He was totally smitten with you.'

'Poor Colm.'

'Well, once he got over the fact that you wouldn't give him the time of day, we got talking.'

'I don't think I was awful to him, was I?' she asked guiltily.

'You probably didn't think you were, but believe me, when you adore another person and they find you an irritant, every knock-back hurts.'

'Oh . . . I see,' said Róisín.

'He visited me in hospital. Brought me bunches of grapes and made me feel like I was special.'

'Do you find him attractive?' Róisín asked.

'God, no,' Liv said. 'It would be like having an affair with my brother.'

'You don't have a brother.'

'You know what I mean,' Liv said.

'So why are your bringing Colm into it?'

'He's nice to be around. He treats me well. He'd do anything for me and he's kind. There are no nasty agendas and I feel safe.'

'So what are you saying? You're going to keep him in the spare room as your little faithful friend?'

'No.' Liv actually smiled for the first time in ages. 'All I'm saying is that there is a man out there who likes me just the way I am . . .'

'Of course, Liv. You're a great person.'

'So I don't need to stay with Martin, do I?'

'No, you don't.'

'But what about the kids? Should I stay with him for them?'

'He rarely sees them as it is,' Róisín said. 'If you let him see them when he comes home, what difference will it make in the long run?'

'It's not quite as simple as that,' Liv said, biting her lip.

'I know that. It'll take a lot of working out and all that . . .'

'His girlfriend is pregnant.'

The words hung in the air as Róisín tried to fathom it all. 'But I thought he said they were finished?' she finally said.

'They are. He's had enough of her and doesn't want the new baby thing again.'

'He should've thought of that a bit sooner,' Róisín fumed.

As they chatted about the options, Róisín was relieved to see that Liv was actually being very level-headed about the whole situation. She didn't want Martin back. She didn't want to deny the children access to him and she had faith in the theory that she'd meet someone else some day.

'I'm aiming for less nerdy than sweet Colm and much less of an arrogant dick than Martin. Do you think he exists?'

'God, I hope so,' she said hugging her sister tightly. 'I hope there are two of them looking for nice women.'

'Will you come with me to tell Mum and Dad?' Liv asked. 'I can't bear to see the disappointment in their eyes. The only thing I did right has failed. They'll be devastated, won't they?'

'Have a little faith,' Róisín said. 'I know all they want is to see us both happy.'

The girls finished their chat and could hear the children downstairs in the shop with Mouse.

'I'd better go,' Liv said. 'Will you come with me later to talk to our folks?'

'Of course,' she assured her. 'Actually, there's something difficult I need to tell Mum, so there might be strength in numbers all round. I won't go into it now, but it's going to upset her.'

Liv nodded. 'What a day,' she said sadly. 'But one thing

I want to say to you, Ro, is that I won't be staggering about any longer. I can't bear the hangovers and I won't allow Martin to drive me to drink any more.'

'Are you giving it up totally?'

'For a while,' Liv said. 'It's not doing me any favours. I need to concentrate on building a new life. It certainly won't happen if I'm half-cut.'

'Good for you,' Róisín said. 'I'm proud of you, Liv.'

Liv left the shop looking brighter than she had for a long time. It was going to be a long road, but Róisín was glad she had at least taken the first step along it.

A while later, Róisín was dealing with a customer when she felt eyes boring into her. Looking across the counter, she saw a very attractive man standing there, just looking at her.

'Hi, can I help you?' she said. Not wanting to crane her neck and get caught staring she asked who was next.

'Do you have any ready meals?' the lady asked.

'Yes, we have a selection to take away and we also have a service where we can fill your freezer. I have a wonderful selection of pâtés, cured meats, smoked fish and cheeses. We bake hand-made breads every morning and there's always a special dish of the day. Today it's summer fish pie.'

By the time they were finished, Róisín had a substantial first order of drinks with food and breads which she brought in to the kitchen but as she turned to go back into the main part of the shop, the attractive man was lurking.

'Hi,' he said, looking shy.

'Oh my God! Rob, it's you!' Her hands shot to her mouth as she felt the heat rise from her toes. She genuinely feared there could be sparks shooting out the top of her head.

'I decided to clean up my image,' he said.

'Wow, you certainly did,' she said swallowing. 'You look . . . you look good.'

'I cut all my hair off, spend a fortune on clothes and get my face defuzzed and all I get is *good*?' He smiled and his eyes lit up.

Róisín actually felt vaguely unstable. He looked utterly divine.

'OK then,' she said, trying to sound nonchalant. 'You look stunning. Amazing. Fabulous.'

'That's better,' he said with a wide smile.

'I can't believe you were hiding under all that hair and stuff.'

'Jeez, you make it sound as if I've been resurrected from a cave and taught how to walk on two legs rather than four!'

She giggled. 'What's brought on the big change?'

'Ah, I thought it was high time I started behaving like a grown-up. So, would it be possible to have a quick chat?'

'Yeah, come on upstairs. We'll be able to talk in the office.' She called over to Brigid and said where she'd be. Brigid gave her a wink that spoke a thousand words and Róisín couldn't help giggling.

As soon as they climbed the stairs and Rob was sitting in such close proximity, Róisín thought she was going to pass out. He was astonishingly attractive. She felt sixteen again, a dizzy schoolgirl. Her palms were sweating and she could barely concentrate on what was being said. She was so conscious of every move he made. His hand brushed off her leg as he settled himself in a chair. She jumped and blushed.

She was so disappointed, she felt as if she might cry.

He'd clearly done all this for his proposal to Theresa. He was probably here to tell her they were engaged.

'So I've been doing a lot of soul-searching,' he said. 'I knew things were hurtling out of control with my life. I was trying to please my father, my friends and most of all Theresa. But it wasn't sitting right with me.'

She swallowed and nodded. The voice in her head was telling her to stay calm.

'So I've made some changes,' he said. 'I've broken up with Theresa.'

'What?' She thought she was going to leap to the roof with delight. 'Eh, really?'

'She wasn't the right girl for me, Róisín.'

'Wasn't she?'

'I knew it all along . . . but it didn't really resonate with me until I met someone else.'

'Oh.' Her hope sank to her shoes as she tried to look pleased for him.

'I met this girl, quite by chance. They say that happens sometimes. You know, when you're really not planning it?'

'So they say,' she said.

'I need your advice, though. That's why I'm here.'

'OK. I'll help you if I can.'

'I don't want to wreck the friendship I have with this girl. She's really amazing and a part of me is terrified to say anything in case she tells me to sling my hook.'

'Do you think she feels the same way?'

'I have no idea,' Rob said. 'All I can say is that she gets me. She understands the way I think and I can always be myself around her. She makes me laugh and on top of all that, she's drop-dead gorgeous.'

'She sounds fantastic,' Róisín said. She stood up. She couldn't listen to another minute of this. If he didn't leave in the next few seconds, Róisín feared she might start blubbing.

'I'd better get back to the shop,' she said. 'I think I heard Brigid calling me. I've a lot of work to do. Good luck with it all. I hope it all works out for you.' She grabbed a pile of pages from her desk, in the hope it would make her escape seem convincing. She was so flustered, though, they fluttered from her hands. Dropping to her hunkers, she gathered them up, trying to stop her hands from shaking. Suddenly, Rob was there in front of her, crouching too. He reached over and lifted her chin. As he stared at her, a tell-tale tear escaped.

'Hey,' he said with obvious concern.

'I'm sorry,' she said. 'I'm being totally stupid.' As she attempted to stand, he caught her and pulled her up. Before she could say another word, he pulled her closer and kissed her.

Róisín felt like she was having an out-of-body experience.

'I don't understand,' she said moments later.

'It's you, Róisín. Don't you see? You've changed everything for me. I was having an uphill battle the entire time I was with Theresa. We weren't suited. When I'm with you, I can be the real me . . . Every time I leave Ballyshore, I try to think of ways of coming back.'

'But my life is such a mess . . . I told you about France and how I could've lost my business . . . and you still want to be with me?' This time the tears that fell were accompanied by the widest smile imaginable.

'I want to be with you no matter what. We have no idea

what the future holds. But whatever pans out with your business, we'll muddle through. Once I have you and you have me, nothing else is important. What matters is finding that person, the one.'

'Oh wow,' she said.

'Remember the dream I told you about? The one where I find the right person to be with me so I can have the family I've always yearned for?' he asked. She nodded. 'You're my one and if you'll have me, I'd like to take this one step at a time and see if dreams come true.'

She kissed him. It was as if she'd been waiting for this moment her entire life. Even though she'd gone through the IVF with Jacques, she'd never felt as close to a person as she did with this gorgeous man in front of her.

'You took my breath away when I saw you earlier,' she admitted. 'You're a dark horse,' she said with a smile.

'I had some help,' he said with a grin. 'I walked into a shop and told the assistant I needed to try to win the heart of an amazing woman.'

'You did that? Really?' she said, taken aback.

'I honestly didn't dare to hope I'd even stand a chance with you,' he said. 'If you'll agree to give us a chance, I'll do anything in my power to make you happy, Róisín.'

'I can't think of anything I'd love more,' she said with a smile.

Their conversation was cut short as her mobile phone rang. She ignored it, wanting nothing to interrupt their moment. When it rang a second, then third time, she sighed and fished it out of her bag.

'Mum!' she said. 'How are you?'

'I'm not great, love. Can you talk for a moment?'

'Eh, I'm with someone, but you can go ahead.'

'Oh, if you have someone there, I'll leave it . . . it's a sensitive subject . . .'

'Is everything OK, Mum?'

'Not really. I need to talk to you about my friend Claus.'

'Claus?' Róisín said. 'You haven't given him any money, have you?'

'No, why?'

'Mum,' Róisín hesitated. 'I've to tell you something. That's what I wanted to talk to you about tonight. I think it might shock you. So I'll talk to you later about it, OK?'

'No, it's not OK, Róisín. Don't treat me like a sensitive little thing, tell me what it is.'

Róisín explained as gently as she could what Rob had discovered about Claus.

'I beg your pardon?' Keeley said in disbelief. She sounded winded. 'I can't believe it,' she said. 'Are you absolutely certain, Róisín?'

'I'm afraid so. It gets worse,' she said. 'Ida was in on it with him. She's not dead, Mum. She shares the proceeds when they con a woman out of money. I'm so sorry.'

'My God,' Keeley whispered.

'And on top of all that, it turns out he is the mystery investor who was attempting to buy the building where Nourriture is now.'

Róisín could hear Keeley choking back tears and her heart broke for her. She had been so affected by the news of Ida's death.

'I'm so very sorry, Mum, but this man isn't anyone's friend. Hey, don't be upset. No harm done, right?'

'No harm done, love,' her mother said.

'Tell her to have nothing more to do with him,' Rob said urgently. 'His real name is Wolfgang Bauer and he's committed more frauds than you've had hot dinners. Seriously, Róisín, tell your mum to stay the hell away from him. He's a crook.'

'Did you hear that, Mum?'

'I did,' Keeley said weakly. 'I understand.'

Róisín promised she'd see Keeley later and then they hung up. She wondered briefly if she should ask Liv to give it a day or two before breaking the news about Martin – there was only so much bad news her parents could take.

'You OK?' Rob said quietly.

She smiled weakly at him. 'Tough times.'

He moved to take her in his arms, where she felt like she never wanted to leave.

Chapter 42

RÓISÍN AND ROB'S ROMANTIC MOMENT WAS LITER-ally just that – the phone on the desk rang loudly and Brigid told her there were deliveries to be checked through and a busload of tourists on the way.

'I got a call from the Irish Tours rep and she said she'd swing by if we can cope? Fifty people in total.'

'OK Brigid, I'll be down in a minute. Put Mouse behind the sandwich bar and ask Steve to do the crepes, he's super quick at those.'

'Will I stay and give you a hand and maybe we can have dinner tonight?' Rob asked. 'As in, a proper dinner date?'

'I'd love that. Once I've had a chance to chat to Mum,' she said.

As he smiled at her, Róisín knew her luck was changing. No matter what happened, if she had an amazing ally like Rob on her side, things could only get better. She and her family would get through this dark spell and find the light again, just as her mother's cards had always promised her. She knew it.

They both ran down to the shop. Rob went into the off licence and set up a tasting station. Róisín sprang into action and showed Mouse how to make that day's special, which was a goat's cheese and locally smoked ham open sandwich.

'It goes with the watercress soup and if we have them ready and looking appealing, it's easy to steer people towards them.'

Mouse nodded and watched intently as Róisín made one.

'Right, I've got it. I'll make a load of them.'

'Samantha, will you stick to the coffee machine while Ricky does soups?' she called out. 'Here we go, let's work as a team and as usual, folks, no chatter until we serve the hungry horde! Listen to one another and shout out your orders, yeah? Communication is where it's at, OK?'

'Yes chef!' they all shouted in unison.

Mouse had the biggest grin on her face.

'This is deadly,' she said as Róisín joined her to speed up production. 'You're like your man Ramsay on the telly.'

The tour bus pulled up and the tourists poured inside. Rob was playing a blinder. The American tourists were loving him.

Róisín ran in and told him to promote his beer, saying people could have a glass of beer with soup and an open sandwich for ten euros.

'You're on,' he said winking.

The next hour was mayhem, but they all thoroughly enjoyed it. The sun was shining and the outdoor area was swarmed with happy customers. By the time the tourists began filing back onto the bus, Róisín felt buzzed.

'That was wonderful,' the tour guide said. 'Can I meet with you to chat about a deal going forward? If you can do a set price for a daily lunch like today, we'll happily add you to our stopover list.'

'I'd love that,' Róisín said.

'We have fifty coaches on the road and we'd bring business your way. For a small commission fee, we could direct lots of traffic in to Nourriture. There's ample opportunity for scenic photographs and I know today's crowd adored the food and craft beer.'

Róisín handed her a business card and said she'd be happy to discuss an arrangement. She whispered a thank-you to the heavens as she waved the bus off, then skipped in to see Rob. If she couldn't buy this building, she felt certain she could make Norriture work somewhere close by. It was the boost of confidence she needed.

'That was mega,' he said. 'I've sold all your stock and had to send one of your lads out to my van. If you could do this more often, I'd be a multimillionaire!'

She explained that it seemed likely and Rob whistled.

'Good job. This place is fantastic to work in, too. I love the atmosphere. Your staff are second to none. Even though it was seriously busy, they knew to offer little tastes of cheeses and cured meats and it seemed as if they had all the time in the world. They sold a shedload of stuff as a result.'

'I'm lucky with this crew,' she said gazing around. 'Mouse did really well too. She's the pretty little girl at the sandwich counter. It's her first week and she flew along. I'll be holding on to her, I can tell you!'

'First week? But why did you hire her if you thought Nourriture was on the way out, as a matter of interest?' he asked.

'She was my kick up the backside,' Róisín answered. 'She was the initiative I needed to keep this business going no matter where I ended up. She's young, hungry and enthusiastic and I knew I couldn't offer her a lifeline and snatch it away again.'

'You're a weirdo, but I think you're amazing,' he said pecking her on the lips.

A French couple approached and asked Róisín a question. She answered in fluent French, letting them know she could organise food for a picnic for eight people for tomorrow. They left looking thrilled.

'Is there anything you can't do, Miss Róisín?' Rob asked.

More customers needed questions answered so she excused herself with a backward glance and a very bright smile.

By six o'clock Róisín's feet were aching. She thanked Mouse and congratulated her on being so quick off the mark.

'You're going to fit in very nicely here. Well done and I'll see you tomorrow. I don't think I'll ever want to let you go.'

The delighted squeal and happy dance that Mouse performed made Róisín laugh.

Róisín noticed there was an older lady waiting in a small car just outside. Briefly, she wondered if she was a relation. Mouse leaned over and hugged the woman and judging by the gestures and wide smile, she was telling her what a successful day they'd had.

Brigid needed to rush off, so Róisín and Rob were the last ones standing as she tilled up. Rob got busy sweeping out the off licence and getting it ready for the next morning.

Róisín would have preferred to go home and freshen up, but she didn't want to leave Rob waiting, so she did a quick fix in her office, replenishing her mascara, lipstick and perfume. She could hear the sounds of Rob's cleaning work downstairs, so she took a quiet moment to herself. She reached up for her box of cards and went through them to find one in particular.

Darling girl

Happy nineteenth birthday! Would you believe this is the age I was when I gave birth to you? If I had one wish it would be that I could live for ever to see you grow and flourish.

Would it be awful of me to pass you the baton? That's what I want to do. I want you to take life by the scruff and go out there and live each day as if it's your last.

Dance as if everyone you've ever fancied is watching.

Laugh and love with every fibre of your being and never accept second best. Nobody is worth hating, life is too short for that kind of nonsense. Embrace the people who make your heart sing. If a relationship needs to be kept a secret, then you shouldn't be in it. Surround yourself with people who help you celebrate the essence of who you are.

Love and light

Mam x

Róisín tucked the card back into the box and sat for a moment. All the relationships she'd been in so far had meant she needed to change or hide something. Rob was the first man who allowed her to act the same way she did with her family and with Jill. In her mother's words, she felt she could hear her blessing over this choice – her decision to love without limits.

She went down the stairs and Rob walked over to her and took her in his arms and kissed her for the longest time.

'The more I see of you, the more I fall in love with you,' he said.

'You . . . you're falling in love with me?' she asked.

'I shouldn't have said that, should I?' he grinned. 'I'm supposed to play it cool and act as if I don't give a toss, right?'

'No,' she said forcefully. 'Let's start as we mean to go on. No games. No pretending and no acting like someone else. If we can keep the friendship we've built and add a little spice to it . . .'

'I think that could be arranged,' he said pulling her close.

Her mobile beeped.

'Oh no, I'm so sorry. It's Liv. I've to go with her to speak to my folks. She's leaving Martin.'

'Hey, no problem,' he said. 'Why don't I go to the Thatch and get a drink and you shoot off and do what needs doing? Meet me when you're free.'

'Are you sure pub grub is OK? Probably not the romantic dinner you had in mind.'

'We'll have so many opportunities for those, you'll be sick of them. Pub grub will be perfect.'

'Are you for real?' she asked with shining eyes.

'Totally. Róisín, I can't believe we're going to be together. I'd wait forever for you.'

'I want to cry,' she said as her eyes filled up. 'Oh my God, I'm being such a sap. You're amazing.'

'Hurry up and get back,' he said kissing her lightly again.

She phoned Liv and told her she was on her way to the B&B. 'Is Dad there with you?'

'Yeah,' she said sounding really nervous.

'Bring him too and we'll have a family meeting.'

'Thanks, sis.'

Róisín drove to her parents' house and was surprised when there was no answer at the door. Walking to the back of the house, she found the door unlocked.

'Mum?' she called out.

'In here,' Keeley said. 'I'll be there in a moment.'

When she appeared, Róisín was astonished to see she'd been crying.

'Hey, what's wrong, Mum?'

'Nothing much,' she said sighing deeply.

'Well, I don't think that's true judging by your swollen eyes.'

'I've been a total idiot,' Keeley said. 'I've made a mess of my life and I ought to know better. Please don't ask me too many questions just at the moment. I'm feeling delicate. But most of all, I'm feeling utterly stupid.'

Before she could delve any further, Róisín looked out and saw Liv's car pulling up.

'Liv and Dad are coming in. We need a family meeting,' Róisín stated.

'Let me wash my face and I'll be with you all,' Keeley said.

The others walked in and Róisín looked around for the children.

'I asked my neighbour's daughter to sit with them for an hour,' Liv said. 'Where's Mum?'

'I'm here,' Keeley said, plastering a smile on her face.

They sat at the table. The awkwardness between Keeley and Doug was swiftly overshadowed by Liv's announcement that she was going to ask Martin for a divorce.

'I'm sorry for letting you both down,' she finished tearfully.

Keeley took her hand. 'You have never let us down. Either of you,' she said forcefully. 'Liv, we will support you any way we can. Whatever you decide is fine by us. Isn't it, Doug?'

He was sitting with a very odd look on his face.

'What?' Róisín asked.

'I could murder that arrogant sod,' he said. 'Well he's the one who's missing out. You won't ever be on your own, Liv,' he said. 'We'll all help you.'

'But what about Martin?' Róisín asked. 'Have you told him this?'

Liv shook her head. 'We have spoken on the phone and obviously he knows I'm very upset, but I think that's something I'll have to say to his face, have a proper sit-down and sort things out between us. I have to do it right for the children's sake and not cause conflict between us.'

Róisín nodded. 'You're being brilliant about this, Liv,' she said gently. 'Brilliant and brave. Billy and Jess will understand later on, I'm sure of it.'

'That brings me to another matter,' Liv said. 'I've been neglecting the children and drinking too much and I deeply regret it. It all ends here. I was so busy feeling sorry for myself that I was neglecting the two most amazing gifts I've been given in life.'

'I'm so proud of you,' Keeley said.

'And I'm going to sign up for a course in the local night college and find an au pair to help out. Martin has agreed to pay for one. Things are going to change. I'm ready to fight back.'

Róisín stayed for another few minutes. There were a few questions she wanted to ask her mother, but not in front of the others and not while Liv was having her moment. The other reason she wasn't delaying was because she knew Rob was sitting on a bar stool, waiting for her. She kissed them goodbye and sped towards the Thatch.

Chapter 43

NELL'S EARS WERE RINGING BY THE TIME THEY arrived back at the lighthouse. Mouse was chattering like a magpie, barely taking a breath.

'I'm delighted you're getting on so well,' she said as they sat down to have something to eat.

'The food is amazing there, Nell. Róisín is so enthusiastic about everything she sells. When the coachload of Americans came in, I thought we were gonzoed. But she was so good at showing me what to do.'

'That's great. Clearly that's how she has managed to make the place a success.'

'Why haven't you gone in there?' Mouse asked. 'I think you'd love it.'

'It's not my type of place.'

'How can it not be? Come in and I'll show you all the stuff.'

'No thanks.'

Mouse stopped and stared at her. 'You're so weird at times, do you know that?'

Nell bit her lip. She could tell that Mouse was upset.

'I know you're very enthusiastic about Nourriture and it certainly sounds as if your boss is delighted with you. But it's not me. I can't help how I feel. It's just not.'

Mouse nodded. 'I might go and have a shower if you don't mind?'

'Sure,' Nell said. 'Aren't you having your dinner?'

'I'm not that hungry. I had a big lunch.'

Nell watched as Mouse grabbed her things from her room and made her way to the bathroom. Swallowing hard, she pulled her scrapbook from the sideboard where she'd left it. Thumbing through the pages she felt suddenly terrified. Was she doing the wrong thing by telling Mouse? Should she leave things the way they were?

The sound of Mouse singing in the shower was like a stab in the heart for Nell. She was so happy. Things were finally going in the right direction for Mouse. What if she ruined everything? She had no right to do that.

She'd take it one step at a time. Shoving the scrapbook into the drawer in the kitchen, she knew what she needed to do first.

'Mouse?' she said as soon as the young girl emerged from the bathroom. 'When you've dried your hair can you come with me? I'd like to show you something important.'

'Yeah,' she said with a shrug. 'If you like.'

Nell knew Mouse was really annoyed with her. She hoped what she was about to share would dispel some of that anger.

It seemed like an hour later when Mouse finally appeared.

'What did you want to show me?'

'Come with me.' They walked to Laura's old room. Nell took the video machine out of the cupboard and produced another large black VHS tape.

'I've seen it,' Mouse said gently.

'I know. This is a different one.'

'Oh . . . sorry.' Mouse sat cross-legged on the carpet and waited for the images to come onto the television screen.

'Hi there!' Laura said, waving at the camera. 'As you can see I'm now enormous.' The camera zoomed in on her tummy, which was as round as a beach ball.

Mouse gasped. 'She was pregnant?'

Nell nodded as tears streamed down her cheeks.

'I don't know how old you'll be when Mum shows you this, but whether you're one or five or ten or twenty I want you to know how happy I've been for the last nine months.'

Mouse rocked back and forth as she crooned and cried and listened to the heartfelt message from Laura to her unborn child.

When it ended with a flurry of blowing kisses and waving hands, Mouse curled into a ball on the carpet and sobbed so loudly that Nell dropped to her knees and scooped her into her arms.

'It's all OK, child,' she said.

'No it's not,' Mouse said. 'It's so tragic. It's so sad. I can't believe you lost her. Did the baby die, too?' Mouse managed to ask.

Nell sat back and took a very deep breath. She shook her head. 'No, the baby survived.'

'What?' Mouse stared at her in shock. 'So what happened to it?'

'The baby went . . . someplace else,' Nell said. Her voice cracked as her body shook with grief. Her animalistic noises of grief made Mouse freeze in fear.

'Nell,' she said, grabbing her arms. She sat onto her hunkers and peered right into her face. 'Nell,' she repeated. 'Where did the baby go?'

Nell shook her head, unable to utter another syllable.

'Please,' Mouse whispered. 'Try to tell me. You need to say it out loud and I need to know.'

Nell swallowed and rubbed her eyes. 'I gave the baby up for adoption,' she said. 'I never planned it. I'd promised Laura I would look after the child. It was my full intention to do just that. I didn't want to give away my grandchild. But I couldn't cope. Laura died when the baby was three weeks old. Laura's body just gave up. The strain of the pregnancy and birth was too much. She'd been warned. The doctors said she was never to get pregnant. Her heart was too weak and her kidneys weren't much better.'

'So how . . .'

'When she was in Australia she met a boy. He obviously knew about her illness. After all, she was missing a foot. It wasn't exactly easy to hide.'

'But he loved her anyway,' Mouse said.

Nell nodded. 'Apparently they were inseparable. Laura thought she'd be one of the lucky ones. She honestly thought that the love she would bestow on the child would be enough to overcome the dreadful effects of her diabetes. She believed she would prove the doctors wrong.'

'That's so sad,' Mouse said, crying fresh tears.

'She arrived back here. A taxi pulled up at the door and she crawled out. The second I saw her swollen belly, I knew she was in grave danger.'

'Were you very angry with her?'

'How could I be? I knew she'd put the final nail in her own coffin. She'd done what the doctors had told her not to do. It was a damned miracle she'd survived as long as she had.'

'Was the baby OK when it was born?'

'Miraculously, yes. The poor little mite was jaundiced and needed to be monitored. But apart from that the tiny bundle was unscathed, considering. Laura, on the other hand, wasn't quite so lucky. Within three weeks she went into full organ failure. I had to turn off the life-support machine.'

'Oh Nell,' Mouse said.

It was strange. All of a sudden Nell felt calmer than she had in a long time. She allowed all the memories of that time to flood back instead of quashing them as she'd done for so long.

'I had to bring the baby to the funeral. Where else could it go? Some of Laura's school friends came along. But it was a small and understated affair. I didn't do a lunch or drinks or any of that sort of thing. Nobody seemed to expect it and seeing as the baby was there, I had the perfect reason to vamoose.'

'What happened to the baby?'

'I had the child here with me for two nights after the funeral and I woke on the third morning and knew I needed to do something. I needed to give that baby the best opportunity in life.'

'Which was?'

'To find a loving family and parents who would do all the things I couldn't. I wasn't fit to mind an infant. I wasn't prepared to go and live in a child-friendly area where there would be other little people around.'

'But Laura was happy being raised here. Why didn't you think her baby would be too?'

'Laura was different, Mouse. She was poorly and more to the point, she was mine. This new little person was Laura's, but I knew the child would be full of vitality, curiosity and life . . . and so deserved to have the type of life that Laura would've wanted. I knew it wouldn't happen with me.'

'So you put the baby up for adoption?'

Nell nodded. 'I did what I thought was right at the time,' she said. 'But not a day has gone by that I haven't thought of the baby and wondered if I did the wrong thing.'

'Was it a boy or a girl?'

'A girl,' she said.

'Have you had any contact with her since?'

'No, I said I didn't want her to know about me,' Nell said looking pale. 'That was the way I requested it to be. In those days that was considered normal. The laws are very different now. But back then it was more usual for babies to be taken in and that was that.'

Nell walked over to the window and looked out. 'I've never forgotten her little face. She was so beautiful. I thought long and hard about giving her up for adoption and I've always hoped I made the correct decision.'

'Have you been tortured living here all alone?' Mouse asked. 'Have you driven yourself half demented thinking about it?'

'In one way, yes. But in another way, there was no alternative. When life gives us a choice, we have to stand by the decisions we make. That's the way it goes.'

'Nell?' Mouse said looking drawn. 'Would you mind if I called my da?'

'No,' she said with a watery smile. 'I'd be delighted if you would. Even if you don't want to see him, I think it would be good if you spoke to him.'

'Is that why you never pushed me to talk to him? Because you knew what it was like to walk away from someone?'

Nell nodded. 'You know me better than anyone else,' she said as she held her arms out for a hug. 'But you've hit the nail on the head. I didn't feel I was in a position to tell you what to do. How could I?'

Mouse left the room and said she'd prefer to be alone while she called her da.

Nell stayed in Laura's room and inhaled deeply. She gazed at each and every inch of the room and closed her eyes, trying to remember the sound of Laura's laughter. She could picture her sitting in a chair just before the baby was born. She was stroking her tummy and chatting to the baby. She was telling the child how much she loved it.

'Baby It, you've no idea how excited I am about meeting you. Some days I know you're a girl. Other days I'm certain you're a boy. Only you know who you are.'

Laura had returned from Australia with a broken heart. The boy she'd thought would stand by her no matter what had run for the hills as soon as he realised the detrimental effect this baby would have on Laura's life. He'd made no bones about the fact that he wasn't prepared to be a single father.

'He said that he hadn't signed up for that. He loved me, but he hadn't realised the extent of what he'd taken on.'

Nell had boiled on the inside when Laura had said that. It was at the tip of her tongue to say that he sounded just like Laura's own father. But she felt Laura had had enough male disappointment at that point. What good would it do to point out the obvious? Her father had shown his true colours when Laura had begun to get weak. He'd booked her a flight and posted her onto the plane like defective goods. Return to sender, this commodity no longer works the way it should, so here you go . . .

Nell had managed to resist bad-mouthing him. What was there to gain by adding to Laura's misery? Instead she'd done what was right. She'd soothed Laura, filled her head with dreams and made a thousand promises about how she would raise her baby.

Nell laughed bitterly as she leaned on the windowsill and stared out at the ocean. In the end, she'd been just as much of a liar and a coward as Laura's father and the baby's father.

For years she'd visited Laura's grave and cried, begging for her daughter's forgiveness. Pleading for her to understand that she'd acted in the baby's best interests.

'Nell?'

The sound of Mouse's voice as she walked back into the room made Nell jump.

'Sorry pet, I was miles away. Did you speak to your father?'

She nodded. 'And?' Nell probed.

'He acted as if I'd only gone to the shops. He said it was great to hear that I'm doing well and I must come back and visit soon.'

'Is that it?' Nell asked, feeling totally flummoxed.

Mouse shrugged. 'Both my brothers are inside. They were done for robbing cars. Da sounded like he was off his face.'

'I'm sorry,' Nell said.

'For what? For caring? For minding me? For giving me a better life? I'm not sorry at all. I know I made the right choice when I left Dublin. And I believe what you said . . . Laura brought me here. We were meant to find each other.'

'You're my second chance too, Mouse. Now you probably understand why I've said that.'

Mouse nodded.

'So sod the lot of them,' Nell said. 'You and me against the world, eh?'

'Sounds good,' Mouse said.

Nell knew it was almost time to put things right. To dot the i's and cross the t's. With Mouse by her side, she knew she could do just about anything.

Chapter 44

NEXT MORNING, AS SHE FINISHED CLEARING THE breakfast room, Keeley looked up to see that Doug had arrived. He stood awkwardly and looked lost.

'May I come in?'

She shrugged.

'What's happening to us?' he asked.

'I don't know,' Keeley said with a sigh. 'This isn't exactly how we planned it, is it?'

Doug shook his head. 'Keeley, I'm more sorry than you'll ever know,' he said. 'I would've come and told you that before, but I knew you were so cross with me that it wouldn't have done any good.'

'I was fed-up being taken for granted. You were treating the house like a B&B,' she said with a tired smile. 'I don't mind the people who pay me acting as if I should run around after them. But we were always a team. You left team us and went off to do something that didn't include me. I wasn't in your thoughts or actions, Doug. I don't deserve that.'

'I know,' he said, looking shamefaced. 'I was a total idiot.'

'There are too many cracks beginning to show right now,' she said. 'We need to take control of our family. I know the girls are grown-ups, but we're still their parents.'

'I agree,' Doug said. 'Can we call a truce?'

She nodded as tears of relief seeped down her cheeks. Doug took her in his arms and for the first time in months, Keeley felt safe.

'Fresh start?' Doug said as he kissed her.

She nodded. Should she tell him that she'd unpacked the suitcase from under their marital bed? Should he know that she'd kissed another man? A con man who only loved the thought of taking her money? Would he hate her and point out the truth, that she was a selfish and horrible person who had betrayed him?

A cold sensation washed over her. If she was being totally honest, she should tell Doug the secret she'd been hiding all these years. She looked up at him and tried to envisage what he'd say if he knew.

She balked. Their relationship was too delicate right now. There were enough issues. She couldn't add to them right now.

The landline rang and Keeley went to answer it, calling over her shoulder to Doug that he wasn't to take any more bookings.

'This place is becoming a home once more,' she said firmly.

'Keeley?'

'Yes?'

'It's Claus.'

'Oh, hello.'

'I wanted to say goodbye. I won't see you again.'

'Oh, I see. I didn't realise you were going back to Germany so soon,' she said.

'I'm not going to Germany. I will travel the world. I am calling to give you the final opportunity to come with me. Will you?'

There were so many things she wanted to shout down the phone at this low-life bastard. She wanted to yell that he was the most dishonest and double-crossing liar she'd ever had the misfortune to kiss. But how could she, with Doug standing right there in the kitchen?

She walked out of the room and into her art room and shut the door.

'Claus, I wasn't able to talk,' she said. 'Doug was there.'

'I see . . .'

'I can't bear to be without you, Claus.'

'You can't?' he sounded delighted.

'You and I both know that we have a connection. You've looked after me so believe me, Claus, I'm going to look after you now.'

'Oh I'm so glad, Keeley.'

'I have a pen ready. Tell me where and when. What flight are you on and I'll book my ticket online before I leave for the airport.'

'This is working out better than I'd hoped. I thought you wouldn't come with me,' he said. 'You're the most astonishing woman, Keeley. I didn't actually dare to hope that you would pick me.'

'Well, we never know what's going on in another person's head, do we? I love surprises, don't you?'

'Oh yes my love,' he crooned. 'So I'm flying to Amsterdam from Shannon at ten thirty tonight.'

'From Shannon?' she said with surprise. 'That's perfect. That flight gives me plenty of time if I leave now. I'll see you at the check-in desk, OK?'

'I can barely wait. I'm so excited.'

'Not as excited as I am, Claus,' she said. 'Thank you for calling.'

'Bye my love.'

Keeley walked back into the kitchen and sat opposite Doug.

'So as you guessed, that was Claus.'

'What did he want?' he asked darkly.

Keeley told Doug about Claus and what Róisín had found out. She omitted to tell him that she'd considered throwing her life down the toilet and being made a complete fool of by him.

'Did you like him?' Doug asked. The pain in his eyes made her stomach lurch.

'He made me feel cherished for a moment,' she said sadly. 'But that was only part of his façade. That's what he does. It's how he gets money out of everyone,' she said with a dry laugh.

'I know Claus or Wolfgang might've been a liar,' Doug said, 'but he was right about something. We have all taken you for granted. That needs to change. And it will. Believe me.'

'No,' Keeley said. 'I'm a bad person, Doug. I knew I'd be punished at some point for what I've done and I'm guessing the clock has caught up with me.'

'What on earth are you going on about?'

'I know something and I've never told anyone. It's haunted me for years and this is how I'm being punished.'

Keeley was so upset, she couldn't possibly tell Doug what she needed to say. But now that she'd started the process, she knew it was time for the truth to come out.

'Whatever it is, we'll get through it together,' Doug said taking her in his arms.

'I need to do something first,' she said. Picking up the phone again, she dialled the police.

'I want to inform you of the whereabouts of Wolfgang Bauer. He's wanted in several countries for fraud. I know where you can pick him up.'

Back at the Thatch pub, Róisín and Rob were having a relaxed and cosy chat. They'd ordered some food and were enjoying a drink.

Róisín filled him in on all the events with Liv and how she was finally getting her life back on track.

'It's funny,' said Rob, 'life can often be like a game of dominos. When one thing goes right, everything else falls into place.'

'I hope you're right,' she said.

About an hour later, Rob's mobile rang. After a brief conversation he hung up and smiled at Róisín.

'That was the police. They've picked up our pal Claus.'

'No way,' she said. 'Where?'

'They caught him at the airport and he's been arrested.'

'I can't say I'm sorry,' she said. 'Poor Mum was totally gutted when she heard what he'd been up to. It seems he'd befriended her and was slowly worming his way into her life. It's a good thing he went when he did.'

'Now that he's in the hands of the law, that means you can go first thing tomorrow and speak with Mr Grace,' Rob said. 'I wouldn't waste another day if I were you. Go and make your offer.'

'I certainly will,' she said. 'Thanks for all your help, Rob.'

'No worries. I'm so happy that he didn't get a chance to ruin everything you've worked so hard to create. I'd hate to see your business going down the tubes. You don't deserve that. Besides, if you keep on making money the way you did today, I could enjoy the notion of being a kept man!'

Even though they'd literally only gotten together, Róisín had a great feeling about him. Clearly he felt the same way.

'Actually,' he hesitated for a moment before continuing. 'I'm so impressed by your passion and the whole concept of Nourriture. I wondered if you had thought about turning it into a franchise.'

'Really?' Róisín's heart literally skipped a beat. 'But how on earth would I do that?'

'We'll talk about it,' Rob said. 'My father has the Midas touch when it comes to business. I've been talking you up to him and I know he'd be on board with rolling out the concept in Limerick, among other places.'

'I . . . I don't know what to say. This is like one of those moments when I feel I could be dreaming.'

As Rob walked over to Joseph to order them another drink, Róisín couldn't quite believe how much of a turn-around had taken place over the last couple of days.

She'd come so far emotionally, too. Jacques had left her with such deep emotional scars. She'd actually wondered if they'd ever heal. But Rob knew all about it and still seemed to want to be with her.

Róisín knew there was one last elephant in the room. She needed to talk to her parents about her adoption. For so long she'd been afraid of hurting them or making them feel as if they weren't enough. But now that she was at a crossroads in her life, she wanted to make sure that she was giving herself the best chance to take the right direction. It was time to be a grown-up. It was time to stop running and hiding from the issues that could potentially mar her happiness. She would put the questions to her parents in the most heartfelt and diplomatic way. But she needed to try and find some answers.

At closing time, Róisín kissed Rob goodnight. She'd already explained that she needed to go back to Liv. Besides, she wanted their first night together to be relaxed and special. With everything that was going on, it wasn't the time for going AWOL.

'If you could spend the night with me, would you?' he asked, holding her close.

'In a heartbeat,' she replied. 'But I can't leave Liv alone.'

'I understand,' he said and kissed her.

Liv was still awake when she let herself inside. In excited whispers, they chatted the way they'd done as children.

'He sounds perfect for you,' Liv said. 'I'm happy for you, Ro. You deserve to find a good man.'

'Thanks Liv,' she said. 'So do you. Martin wasn't the man you fell in love with. He's weak and doesn't deserve all of this,' she said looking around.

'He was the first man who made promises and I believed them,' Liv said. 'He's taught me a lesson though. He probably thinks I'm going to lie down and sob for the rest of my life. But he's made me stronger, Róisín.'

'How are you so amazing about all of this?' Róisín asked in awe.

'Because of your birth mum's letter,' Liv said.

'What?' Róisín was astounded. 'What do you mean?'

Liv sighed. 'When I read her words that day, Róisín, they touched my heart. I saw the person I used to be. The one who loved her kids and was delighted by the whole journey of motherhood. I used to be patient and content, you know? Then I saw what I'd become . . . this narky, joyless, bitter person. It cut me to the quick, and for a while it made everything harder. The guilt and shame seemed to push me further away from where I really wanted to be. But now that I've faced that negativity and given myself a serious talking-to, I hope I'm headed in the right direction. Every time I think of those words, they help me through. They actually help me to be brave.'

Róisín could feel tears welling up in her eyes. 'That's so incredible, Liv,' she managed to say. 'Thank you for telling me that.'

'The truth is,' Liv went on, 'I did all my crying and grieving while I was still married to Martin. As the years rolled by I was sinking deeper and deeper. I suspected a long time ago that he was being unfaithful,' she said. 'I questioned him so many times and each time he looked me right in the eye and insisted I was imagining it.'

'That's awful,' Róisín said. 'When you're so sure of something and another person convinces you it's not true . . .'

'It's soul-destroying. I used to think I was going insane. I thought I had postnatal depression at one point. Then I figured I was probably just paranoid. But the more I turned it over in my mind, the worse it got. He let me believe it was all in my head. We were discussing the idea of me seeing a psychiatrist when I found a load of text messages on his phone quite by mistake.'

'How did you find them?'

'Billy was playing with his phone and opened the messages by mistake. He had her name saved as "Frank" so I wouldn't suspect.'

'It must've broken your heart to read the texts,' Róisín said, stroking her hand.

'Do you know what? It was a relief. I was angry and

hurt, needless to say. But there's nothing like knowing you're not a lunatic.'

'I agree,' Róisín said, sighing. 'I've lived with the thought that I'm not worthy of being loved by any man since I left France. And writing that e-mail to the clinic was so hard, but I think it was the right thing to do.'

The two sisters curled up together in Liv's bed.

'For the record,' Liv said, 'I think you made the right decision. It was best that you came to your own conclusion, too.'

'Really?' Róisín stared at her in the darkness.

'Mum would've had you on the next flight back to France to try and retrieve them. I know she would. But it wouldn't have been right for you.'

'It's such a difficult subject. It's not something I thought I would ever discuss until I told Rob.'

'You told Rob?' Liv said. 'I'm gobsmacked. You really have told him a lot, haven't you?'

'This is what I'm trying to explain . . . I think he's my soulmate, Liv.'

'Sounds like it,' she said. 'Clearly he didn't judge you either?'

'No, bless him. I know there are many people in the world who would never want to be in the same room as me again because of that decision. This might sound crazy to you, but I want to bring a baby into the world in a more traditional way . . . with Rob, if I'm lucky . . .'

'I honestly thought Martin and I would make it,' Liv said.

'Oh Liv, I'm sorry! I didn't mean to sound like I'm preaching. I know you had your babies hoping you and Martin would last the test of time together.'

'I really did,' she said. 'But that hasn't happened. So I guess what I'm saying is that I don't judge you either because you also acted in good faith when you went for IVF with Jacques. We can only do what we think is right in our hearts.'

They lay in silence for a long while, both women caught up in their thoughts.

'Thanks for being my sister,' Róisín said as she was about to drift off to sleep.

'Thanks for being mine too,' she said. 'An angel was watching over me when you were sent to my life.'

When Róisín's mobile phone rang, it made her jump a foot off the bed.

'Hello?'

'Hi, it's me,' said Rob. 'Are you two finished talking yet? I'm outside at the gate and it's kind of cold.'

'What?' she giggled. 'You're here?'

'I asked where Liv lives and that nice fellow Joseph gave me a lift. Can I come in?'

She hung up and jumped out of bed. 'Sorry sis, you're on your own tonight,' she said with a skip in her step.

'Go for it Roisin,' Liv smiled sleepily.

As soon as she opened the door, Rob picked her up in his arms. She directed him to the bedroom and she kicked the door shut.

Chapter 45

RÓISÍN WOKE EARLY THE NEXT MORNING AND reached over to check that Rob wasn't a figment of her imagination.

'Morning, sleepyhead,' she said stroking his face.

'I could get used to this,' he said. 'Waking up and seeing you.'

Before they could have an encore of last night's antics, the door flew open.

'Auntie Ro-Ro,' Billy said and stopped in his tracks.

'Eh, look who's here,' Róisín said. 'You remember Rob, don't you?'

'Hi Rob,' Billy said, running and jumping onto the bed. If the child thought it was remotely odd to find this man in his auntie's bed, he certainly didn't show it.

'Guess what?' he said sitting cross-legged facing them.

'What?' said Rob.

'We're having a day out with Mum today,' he said. 'We're going to the adventure park and we're going on climbing frames and swings and everything.'

'And we're bringing a nic-pic,' said Jess as she ran in too. 'Hi Rob,' she said, waving happily. Róisín laughed at the innocence of them.

'Mum said she is sorry that there's been lots of shouting here, but that it's all finished now,' Billy said.

'That's fantastic, isn't it?' Róisín said, feeling as if her heart might break.

'We had a lovely talk yesterday, didn't we, guys?' Liv said, walking in and leaning against the door. 'I explained that I haven't been behaving like a fun mum for a while. But I'm going to try and make it up to them.'

'You'll do a fabulous job,' Róisín said, blowing her a kiss. 'Now if you don't mind, we might take a little minute to wake up before we join you for breakfast.'

'Sure,' said Billy as he jumped down off the bed.

'You can come to the adventure park too if you like, Rob.'

'Oh thanks Jess, but I might have to go to work today.'

'Ah pity,' Billy said as he and his sister skipped away.

'You'll have to find a bolt for that door if you want any privacy in this house,' Liv said with a grin. 'Fair play to you for not balking at your little visitors. I think you'll fit in very nicely around here,' she said as she closed the door.

Before Róisín and Rob had a chance to even catch their breath, there was a sound of car tyres on the gravel outside.

'Granny and Granddad are here!' Billy yelled.

'Oh dear Lord, do you think I could at least put some clothes on before I meet your folks?' He laughed.

'You get yourself sorted and I'll go and see what's going on,' Róisín said, kissing him.

Liv opened the front door and welcomed Doug and Keeley inside.

'To what do we owe the pleasure of your company at the crack of dawn?' she asked nervously.

'We were awake early and figured we'd pop over to explain what's happening,' Doug said. 'We owe it to you both.'

Liv made porridge for the children and allowed them to eat it in the garden, which they were delighted about. Róisín slipped back into the bedroom and gave Rob permission to slip away. He said he'd walk back to the village and pick up his car.

'I'll call you in a while,' she promised.

'I feel like a naughty teenager!' he grinned.

As she joined the others at the table the children were eating happily outside. 'OK, the coast is clear for a few minutes. What's happening?' Róisín asked in concern.

'Well, we wanted to say that now we know what's happened with Martin, we're here to help any time.'

'Thank you,' Liv said with glassy eyes.

'Mum and I feel we must be partially to blame for your stress and drinking lately,' Doug admitted.

'How do you figure that one?' Liv asked.

'Well, I've been gadding about like a teenager and your mother has been left to carry the can. In turn she's been snowed under with all the responsibility,' Doug said. ' Our family was beginning to fall apart. That'll all change now.'

'Yes,' Keeley said. 'I'm winding up operations at the B&B as you know, so there'll be lots of time to help out.'

'We need to be there for you as well, love,' Doug said, turning to Róisín. 'We need to look at how we can help with Nourriture. Mum and I were thinking of selling the house. We'd get a good price for it. The books show how successful it is, so it would be ideal for a younger couple or anyone wanting to take on the business.'

'But where would you go?' Róisín asked.

'We'd buy something a lot smaller and give both you and Liv some cash. It would take the pressure off for you both,' Doug said.

'We want to help and there's no point in us sitting in a big house when it could be put to good use,' Keeley said.

'Well,' Róisín said, 'I have news of my own. Claus has been arrested.'

Doug and Keeley exchanged a glance.

'We know,' Doug said.

'How did you find out?' Róisín asked, puzzled. 'It only happened last night.'

Doug grinned. 'It's a long story, but let's just say Miss Marple has nothing on your mother. She snared him good and proper and now he's going to pay for the havoc he caused around here.'

Liv and Róisín stared at each other open-mouthed. This was a lot to take in pre-coffee.

'Well,' Róisín went on, 'however it happened, it's good news for me because his offer to buy Nourriture is off the table. So I'm going to find Mr Grace today to explain, in the hope that he'll accept my offer.'

'That sounds wonderful, Róisín,' Doug said.

Keeley began to cry. Doug wrapped an arm around her and she leaned into him, covering her face with her hand.

'Oh no, Mum, what is it?'

'Sorry, but I'm just so relieved. Things could actually turn around for us. We really might be OK.'

'Of course we will,' Doug said, hugging her hard. 'We've been through thick and thin over the years, us four. We're not going to fall apart at the seams now.'

Róisín's mouth was dry. She knew this was the moment she'd been both waiting for and dreading for a very long time. But there wouldn't be a better moment than this.

'Can I ask you both something?' she said. Her voice sounded so wobbly her parents looked up in surprise.

'What is it, love?'

'I want to prefix this entire conversation with the fact that I love you both with all my heart and soul.'

'Thank you,' Keeley said.

'That's nice to hear, pet,' Doug said.

'May I ask you about my birth parents?' Róisín asked. 'I've wanted to for a very long time, but I never wanted to hurt you. You've been so open about the fact I was adopted, but I've never had any information after that . . .'

'You get your cards every year,' Doug said. 'That's a nice thing, isn't it?'

'Of course,' Róisín said. 'But I'm wondering if the people mentioned anything when you adopted me? Did they say who my mother was? Where she came from or anything about her?'

Keeley and Doug looked at one another.

'They gave us a photograph of you the week before we got you,' Doug said. 'We had it propped up on the window-sill in the kitchen and it was like looking at our dreams come true.'

'We cherished it so,' Keeley nodded.

'The day we finally got you, it was all very low-key,' Doug recalled.

'When you signed those papers,' Róisín pressed, 'did they mention my mother's name?'

'Oh no,' Doug said. 'Nothing like that. We were only presented with our own set of paperwork. We didn't get to see the stuff from the other side.'

'Doug was the first to make physical contact with you,' Keeley said. 'He stood and walked over and put his finger into your tiny hand. You gripped it tightly and he turned to smile at me. I will never forget the look in his eyes.'

'We were blessed to get you, Róisín,' Doug said. 'And I'm so sorry we can't tell you more, but honestly, things were so different in those days. The nuns weren't into background checks and the like, and they weren't into keeping records either. The way they saw it, you would come to us and that would be an end to it. They wouldn't have been thinking in terms of you coming looking for information later, especially not when your mother had passed away.'

Róisín nodded and hugged her parents and thanked them for talking to her. But deep down, she was gutted. She'd always held a tiny hope that her parents did actually know where she'd come from and hadn't said. That once she found the courage to ask, they'd be able to tell her. It was devastating to hit a blank wall immediately.

The only way she could get information was by hiring an investigator. She'd spent many hours online looking at other stories of men and women who'd wasted time and money trying to trace their parents. There were so many gaps in the Irish adoption records that she knew she would probably end up disappointed. She would have to accept defeat.

As the children ran in from the garden looking excited about their day out with their mum, Róisín realised she was lucky. So many people had families that didn't give a damn about them. She was, and always would be, loved by these extraordinarily generous and giving people. The fact they weren't blood relatives didn't really count. What mattered was that they loved and adored her. That was enough, wasn't it?

Pulling up opposite Nourriture a short while later, Róisín got out of the car and stared across at the ocean. Early morning seagulls were swooping noisily as they argued over their finds. Looking across at Nourriture made her heart jolt. She adored what she'd created. She had so many new ideas, too. If she could secure the building, she planned on moving into the flat for a while. Once she had things ticking along nicely, she wanted to expand and open a restaurant on the upper floor. From that height it would boast one of the most stunning views in Ireland.

The possibility of franchising this concept and opening in other venues made her giddy with excitement. Rob was adamant that his father wanted to invest.

Just then, Róisín spotted Mr Grace wandering up the road toward her. His old and faithful dog was waddling beside him, looking just as decrepit as its owner. It must be fate, Róisín thought, smiling to herself.

'Good morning, lass,' he said, lifting his walking stick in greeting. 'Isn't it a gorgeous morning?'

'It certainly is,' she said with a smile. 'There are few places I'd rather be.'

He paused and looked into her eyes. If she wasn't mistaken, Róisín saw a flicker of regret.

'Mr Grace,' she said. 'I was intending to visit you this morning, as a matter of fact. Could I call over in a while if you're not too busy?'

'Now is a good time unless you've something on?'

'Of course,' she smiled. 'Come inside and I'll make you a coffee.'

Róisín opened the shutters and wasn't surprised to see Brigid inside, beavering away busily.

'Hi Brigid,' she said. 'Only me. I'm having a quick meeting with Mr Grace and I'll be with you shortly.'

'No problem,' she said. 'Morning, Mr Grace. I don't

suppose you'd have a quick taste of my *pain au chocolat*? I used a new ingredient and I'm not sure how the customers will take to them.'

He grinned as Róisín set a frothy latte in front of him.

'I'll wander up here more often,' he said before looking guiltily at the floor. 'Oh,' he said. 'I'm sorry. I'm forgetting . . .'

'That's what I need to tell you, Mr Grace.'

Róisín started from the beginning and explained everything she knew about his generous investor.

'Wolfgang Bauer you say . . .' He nodded calmly.

'Aren't you surprised?' Róisín asked.

'Not hugely,' Mr Grace admitted. 'I've been watching him for the past few weeks. He disappeared for days on end and was always cagey when I tried to speak with him. I put it down to being foreign and not wanting to fraternise with the locals.'

'So, his offer to buy this place won't stand any longer.'

'No,' Mr Grace said.

'So I would like to submit mine. I know it's not as much as Claus was offering . . .'

'It's much more than he was offering,' Mr Grace corrected. 'For a start, your money is legitimate. Secondly, you are breathing life into this village. You are attracting more tourists than the view and that's saying something!'

'So would you consider my offer, please?'

'No, I won't consider it, Róisín. I'll accept it and be glad of it.'

'Really?' Róisín leapt out of her chair and hugged him.

'You deserve it, my girl. I wasn't finding it easy to live with myself these past weeks,' Mr Grace said. 'I knew I was being ruled by greed. That's a nasty way to be. I'm ashamed of my behaviour and I sincerely hope you can forgive me.'

'Of course,' Róisín said. 'Business is business,' she said with a shrug.

'I've realised another thing,' Mr Grace said. 'My two boys are idle good-for-nothings. I've told them in no uncertain terms that they won't be splashing my cash. I've told them to get jobs and sort themselves out.'

'Wow, good for you,' she said. 'How did they take it?'

'Surprisingly well. Sean thinks he has work with a fisherman friend of his and Liam is in Galway since yesterday, working in a hotel.'

'Will you be lonely without them?' Róisín asked.

'It's hard to be lonely on a cruise,' he said, laughing. 'That's what I'm going to do. It's a golden years one, so it'll be a ship full of old fogies like me! Who knows, I might even make some new acquaintances.'

Róisín promised to have the final documents ready for them both to sign as soon as possible.

'I really am delighted for you, Róisín,' he said. 'Seeing this place turned into one of those gaudy supermarkets would've been a travesty. This is better for everyone.'

As soon as Mr Grace and his dog waddled back down the village, Róisín let out a happy scream and dropped to her knees with her hands clasped above her head.

'Thank you God,' she shouted.

'Eh, have you lost your marbles?' Brigid asked as she stood with a spatula, staring at her from the back kitchen.

'No, my darling Brigid, I've found them! I'm buying this building. Nourriture is here to stay and I've so many plans!'

'Oh cripes,' Brigid said. 'You're going to expand and find more things for me to do, aren't you?'

Róisín burst out laughing and Brigid hugged her.

'Nobody deserves this more than you. Well done. I'm thrilled. But promise me one thing?'

'What's that?' she asked.

'Don't lose the run of yourself. You're already dedicated to this place. Don't forget to live too.'

'I won't,' Róisín said. An image of Rob and the night she'd just shared flashed through her mind and she blushed as she ran up the back stairs to her office.

Checking her e-mails, she was delighted to see confirmations for things she'd bought for her mother's party. This party would be one hell of a celebration, after all. Keeley deserved to be thanked for all the wonderful things she'd done over the years and Róisín was going to make sure Nourriture got a little nod of appreciation too.

Clicking on to the long-term weather forecast, she was delighted to see a period of settled weather ahead. If the sun and warmth could last until Saturday week, she'd be a very happy bunny. The marquee company that had provided the tents for the festival had confirmed they would return with a similar one for the party.

The feelings of dread and fear were all gone. Róisín couldn't wait to finally take the reins and see just how bright her future could be. She dialled Jill's number and grinned as her beloved friend cried happy tears for her.

She texted Rob and asked him to pop in whenever he could. She wanted to get the ball rolling on Nourriture, the franchise. She also wanted to see him again. Love was a drug and she was well and truly hooked.

Chapter 46

MOUSE WAS PACING THE KITCHEN FLOOR LIKE A caged tiger.

'You need to calm down,' Nell said. 'I know it's soon to take your test, but if you don't try you won't have an idea of where you're going wrong.'

'But what if I can't read the questions?'

'We've gone over them in the guidebook. You know the answers and your writing is clear. Take your time and you'll be fine.'

Nell had applied for Mouse to do the driving test. She'd heard the test centres were backlogged and it could take up to a year for a slot to become available. As luck would have it, the centre outside Ballyshore wasn't exactly inundated with applications, so Mouse was going this morning.

'You remembered to tell your boss you'll be late in, didn't you?' Nell asked.

Mouse nodded and bit her nails. 'I don't think this is a good plan, Nell. I've never passed a thing in my life.'

'You've never taken a test in your life,' Nell pointed out.

Mouse looked utterly stricken. Nell softened.

'OK, I'll tell you what, if you fail and they say you didn't manage to do any of it correctly, I'll eat my words.'

'That's big of you,' Mouse said.

'You don't know unless you try,' Nell repeated. 'Besides, what's the worst that can happen? They tell you a visually impaired goat could drive better than you and that your writing is worse than a drunk spider? Who cares? You go away and try harder.'

Mouse swallowed. 'You won't tell anyone if I make a balls of it, will you?'

'Who would I tell?'

'OK,' Mouse said with a sigh, 'let's do it.'

'Atta girl,' Nell said.

They sat in silence as Nell drove them to the test centre.

'Good luck. No matter what happens, I'm ever so proud of you,' Nell said.

As Mouse got into the car with the examiner, a wave of loneliness and regret washed over Nell. Why had she given Laura's daughter away? She could've had all the years of watching her grow and mature. She would've had companionship and love and laughter . . .

But it wouldn't have worked like it did right now with Mouse. The poor girl hadn't exactly been given many opportunities over the years, but she'd still been out there, living in the world . . . seeing things, albeit the more dingy end of life . . . that baby would've been thwarted if she'd stayed with her, wouldn't she?

Nell stayed in her own car while Mouse did the test. She didn't want to sit chatting to some random stranger about the difficulties of the driving test in the waiting area. She'd rolled her seat back and closed her eyes. She knew she wasn't going insane, but Nell was starting to hear whispers. She wouldn't call them voices per se. Just suggestions that it was time to move on. Time to play out the end of her life in a more positive way. She knew that in order to do that, she needed to set things straight.

Mouse came out to the car a while later. Her head was hung low and she looked defeated.

'Hey, it was all too soon,' Nell said as soon as she sat in. 'It's my fault Mouse, I shouldn't have pushed you to take the test yet. You weren't ready . . .'

'I PASSED!' Mouse shouted, shaking her fists in triumph. 'I've never passed a single thing in my life, Nell.' She threw her arms around Nell, almost strangling her as she mashed her into the driver's door with the force of her enthusiasm.

'I am so unbelievably proud of you. You are some force of nature. This is the first test you've ever taken and you passed. Have you any idea how amazing you are?'

'I can't believe it,' Mouse said. 'I'm not as thick as I thought I was.'

'You're as far from thick as it's possible to be,' Nell said. 'Don't you ever put yourself down. There are enough people in this world who'll jump on the bandwagon of trying to crush others.'

'I know,' Mouse said, sitting back onto her own side of the car and throwing her arms above her head and grasping the headrest. She stretched luxuriously and laughed.

'I was able to read all the questions too,' she said. 'You were right. They were all the same words as the ones we'd seen. Some were in a different order, but I was able to sound them out. Once I was halfway through a question, I had a pretty good idea of what they were asking.'

'I'm delighted for you,' Nell said. 'Now you can drive yourself to work some days. It's not as if I use my car all that often.'

'Speaking of work,' Mouse said. 'I need to get there or I won't have a job to drive to. I told Róisín I'd be a bit late. But I don't want to take advantage.'

Mouse allowed Nell to drive, saying she was too overcome and might drive them into a tree.

'I'm that excited I don't trust myself.'

Nell waved as Mouse ran in the door of Nourriture and splayed her arms and announced to all and sundry what she'd done. Nell drove away smiling.

Nell had lots of bookwork to catch up with. Normally at this time of the year the fellow from the council appeared looking for his bits and pieces. In former years, Nell would have them ready and waiting with weeks to spare. This time she was actually anxious about how far behind she might be.

The day flew by as she got stuck into her work. There was barely enough time to drive back and collect Mouse.

The girl was still buzzing after her day. 'Ooh I have an invitation for us too,' she said. 'Promise me you'll come,' she said.

'What's it for? A party for passing your test?' Nell asked.

'No. Nothing like that,' Mouse said. 'My boss's mother is turning sixty. She's doing a surprise party for her in a marquee across from Nourriture. The same one that was there for the festival.'

'Oh I see,' Nell said. 'And she invited us?'

'Certainly did,' Mouse said. 'She said it's a case of the more, the merrier. Her ma is a great woman by all accounts and she wants the whole village to come out and celebrate with her.'

'It's not my sort of thing,' Nell said. 'But I'll drive you over and collect you afterwards.' Nell figured the subject would be dropped and thought no more of it until Mouse appeared after her shower a short while later. She was carrying a hanger that contained a dress and wrap.

'I was rooting in your wardrobe just now,' Mouse said.

'You shouldn't do that, Mouse,' she said in shock. 'That's not polite.'

'Ah yeah,' Mouse said. 'We won't worry about that. We both know I wasn't raised. I was dragged up. So we'll excuse my ignorance. Anyway, I think you should wear this to the party. You'd look very elegant.'

'I told you,' Nell said. 'I'm not going to the party.'

'Ah but you are,' Mouse said firmly. 'We won't talk about it all the time and we won't fall out over it. But you'll come and I'll be thrilled because I'll feel like my own ma is with me. You wouldn't let me go with nobody to call my own, sure you wouldn't, Nell?'

She was ready to scoff and tell Mouse to stop her nonsense when she realised the young woman was crying.

'Ah stop that now,' she said. 'That's not fair. You're using emotional blackmail and that's not right.'

'I'm not doing it to annoy you,' she said. 'But all the other workers at Nourriture are full of the joys, talking about the party and how they can't wait. I'd die if I have to go alone.'

'But won't you be working essentially?'

'For a bit, but after that I'll be standing there like a spare part. Don't do that to me. Please Nell, I'll never ask you to come to anything with me again.'

Nell felt her heart drop like a stone. Here she was, full of great intentions to get more involved with life in general and she'd fallen at the first fence. Taking a deep breath she made a decision.

'OK, I'll go.'

'You're a star,' Mouse said. 'Thanks a million. My own ma never came to anything with me and if she did, she'd be too pissed to be of any use.'

Nell inhaled deeply. This kid really needed to be supported. She might have missed out on doing anything good with Laura's baby, but this was most certainly her second chance.

'I don't think I can wear that outfit, however. It's over thirty years old. We might have to go shopping.'

'Will we go to the city again?' Mouse asked.

'No, I don't think I can bear it. There are boutiques in Clifden. That's only half an hour's drive. Maybe tomorrow. You're on a day off aren't you?'

Mouse was so enthusiastic, Nell felt ashamed. How could she have considered not going if it meant this much to her?

They shared some fish stew that Nell had cobbled together and chatted about how important it was to tell people what they mean.

'The only consistent feedback I got as a kid was how much of a nuisance I was. I didn't try to annoy people, but that was what happened. I wish I had some memories of nice things Ma had said.'

'What about your da?' Nell asked. 'Did he mind you much?'

'Nah, he was all about the boys. I remember he took me on a job one time. He was robbing a house and wanted me to get in a small window. I was to run to the front door and open it so he and my brothers could get in and steal stuff.'

'Did you do it?' Nell asked.

'No,' she said. 'I cried and said I didn't want to get put in a police car. I was terrified of getting caught . . . I also knew it was wrong. I didn't want to help them rob other people's things.'

'What happened?'

'He smacked me so hard it winded me. I ran all the way home in the dark and hid under my bed.'

'How old were you?'

'Six or seven,' Mouse said. 'In fairness to Da, he never hit me much after that. He wrote me off, though. He used to act as if I wasn't there. For months he blanked me totally, refusing to answer if I spoke to him.'

'How did that make you feel?'

'Horrible. I figured it was my own fault. My brothers did what he wanted and they got on like a house on fire.' She shrugged. 'But I couldn't be what he wanted. I wasn't born that way. God only knows where I came from. Maybe Ma was a good person underneath her problems.'

'Did you have a better relationship with her?'

'Yeah, I suppose I did . . . when she was sober, which wasn't often, we got on great. She was funny. Knew how to look at things in the world and make them seem like a laugh. She loved me, I know she did. But she was too messed up to be able to mother any of us.'

'That was the way for a lot of kids when I grew up in the flats,' Nell said. 'You've a wise head on young shoulders, Mouse. It's taken me many more years, decades even, to come to the same conclusion as you.'

'Did none of your family come here to visit you?' Mouse asked.

'No. I was a bit like you. I disappeared and nobody seemed to mind. I know it would sound totally crazy to a person with a loving family, but mine were probably relieved I went.'

'I get it.'

'I know you do,' Nell said. 'I know when Laura's father left me at the altar, everyone assumed I'd go off my rocker. I probably would have if Laura hadn't needed me so badly. I came here because I knew she'd be safe.'

'I know,' Mouse said. 'And for the record, I think you did the right thing. When I see her in those videos, it's obvious that she was so happy with life.'

'I miss her,' Nell sighed. 'I've learned to live without her for certain. But I've never stopped longing for her.'

They went to bed and Nell slept better than she had for a while. Mouse was up early the next morning. Nell was up at the observatory doing her morning routine.

'What time will we go to Clifden?' she asked. 'Can I drive?'

'Sure,' Nell said. 'We'll go in the next half hour.'

They mooched around, each doing her own thing and gravitated toward the car at the same time.

Nell smiled as Mouse drove them away from the lighthouse. They'd fallen into step with one another. They were kindred spirits and it felt great.

Nell was pleasantly surprised by how much the town of Clifden had come on. It was a long time since she'd been there. The array of high quality gift shops, boutiques and restaurants was impressive. Once she'd picked an outfit, which Mouse insisted looked 'stunning' on her, they visited the bookshop.

'I've never been in a bookshop before!' Mouse said with excitement. 'I love the smell and the fact there are so many stories waiting to be discovered.'

Nell spoke to the owner as Mouse browsed. She expertly directed them to a section of books that would be suitable for Mouse, taking her reading level into account.

'She's eager and very quick to learn,' Nell assured the lady. 'But I don't want her to get bogged down with a novel that will put her off. I don't want to put a halt to her gallop at this stage.'

Nell needn't have worried. Mouse was like a child in a sweet shop and took the lady's advice.

They went to a gorgeous fish restaurant for lunch and Nell enjoyed every morsel. The best part was when the waiter offered them the dessert menu.

'For madam,' he said in a French accent, 'I would recommend the *tarte au citron*. And for your daughter, the salted caramel and chocolate sundae.'

'Sounds lovely,' Nell said as she winked at Mouse.

'Yep, I'll go for that,' Mouse giggled.

'Do you hate it that he thinks I'm your mother?' Nell asked staring intently at Mouse after he'd left.

'No, it makes me feel great,' she said. 'I never thought I'd have a mother again. You're my second chance, Nell. My life began when you found me.'

Nell stared at Mouse and shook her head. 'I know you were sent to me,' she whispered as she attempted to swallow the large lump in her throat. 'We're so damn lucky to have each other.'

Chapter 47

CLOSING DOWN AND MOVING ON WAS PROVING easier than Keeley had anticipated. Once she'd decided to close with immediate effect, she'd had to organise alternative accommodation for her bookings, and happily had been able to pass on the business to two extremely grateful nearby establishments. She'd spent an entire morning calling guests and explaining her situation and asking them to move to the other B&Bs. Keeley found it very bittersweet when people said lovely things to her.

'We've enjoyed every stay at your place,' one lady said. 'You've made us feel so welcome and it won't ever be the same in Ballyshore for us. But we wish you well.'

Keeley felt more at ease than she had for such a long time. She and Doug needed to rebuild their relationship, but those changes were already taking place. Liv needed support and Róisín needed to know they were behind her every step of the way, too. This way, with more free time, they could attend to themselves as well as to their daughters.

'It would be lovely to buy a cottage near the village,' Keeley said with excitement. 'One that only has two or three bedrooms. Can you imagine how easy it would be to keep?'

'Can we find somewhere with a little garden so I can have a small man shed?' Doug asked sheepishly.

The estate agent had come that day and was confident the B&B would sell in no time. 'Summer is the optimal time for selling houses like this one. People don't have to imagine what it all looks like with the sun making the water glisten and the flowers are divine. This place is immaculate and it would be a luxurious family home if the new owners don't want to continue the business.'

Keeley had thought the entire process would take months, but it seemed property was shifting at a good pace.

'This has been the busiest summer for sales in I can't tell you how long . . .' the estate agent said. 'I have two properties I'd like to show you both. One is on the market and the other has literally just come to us. It's not officially for sale, but I can give you a sneak peek.'

So that's exactly what they were doing today, sneaking and peeking.

As soon as they drove up to the property Keeley got a good feeling. 'It's perfect,' she said to Doug.

'Shush,' he said. 'Don't let Jack-the-lad hear you being so enthusiastic. He'll add another ten grand to the asking price.'

Keeley smiled. Doug was always looking for a bargain and this time was no exception.

The cottage was newly refurbished and ready to move into. It was decorated in simple rustic fabrics, in tones that brought the garden and ocean together sympathetically.

'The couple are moving to England to be with their daughter as she's just had a baby. They're looking for a quick sale,' the estate agent explained.

Doug went into bargaining mode. 'We were looking for something with a much larger garden,' he fibbed.

'It's all in immaculate condition,' the estate agent shot back.

'I'd need to buy a shed,' Doug said.

'There's a very nicely appointed outhouse to the rear left,' he said. 'If you'd like to follow me, I'll show you.'

Doug and Keeley looked at one another and followed him out the back. What looked like a miniature version of the cottage sat prettily surrounded by blossom trees.

'The occupier worked as an architect before his retirement and this was his office-cum-workshop.'

Doug's eyes lit up as he walked in. There was enough space to have his tools along with an art area for Keeley. And it was properly insulated, heated and lit.

'It even has a feed to the satellite dish so you can watch sport out here,' the estate agent said.

Keeley laughed out loud as Doug turned to look at her. Gone was the hardball poker face. She knew he'd been drawn in!

Keeley left them to poke about in the man-cave as she returned to the house. Standing in the open-plan kitchen area, she could clearly see herself living here.

The three double bedrooms with one en suite were immaculate too. She wouldn't even change the colour of the bed linen, she loved it all so much.

By the time the men joined her at the front door Keeley had made up her mind.

'We'll take it,' she said firmly. 'We'll give the full asking price and we'll go for it.'

'Keeley!' Doug said. 'That's not the way to play the game.'

'I'm fed-up playing games, Doug. We've worked long and hard for what we have. Once this kind gentleman can sell our place, let's do a deal.'

'But . . .' Doug looked astonished by her unbending manner as she folded her arms and stared him down.

'I don't see an issue with selling your house,' the man said. 'You'll end up with a nice nest-egg at the end of it all too.'

'Precisely,' Keeley said. 'We won't find anything nicer and besides, I knew from the moment we drove up here that it felt like home.'

Doug threw his hands up in surrender and hugged her. 'I like this new bossy version of you.'

Keeley was oozing with excitement as they sat having a cup of tea back at the B&B.

'It's a new beginning for us,' she said. 'We'll be able to help the girls financially and it means we can sit back and enjoy the time we have left.'

'You're making it sound as if we're both on the way out,' Doug said.

'I don't mean it like that,' Keeley said. 'But I think we both deserve to enjoy the next chapter. Are you excited?' she asked.

Doug took her hand from across the table. 'I can't wait,' he said.

Over the next few days there was a steady stream of viewers at the B&B.

Keeley was delighted with the snippets of information she gleaned about the party the girls were organising.

'I wish you'd let me help,' she said.

'No way,' Liv said. 'It's our turn to spoil you.'

The girls had insisted that Keeley buy a nice dress for the party. Doug had brought her to a boutique and paid for everything, from the dress to the shoes and a matching wrap.

'If you don't look knock 'em dead fabulous in new gear, the girls will have my guts for garters.'

Keeley knew the party was on Saturday and she was to be there at eight o'clock, but that was it. Her friends refused to discuss it and most of the times she walked into Nourriture, or anywhere else for that matter, people stopped talking and looked at her with a grin.

'I'm getting a bit nervous about this party,' she confided to Doug. 'What if it's not organised properly? I'd prefer to speak to Róisín about it and see if I can help out.'

'I wouldn't do that if I were you,' Doug said. 'You'll risk having your head bitten off.'

'Róisín is a bit of a control freak, isn't she?' she mused.

'She didn't lick that off the stones either,' Doug smiled. 'She's so like you. Most of the time I forget she was adopted. She's more like you in mannerisms than Liv.'

'I agree,' Keeley said. 'I hope poor Liv manages to find her feet. She's had a tough time of it. Both of them have, as a matter of fact.'

'It's called life,' Doug said. 'But I think both of them will come out the other end. They're both strong women in their own ways.'

Keeley knew Doug was right. She did wish she could shield her girls from all of life's upsets. But no mother could ever do that. When Róisín arrived and once she'd had Liv, she'd vowed she would do everything in her power to help them grow into independent and happy women.

There were many years ahead of her girls and neither of them was perfect, but Keeley was incredibly proud of both. For the first time in a long time, she was truly excited about the future.

Chapter 48

RÓISÍN WAS WALKING ON AIR. IT WAS THE BEGIN-
ning of August and the papers were signed and it was
official – Nourriture and the building it inhabited now
belonged to her. Not wanting to waste another second,
she typed up a letter and slipped it under the door at the
flat. She apologised to the tenants, but explained that she
would need them to move out and gave them a month's
notice as per their letting agreement.

By this time next month, she would be installed there
for the next while, enjoying the best commute in the world.
Her dream of opening an upmarket restaurant in the
converted flat was going to become a reality. She was
certain of that. For now, she would use the flat as her
home and that would afford her more time to find somewhere convenient to live.

Keeley's big day had arrived, and it was all systems
go. The marquee for the party was erected across from
Nourriture and Mouse was working diligently as she
helped Steve to string bunting and place bunches of
balloons on the tables. The giggling and horseplay
between the two of them made Róisín stop and smile.
She'd noticed a little bit of flirting between them before,
but had put it down to friendly banter as they were a
similar age. But now that they'd gotten to know one

another a little better, it was obvious they were very well suited.

Róisín turned her attention to the food for the party. She marched purposefully toward the marquee with a list of things in her head that needed doing. As she walked in, she was caught by surprise. Mouse and Jill had done the most amazing job of the décor. They'd gone so far as to set the tables and had carried the colour theme throughout.

'Mouse and Jill,' she said in awe. 'How did you learn to do all this?'

'Is it OK?' Mouse asked, looking critically at the space.

'OK? It's utterly fantastic. Mum and all the guests are going to be gobsmacked when they see this. You're so clever, well done!'

'I was second in command, I would like to point out,' Jill said. 'I only arrived a while ago so I'm not taking any of the credit here. It was all down to Mouse.'

'Ah cheers,' Mouse said with a wide smile. 'I had a vision in my head and it happened to work. I hope your ma enjoys her night now.'

'I'm sure she will,' Róisín said.

'I need to finish off the entrance area and I'll be happy,' Mouse said walking off and making it clear she was finished chatting. Róisín smiled in spite of her stress. Mouse was one in a million and she had a good feeling that she was going to become a wonderful asset to Nourriture.

The rest of the day seemed to slip by in a flash as Róisín helped the others put the finishing touches to the party. The DJ had set up and the hog roast was well under way. Instead of fiddling around with lots of different drinks Róisín had decided to offer a whittled down version of a bar, sticking to Prosecco, red and white wine, two signature cocktails and Rob's Celtic beer. Rob had kindly offered to come and pour drinks while cheekily winking and saying he was going to be pushing his own product.

'I can just see you doing that too,' Róisín said. 'You'll have Mum's gardening club members swigging out of bottles by the end of the night.'

'With a bit of luck,' he said.

Róisín had invited Melvin, Rob's dad. He was apparently delighted with the invitation and was bringing one of his bridge buddies as his plus one. Róisín had booked them two rooms at the Thatch. Jill had invited Róisín and Rob to stay at the cottage.

'Better to have a bed within staggering distance,' she said.

Róisín was a bit nervous about introducing him to her parents as her official boyfriend, but she felt it was essential that they know how important he was to her. This definitely wasn't a flash in the pan thing, so they were going to have to get used to him.

By the time the shop was closed Róisín hadn't time to go home and change, so she slipped into the office and did a swift patch job on her make-up and pulled on the black bandeau dress she kept there on a hanger to see her through most eventualities.

'Looking good,' said a voice from the marquee as she tottered across the road in her high heels.

Róisín gazed with appreciation at Rob. He was wearing a very tight-fitting short-sleeved shirt with indigo blue denims. Not a look she would've loved the idea of on paper, but it showed off his taut physique to a tee.

'You're not looking too shabby either,' she said, hoping

she didn't look like a love-struck teenager. He pulled her close and kissed her. 'This is supposed to be my mother's party,' she said breathlessly. 'But already I feel as if it's my birthday and Christmas rolled into one.' The smile that lit his eyes made her want to stamp her feet in a happy dance right there in front of him.

Róisín could've stayed in his arms for the entire night if guests hadn't started to arrive.

'Wow, this is the difference between sixty-plus-year-olds and young pups,' Róisín said. 'The invitation said eight, it's five to eight and they're all pitching up!'

The DJ started the music, which was a mix of everything from fifties and sixties right up to Michael Bublé. The sound level was a far cry from nightclub booming, but just loud enough to create a party atmosphere.

By the time Keeley, Doug, Liv and the children arrived, the marquee was buzzing. Keeley looked teary yet exhilarated as she milled around, being kissed to within an inch of her life.

'How are you doing, Mum?' Róisín asked as she finally got to say hello to her. Liv walked over, looking better than she had in years.

'This is simply wonderful. I really cannot thank you both enough for all of this.'

'You deserve it,' Liv said. 'If my two love me half as much as we love you in years to come, I'll be a happy lady.' They both watched with a smile as the children played on the dance floor in front of the flashing coloured lights.

'They're such gorgeous children,' Keeley said. 'They need their mum. The difference in you these past couple of weeks is astonishing. Well done, Liv.'

'I agree,' Róisín said, hugging Keeley and kissing Liv's cheek.

'Dad and I have bought a new house, by the way. The cottage before the beach, on the left.'

'No way!' Róisín said. 'You two don't waste time, do you?'

'We've actually organised ourselves so that we don't have many things to interfere with our time for the foreseeable future.'

Doug came over and joined them.

'I'm telling Róisín and Liv about the cottage,' she said.

'And,' Doug said, 'it's looking as if we've got a buyer for the B&B. A young couple with four children no less. They're moving from the city to the country to raise the children and wanted a place with lots of space.'

'I'm so happy for you both,' Róisín said as she hugged them in turn.

Rob walked over and Róisín turned to hug him.

'Mum and Dad, I want you to officially meet my boyfriend,' she said with a little giggle. 'This is Rob.'

He shook their hands and duly introduced his father Melvin and his friend Amelia, a dainty little white-haired lady in a gorgeous matching dress and frock coat.

Melvin handed Keeley a small gift-wrapped box.

'I used to adore making wooden presents for my late wife,' he said. 'So I hope Doug doesn't mind that I took the liberty of making something small for you.'

'How lovely of you,' Doug said, nodding and impressed.

'It's a little carved frame and I thought you could put a photograph from tonight inside that you can cherish. The date is inscribed on the back to remind you how young you are!'

'Oh thank you, Melvin, I'm thrilled,' Keeley said.

'Wait until you open it,' Melvin said. 'My old eyes aren't as sharp as they used to be. It could be dreadfully bockety!' They all laughed as Róisín looked up at Rob. His father was so thoughtful and an utter gentleman. He was further proof, not that she needed it, that she had found a truly good man.

After an hour and a half, Róisín asked the DJ to announce that food was now ready and invited people to come and fill their plates. The atmosphere was one of warmth and celebration as the tables filled with chattering and laughing guests.

So far, so good, Róisín thought happily.

Chapter 49

AS NELL AND MOUSE GOT INTO THE CAR, NEITHER of them was feeling overly confident about turning up at the party. Mouse had insisted on coming back to the light-house before the party, knowing full well that given half a chance, Nell would back out of going.

'Do we really want to go?' Nell asked.

'Yes, we do,' Mouse said firmly. 'You look fantastic in your new gear. Your make-up is beautiful too, even if I say so myself.' Mouse had sat her down and made her close her eyes as she applied what felt like an entire palette of eye shadow to her lids.

'I'll be like a panda,' Nell protested.

'No you won't,' Mouse insisted. 'I'm doing shading and most of it is iridescent, so it's not as if I'm drawing dark brown all over you.'

For her part, Mouse had curled her hair gorgeously. With her imperfections evened by the foundation and the smoky eyes and pale glossy lips, she looked like a doe-eyed beauty.

'You're so pretty,' Nell said. 'I hope there's a nice fella waiting for you tonight.'

'I might have done this for me,' Mouse said.

'Or you have your perfectly mascaraed eye on someone,' Nell said as she walked to a mirror to inspect her look.

'Wow, are you sure you didn't use a magic wand? Good job, Missy Mouse.'

They trundled along in the car and Nell felt sick with nerves. It was almost forty years since she'd been to a party. She couldn't possibly voice that to Mouse. Even admitting it in her own head was bad enough.

Guessing the village would be parked up, Nell found a spot just before Ballyshore and turned the car.

'Always have your escape vehicle lined up and facing in the right direction,' Mouse said. 'I learned a thing or two from Da.'

Nell laughed heartily, glad of the light relief. As they climbed out of the car and walked toward the marquee, which was humming like a beehive, Nell wanted to beg Mouse to stay by her side. But sense prevailed and she knew she needed to pretend she was at ease. The poor girl was living for this party and she couldn't become a burden on her. Besides, Nell mused, she was an adult. She could get in her car and drive away if the mood took her.

Much to her astonishment, Nell found herself smiling the second she walked into the tent. The atmosphere was relaxed and unpretentious.

'You did an amazing job, Mouse,' she said. 'When you said you'd wound bunting around things, you didn't make it sound quite as wonderful as this.'

Nell took a glass of wine. She had no intention of drinking more than one glass, but felt it would take the edge off her nerves.

Mouse pulled her over to meet someone called Steve. Instantly, Nell knew why Mouse had been so eager to get to the party. The looks of mutual infatuation that floated back and forth on the invisible line of heightened tension between them brought Nell back. Ah, young love and the incredible feelings of expectation, she thought.

Food seemed to be in full flight and Nell was advised to take a plate before it was all gone. She hadn't thought she was hungry until she spied the hog on a spit and the mouthwatering spread of salads and breads. She and Mouse joined some of the other staff from Nourriture at a table toward the rear of the marquee. The others were incredibly welcoming and Mouse had obviously fit in with ease.

'So tell us about Mouse,' another rather hairy-faced fellow said. 'Was she a nightmare when she was younger? I'd say she was a little monkey!' he scoffed.

Nell looked to Mouse for guidance.

'I didn't grow up with Nell. I'm only living with her for the last while. She's my family now though.'

'Oh sorry, I didn't realise,' he said blushing wildly and looking uncomfortable. 'I just assumed you were related. You have that kind of relationship.'

'Yes, we do,' Nell agreed. 'Mouse and I were meant to be together. Like bangers and mash.'

'Beans and toast,' Mouse shouted.

'Tea and cake,' Steve added.

They all laughed and the awkwardness was momentarily forgotten. Nell finished her food and excused herself.

'Give me the nod if you want to go or if you need me to rescue you,' Mouse said.

Nell smiled and walked to the far side of the marquee where she stood and observed. She scanned the room for familiar faces. She recognised some of the local bigwigs who turned up week after week in the local newspaper. Mo hadn't been invited, much to her chagrin. Nell had promised to fill her in on as many details as she could, which the other woman had agreed was as good as being there, if not better.

'John-Joe hates tents. They make him sneeze, so it would be preferable if you could give us a blow-by-blow account of the evening instead.'

The music wasn't exactly loud, but everyone noticed when it stopped all the same. The sound of someone tapping a microphone silenced the crowd.

'Sorry to interrupt, folks. I won't keep you long, I promise. There's nothing worse than someone warbling into a microphone when all you want to do is have a good time!'

Nell stared intently at the man, drinking in everything about him. He was well dressed and seemed likeable. He had smiling eyes and an easy manner that she reckoned would endear him to most.

'As you all know, we are here to celebrate Keeley's sixtieth birthday.' A round of applause rippled around the tent. 'Anyone who has had any contact with my wife over the years will confirm that she deserves this party.' More applause. 'On behalf of our daughters, Róisín and Liv, I would like to thank you all for coming and welcome you here tonight.' He looked nervous all of a sudden. 'Keeley is usually the one who organises all the surprises. She does it with ease and flair. So I wanted for once to turn the tables. Can you come up please, Keeley?'

Nell craned her neck as a pretty, wavy-haired woman in an elegant royal blue silky outfit walked to the microphone amidst further applause. Nell had seen her before, but not for a long time. She looked marvellous.

'Keeley, the word roller-coaster is often used to describe

marriages. We've certainly had our fair share of tumultuous times over the years. But no matter what has been thrown at us, we've survived.' There was a communal *aww* from the crowd. 'I know I'm blessed to have you in my life. Keeley and I are both officially retired and we will move to our new home in the village shortly,' he said.

There seemed to be massive surprise at this news. Nell listened as a ripple of chatter behind hands commenced.

'Happy birthday, Keeley, and tonight I'd like to put a new ring on your finger. This time I'm asking you to remain as my wife as we look to our retirement together.'

He got down on bended knee as Keeley struggled to hold back her tears. A standing ovation followed as Keeley admired her beautiful ring, which sparkled in the lights.

Nell wrapped her arms around herself as she tilted her head to the side and wondered for a moment what her life might've been like had she found a man like this. Instead, she'd picked a coward who'd abandoned her.

Her daydreaming ended as Mouse's boss, Róisín, took the microphone. Nell listened and watched intently as she praised her mother and told the guests how lucky she'd been to have such an incredible role model.

'Mum,' she said taking her hand, 'you have made me the woman I am today. Nothing was ever too much trouble for Liv and me growing up. If I end up being even half the woman you are, I know I'll be happy. Liv is insisting she won't speak,' Róisín said looking to her sister who waved her hands in resistance. 'So from both of us, thank you and we hope you have a brilliant night. Please stand, everybody, and toast our amazing mum.'

Everyone did as Róisín bid and toasted Keeley.

The music came back on and the chatting slowly moved

from a rumble to a full-blown party once again. Nell was attempting to figure out what she ought to do next, whether she'd stay or go, when she felt someone touch her elbow. Spinning around, she came face to face with Keeley.

The breath left her body, but she managed to whisper, 'Happy birthday.'

'Thank you,' Keeley replied. She looked at Nell with such intensity, it jolted her. Neither of them moved a muscle. It was as if the sounds in the marquee had been faded to mute. The flashing lights in the background disappeared and all that remained was this woman's gaze.

'Would you walk with me a moment?' Keeley asked.

Nell swallowed and nodded. The evening air was balmy and sweet. The sounds of the waves lapping against the rocks below offered little comfort. They walked a short distance from the marquee and turned to face each other once more.

'You know, don't you?' Nell said quietly.

Keeley nodded as her face crumpled. She swayed horribly and for a terrible moment, Nell feared she would collapse.

'It's OK,' Nell said. Her voice sounded strangled. Not like her own. Like a stranger she'd never met before. 'How did you know?'

'I saw,' Keeley said through sobs.

'Saw what?'

'I saw the papers you signed when you gave the baby up for adoption.'

Nell's head reared back as if she'd been boxed.

'But if you knew . . . why didn't you ever . . . My God, who else knows?' she asked, the words tumbling from her mouth.

'Nobody knows. Not even my husband, Doug. I never told a soul.'

'So all this time, you knew and never approached me?'

'Why didn't you approach me?' Keeley shot back.

'I was so eaten up by what I'd done. It took me years to even look in a mirror I was so traumatised. But I knew I couldn't offer Laura's baby the life she deserved.' Her voice was barely above a whisper. Nell gasped as her body shook and she attempted to cover her face with her hands.

Keeley stepped forward and gently removed her hands, holding them firmly in her own.

'I shouldn't have come,' Nell said. 'I feel like the black fairy at Sleeping Beauty's christening.'

'I'm very glad you came. You gave me the most wonderful gift imaginable. You're my fairy godmother, Nell. The only reason I never told a soul and never contacted you was because I was terrified you would change your mind and take Róisín back. When I heard people say your name, I nearly lost my mind. I was so scared of you. Then I convinced myself it was a coincidence. But in the back of my mind, I always knew, but I was just so scared you'd take my Róisín from me.'

'Oh Keeley,' Nell said, tears rolling down her cheeks, 'she wasn't mine to take. She's yours. Yours and Doug's. I would never have dreamed of ripping her from her happy life. I just wanted to be near her. Stupid, I know, but I couldn't help it.'

'Did you know she was happy?' Keeley asked.

Nell nodded. 'I kept scrapbooks over the years. Any time she was mentioned in the local papers or even the national ones for Nourriture, I snipped the picture out and kept it.'

'God help you,' Keeley said sadly. 'You've watched your granddaughter from afar and had the incredible restraint to refrain from interfering.'

'You must think I'm cold and selfish.'

'Oh no,' Keeley said shaking her head vehemently. 'I think you're the strongest and most giving person I've ever met. You bestowed the gift of a daughter on us when we thought we'd never, ever have a family. For that I can never thank you enough.'

The women were still holding hands and crying openly when they heard a voice coming from behind them.

'Mum?'

'Oh Jesus, help us and preserve us,' Keeley said as she wiped her eyes with the back of her hand. Her eye make-up smudged all over her face, making her look ten times worse than before.

'Mum?' Róisín said rushing over. 'Hello there,' she said nodding at Nell. 'What's happened?'

Nell took a small step back. She caught Keeley's gaze and nodded her head ever so slightly. Keeley took a deep breath and lifted her hands to rest them on Róisín's shoulders.

'Róisín, there's never going to be a great or right time to tell you this.'

Róisín looked from one woman's face to the next. Nell honestly wanted to run and never return. Keeley took her hand and manoeuvred her body around so they were both facing Róisín.

'This is Nell.'

'Hello Nell, you're the lady Mouse lives with, right? You live out in the lighthouse? Keep yourself to yourself,' Róisín said, smiling.

Nell couldn't find her voice so she simply nodded. With Róisín staring at her at such close proximity, she could examine her face properly. She had Laura's eyes. She shared a similar steely determination.

'Nell . . .' Keeley said closing her eyes and shuddering. 'Róisín . . . Nell is your maternal grandmother.' The words hung in the air. Nell cowered, expecting Róisín to explode. She'd imagined angry tears and hateful expletives should this moment come to pass.

'Róisín, I hope some day you can forgive me,' Nell managed. 'Your mother was my daughter, Laura. She died of organ failure due to severe diabetes after you were born. I couldn't . . . I wasn't able . . . I brought you to the nuns for adoption.' Nell couldn't bear the tension a second longer as she dropped to her hunkers and tried to curl into a ball. She prayed she'd either pass out or die of shame.

She jumped when Róisín put one hand on her tightly folded arms.

'I can't believe you're my maternal grandmother,' she said softly. 'Please look at me.'

As they looked directly into each other's eyes, it was as if the rest of the world had melted away. Róisín guided Nell by the elbows to a standing position.

'I've wondered all my life about where I came from,' Róisín said. 'I was very happy always. But I have always had a curiosity about who I really was. And it's been so much worse of late. It's actually been eating me up. I could barely understand it myself, but I just felt there was something else I didn't know, but no one could tell me what it was.'

'I told her from the time she could understand that she

was adopted,' Keeley said. 'But we only got one little file with barely any information. You remember how it was then, Nell, the convent didn't expect anyone to come back looking for more. So I wasn't able to tell Róisín anything, but then . . . then,' Keeley said, dissolving into tears.

Róisín turned and held her arm out. 'Come here, Mum,' she said with a watery smile. 'You've been the most incredible mother. I couldn't have been happier. You put me in the right hands,' she said to Nell. 'But I've always felt that there was a piece of the jigsaw puzzle missing.'

Keeley's shoulder shook violently as she covered her face with her hands. Róisín embraced her and rocked her back and forth.

'You're a wonderful woman,' Nell said. 'I know my Laura would be proud of you, darling girl.'

As soon as she said the words, Róisín's head spun around.

'What did you call me?' she whispered.

'Darling girl,' Nell said as tears rolled down her cheeks.

'Nell,' Róisín said. 'Did you write my birthday cards?'

Nell nodded. 'Yes, that was one wish I did carry out properly for Laura. In the end, her strength was waning, so she dictated them to me and I wrote down every word. Her last request was to make me promise you would receive them.' Nell regarded her gently. 'She adored you, Róisín.'

'What about the letter?' Róisín asked.

'That she was determined to write in her own hand. She gave it to me in a sealed envelope and asked me to make sure you received it on your thirtieth birthday. I believe she felt you would be ready to read it by then. I have no idea what was in it.'

Nell turned to Keeley. 'I'm so sorry for intruding on your birthday. I had no right.'

'Nell,' Keeley said with a heavy sigh. 'You have lifted the veil. Who knows what the future may hold? But I know one thing for certain. Secrets are better shared.'

'I have so many questions,' Róisín said. 'Please don't disappear again, Nell. Don't you agree, Mum?' she said, beseeching Keeley to say something.

'Róisín's right,' Keeley said. 'There's no reason why you shouldn't get to know one another. I know I'm her mother. But she could do with a grandmother who loves her. Someone else to watch over her.'

Nell nodded and a bright smile lit her eyes.

'I have lots of things belonging to Laura,' Nell said. 'I have a video message she wanted you to have. If you'd ever like to see it, I would be delighted to give it to you.'

Róisín's smile matched Nell's as she nodded vigorously.

Suddenly Keeley's face crumpled. 'Róisín,' she said. 'I have a confession to make. But I'm afraid. I'm afraid you'll hate me or think I'm evil . . .'

'My God, Mum, there's more. What is it? And I could never think that of you, so don't worry. Please, what is it?'

'I feel so guilty,' Keeley said, covering her face with her hands.

Nell nodded and reached over and patted her arm.

'Róisín, I knew Nell was your grandmother. I saw her name on the adoption papers when the nuns were giving you to us. I knew I wasn't meant to see that page . . . It was only a glimpse, but I saw it.'

'Does Dad know?' Róisín asked in astonishment.

'Nobody knew, ever. It's been eating me up inside all

these years. Her name was burned into my brain, and then when a woman moved into the lighthouse and they said her name was Nell Daly, I was absolutely petrified that she'd changed her mind about you. I've lived in fear that Nell would come and take you . . .'

'Oh Mum,' Róisín said pulling her into her arms.

Nell had never been a touchy-feely type of person, but she had a sudden compulsion to join the two women. Stepping forward, she wrapped her arms around both of them. In turn, they took her into their embrace.

'Tonight is supposed to be about you, Mum,' Róisín said. 'But I've got a feeling this is only the beginning of a whole new chapter in all our lives. Now is not the time for any new announcements. I think poor Mrs Bird inside will go to her grave with her jaw on the floor after Dad handed you the ring. If we told her all of this, we'd be taking her out of that tent in a pine box!'

'My goodness, this has been a birthday I'll never forget,' Keeley said.

'Me too,' Nell said.

'Me three,' Róisín added. 'I suggest we all find some make-up followed by a stiff drink and try to see this night out without looking like a herd of deer in the headlights.'

'How are you so calm?' Keeley asked Róisín.

'Her mother was the very same,' Nell said without thinking. She clapped her hand over her mouth. 'Sorry.'

'Don't be,' Keeley said. 'These are precious details that Róisín has a right to know.'

'Thanks Mum,' Róisín said. 'Now that Mouse is a connection, perhaps we can take baby steps and get to know one another?'

'Keeley?' Nell implored with a hopeful gaze.

'Absolutely,' she said. 'I have a bit of explaining to do with Doug and Liv. But life is short and it's ever so precious. Let's not waste another day hiding behind the shadows of the past.'

'I'm more than ready for the light to shine,' Róisín said. 'Just like my other mum . . . Laura . . . always said it would.'

As they gathered themselves to rejoin the party, all three women felt a sense of calm contentment as never before.

Chapter 50

IT WAS TWO WEEKS SINCE KEELEY'S PARTY AND SO many changes had come to pass.

Keeley had dreaded Doug's reaction when she told him the secret she'd been holding inside all these years. But in typical Doug style, he was calm and supportive.

'I don't understand why you didn't tell me, love,' he said. 'I can't say I would've done anything to help, but surely you know I wouldn't have done a single thing to hurt our little family.'

'I knew you wouldn't hurt us, darling Doug.' She stroked his face. 'But I shouldn't have seen Nell's name. The nuns were clear that Róisín's mother wanted us to have no contact.' She looked at him and the anguish was written all over her face. 'That suited me just fine. Don't you see? I was happier to put up with the guilt and go it alone rather than risk losing Róisín. With every day that passed I loved her more. The force of that love was unstoppable. I would have put up with anything to keep her.'

'I know, but I wish you hadn't pushed me out,' he said sadly. 'But for the record, if the tables were turned, I would've done the same thing.'

'You would?' she said, as a smile broke out on her face.

'Damn right I would.'

'Thank you for saying that, Doug. It makes me believe that some day you'll forgive me for keeping it from you.'

'I already have,' he said sincerely. 'You fought for our family. End of.' As he took her hand in his, she looked down at the diamond ring he'd given her for her birthday.

'Where did you get the money for that?' she asked. 'It's beautiful, but it has worried me slightly.'

'I sold the boat. Jimmy is going to live in Spain with his daughter. I've had enough of bobbing about on the ocean. I was trying to find myself, silly old git that I am. I should've looked in the mirror and right here under my nose.'

'I hated that bloody boat,' she said with a laugh. 'I think it looks so much better as a diamond!'

The old-fashioned brass doorbell of their newly acquired cottage pinged.

'Hello?' came Liv's voice. 'Anybody home?'

'In here, love,' Keeley said as they turned to hug her. 'Where are the children? I thought Dad was going to mind them while we go out.'

'Martin is with them. They're spending the night in a hotel in Galway. The children think it's the best treat ever.'

'How are you feeling, pet?' Doug asked.

Liv's shoulders shook and she waved her hand in front of her face. 'I'm sorry for crying,' she said. 'I'm actually fine, you know?' She nodded. 'I thought I'd be totally shattered when Martin walked into the room. We decided to meet on neutral ground, so we went to the Thatch. But as soon as I saw him, I knew it was over for me.'

'Was he at least polite?' Doug asked, looking furious. 'I wish I could get him in a dark corner. The things I'd like to say to him . . .'

'Enough now, Doug,' Keeley said. 'That's not helpful. We need to learn to develop a new and different relationship with him. He'll always be Billy and Jess's father.'

Doug shrugged and looked like a petulant child. 'It'll take a long time before I'll talk to that bastard,' he said. 'Political correctness can take a running jump. Tell him from me that he'd better run if he sees me coming.'

Liv laughed through her tears and Keeley handed her a tissue.

'I didn't realise until I saw him today that I'd stopped loving him a long time ago,' Liv admitted. 'This is definitely the best decision for all of us.'

'That may well be the case here and now,' Doug fumed. 'But he two-timed you and chose to forget about his wedding vows. He's a . . .'

'It's OK, Dad,' she said. 'I hear ya. Believe me, I've had many worse thoughts involving everything from sharp garden shears to a hitman. But none of those things are going to change the fact that my marriage is over. I need to look out for my children and forge a new life for us.'

'Well done, Liv. We're so proud of you,' said Keeley.

'Thanks, now let's get going. We don't want to be late,' Liv said.

Doug kissed them both and wished them well.

'You're sure you don't want to come?' Keeley offered. 'Now that the children aren't here, you could if you feel like it?'

'Nah, you girls go and get acquainted and I'll come another day.'

Keeley and Liv walked up the village, past the Thatch and on toward Nourriture. Róisín was waiting outside.

'Hi,' she said, kissing them both. 'How are we all?'

'Nervous,' Keeley admitted.

'Me too,' said Róisín. 'But I'm also excited.'

'We all are,' Liv assured her.

Róisín insisted on driving them in her Fiat 500, so they piled in and hurtled toward the lighthouse.

'It was nice of Nell to invite us all,' Keeley said. 'I think this is more of a big deal for her than we realise. She's barely left this place in forty years, you know?'

'I can't believe I'm going to see a video of my mother,' Róisín said as she opened the window. 'I need air.'

'Take your time,' Keeley said.

As the lighthouse came into full view they all peered up. It was more majestic than they'd realised. When they drew up out front, Mouse came out, waving.

'Hey Mouse,' said Róisín smiling. 'It's great to see you.'

'I'm the one who knows all of you, so it's my job to try and stop you all wanting to puke with nerves, OK?'

They laughed and already Mouse had done her job. Nell walked outside and held her arms out to Róisín.

'It's thirty years since you've been here,' she said. 'I kept you here for three weeks before bringing you to the nuns. I never dreamed I'd have a chance to hold you in my arms again. You're welcome back.'

Róisín could feel the older woman's heart thudding like a bass drum as they embraced.

'Thank you. It's great to be here,' she said. Taking Keeley's hand, Róisín let all the women chat for a moment.

'Right, enough smalltalk,' Mouse said. 'In with you. The video is the main attraction and if I were you lot, I'd be gagging to see it. So why don't we cut the crap and watch it?'

'After we do one thing first,' Nell said with a smile. 'Follow me.'

She walked them to the far side of the lighthouse, where they came upon a tiny grave.

'Laura's ashes are here,' she said. 'I wanted to keep her close and I knew I'd never leave here. So there was no point in going to some weird place in a city or town.'

Róisín dropped to her hunkers and read the neat plaque.

LAURA DALY

CHERISHED DAUGHTER AND PROUD MOTHER

TAKEN TOO SOON, NEVER FORGOTTEN

'I never knew that was here,' Mouse said in awe. 'Did you get permission?'

'It's only her ashes,' Nell said with a smile. 'And of course I didn't.'

They stayed there for a moment and joined hands as each of them thought of the girl who was taken too soon.

'Now can we watch the video?' Mouse asked impatiently. 'I've seen it about twenty times, but I can't wait for you to all see Laura.'

'She's saying all the things I wish I could say,' Liv whispered to Róisín.

'I know!' Róisín said. 'Isn't she brilliant?'

The ladies all marvelled at the interior of the lighthouse and how homely it was.

Knowing that the time had finally come, Nell led them to the spare room. 'I've never moved the video player or television from in here. So I don't want to do it now.'

They all nodded, unable to really speak. The atmosphere as Nell pressed the Play button was electric.

As Laura waved and moved about and delivered her message, Róisín felt as if something inside her had finally clicked into place. It was like something that had been constantly jarring suddenly found its groove and everything felt smooth.

'She was so beautiful,' Róisín said, turning to Nell. 'Now I feel complete. Thank you.'

Nell hugged her tightly

'I'd like you to know, Nell,' Liv said quietly, 'that I read the letter that Laura sent to Róisín for her thirtieth birthday.'

'You did?' Keeley and Nell said together. Liv nodded.

'The words gave me such courage and strength. Laura's letter was the catalyst I needed to get my own life back on track.'

'She'd be so proud to know that,' Nell said gratefully. 'It's kind of ironic that she seemed to give you good relationship advice when she hadn't much luck herself.'

'That was a bit of a pattern, now that I think about it,' Róisín said.

'What? We all picked stupid gits who skedaddled once they'd made us fall in love with them?'

'Yeah,' Róisín laughed. 'Although the one I've just found is going to break that mould. I just know it.'

'Hallelujah for that,' Nell said.

'Would you like to read the letter?' Róisín asked Nell. When Nell, Keeley and Mouse all nodded eagerly, she knew the best thing would be to read it out loud so everyone could hear.

She took it from her bag and carefully unfolded it.

My darling, my beautiful, my daughter,
You are ten days old and we don't have long left together.

Panic is a terrible thing. It takes away all rationale. But my love for you has spurred me on and helped me find a way to leave you a part of myself.

As she read through the letter, her tears didn't stop her voice. When she came to the final part, it was Mouse who seemed the most affected.

I will watch over you always and I know we will meet again some day. There is nothing more I can say except that I love you. I love you. I love you. I love you, my darling girl, my perfect gift.

'Right, feck it,' said Mouse. 'That's it. No more messing about. I'm out of here.'

'Where are you going?' Nell said in alarm.

'To find Steve and tell him how I feel. I'm going to kiss him and hope to God he doesn't turn his back on me.'

'You go, girl!' Róisín said, as Mouse ran from the room.

They made their way to the kitchen, and Nell handed Róisín a wrapped box.

'What's this?' she asked.

'Open it and see.'

Liv and Keeley peered over as Róisín removed the wrapping paper. It was a picture frame with two handprints, one large and one tiny. Beside it was a photograph of Laura holding baby Róisín.

'It's the only one I have. It's the only picture of you and your mother together. It was meant for you always, and I'm so glad you finally have it.'

'Thank you,' Róisín said, drinking in every detail of the image.

As Keeley put her hand on Róisín's shoulder and Liv reached over to touch her hand, she looked over at Nell.

'I promised Laura you would be loved,' Nell said to Róisín. 'I now know that though I was tortured by my decision, I did keep my word. Thank you for coming back today.' She turned to Keeley. 'Thank you for doing what I couldn't.'

Keeley smiled at her through tears. 'We both acted out of a mother's love, in our own ways,' she said softly. 'And that's the perfect gift, isn't it?'

Nell could only nod in response.

Róisín took Liv's hand in hers and smiled at the women who loved her. She remembered her mother's words. *Whatever your gifts are, I wish that life will deliver them to you.* And in that moment she knew she had everything she could ever wish for. Right now, right here.

Acknowledgements

ALL MY BOOKS ARE THE RESULT OF TEAMWORK. I am privileged to have a dedicated bunch of cheerleaders who work tirelessly to help me shape and develop my books. The work that goes into cover designs and marketing is a whole other story again!

Massive thanks to the team at Hachette Books Ireland. As always, Ciara Doorley has been patient and encouraging with edits, and always sees the best in my work. Ruth Shern is tireless in her enthusiasm, and I adore tagging along with her for signing tours. Thanks also to Breda Purdue, Jim Binchy, Siobhan Tierney, Joanna Smyth and Bernard Hoban for all the work you do on my behalf!

I am so grateful to team Headline in the UK. Sherise Hobbs, you are so enthusiastic and positive with your editing skills, and I know I am lucky to have you on my side. Thanks to Fran Gough, Jo Liddiard, Beth Eynon and all the team for your constant championing of my work.

Thanks also to Rachel Pierce for casting a fresh eye over the book, and doing a wonderful job of the copy edit.

My agent Sheila Crowley has never faltered, and always goes above and beyond the call of duty. Thank you for your business advice, wisdom, chats and friendship. You really are a Jack of all trades – or should I say Jacqueline?

Thank you, thank you, thank you! Thanks also to Susie Cronin for your kind help with PR.

This book is dedicated to the people who live my life with me and know me better than anyone else. These people are an extension of me, and I cannot imagine a day without them. My husband Cian, our children Sacha and Kim, and my parents Denise and Philip. I wouldn't manage to exist without each one of you.

Thank you to all my cousins and extended family and friends. You all make my life worth living. Thanks also to my brother Tim, his partner Hilary, and their cats Teabag, Sid and Murray. You are wonderful furry cousins to Herbie-Doodle and Tom puss. Thanks to Fiona Cullen and Michael Walsh for minding Tom when we go away. Teddy and Jo-Jo are lucky to have such dedicated puss-parents.

Also, huge woofs and sniffs to Joey Crowley and his owners Angela, Ger, Niall, Meghan, Fionn and Donnecha for putting up with Herbie's regular uninvited and very enthusiastic visits to your garden. Thank you especially for minding him when we desperately needed it! Joey is welcome to come and stay with us any time.

Thanks to Keith Hayden for rescuing Herbie when he goes on adventures, and to the many kind and lovely people who phone when they see naughty Doodle-boy gleefully escaping. We would all be heartbroken if anything happened to him, yet he seems to think it's all so much fun . . .

Thanks to Loretta and Stephen O'Toole for all the help and kindness in Connemara. You ensure our home away from home is always perfect. Thanks also to Kay McEvilly and all the staff at Cashel House, for feeding and welcoming us so often!

I can never forget Dr David Fennelly and the staff of Blackrock Clinic oncology unit. My cancer treatment is ongoing and, without your care and expertise, I wouldn't be able to do the job I adore or enjoy the life I love. I am beyond grateful for everything you all do. I am in awe of you all, and I know I wouldn't be here without you.

Love and gratitude to Aisling Hurley and Sam McGregor from Breast Cancer Ireland, for the amazing work you do in raising money for cancer research. I am honoured to be an ambassador for such a progressive and worthwhile cause. The work you do saves lives. The work you do has saved *my* life. Please log on to www.breastcancerireland.com for more information.

Massive thanks to all the booksellers who work like Trojans to keep folks interested in reading. The support you show by putting my books on display and by recommending them never goes unnoticed. With each and every book that hits the shelves, I have several moments of breath-stopping fear. You see, I'm terrified my loyal and wonderful readers will hate it! So, I'm hiding under the stairs with my fingers crossed and my eyes squeezed shut, in the hope that you'll all enjoy this one . . .

The letters, e-mails, tweets, Facebook messages and cards I receive are, quite simply, a gift. Thank you all for taking the time to read my work, and for letting me know how much you enjoy it. Thank you all from the bottom of my heart for the tsunami of support you all send my way while I'm battling cancer and trying to make sense of it all. It never ceases to amaze me how generous and giving you all are with kind words and messages. They really have such a positive impact on me. Thank you.

Please keep the letters and banter going – it really makes

my day to interact with all of you! You'll find me at www. emmahannigan.com, @MsEmmaHannigan on Twitter or /Author-Emma-Hannigan on Facebook.

I am incredibly proud (in spite of hiding under the stairs) to present *The Perfect Gift*. This is my eleventh book and my tenth novel. I cannot believe I've written so many words! I've loved every second of it, and I'm thrilled to say that there are many more novels in the pipeline.

I really hope you enjoy this story, and thank you kindly for buying it.

Love and light,
Emma

Emma Hannigan

The Perfect Gift

Bonus Material

What my mother means to me...

MUM IS THE FIRST PERSON I PHONE EACH MORNING. We see each other all the time too!

I've battled cancer many times and I know I couldn't have coped without my mum. When I was too sick or too weak to mind my own children, both of whom are now teenagers, Mum stepped in seamlessly. She never made a fuss and I know for a fact that my children don't remember my being absent when they were small. Mum is serene, smiling and always there for me.

I hope that I have carried some of Mum's warmth through to my children. Like most teenagers, they predominantly want to be with their friends but that's normal. My son hugs me daily and tell me he loves me; he's nearly six foot and doesn't care who sees or hears. My daughter writes cards and draws pictures and bakes me cakes on a regular basis. So I guess some of my personality has rubbed off on both of them!

Each time I've been diagnosed with cancer, we've had to face the inconceivable thought of not having one another, but I don't believe that is why we are close. I put it down to how I was raised. Mum treated me to such an idyllic and wonderful childhood that I was easily in the position to pass that on.

It's only in adult life that I realise just how incredible my mum really was as I was growing up. She worked as a Montessori teacher when my brother and I were children and she instilled a wonderful sense of purpose in both of us. She read to us and taught us both to read fluently by the age of four. She brought us on nature walks where we collected wild nuts and berries to be kneaded into bread or boiled into jam. We picked flowers and leaves for pressing into home-made cards for friends. She stood by and gently instructed as my brother and I destroyed the kitchen making everything from simple cakes to delicious stews. She showed us how to make stamps from raw potatoes and use them to create pretty pictures with poster paint. She taught us to care for our pets and let me know that cats don't really like wearing T-shirts and tights. She encouraged me to speak my mind without being offensive but, most of all, I always felt heard. I always felt loved. I always knew Mum was there for me, no matter what. Her *joie de vivre* is infectious. She did things that I thought *all* mums did. Hindsight has taught me that she was actually quite unique.

I hope you have some lovely memories of your childhood and your own mother. If, like me, you are lucky enough to be a mother, I hope you remember to have fun with your children, creating their own memories for the future.

To mums everywhere, I salute you!

Love and light,

Emma

A special home-made treat for your mum...

To make a pressed flower card

- Pick some pretty flowers – smaller ones, such as primroses, work best
- Arrange the flowers face down inside a hardback book (a cookery book works well) or if you have a flower press use this!
- Close the book and lay on a flat surface with several heavy objects on top
- Leave for a couple of days
- Once the flower is dried and fully flattened it is ready to use
- Using school glue, stick to the front of a folded piece of card
- Write your own special message for your mum inside

To go with the card how about some hand-made truffles?

Chocolate truffles

Ingredients
225g good quality chocolate (milk or dark depending on your mum's preference)

85g butter
2 tablespoons of cream
1 tablespoon of Tia Maria or orange juice
85g chopped hazelnuts or ground praline
cocoa powder to coat

Method
- Melt the chocolate
- Bit by bit, stir in the butter
- Add the cream and Tia Maria or orange juice
- Stir in the finely chopped nuts or ground praline
- Refrigerate for approx 30 minutes to ensure the mixture is set
- Take a teaspoon of mixture and roll it gently and quickly between your palms
- Immediately roll in cocoa powder
- Place in a pretty petit four case (available from most supermarkets or baking stores)
- Store in the fridge before putting in a pretty box or cellophane bag tied with ribbon

Emma
Hannigan

The Secrets
We Share

**Don't miss this beautiful moving story
of heart and home . . .**

Devastated after a tragedy, Nathalie Conway
finds herself on a plane to Ireland. She is on her way
to stay with her grandmother Clara. The grandmother
who, up until now, Nathalie had no idea existed . . .

As Clara awaits her granddaughter's arrival,
she is filled with a new sense of hope. She has
spent the last twenty years praying her son Max
would come back into her life. Perhaps now he can
find a way to forgive her for the past. And her
granddaughter may be the thread to stitch the
pieces of her beloved family back together.

Uncover the magical secrets of Caracove in Emma Hannigan's glorious novel

A little magic is about to come to
sleepy Caracove Bay . . .

Lexie and her husband Sam have spent years lovingly
restoring No. 3 Cashel Square to its former glory.
So imagine Lexie's delight when a stranger knocks
on the door, asking to see the house she was born
in over sixty years ago.

Kathleen is visiting from America, longing to see
her childhood home . . . and longing for distraction
from the grief of losing her husband.

And as Lexie and Sam battle over whether or not to
have a baby and Kathleen struggles with her loss, the
two women realise their unexpected friendship will
touch them in ways neither could have imagined.

In Caracove, there's more than a pot of gold
at the end of the rainbow.

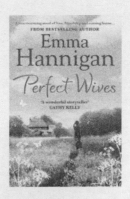

A heartwarming novel of love, friendship and coming home from this bestselling author . . .

When actress Jodi Ludlum returns to the Dublin village of Bakers Valley to raise her young son, she's determined to shield him from the media glare that follows her in LA. But coming home means leaving her husband behind – and waking old ghosts.

Francine Hennessy was born and raised in Bakers Valley. To all appearances, she is the model wife, mother, home-maker and career woman. But, behind closed doors, Francine's life is crumbling around her.

As Jodi struggles to conceal her secrets and Francine faces some shocking news, the two become unlikely confidantes. Suddenly having the perfect life seems less important than finding friendship, and the perfect place to belong . . .

A delightful, irresistibly romantic e-short featuring much-loved characters from Emma Hannigan's novels, *The Summer Guest* **and** *Driving Home for Christmas.*

Tess can't quite believe her luck – she's marrying Marco, the man of her dreams, in an exquisite traditional Italian wedding, surrounded by her adoring family.

But when an ex puts in an unexpected appearance in Rome, Tess is instantly taken back to glorious Huntersbrook House and the warmth and joy of the Craig family. Memories she thought she had long buried and left behind in Ireland suddenly resurface at the worst possible moment.

Forced to face both her past and future on the evening of the rehearsal dinner, Tess is thrown into turmoil. Which man – and moment – will win out?

Discover Emma Hannigan.
Stories you'll want to share . . .

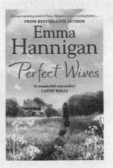

A | Z
BOOK ENDS
P R O M I S E

Emma Hannigan's THE PERFECT GIFT has been loved by readers and critics alike. At Bookends we are sure that you will love THE PERFECT GIFT too. However, as part of our Bookends Promise, we are offering our readers a free book (chosen by us) if you buy this edition of the book and are dissatisfied with it.

To claim: send your valid receipt along with a letter containing your name and full postal address and stating the reasons why you are dissatisfied to the address below, to arrive no later than
31st October 2016.

**Bookends Promise / The Perfect Gift
Marketing Department
Headline Publishing Group Limited
Carmelite House
50 Victoria Embankment
London EC4Y 0DZ**